SAINT DEATH

A Reagan Moon Novel

τ

By Mike Duran

BLUE CRESCENT PRESS

Mike Duran
SAINT DEATH
A Reagan Moon Novel

© 2016 Mike Duran
Published by Blue Crescent Press
ISBN-10: 0-9909077-5-9
ISBN-13: 978-0-9909077-5-6

ACKNOWLEDGMENTS

I've come to see writing as more of a journey than a destination. Along the way, I've met many fellow travelers who have shared the trip and inspired me to keep moving forward. Some of the ones which currently come to mind are: my mother, who always encouraged me towards creativity; my wife Lisa, who has endured my artistic adventures with grace, resilience, and a loving side-eye; my writing partners, Merrie Destefano, Becky Miller, Rachel Marks, and Paul Regnier, who help me keep the lap bars in place when the roller coaster is in motion; my beta-reading friends, Kessie Carroll, Johne Cooke, and Kat Heckenbach, for their catches, critiques, and encouragement; the many wonderful writers and readers I've gotten to know and appreciate including Tosca Lee, Kerry Nietz, Kevin Lucia, Sharon Thomassie, Lyndon Perry, Lelia Rose Foreman, Joe Sacco, Steve Laube, Donovan Neal, Richard Laffin, Mark Carver, E. Stephen Burnett, Randy Streu, Gina Hernandez, Lee Thomas, Tim Greek, Gretchen Engel, Christian Jaeschke, Janeen Ipolito, and so many more whom I am remiss for not mentioning; my editor, Jill Domschot, for her typically stellar work; and Kirk Douponce of Dog-Eared Design, for capturing the vibe of Saint Death (and the Hawaiian shirt!). It's been a surprising, grueling, but deeply rewarding journey, which so many of you make all the richer.

OTHER BOOKS BY MIKE DURAN

The Ghost Box: A Reagan Moon Novel (Book One)
Subterranea: Nine Tales of Dread and Wonder (anthology)
Christian Horror: On the Compatibility of a Biblical Worldview and the Horror Genre
Winterland: A Dark Fairy Tale (novella)
The Telling
The Resurrection

"The wounds received in battle bestow honor, they do not take it away."

– Don Quixote

CHAPTER 1

The moment I saw the shrine, I knew I was in for a long night.

"Bernard," I whispered. "You here?"

Bernard was my guardian angel. I'd given him that name, but he didn't like it. Angel names were usually a lot fancier—*Bazazath*, *Jael*, *Metatron*. Things like that. *Bernard* was probably too ordinary a name for my glowing celestial bodyguard. However, at the time, christening him thus was the only way I could cope with seeing invisible beings.

However, I've gotten used to seeing invisible beings now.

Bernard didn't answer. Which was about as surprising as the Pope being Catholic.

I scanned the barn again and then looked behind me, up towards the road. I could make out the shadow of the Cammy, my vintage El Camino with faded racing flames, parked thirty to forty yards away on the windswept berm. It was framed against a beautiful Technicolor sky. After living almost a decade in Los Angeles, I could attest that no amount of CGI and Hollywood neon can compete with live sunsets on the Pacific Coast.

The large wooden gate I had entered by stood open. Somewhere in the foothills, the whinny of a horse sounded. A soft breeze rattled the cacti bordering the property. I was close enough to the Pacific to feel the ocean air, and far enough away from downtown Los Angeles to not smell the smog. However, Rolling Hills, located on the beautiful Palos Verdes peninsula, was known for its gated community, high-dollar ranches, and equestrian trails, not for its shrines to the saint of death.

Yet there it was.

I stood at the doorway to the barn with my backpack slung over my shoulder. In the corner were two dozen smoldering vigil candles—black candles—surrounding a life-sized statue of the grim reaper. She was wearing a lacy gown and holding a scythe. The flames cast an eerie glow upon the statue's skeletal face. An assemblage of odd mementos were heaped at the base of the statue, fruits and small fleshy things scattered amidst trinkets and amulets. Definitely not your typical mom and pop shrine.

It was Santa Muerte.

I'd seen them before, shrines like this. Usually they were accompanied by murder and mayhem. The Santa Muerte religion had been migrating from Mexico into the southland for the last half century bringing with it a toxic mix of old world esoterica, spiritualism, and crime. Its central deity was sometimes displayed as a Virgin, a bride, or a queen. Some called her the Grim Reapress, others the Bony Lady.

But mostly she was known as Saint Death.

Over time, she'd become the patron saint of drug lords and hit men; the Mexican cartel had adopted her as their own, splaying untold victims upon her altars. Saint Death's protection and blessings were routinely sought, as was her vengeance. Whether one was seeking to guarantee safe passage of a drug shipment, smite a foe with the *necrotizing fasciitis*, or be protected from such curses, Saint Death was all ears.

I didn't require intuition or supernormal power to know I was on dangerous turf.

"Bernard?" I whispered again. "Hello? I can use some assistance."

Bernard was nowhere to be found. Figured. Angels were not genies. There was no magic lamp you could rub to make one magically appear. Not that Bernard would lower himself to such a level. Either way, we had a weird relationship. He showed up when he wanted, if he showed up at all. Yet he saved my life once which makes me indebted to him. Although his methodology and timing can be questionable, he seemed to be helping me limp my way to some higher calling. God bless him.

I studied the barn for Invisibles, but saw nothing. At one time, I required crazy visors to be able to see the complex, exotic world of angels and demons that lived behind the curtain of normal sight. The Accident had tweaked my senses, rewired the circuitry inside me. Think of it as a personal Singularity, an event horizon of my own destiny. Now I didn't need the visors to see the Invisibles. Angels, demons, and other assorted inter-dimensional interlocutors could pop into view at any time. Mostly at unexpected times. You could say it was my own peephole into the Great Beyond. Either that, or cruel punishment for having been a skeptic for so long.

I scanned the barn for Invisibles, but came up dry.

So I stood my ground and studied the shrine and its surroundings. The barn was immaculate—fresh hay bales, bright, neatly rolled ropes. A lone pair of polished leather boots. The water troughs were empty as were the stables. This place hadn't seen a horse. Like, ever.

My flesh was clammy. This wasn't feeling right.

"Dammit."

I glanced back up at the Cammy, and then to the nearby house.

It was a ranch style house, probably a bit rustic for these parts. A single story, but sprawling. The porch light was on. When I'd first arrived, I knocked on the door and made my presence known. To no avail. Felix Klammer had sent me there looking for someone named the Shroud. What I was supposed to do when I found him remained a mystery. But that was how Klammer, the secretive billionaire, rolled.

I suppose you could say that he was my boss now. Klammer had been paying me for odd jobs. And when I say odd, I mean really odd. Paying me quite well, in fact. So much so that money had stopped being a big issue for me. Of course, it helped that my tastes were simple. But this particular job appeared to involve more than just miscellaneous knowledge of the occult and Southside dives. Klammer was always after more than casual sleuthing. He was in it for something bigger.

3

Something more grandiose, more cosmic. At this stage, I was simply along for the ride. This ride, however, had no safety bars or guarantees of a happy ending. What Klammer ultimately wanted still remained a mystery.

Mostly, I guess, he wanted *me*.

So I remained there with the sunset behind me, staring forlornly into a barn containing a pagan shrine.

I slung my backpack off, removed my camera, and started taking pictures. As a photojournalist, this was my default practice. Especially if Santa Muerte shrines were involved. I found them colorful, occasionally artsy. And creepy as all hell. However, I did not approach the shrine. I stood outside the barn and reeled off two or three dozen shots, zooming in and out, before capping the camera and stuffing it back in the pack. I debated my next move.

The ranch rested in a horseshoe of small hills whose peaks were now glazed with the final luster of sunset. Shadows grew longer as I grew more restless. Somewhere in the brush, a night bird trilled. Dust swirled behind me, whipping grit and particles of straw into my face. I glanced back at the ranch house.

The Shroud.

Exactly who was I looking for? *What* was I looking for? Klammer rarely gave specifics. He seemed intent on leading me to water and letting me figure out if the well was poisoned or not. In this case, bad vibes were everywhere.

I seriously thought about getting the hell out of there when a figure dropped from inside the barn and into the doorway. Without hitting the ground, it swung towards me like some maniacal trapeze artist, feet extended, aimed square at my chest. I was quick enough to dodge direct impact. Nevertheless, the blow glanced off my shoulder, lifted me off my feet and catapulted me backward, spinning as I went through the air. I plowed into the ground face first, eating dirt as I went.

The impact had apparently rendered me partly unconscious because somewhere in a distant part of my brain, I could feel my body violently lurch. I was being dragged into the barn. By the time I was lucid enough to regain control of my motor skills, my attacker flung me at the base of the shrine.

Being that my intuitive circuitry had significantly improved after the Accident, I cursed myself for not having seen this coming. However, I did not have time to wallow in self-judgment as my attacker straddled me, grabbed my shoulder and flipped me onto my back. I spat dirt, fighting to zero in on this mystery foe.

It was a young guy with greased back doo-wop hair and a T-shirt, sleeves rolled up, revealing heavily tattooed arms. He stood over me, drooling. And, oh yeah, he had fangs.

A rockabilly vampire? No shit.

He must have noticed my utter surprise because he laughed.

"Whath?" he slurped. "You weren'th exthpectin' me?"

He was slobbering all over my Pink Floyd shirt. Gross!

I've never encountered what I consider a real-life, honest to goodness, vampire before. Yet in this stage of my life, I was far more open to the possibility. During my years working at the Blue Crescent, I'd run into many claims to revenant fame. However, if the reports didn't prove complete fabrications, they usually involved some mentally unstable individual who hung out at Goth clubs, fetishized body modifications, and got way too involved in role-playing games. Perhaps this was why my initial reaction to the rockabilly vampire was not to avoid being bitten by him, but to keep him from drooling all over one of my favorite print shirts.

Before I could make a move to escape, he reached into the shrine and removed a dagger. It was a long ceremonial type blade. Uniformly black, of a strange lusterless material. I glimpsed ornate inscriptions along the shaft as he drew it to my throat.

Then he spat out the pair of fake plastic teeth.

"You didn't think I was a real vampire, did ya?"

Before I could answer, he got on one knee and with his opposite hand, reached down, took hold of the bottom of my shirt, and prepared to pull it up. I instinctively flinched and he jammed the blade dangerously close to my artery. I raised my hands in a show of compliance. He smiled and yanked my shirt up, exposing my chest.

He knelt there, breathing heavily, eyes fixed. He was staring at the scar on my chest.

"Then it's true," he finally said. "You *are* the Seventh Guardian."

I swallowed hard and my Adam's apple jostled the tip of the black blade. "Most people just call me...Moon. Reagan Moon."

Apparently, my words didn't register. Or he didn't like what he heard. Because he reared back and howled. His voice echoed off the foothills, inciting some neighborhood dogs to follow suit.

He quickly returned his gaze to me, looking more skittish than before. "Then I'm the chosen one. The one she spoke of. The Empress. *Gracias dulce dama.*" He tipped his head toward the shrine. "And the spoils go to me. Ha! Game over. So I'll kill you. Do ya hear me? Whatever you are, I'll kill you. Before the waning. I'll take the mark and offer you up. A sacrifice to the Bony Lady. Oh God, I think I pissed myself."

He repositioned himself and switched the blade to his opposite hand. His body was trembling. He stared at the scar as his smile grew lunatic.

That's when the first sensation came.

It began in my chest—a tingling impression where the scar of the Tau had infused itself. It was as if some invisible energy was leaving me, or perhaps pulling me forward. It came with a weird sense of motion.

I'd been having many strange sensations since the Accident. I guess that's bound to happen when you're struck by a thousand volts of raw electricity. Sometimes I would find myself thinking about quantum possibilities, contemplating orbital mechanics and angular momentum, things I didn't fully understand and couldn't explain. More than once, I woke up in a cold sweat and started sketching contraptions that I'd never seen before. Sounds, smells, and bizarre cravings often rose inside me, leaving me perplexed and feeling alien. Sometimes I needed a drink or two just to be able to cope with it all. Three or four to temporarily forget about it. But this was something different.

It was a feeling of…motion. Relocation. But it had nothing to do with my body. It involved my mind.

My assailant's eyes glistened in the candlelight from the shrine. He continued staring at the scar on my chest. "It's beautiful," he said. "Do ya know that? Ha! Of course. But it's mine now. Oh. Pardon me. You don't mind if I remove it, do you? Of course ya don't. The Shroud will reward me. Ha! Me! This is it—the reward. I've been a good boy, done just what they said. Yeah. The Shroud'll reward me for somethin' this big."

The Shroud. Welp. Guess I was at the right place.

Despite being straddled by this maniac and the threat of having the Tau scar cut from my body, I was preoccupied with a mounting sense of power. From my position, I could see past the barn door. Slight furrows marred the earth where I'd been dragged. My backpack lay just outside the entry where it had been knocked free upon my attack. The porch light shone in the gloaming. And this light seemed to illumine a trajectory, a line of sight that was boring through space itself.

I tilted my head to get a better view of this anomaly. The man's leg was blocking a clear line of sight. But there was enough to envision a path of escape. A channel. Everything on the periphery of my vision grew murky, indistinct. Only this thoroughfare through space seemed important.

As did the strange confidence that I could traverse this space in an instant.

The madman yanked my shirt down and laughed. His eyes were feral. Jaundiced. If I looked deeper, I was sure I'd see that this guy was a carrier, a host to multiple demons.

"She wants blood," he said. "The blood's the life. The blood's power. Ha! Much power." He adjusted his grip on the blade and hunched forward, so close I could smell herbs and garlic on his breath. Which only confirmed my suspicion that he was a mentally unstable person with a vampire fetish.

Why is it always a vampire fetish?

"Wait!" I practically coughed out the word. "The Shroud—*kech*—he wants me—*erck*—alive."

I felt the pressure on the blade slightly lessen. This idea niggled into his brain, which gave me a chance to refocus on the field of power that seemed to be growing around me.

I could envision myself, my body, sweeping from this space to another. Through the barn. Over the dirt and straw. Past my backpack. To the porch. This feeling, this sense that my mind had gone ahead of me to another location, produced a rush. My stomach dropped. It was the same feeling you have on a roller coaster, as if actual space and perceived space are suddenly disjoined. Or accelerated. Except I hadn't really moved. Quickly my mind snapped back into my body. The whole process left me feeling queasy and tingly and really alive.

Meanwhile, my attacker had shaken off my attempted deflection and repositioned the blade. This time, he was prepared to drive it through my throat and stake me into the ground. Oddly, I knew that he chose my throat rather than my heart because he did not want to damage the scar he intended to remove. Which made me more intent on getting the hell out of there.

He stared forward into the shrine. "Most Holy Death, Empress of the Darkness, rewarder of the faithful, receive this offering."

I turned away. Eyes fixed on the porch. Not sure why. But believing that mattered.

"May your enemies be defeated, oh Queen of the Darkness."

I knew—somehow, I knew—that I had to see the spot in order to actually get there.

"May your servant Marty receive blessings for this thine sacrifice."

Some actions are best accomplished by letting go, surrendering to a force or movement. Or a decision. This wasn't one of them. I did not let go. I reached out and took.

"Blessings and power!" He was drooling again.

I think good 'ol Marty, the wannabe rockabilly vampire, wept in ecstasy when he raised the ceremonial blade and prepared to spike me into the earth with it. However, in that brief instant, I willed myself forward. Towards the target I'd cordoned in my field of view.

I think I momentarily left my body. Or had my body left me?

—*is again.*

—*into a secret place*—

Voices. Snapshots of images. Shadowy faces watching me and my passage through space.

—*a barrier between the two.*

Was it teleportation? No, that involved a disassembly of matter. And I didn't quite feel atomized. Not that I would know exactly what being atomized felt like. Everything blurred past. My assailant. The barn. The beautiful Pacific Coast skyline. Momentarily, I was semi-weightless. Blistering with kinetic energy.

I saw, rather than felt, my body somersault ahead of me, flipping head over heels into the dirt just beyond the barn where I had been held just seconds ago. In that brief, disembodied instant, I witnessed my attacker's eyes widen as he was flung forward into the spot my body had vacated. Driving the blade into empty earth. Screaming in agony.

My mind snapped back into my body. Pain burst into my back from the crazy somersault. The air was bristling. The scar on my chest seethed. Even though the man was shrieking behind me, I didn't have time to turn and calculate the danger quotient. The spot on the porch was still illumined in my eyes, like a finish line beckoning me to run towards it. Only, in this case, the running was *thinking*. And the moment I entertained the thought of movement again, the strange experience repeated itself. With equally awkward results.

The air was sucked out of the world. A convulsion of colors mixed with shadow figures, watching me.

—him!

A station there for—

I slid across the porch and slammed into the door of the house. The barn was now behind me and I was hyperventilating.

I did not have time to understand what had happened. I had to survive. First, I needed to locate my attacker. He was in the barn where I'd left him. He had tumbled forward into the shrine and was grappling at the stump of his leg. It only took me a second to realize the reason for this. My body had passed through his leg, severing it. The bone did not shatter, it was basically vaporized. However, this did not make his pain seem any less real. As he writhed at the foot of the Grim Reapress, the shrine burst into flame. Vigil candles, straw, and other combustibles tumbled into an explosion of fire.

Neighbors were yelling now. Dogs howling. Somewhere a car alarm went off. Between the man's shrieking and the flames now engulfing the barn, this was becoming a spectacle of front page proportion.

After what had happened, I wondered if my body could still move or if my atoms had been sprinkled through the air like fairy dust. I tried to get to my feet and collapsed. I had to call the cops. Call someone! But my cell phone was in the Cammy. And the rush of confusion was overridden by pain. My chest burned like hell. Like someone had doused my scar with gasoline and torched it with a cigarette. I had to do something.

That's when the porch door opened. Which changed everything. For standing in the doorway peering down upon me was a figure that reeked of demon.

And something much worse.

CHAPTER 2

I quickly scanned my body to make sure I was all in one piece. Whatever had just happened, I appeared fully intact.

Welcome to my strange new world.

I called them "the storm gifts," but doubted that thunder and lightning could, all by themselves, generate the new talents I now possessed. And the jury was still out on whether these talents were an actual upgrade or a big fat pain in the ass.

As I lay on the porch and looked up at a dark figure in the doorway, I had the distinct impression that I was in for trouble. On the scale of defcon four trouble. My chest was on fire. My inner compass spun wildly. Behind me, the barn had become a pyre. My attacker's screams were now hideous cries of torment. Nearby, horses whinnied and neighbors shouted.

But none of that could outweigh the force of this person before me.

It was a woman. The fire sent shadows dancing across her face. She stepped closer, looking down upon me. And with her came a shadow unlike anything I'd ever felt.

Pale skin shone bright against a persona of black. She wore thick eyeliner, so thick it was almost clownish. But she was anything but a clown. Black lipstick and nails. Large silver hoop earrings with spindly spider webs glistening inside them. Lots of jewelry, multiple rings, and a circular pendant with an image of a thin crescent bowl containing three droplets hugged her throat. Her arms were looped with fine lace and covered with tattoo sleeves. Gothic shit like skulls, candles, and bats. And she oozed poison.

The atmosphere around her seemed to smolder, not with heat, but with concentrated evil. My skin bristled and the hair on my arms stood on end when she came near. She had the kind of aura suited for fiery infernos. Just one look and I knew this woman dined at the devil's table. Hell, she'd probably birthed his child. I wondered if the earth curdled under her feet as she walked, or if cancer cells sprang to life when she passed. Surely, death followed her and hell was not far behind. Unlike the faux vampire being roasted behind me, this chick was a bona fide bad ass. She was packing more than demons—she was breeding them.

The entire area was now bathed in light. Flames raced up the sides of the barn and licked the twilit sky. Timbers creaked and crackling ash settled about us like hellish snowfall. Sirens wailed in the distance and grew louder by the second.

Yet it was to *her* that my attention was drawn.

"Now *that* was quite a show," she said, her eyes sparkling wickedly from the conflagration.

I remained panting, staring up at this woman, unsure if my legs still worked or if I had enough power to repeat my teleportation trick.

"Looks like Marty will need a new leg," she said. "Please tell me you intended that."

"Me? I, uh—"

The roof crackled and collapsed behind me and Marty's hideous screaming was mercifully terminated in the roar of flame.

"Oh, well," she said. "So much for the new leg." Then she tilted her head. "You've got... energy. All over you."

This was unnerving. She could see me, see the storm gifts. See the power. I massaged the burning scar on my chest and just stared at her. Truth be told, I was afraid to engage this woman. At least until I knew my legs worked well enough to get me the hell away from her. But I feared that standing would only lead to embarrassment, so I used the moment as a chance to continue to recalibrate my equilibrium and devise some plan of attack. Or plan of escape.

"You're looking for the Shroud," she said.

"Yeah."

"And what do you hope to accomplish by doing that?"

"To tell you the truth, I'm not exactly sure."

This seemed to surprise her. "Let me get this straight: You don't know what's going on inside you or why you're even here."

"Crazy, huh?"

She smirked. "And you're the promised one?"

I stared at her. What did that mean? I cleared my throat. "Look. I was sent here to talk to the Shroud. That's all I know. Where can I find him?"

She smiled and peered off into the fire.

"Do you even know what you're getting involved in?" She spoke with deft precision, each word a single pin into a voodoo doll bearing my likeness. Her hair swirled around her face. Hot wind carrying smoke and fleeting embers whorled by us. I gritted my teeth, but she stood there, hair dancing on the broiling air as if she was at home in fire and brimstone.

"Okay," I said. "You're right. I'm way out of my league."

"It's not the first time, is it?"

"Lately, it's my regular practice."

The surrounding properties were now alive with the sound of anxious shouts and barking dogs. Some cars were parked on the berm above where a crowd had assembled to watch and record the fiery event on their phones. Perhaps if I stalled, I could detain the Queen of the Damned long enough for the authorities to interrogate her about the shrine and the dead guy who tried to kill me.

Feeling that my body had sufficiently realigned with the laws of gravity, I climbed to my feet and stood wobbling. It felt like I had borrowed someone else's legs. I gripped the porch rail and turned to face her.

"We were told that someone new had arrived," she said. "Someone who would save them, reunite the Imperia. I just can't believe you're it."

The Imperia! How did she—? Instead, I played it off. "Um, I've been known to disappoint."

14

A flash of anger passed through her features. She didn't like being messed with. The anger quickly passed, a smile returned to her face, and she straightened.

"It's too late, errand boy. The wheels are already in motion. Your time has run out."

"I didn't know I was on the clock."

She approached, slipped her forefinger under my chin, steered me to herself, and kissed me on the lips. It was more out of shock that I did not recoil. She stepped back. Her eyes were big and dark. And I got the strange sense that if I looked into them too deeply, I'd be cut into ribbons.

"You remind me of someone," she said. "Someone who doesn't belong here."

"Look, I'm—" I wiped my lips with the back of my hand, checking for black lipstick. "Should I know you?"

"You will. My name's Etherea. They said you could pose a problem. But seeing you now—?" She shrugged. "We have nothing to fear."

The sirens were almost upon us.

Etherea started to leave.

"Wait!" I said.

She turned. "You know, if I still had a soul, I'd be worried for you." Glancing up towards the road, she said, "The Tenth Plague's coming, errand boy. Get ready."

Suddenly, a car screeched into the driveway, its headlights swiping across the porch area as it barreled down into the property. Etherea laughed and bolted into the house, appearing far more agile in fleeing than I would have guessed she was.

The doors of a police car flung open.

"Moon!" shouted a familiar voice. "Moon! You okay?"

It was Jimmy Pastorelli, neighborhood conspiratorialist and Special Investigations unit lead.

"Inside! There's someone inside, Jimmy!" I pointed into the house, not venturing with my own pursuit of the chola priestess.

Jimmy squinted at me, shielding his face from the inferno. He was trying to wrap his brain around this melee. A fire truck navigated onto the turnoff, and its crew began spooling out a hose and working it down the driveway to the barn. Another police car skidded down the driveway, stopped, and its doors flung open. Jimmy barked some orders, and several law enforcement compadres spilled out of the car with guns drawn.

I stumbled off the porch as the officers took it and demanded that the occupants of the house come out with hands raised. But no one did. A riot of commotion ensued. Between the crowd on the street, and the police and the firemen hustling in opposite directions, it was chaos.

Jimmy jogged up. I was still wobbling. In fact, I was so disoriented that I had to watch my feet as I walked to coordinate my motion with my actual footsteps. The pain in my chest now radiated into my pecs and shoulders. What the hell had happened to me?

"What did you do, Moon?"

"Me? I just showed up."

"Exactly." Jimmy's bald head shimmered in the glow of the burning barn.

"There's someone in the house. And the barn. Jimmy, they tried to kill me."

Jimmy stared into the barn and then back at me, still trying to make sense of the chaos.

As the firemen hosed down the structure, the smoke became a thick white column spiraling into the night sky. Glowing ash settled upon us, blanketing the area in a surreal pall. That's when I saw my backpack, dangerously close to the fire, but lying where it had been deposited. Intact. With my camera. And accessories.

I squatted gingerly, sensing that I'd regained enough of my capabilities. I excused myself and headed for the barn.

"Moon," Jimmy said from behind me.

Then I began speed-walking.

16

"Hey!"

Then running.

"Moon!"

The firemen lugging the hose yelled something indistinguishable as I passed under the spray of water. The remaining structural beams crackled and plumes of smoke unfurled in majestic display. I snatched the backpack. The heat was so intense that sweat broke out on my flesh. A section of the rooftop had pulled free and the twilight sky shone between it and the bonfire. The Santa Muerte shrine was now just a molten heap of wax. The skeletal statue of Saint Death tottered to one side and collapsed. As I stumbled back, I glimpsed Marty's body, a charred heap in the inferno. Missing the bottom half of one leg.

Someone grabbed me and yanked me away from the barn.

"Are you freakin' nuts?" Jimmy had me by the arm.

I held the backpack up. It was hot, but unburnt. "Do you know how expensive film equipment is these days?"

He dragged me away from the commotion and led me back towards his car.

"What'n the hell's wrong with you, Moon? Do you have a death wish or something?"

He pushed me rather rudely against his cruiser.

Just then, a detective emerged from the ranch house and hustled up. He had surgical gloves on and carried a brick of dirty pink powder encased in plastic. The plastic brick was sliced in half. The detective opened it for Jimmy to see.

"You don't say." Jimmy glanced at me.

Lerium.

The marijuana dispensaries had dried up long ago thanks to the lerium trade. Even the genetically modified versions of the plant could not compete with the smart drug that had swept the city. Of course, the side effects of lerium were substantially worse than anything good old hemp could ever manage. Or *better*, depending if you actually survived usage.

"We got ourselves a lab down there," the detective said. "Cellar. Tunnels. Crawlspaces. The whole deal. There's a hundred, maybe two-hundred pounds of this stuff."

"Ho-ly shit." Jimmy glanced at me again, this time with great suspicion.

"The lady," I said to the detective. "There was a lady."

The detective hesitated.

"He's okay," Jimmy said gruffly. "Go ahead."

"No lady," the detective said. "At least not yet. Could be miles of tunnels down there. But this's huge, Jimmy."

Jimmy nodded and sent the detective back to his work. He turned and pointed at me. "You, stay here."

Getting into his car, Jimmy radioed for an investigative unit and other assistance. The firemen were bringing the flames under quick containment. But not in enough time to save half the barn from caving in on upon itself. They'd be lucky to extract any evidence of the shrine from that mess.

Jimmy returned. "Okay, Moon. Here's where I ask questions and you give answers."

"I'll try my best."

"So what brings you to an obscure ranch in an upscale neighborhood?"

"That's what I was going to ask you."

"Well, being that there's a lerium lab inside the house, a dead man inside the barn, and a barn that's now a bonfire, I think you should go first." Jimmy folded his arms at his chest.

"Right. Well. Remember that unnamed source I told you about?"

"Him again?"

"He's paying me well. Sent me looking for someone named the Shroud."

"*The Shroud.* That some comic book villain?"

"I don't think so. I showed up and found a shrine in the barn. Santa Muerte."

Jimmy unfolded his arms. "Again? Now this is getting interesting."

"I took some pictures. Next thing I knew, I got attacked by a wannabe rockabilly vampire."

"That's new. And the fire? Did you do that?"

"Well, sort of. I was just trying to get away. The vampire guy knocked over some candles. Everything caught fire."

"And the lady?"

"Never seen her before." I wiped my lips again. "She said the Tenth Plague was coming and that I should get ready."

"Tenth Plague, huh? Sounds biblical. So this unnamed source, how well do you know him?"

As I prepared to answer, I stopped. Something about Jimmy Pastorelli suddenly struck me as odd. No, not odd. *Disconcerting.*

"Moon. The guy that sent you here. What do you know about him?"

I peered at Jimmy, allowing my second sight to take over. The world around us became gauzy and indistinct. He, however, became crystalline. Something in his aura. Something inflamed, diseased, burned into my brain.

"Moon? Hey."

Despite the fire, the panicky neighbors, and the police tromping in and out of the house, it was as if I could hear the blood rushing through Jimmy's body. The brain cells colliding behind that bald dome of his. Something foreign was growing inside him. Something… *cancerous*. In his gut. *No!* He stared at me angrily. He was saying something, but I was fixated upon my friend and the growing awareness of his condition. I gaped, unsure whether to warn him or try to invoke some power for healing. It was then I realized that he already knew about this malady. He'd been seeing the doctors and receiving treatment. Yet even though he was deeply concerned, he was playing the tough guy and keeping a stiff upper lip.

"—to it, Moon!"

Jimmy jammed his open palm into my chest, shoving me stiffly, and the pain exploded. It snapped me out of the premonition.

He glared at me. "What'n the hell's wrong with you? Geez!?"

I grabbed my sternum and grimaced as the emotional echo of the vision reverberated into silence. Jimmy stared, puzzled at me. Then he gritted his teeth and returned to playing the tough guy.

"Listen, Moon. I don't know what's going on here. Or what you're hiding. But if you ask me, it's an odd damn coincidence. You just *happen* to show up at a ranch with a lerium lab and enough narcotics to fry the brains of the entire West Coast? Either this guy you're working for has uncanny intuition or he's got first-hand knowledge of this operation. Which would make him, and you, complicit.

I opened my mouth to object, but Jimmy silenced me.

"No! That stuff about the shrine—let's keep that quiet, shall we? Until we know more, this is an LAPD crime scene investigation."

"Yeah, but I was first on the scene."

"Which is suspicious and why you're gonna stay really close. Like, no weekend trips to Tijuana. *Comprende*?"

I prepared to answer.

"Good. I got your number. Be expecting my call. Now if you'll excuse me." Jimmy turned and began heading to the house.

I watched him go, wondering how he'd known to show up here. Kanya didn't know anything about this adventure. The Crescent staff didn't know. Only Felix Klammer. But why would he send me here to find the Shroud and then send Jimmy to rescue me? Or had he? It didn't make sense.

"Hey!" I called after Jimmy.

He turned.

"How'd you know?" I yelled. "To come here? Who told you?"

Jimmy smiled and walked back to me shaking his head. "You are a mess, aren't you. Apparently someone's got your back, Kolchak. We got a call from a woman. Said I would find you here and that you were probably in trouble." Jimmy nodded towards the now collapsing barn. "Looks like she was right."

"A woman? What are you talking about?"

"I'm talking about someone who called the station and asked for me. She said you were in deep shit and that if I didn't get out here immediately, your ass was history. Thought it was a crank call at first, but I listened. And obliged. Good thing I did."

Jimmy turned to leave.

"Wait!"

"She called herself Audra," Jimmy said. "Sounds like a stage name if you ask me. Okay? I gotta go."

I watched Jimmy as he walked into the house. My head was swimming.

When I left, the police were cordoning off the property with barricade tape. A police helicopter circled overhead, with a couple news choppers on the periphery. Between the fire and its extinguishing, mud and ash had collected and left the place reeking of charred death.

Audra. Who was this mystery woman? How did she know I was here, and why had she sent Jimmy to rescue me? Either I had another guardian angel, or this secret admirer was saving me for something worse.

CHAPTER 3

I unlocked the Cammy as half a dozen more cop cars entered the property. The Rolling Hills ranch would probably end up being one of the biggest lerium busts on record. Crazy. Yet so many questions remained.

I tossed my backpack onto the passenger seat, got into the Cammy, closed the door, and turned on the dome light. Then I angled the rearview mirror down and pulled my shirt up.

The Tau scar was rimmed with fiery, inflamed tentacles. Fleshy veins had pushed outward, reaching towards my pectoral muscles and shoulders. It was as if a growing web had been etched into my chest and irrigated with liquid fire. I touched the scar and winced. Whatever had happened at the ranch, whatever power I had tapped into, it had awakened the Tau. The storm gifts were roused.

I let my shirt fall back into place and just sat there. What the hell was happening to me? I studied my hands and appendages. Everything seemed intact. Had I actually transported? If I had, I'll be damned if it was a talent I knew how to reproduce. Nausea rose inside me just thinking about the experience. Had my molecules disassembled and reconstituted themselves? No. I didn't have the power for something that fantastic. Did I? Besides, disassembled matter could not sever someone's limbs. Could it?

I turned off the light and watched the commotion on the street. If Klammer was in a hurry to locate the Shroud, he was going to have to wait. Besides, trying to figure out Felix Klammer's modus operandi was a losing battle. The hooded billionaire was about as easy to read as a compass in a magnetic storm. Despite Etherea's ominous warning about the Tenth Plague, it was Jimmy Pastorelli and his condition that weighed heaviest upon my mind.

It was pushing 10 p.m. I retrieved my phone from the glove box and checked it to see I'd missed a couple calls from Jimmy earlier. Arlette had messaged me. She was at the Blue Crescent and had a story she wanted me to start. At the moment, working on a new story for the paranormal mag was the last thing I wanted to begin. But getting back to the office would give me a chance to do some research on Etherea, the Shroud, and the Tenth Plague. Rockabilly vampire research would have to wait. I responded to Arlette's message that I could be there within the hour.

I fired up the Cammy and let it idle. As it did, I opened my backpack. The contents smelled like smoke, but the camera appeared undamaged. I turned it on and began scrolling through pictures of the shrine. It was not unusual to find the Grim Reapress in proximity to a drug house. Just recently, San Diego sheriffs had discovered a dismembered body on a remote roadside. The parts belonged to a dealer and were arranged in the shape of a hexagram with the victim's heart removed and placed in the center. A warning to the competition. The Los Angeles prison system was now thick with criminal devotees of the Bony Lady. They believed that the skeletal saint could be petitioned for help, whether vengeance or prosperity, and often sported elaborate tattoos of Saint Death on their arms or back.

The religion's stream flowed from many tributaries, some tracing as far back as Mayan death gods. This confluence of primitive occultism and old world Catholicism eventually merged into the dark religion of Santa Muerte. At one time during the Spanish colonial period, the Catholic Church had attempted to eradicate veneration of the bizarre folk religion, only to drive it underground. Now it existed on the fringes of society, occasionally accompanied by chilling tales of execution, torture, and human sacrifice.

As I scrolled through the digital pictures, perhaps what intrigued me most were the black candles filling the shrine. Santa Muerte used colored candles to signify different purposes. A red candle was used for love and passion. Gold for prosperity and abundance. Purple for healing. Black, however, was often used for the most nefarious purposes—protection and revenge. It made me wonder whether this shrine—or Etherea's drug operation—wasn't evidence of a much larger, more ominous, endeavor.

I was about to turn the camera off when I scrolled to a picture of Kanya and stopped. I had forgotten I'd taken the picture. It was from her father's memorial service. She was standing next to Father Eufemio, who'd officiated the service. Apparently, Matisse considered the man as his priest. Although it was unclear exactly how much Father Eufemio knew about Matisse's occult obsession. The Mad Spaniard's ashes were now interred somewhere inside the vast warehouse he'd named the Asylum. But it was Kanya's image that drew my attention. She wore a black, sleeveless dress with a light, grey sweater and knee-high laced black boots. Kanya's style was unorthodox, but impeccable. However, it was her hazel eyes and the look on her face that captivated me. Slightly puffy eyes revealed that she'd been crying. She smiled politely next to the priest. But it was the look of resolve, of steely certitude, that seemed to intensify her features and mark her these months after her father's tragic death. Seeing her picture reminded me we hadn't talked in a while and that I needed to pay her a visit. I'd given Matisse my word to watch over the Asylum, which also meant keeping an eye on his daughter. Something I did not mind doing. I nodded to myself, shut the camera off, and stuffed it back into my backpack.

I put the Cammy in gear and navigated through the Palos Verdes peninsula back to the 110 freeway. I took it north to the 101 and exited on Hollywood Blvd. The traffic was awful there. Hollywood wakes up at 10 p.m. Tonight's traffic was made worse by some local kooks who'd been predicting the end of the world. It involved an odd celestial event called the Regulus Effect. Arlette had decided not to do a spread on the event simply because of the mainstream media's coverage.

Sure, it was mostly filler. But the L.A. crowd kept up on such bizarre happenings. Apparently, the Regulus Effect was the alignment of three stars, one being Regulus itself, and a waning crescent moon. The event happened once every half century or so. And now we were two days away from the next one. Survivalists were using it as a portent for global apocalypse, earthquakes, and tsunamis. The usual stuff. The doomsayers saw it as the ushering in of a new age. Which meant that every other street corner was occupied by some nut preaching repentance or hawking freeze-dried food. Typical L.A.

I arrived at the Blue Crescent just as Ashton was leaving. We met at the back door. He wore his leather jacket and held his motorcycle helmet at his side.

"Moon," he said coolly. "You have a visitor."

"Now?"

"Why not now? You're a celebrity, remember?"

"Oh yeah. I forgot."

"Pretty soon, Arlette will be rolling out the red carpet for you and making us bottle the glitter after you pass."

"Dude, let it go."

"What? Everybody wants to meet the guy who took down Spiraplex. Own it, baby. You're boss."

"And here I thought they just liked my cutting-edge reportage."

"Yeah, that too." Ashton prepared to put his helmet on. "Anyway, she's waiting for you."

"*She?*"

He put his helmet on, straddled his ninja bike, fired it up, and peeled out of the alley.

Neville stood at the back door, waiting for me. "He's still pissed at you."

"Don't break my heart."

"Dude, I could care less either. Too much good stuff going on right now to worry about him. Subscriptions are up. Web traffic's almost doubled. The Crescent's finally on the map. Yes!" Neville thrust his fists skyward in celebration. "Now, if only that could translate into chicks."

I approached and patted him on the shoulder. "Good luck with that."

As I passed, Neville said, "Hey, Arlette is lookin' for you."

I flashed him a thumbs-up.

After the Accident, I'd taken some time off. With Arlette's permission, of course. I only visited the Blue Crescent sporadically to tinker around with some miscellaneous projects. Mainly, I showed up to borrow some books from our library for the new sketchbook I'd started. I had entitled it *Of the Invisible Order and Its Inhabitants*. Like Lewis & Clark, I was determined to catalog my journey into a new world. Unlike those intrepid explorers, my journey did not involve bison and beaver. The realm of the Invisibles was far more exotic. From what I had gathered, demons were the lowest in the food chain, the base of a family tree that blossomed into the most wickedly florid creatures one could imagine. I'd encountered griddlebacks, halfhounds, and narvogs. Like Adam in the Garden, I gave names to them and sketched out their peculiarities. The way things were going, I was just skimming the surface of a vast invisible ecosystem.

Penny poked her head out of her work station. "Well, hey there, stranger."

"Hey, Penny."

She stepped into the hallway. Penny was wearing some skinny jeans and a tight checkered tee. Her hair was pulled back to one side. When it wasn't dyed neon pink or green, it was jet black. She was in a jet black phase, which did not exactly coincide with her persona. You see, Penny is a bubbly, rather optimistic person. More than once she had issued a timely word of encouragement to me when I was down. Penny was a great argument against trusting first impressions. She manned our police scanners most of the time, but was slowly making her way into the journalistic end of things. Currently, she was working on a piece about the downtown subway project.

Penny fiddled with her oversized necklace of charms. "Did you hear they closed down the subway project again?"

"Again?"

"Yeah. Rumor is they unearthed something."

"Not extraterrestrials again. Please."

"Extraterrestrials were the last rumor."

"Thank God."

Unlike New York or Chicago, L.A. is not known for its subway system. Several attempts to upgrade and expand the system had repeatedly been made. Yet the project had been a political hot potato, passing through various stages of funding and non-funding. Until NeoKor, the urban developing conglomerate, recently got involved again. The original subway had long been condemned. Metro 417, high-end luxury apartments near Pershing Square, had been erected over the site of the original terminal. The web of abandoned underground tunnels, containing the original architecture from the 1920s, was said to have been left intact. It was only recently as the new digs had begun that they bumped into something out of the ordinary. Allegedly.

Penny glanced back into her cubby as the scanner crackled. "Apparently they found something different."

"Like…?"

"An altar."

"As in—"

"Religious rites. Pagan hoodoo. Human sacrifice. You got it."

"Wow." I stared into space, pondering the implications. "Fifty feet below the City of Angels? I didn't see that coming."

"Don't think anyone did. Supposedly, during the dig they broke through into some kind of catacombs. An ancient burial site with bones. Human remains. Whatever it was, it was enough to scare off half their crew. Some even had to be hospitalized. From what I hear, they were forced to shut the

27

whole operation down. In the meantime, NeoKor put the lid on the PR. Which means getting any more info will require a lot of…digging."

"Funny."

"I couldn't resist."

"Well, it sounds like our kind of story. Let me know if you need any help."

"Hey. I might take you up on that."

I noticed that Arlette's door was open and excused myself.

"Glad you're back," Penny said as I turned to leave.

"Yeah. It's good to be back."

I wasn't lying. As much as my life had changed, the Blue Crescent was like a home and its quirky staff like family. Of course, like every family we had our squabbles and problem people. But between the crunch of deadlines and the constant surprises of keeping up with the weirdness of "weird L.A.," there was laughter and friendship. One day, I reckoned, this fact alone would save me. If it hadn't already.

My boss was standing at her desk. I didn't realize until that second how long it had been since I'd actually seen her. Arlette looked good. In a purely professional sense, of course. She was growing her bob out and had lost a few pounds. Not that she needed to. Apparently, being single again suited her. However, my hunch was that the break-up with her ex had taken more of an emotional toll than she would ever admit. Arlette was a good woman. Strong-willed but not calloused. She deserved better than that two-timing louse she'd once called her husband.

"Well, well." Arlette straightened. "I trust that you're sufficiently refreshed and ready to dive back into things?"

"Heh. I kind of already have dived back into things."

Her eyes creased in suspicion. "If it's anything like your last adventure, I don't think I want to know."

"That's understandable."

"So I have a job for you."

"As long as it doesn't involve rockabilly vampires, I'm game."

"No rockabilly vampires."

"Or extraterrestrials."

"Them either. But there may be a killer ghost."

"Sounds juicy."

"I knew you'd think so."

Arlette lifted an electronic tablet from her desk and began scrolling through some pages. "Check this out."

I approached and stood next to her.

Arlette had changed perfumes since the last time I'd stood next to her, replacing almond with something musky. This had a certain import that I did not now intuit.

"Whoa," she said, leaning away from me. "You smell like smoke."

"It's a new cologne—*eau de bonfire.*"

"Yeah? I'm tempted to ask what the hell you got yourself involved in, Moon."

"I thought you didn't want to know."

She stared at me and then shook her head. "You're right. It's best I don't." Instead, she brought up a video on the tablet, turned it on, and handed it to me.

By the looks of it, someone had recorded images on a surveillance monitor. It appeared to be the video feed of a hospital room. However, an amorphous black blot partly covered the bed. At first, it was unclear what I was supposed to be looking at. Was this an object blocking the camera's view, or was something on the lens? Just then, the black shape moved, revealing an elderly man lying on the hospital bed behind it.

"We received it from a nurse. She was working the nightshift at Saint Vincent's. Captured what she thought was—" Arlette looked sideways at me "—their resident poltergeist."

"You mean, Eve?"

"*Weeping* Eve."

"Ugh. Not another *ghost caught on camera* stunt."

"Just watch."

The images were grainy. It appeared to be an ICU unit. A ventilator, monitor, and other equipment stood next to the bed. A man lay there. Bald, partly bandaged head. Multiple tubes and cords trailed from his body. He was gripping the sheets and pulling them up to his chin, his eyes seemingly fixed upon the black shape between him and the camera. Suddenly, the figure moved again, changed angles. Perhaps it morphed. Because now I could make out a crooked form, hunched over the man. Objects appeared to stream behind it, something like multiple appendages. Or hair. Or was it wings?

"What the—?"

"Keep watching," Arlette said.

The picture shivered as the person filming the monitor moved. In the background, indistinguishable voices sounded, followed by a gasp. The man's eyes grew wide with terror as the black image repositioned itself, now seated directly on his chest like some shadowy gargoyle. The transmission shuddered. The black figure straightened and turned toward the camera as the recording snapped into static.

"That's it?" I said.

"Not exactly. Apparently, they found the patient dead. Their third patient in as many nights. All cardiac arrests. When they got to the room, nobody else was in there—no ghost, no monster. No one. Only the dead guy."

"That's creepy. And you're sure the video hasn't been tampered with?"

"As sure as I can be. But I'm no expert."

I handed the tablet back to Arlette. "And they think it's Eve?"

"Wouldn't you?"

"Not necessarily," I said. "Eve was a suicide victim, wasn't she?"

"Allegedly."

"So why would she be killing people?"

"She's a ghost, Moon. Who knows—revenge, attention? Headlines? It's why I want someone on this story. And you're pretty good with poltergeists, anyway."

"Me?"

"Sure. Remember the Biltmore hubbub?"

"That wasn't a poltergeist. It was some cleaning lady who went berserk."

"Because she was possessed. The Biltmore Twins drove her to murder those people. Isn't that what she said?"

"She said that because she was schizophrenic."

Arlette heaved an exaggerated sigh and put the tablet down. "Anyway, about St. Vincent's. They all died of natural causes. So the deaths are not being called murders. That's an angle I'll leave to you after you do some research. Either way, the staff is pretty shaken up."

"Well, I don't blame them. But I'm not sold that this is anything other than a..."

"Forgery?"

The image of the shadowy black form was rattling around in my brain and it wouldn't stop. "Look. Don't you have something maybe a little less grim?"

"*Less grim?* You mean like something about rehabilitated criminals? Or maybe a lost dog that finds its way home? Sorry. I'm all outta feel-good stories. Besides, when did you become allergic to *grim?*"

I shook my head, at a loss. "Okay, *Haunted Hospital* it is." I set the phrase in air quotes.

Arlette stood watching me. "You sure you're ready to go, Moon?"

There was that tenderness in her voice that I was talking about.

"I'm ready, boss." I smiled. "Thanks for asking."

She ripped a piece of paper from a notepad and handed it to me. "Saint Vincent's Hospital. Alma Curtain. ICU nurse. She works the night shift. With any luck, you might catch her there tonight."

I took the paper. "Can you send me a copy of the video? And do you have a timeline?"

"Next issue."

"That soon?"

"You said you were back, right? And can you put a little meat on this story, please?"

"Uh, don't I always?"

"Readership has been up. Let's try to ride the wave, shall we? And, don't forget." She pointed down the hallway.

"Forget what?"

"Your visitor. In your office." She peered at me. "You sure you're okay?"

The reminder that someone was waiting to see me made me tense up. I'm not sure why. With everything that'd gone down that night, what was another surprise?

I grunted and turned into the hallway. As I walked toward my office, I scratched at my chest. The scar tingled and the pain evoked the memory of the incident at the ranch. Could I teleport again? Did I control this power or was it a spontaneous occurrence? And if it was random, there was no telling the kind of damage I might cause if it happened in the wrong place. I found myself wishing that someone had written a how-to manual for being an earth guardian.

My office is more like a large corner. Pre-Ashton, I'd been offered to move into the room he now occupies, but turned it down. As much as I needed relative quiet when working on a story, there was something about chatter, ringing phones, and interruptions that kept me focused on a story. Kind of like how getting shot at makes you feel alive, and at peak concentration.

A single wooden chair sits opposite my desk. I rarely have visitors. But a woman sat there. An Asian woman with dark, striking features. Thick and leggy. Her brunette hair was pulled back tightly and held in place with dark wooden hair sticks, accentuating defined cheekbones heavy with blush, penetrating Hazel eyes, and a thin scar running almost the full length of one cheek. She wore a dress and black nylons underneath. She was a lot older than I was, perhaps mid-forties, but carried a sense of age greater than her actual appearance. She rose when I walked up and extended her hand. She looked awfully familiar, and I began scanning my memory banks as I approached.

"Reagan Moon," she said. "We finally meet."

I shook her hand. "I'm sorry, but do we know each other?"

"Forgive me. We don't. At least, you don't know me."

I hesitated, trying to read her. But I came up empty. If she was a carrier, I couldn't tell. Her face seemed oddly familiar. Underneath her fair complexion, she was hardened, not just because of the scar across her cheek, but the weariness in her eyes. Or was it anger? She'd been through a lot, this woman. Drinking. Fighting. And losing. But my sense was that there was no chip on her shoulder as a result. In fact, if anything, there was some baggage she was dying to jettison.

"Please." I motioned to the chair, feeling a tad guilty for not keeping a cleaner place of work.

She sat down again and promptly began examining the hourglass I had on my desk.

"This is a beautiful piece." She lifted the hourglass and turned it over.

"Thank you," I said. "I bought it in Chinatown. I have a friend there. We do business on occasion."

I did not tell her that Casey Song was always a pain in the ass to deal with. He ran a traditional Chinese medicine store, provided acupuncture and dermatology services, and claimed to have the only key to unlock the golem prison underneath Broad Street Shul. When he traded me the hourglass he said the piece, when combined with the correct spell, had the ability to freeze time. Of course, I'd never learned the spell or frozen time. To my knowledge, the only upside of that exchange with Mr. Song, despite now owning a cool hourglass, was his promise for a lifetime supply of ginseng root. Which was about as useless as a lifetime supply of Kryptonite.

She smiled politely, watching the particles of sand tick away the moments inside the hourglass.

"My name is Audra," she said.

"You're the one who called Jimmy."

"I did."

"Well," I said, "I suppose I should thank you."

"No worries. I've needed my own share of interventions. Trust me."

Someone had walked into the hallway, and Audra looked that way. When she did, I quickly studied her. Who was this woman? How did she know I was at the ranch? How did she know Jimmy could help me? Audra was not some damsel in distress. Far from it. She knew how to drink with the boys and, probably, kick their asses when they got out of hand. Unless she had a Luger under her dress, the kind of heat she was packing seemed purely genetic. I wanted to say there was something reptilian about the woman. Not sure why. She didn't have scales or a forked tongue. Yet there was something oddly alien about her. She turned back and met my eyes.

Before I could sit down at my desk, she said, "I want you to come with me."

"Come with—? Now? Where?"

"Not far. Beverly Hills. There's something we need to discuss. At my place."

"Um..." I glanced about my office, attempting to buy a few seconds. Beverly Hills? She didn't quite look like part of the rich and famous crowd. Not enough silicone and despair. But the bigger question was whether I could trust her. And why we needed to go to her place to do it.

"Listen." I cleared my throat. "Things are happening kind of fast right now."

"I understand. Take your time." She folded her hands politely on her lap.

I nodded, but felt a bit lost in this exchange. "So, can I ask what this is concerning?"

"You can ask." She smiled politely.

The soft patter of falling sand crystals was the only sound in the silence.

I shifted my weight. "Well, I'm asking."

She issued a pained smile and looked away. Then she returned her gaze to me. "Let's just say I've been following your career and, well, I have a story that I think will very much interest you. It involves conspiracies and the supernatural. But mostly it's about someone you saved. Someone who's indebted to you. And someone who will kill you the second they get the chance."

CHAPTER 4

I had known this woman for only ten minutes and had already agreed to go with her to an undisclosed location in Beverly Hills. At almost midnight. Without exactly knowing why. This clearly wasn't the smartest thing to do. But being that Audra had saved my life and had info that would, allegedly, keep me breathing, I figured I'd roll the dice.

Audra insisted that she drive. In a way, I was relieved by this. After Kanya's initial dislike of the Cammy, the last thing I needed was another female passenger dissing my vintage ride.

Audra drove an old model sports car. Old enough that it had a stick shift. And boy, did she know how to use it. She took corners and accelerated around slow drivers without mercy. I was tempted to inquire about our hurry, but snide comments would probably only add a few miles-per-hour.

Her window was slightly open, and loose strands of hair whipped about her face.

"I love the city at night," she said.

I really wanted to concur, but at this speed I wasn't sure how much more of the city I'd live to see at night.

She sped west on Sunset, zig-zagging through traffic. Braking hard at stoplights and tapping the stick shift as she waited impatiently at lights. This was not the type of temperament suited for L.A. driving. Type A drivers didn't last long around here. At least without medication and lots of dented fenders.

"I've only been in the city a few years," she admitted. "The congestion drives me crazy."

"I can tell."

She looked sideways at me with a wry smile.

"You enjoy living on the edge, don't you, Mr. Moon?"

"Actually, I prefer the mundane and low-key."

"Really? It must be difficult reconciling that with being an earth guardian."

What the—?

She changed gears, and I clung to the seat as we launched into another turn. Something flashed on her hand as she gripped the shifter. It was a ring on her index finger, mounted with a smooth amber cat's eye stone. Amber was believed to have magical properties. But any inquiry into Audra's possible commitment to such magical purposes would have to wait. At the moment I was reeling from her reference to my being an earth guardian.

I kind of loathed that term—*earth guardian*; it sounded so pretentious and highfalutin. The moniker had come with protecting the Tau, and I had little idea what it really meant. Or who it was supposed to impress. Besides, I had enough problems protecting my own self, much less the earth. Either way, Audra apparently knew enough about me to guarantee a stimulating time together.

She turned north on a side street and jetted up towards Coldwater Canyon. Beverly Hills is a throwback to Hollywood's Golden Age. Lots of estates and luxury homes occupied by rich, white, highly-educated, bores. There were more ass implants and silver spoons per capita here than anywhere on earth. And it was one of the few places in L.A. that didn't require safety bars on your doors and windows. Audra navigated up a winding road overshadowed by massive oaks before pulling into the driveway of a large two-story Spanish style home. The car idled before a tall ornate wrought iron gate. Hmm. Maybe I was wrong about her.

She pressed a device above her visor, and the gate retracted. The car's headlights revealed a long gravel driveway that bordered a cottage or bungalow, tool shed, and a well-manicured grove of trees further down.

"You didn't think that was mine, did you?" She motioned to the two-story as we drove past and the gate shut behind us. "I'm just renting the back place. They needed

Mike Duran

someone to keep an eye on the property when they travel. And feed the cats."

We stopped in front of the cottage and got out. A path led from the small white stucco cottage to a tool shed further back where wooden crates were stacked and gardening tools leaned. On the side of the cottage, I could make out what appeared a cellar door below ground with crates of canning jars stacked nearby. A tall white stucco wall bordered the property.

I glanced up at the sky and did a double-take. The waning crescent moon had reached its zenith. In two days it would align with three stars and the world would come to an end. Allegedly.

"Regulus," Audra said.

I looked at her. "You're a believer?"

"Oh, not really." She used her keys to unlock the door. "But I can't stop others from believing. And depending on *what* they believe, that can sometimes cause problems for both of us."

She opened the door and invited me in.

For its size, she'd done it up nicely. Either Audra had some cash, or her landlord didn't mind putting money into the guesthouse. Lots of woodwork and deep leather furniture. A massive fish tank glowed at the opposite end of the room where a cat kept sentry on the arm of the couch, watching the fish. It glanced at me in disregard. Damn cats.

Audra invited me to sit while she walked behind a small bar, laying her keys on the dark polished top. "Would you like something to drink, Mr. Moon?"

I declined. She poured herself a half tumbler of gin and tonic, and inserted two lime wedges.

"From what I understand, this whole area was a grove at one time," she said, joining me on the couch. "Avocado and citrus. Beehives. There's even a cellar outside. They used to can and store everything. Hired labor lived here, I guess. And then property prices skyrocketed and it became more economical to build homes than sell oranges. Sad how the earth

38

always gets sacrificed for the sake of human progress." She sipped her drink, slid a coaster over and set the glass on the end table. Then she turned to me.

"Your resume indicates that you have some background in occult artifacts."

"My resume says that?"

"And anomalous conditions."

I peered at her. "I'm not exactly sure what you mean by that, Miss…"

"Audra. Just call me Audra." She crossed her legs. "*Therianthropy*. Have you ever heard of it?"

"Sure. That's the ability to shift, to change forms."

"Partly true. In some cases, such changes are not abilities as much as they are survival skills, defense mechanisms. Beyond the victim's control and resulting from a primal reaction to threat or fear. Sometimes, depending on what school of thought you hold to, the changeling or shapeshifter can be controlled by forces outside herself—lunar conditions, herbal concoctions, even spells wielded by an adept."

"Okay," I said, waiting for the punch line.

"My daughter is one such person."

"My condolences."

She stared at me and then smiled. "She was unique in that she could not morph into animal forms, only human forms. Namely persons she physically touched. Possibly a type of genetic replication. We weren't sure. But if she snapped, she could put people at risk, sometimes even herself. She's fierce in such a state, Mr. Moon. A force of nature."

Audra looked at me all dead serious, as if she could burn her words into my brain with her eyes. She continued.

"We were unclear as to the source of her condition. Had she been cursed? Or was this somehow genetically inherited? There was even conjecture that she may have fae blood, or possibly even something more sinister. It didn't help that her father was mysteriously murdered when she was young, leaving his own family tree somewhat of a question mark. It made my daughter a bit of an anomaly. How had she become therianthropic? Was this some genetic mutation? And then there were her rather legendary fighting—sometimes killing—sprees. I suppose it was all of this that attracted the Summu Nura to her."

The mention of the Summu Nura stunned me. This lady was full of surprises. But I was beginning to get the feeling I was being played.

"Okay. Time out." I scooted to the edge of the couch. "Let's stop the games, all right?"

She raised an eyebrow.

"Earth guardians?" I said. "The Summu Nura? What else do you know about me?"

"I said I've been following your career."

"Yeah. But this sounds more like stalking. You know where I work. You knew who to call to rescue me from that ranch. Except no one knew I was even going to that ranch."

"Except Felix."

"Exactly! That's my point. How do you know about Felix and the Imperia? How do you know about any of this? And what the hell does this have to do with your daughter? Look, I'm not sure where this is going, Miss Audra. I've been courteous enough to join you at late notice. But I've had a rough night. I burned down a barn. Got threatened by some witch. And, to top it off, I got drooled on by a rockabilly vampire. So can we please just cut to the chase?" I forced myself back into the sofa, somewhat embarrassed with my brief outburst, but satisfied that I'd made my point.

Audra just stared at me with her lips slightly parted. Then she took a deep drink of her gin and drew her fingertips across her lips. The cat was looking at us now, its back straight, its eyes glistening.

"You're right," she said. "I've been far too cryptic. I apologize."

I nodded.

"Kanya is my daughter, Mr. Moon."

I managed to spit out a single word: "What?"

"I know. She probably doesn't speak of me anymore, does she? I deserve it. I deserve every damned bit of resentment that she can muster."

Audra hung her head. But I'd been thrown for a loop. I wasn't sure if I should console her or start digging for information. *This was Kanya's mother?* Perhaps that's why Audra's appearance had rung a bell. I couldn't recall any instances where Kanya had ever referenced her mother. All I'd ever known was that Matisse was her adoptive father. That's all I *needed* to know. However, this revelation potentially held an important piece to a complicated puzzle.

Audra looked up. Her eyes were moist with tears. She hadn't struck me as the emotional type. Guess I was wrong again.

"I was a queen once, believe it or not. A long time, maybe twenty years ago. Of course, in your culture, royalty is an archaic concept. I was young and had inherited the rule when my husband was mysteriously murdered. The Nam Jook River valley in Laos—that was our home. It's where Kanya was born. We were part of the forest peoples and could trace our lineage back hundreds and hundreds of years. Today, such peoples have either been domesticated or pushed into the remote parts of forests of the Malay Peninsula and Borneo. Sometime in the nineteenth century, French explorers passed through. Some intermarried, remained among the tribes. Others left mixed race families up and down the delta. My husband, Kanya's father, was from one such family."

"Forest people? For real?"

She smiled. "It's not like we lived in trees or anything. We grew sugar cane and owned rubber plantations. We were well-off by the region's standards."

"And the Summu Nura? How do you know about them? And why were they interested in Kanya?"

"The Summu Nura." She nodded ruefully. "They were more than just interested—they coveted her. She was something they had not yet seen before."

The cat sauntered over to Audra and leapt onto her lap, where she began stroking its fur. "Of the many villages that dwelt nearby, the Noi were the most primitive. Among their shamans rose a man who claimed to speak for the old ones, the gods of the mountain. It was the Summu Nura, *Those Without Light*. Our legends had spoken of these evil gods and we knew not to reverence them, nor seek their power. They possessed the shaman and expanded their reach. They brought knowledge and industry, but at great cost. For they possessed the bodies of the living, consumed the Noi. Strange experiments were conducted. Stories about inhuman entities emerged, half-human, half-spectral hybrids that roamed the mountain forests. Strange phantoms caught between worlds. The Noi gained strength, leveled surrounding villages, and farmed the people of the valley, advancing the reach of the Summu Nura. Eventually, they came to us."

"I think I've heard this story before."

"Not a surprise. This has been the Summu Nura's MO since they started visiting earth—possess a small contingent and then broaden that influence. Thankfully, there have always been those to stand up against them."

"So you fought."

"Not exactly. Mr. Moon, we were a simple people. The country was largely pacifist. We had never seen evil of this order. They took our village and killed us. Tortured us. And I was partly to blame."

She reached up and touched the scar on her cheek as she stared off in thought. The cat lay purring on her lap.

"Had I been wiser, more experienced, I would have prepared us to flee. Or fight. But I wasn't. There was no escape. Until the Noi offered me an ultimatum. They'd heard the rumors about the changeling child. If I agreed to let them study her, they would spare our village."

Audra turned away slightly. The air in the room seemed to grow cold. Or was it the ice water that now seemed to flow in this woman's veins?

I peered at her. "Please don't tell me—"

When she returned my gaze, her eyes were steely. "You don't understand, Mr. Moon. I watched friends tortured. I saw children slaughtered. I knew that Kanya could take care of herself. I believed that she could survive, if not destroy them all. There was no other way."

"Damn."

"I gave up my daughter for the sake of the tribe."

I just stared at her, letting this information sink in. And the more it did, the more unnerving everything became.

"So I led our people south," Audra continued. "More coastal. We safely resettled. The city is still there. Different, but the same. They don't need kings and queens anymore. But many of those that were saved are still alive. I suppose that's my only credit.

"I never saw Kanya again. Of course, I always held out hope. Eventually, there was news of a powerful warrior sent from heaven to defeat the Noi and the Summu Nura. It was one of the Imperia. Later I learned that Kanya had indeed escaped. Like I knew she would. But she never returned home, never sought me out. I can't blame her."

I was torn between sardonic remove and reprehension. Finally, I said, "To tell you the truth, neither can I."

Audra glanced at me, picked the cat up, and dropped it to the floor. Then she rose, took her drink, and finished it in two great gulps.

How many years had this thing smoldered inside her? And what kind of hell had those cosmic leeches put Kanya through? This was turning into the mother of all family issues.

"So what do you want me to do?" I asked, rather exhausted from the whole affair. "I'm not a family counselor. And even if I was, you'd probably need a lifetime's worth of sessions."

Audra went to the bar and set her glass down. She looked weary. Fatigued, but not defeated. When her eyes finally engaged mine, they seemed to possess a strange resolve.

"I live for one thing now, Mr. Moon. You don't have to believe me. I won't begrudge you if you don't. I want to revenge her. The life they stole from me. I'll stand against those monsters if it's the last thing I do." She clenched her fists. When her rage passed, she calmly said. "Judge me if you want. I've lived with this for a long time. Now I only want one thing, Mr. Moon—to see her again. I want to make amends, if possible. It's why I've come here. It's why I've followed the Imperia. From one rumor to the next. It's why I've joined their fight."

She stepped out from behind the bar and brushed her hair out of her face.

"I want you to help me, Mr. Moon. You're the Seventh Guardian. The healer of the breech. Please, save Kanya from her hatred. Before she kills both of us."

CHAPTER 5

If you thought that confessing would have slowed Audra down a few RPMs, well, you'd be wrong. She took the roads with the same abandon, cutting close corners and accelerating every straight-away. What was up with this lady? We reached Hollywood, and Audra pulled into the alley behind the Blue Crescent. I was relieved to have stopped.

Having had some time to gather fragments from the bombshell she'd dropped on me, I ratcheted back the snark. "Look," I said, before exiting her car. "I apologize if I came off a little callous back there."

"No apology necessary."

"It must have been a really hard thing. Honestly, I can't say *what* I would have done in that situation."

She nodded.

"But as far as orchestrating some *reunion* between you and Kanya." I shrugged. "I'm going to have to think about it. I haven't spoken to her in a couple weeks. Maybe this will be a good excuse to do so."

"I trust your judgment, Mr. Moon. Now you know the players, and what's at stake."

As I exited the car, Audra reached into her purse and pulled out a small object.

"When you see her, I want you to give her this."

I reluctantly reached out and she pressed a small hard object into my open hand. I held it up to the vapor lamp. It was a pewter icon in the shape of a five-petaled flower.

Five.

Five is a complicated number. It's the most dynamic and energetic of all the single-digit numbers. It is unpredictable, always in motion and constantly in need of change. But after my last adventure, my fixation upon numerology had taken a back seat to other more fantastical trivia. Still, it seemed fitting that Kanya be associated with such a number.

"Kanya means 'poisonous flower,'" she said. "Did you know that?"

"Yeah. I've heard that somewhere before."

"I used it as a totem to calm her down, to draw her back to herself when she morphed. It was a point of contact. A mental marker, a reminder of who she really was. But after the experiments, I don't know what she does now, or how she survives. Take it. I have a feeling you'll need it."

I stuffed the icon in the pocket of my jeans.

"I'll be in touch, Mr. Moon. Or, if you need, feel free to drop in. RSVP is not required."

She smiled and drove off. I stood there, listening to her tires squeal into the night. If Audra managed to survive her stay in Los Angeles, she might want to consider a stint in the Formula racing circuit. Say what you will about her extraordinary story, I was confident that what she'd told me was not a lie.

And that she still knew a whole lot more than she was saying.

Before entering our offices, I searched the night sky for the moon, hoping for a glimpse of the celestial phenomenon that would grace us in the next couple nights. However, when surrounded by hotels and high-rises, such glimpses are rare. The moon was nowhere to be seen.

It was pushing one o'clock, which most likely meant that someone was still working. I wasn't surprised to find Neville posting some news items to our website. He brushed his mop of hair back as I passed his office, and swiveled in his chair.

"So who was the vixen?" He smiled wolfishly.

"Dude, she's twice your age."

"Yeah? Well, she's had her eye on *you*. Been here three times the last few days, asking lots of questions."

"It's not what you think, Neville. Trust me."

"But you're a celebrity now." He pumped his fists. "Money, chicks, fame! Woo-hoo!"

"It's getting late. You should go home."

I went to my corner-office, plopped into my chair and just sat there. What was happening? What was happening *to me?* I spread my palm over my chest, touching the scar of the Tau. The smell of smoke arose from the fabric. God, I needed to change this shirt.

I stared at the computer screen. *Jimmy. Etherea. Saint Death. Audra.* I wasn't sure where to begin. I heaved a deep sigh, logged into my computer, and gathered up some info on the St. Vincent Hospital. More specifically, *Weeping Eve.*

She was a patient back in the mid 1950's, hospitalized with some strange, long-term condition. Nothing more than a young pretty girl unfairly sucker-punched by life. She used to walk the halls, weeping. No one knew why. Eventually, they found her hanging in the basement one day and called it suicide. Although claims of foul play were always hovering on the periphery. Thus began the legend. Staff claimed they started to hear Eve's ghostly weeping at night. Some swore they saw her apparition wandering the halls. Attacking people and forcing cardiac arrest did not seem to fit Eve's character. Although I'm no expert in poltergeists.

I fished out the note that Arlette had given me. Alma Curtain. She worked the night shift and was the one who filmed the poltergeist. Or should I say, filmed the *alleged* poltergeist. St. Vincent's was on the way back to my apartment. I could drop in, do a little snooping around, and possibly catch Alma Curtain to boot. If anything, this story might help me take my mind off the crazy events of this evening.

I put a paper tablet and a few fresh pens into my backpack. Made sure my cell phone was charged, unplugged it, and slipped it into my pocket. As I did, I felt the icon and removed it.

Poisonous flower.

I studied the totem and shrugged. *Why not?* I removed the phone from my pocket and called the Asylum.

Being that the Asylum was encased in a lead-lined perimeter, cell phone communication was impossible. The call went to their landline. I was sure Kanya would be awake. That girl was alive in the night. Sometimes I wondered if she ever slept. But whether or not she was there was another story. Before her father died, I'd promised him that I would watch after the Asylum. I made the promise reluctantly, out of obligation more than desire. But as much as I can be a slacker, I do not renege on my word. Which is also why hearing her voice made me feel a little guilty.

"Hey," I said. "It's Reagan Moon."

"Well, hey Reagan Moon." A rustle sounded on the other end. "I was wondering if I'd hear from you."

"Let me guess—you're ready for that Mexican omelet and walk on the Santa Monica pier I promised?"

She laughed. "Sure, I'd love to."

This caught me a little off-guard.

I have mastered having no plan of attack. In fact, ad-libbing was probably one of my earliest superpowers. Apparently, this conversation would be a perfect opportunity to display such powers.

"So how you been feeling?" she asked.

"You mean the scar?"

"Yeah."

I thought about the inflamed tentacles growing along my chest and the tingling energy that seemed to fuse the Tau scar into place. "Uh, not so great."

"It's still burning at night?"

"Sometimes. Lately, it's been…growing."

"Reagan. That's not good. Someone needs to take a look at that."

"Do you know of any witch doctors?"

"Funny."

48

"Well, I'm just on my way to the hospital. Maybe I can have them take a look at it."

"The hospital?" Ruffling sounded again. "What's wrong?"

"No, nothing. I was kidding. I mean, about having someone take a look at it. But I *am* going to the hospital. It's just a story I'm starting. I'm finally getting back into the swing of things. St. Vincent's. My boss has me researching a story about their beloved poltergeist."

"You mean Weeping Eve."

"Right. Well, apparently, Eve has turned into the grim reaper. Three people have died and they have a video of the third being straddled by some creepy figure."

"Interesting. We haven't picked that story up yet. The Regulus event is the big thing now. But it's fairly tame by our standards. No one of note has really claimed it as anything more than just a unique celestial happening. I've just been busy trying to organize things. Matisse was great at getting things into circulation. Cataloging them was another story. But I still miss him."

The line went quiet.

I said, "I know what you mean."

There'd always been a sweet melancholy about Kanya. You could call it brokenness. And after what I'd learned from Audra, that brokenness would not only be understandable, but warranted. Cricket, Kanya's mysterious alter ego, was another story. Yes, she'd saved my life. But that didn't mean she still hadn't scared the shit out of me.

"So maybe I can drop by sometime," I said. "I promised Matisse I'd help with the Asylum, you know."

"I could sure use the help. It's a huge mess around here. And Mace just got back from North Africa, or somewhere. Which really doesn't help matters. So, yeah, anytime."

"Good. Then I'll drop by. Tomorrow's okay?"

"I'll be here."

As we prepared to hang up, I added, awkwardly, "Hey. I, uh—there's something else."

"Like what?"

"It's something kind of weird."

"Yeah?"

Suddenly, I was wishing I could take the whole thing back, start over, and query her another time. So much for my ad-libbing skills.

"What is it, Reagan?"

"Yeah. It's just—" I held the icon in my fingers, flipping it over and back.

Poisonous flower.

"I don't know," I said.

"Okay," Kanya said firmly. "What's going on? You called me. You want to tell me something, so just say it."

"Right." I took a deep breath. "Someone showed up at my office tonight. In fact, she...she sort of saved my life."

"Oh? Go on."

"Her name was... Audra. She said she was your mother."

The line went quiet.

"Kanya? You there?"

"Yeah."

"So...I didn't even—"

"What'd she want?"

"Well, she said...She told me what happened. When you were a kid, and about the Summu Nura. She's been looking for you, I guess. And following the Imperia. Listen, she wants to apologize. She wants to help you. Help *us*."

Again, the line went quiet.

"She gave me something for you. Kanya? Hey, you all right?"

The rustling sounded again, this time followed by a muffled exclamation. Something crashed as the line went dead.

"Kanya? Hey! Hello?"

I fumbled at the phone and quickly redialed, but the call went straight to the answering machine. *Dammit!* So much for spontaneity and ad-libbing. I should have just kept my mouth shut. Should have waited for a better time and place. I grabbed my backpack and hurried down the hall.

Neville had his headphones on and was hastily tapping away at a gaming console in front of his computer, splattering virtual aliens across their digital domain. He saw me passing and I signaled I was leaving. The Cammy was out back and before I got in, I called the Asylum again. This time, I left a message, apologizing to Kanya, pleading with her to answer the phone, and then telling her I was on my way over.

Audra would have been proud at how quickly I reached my destination.

I arrived in the Warehouse District and parked near the alley that led to the Asylum. A low fog hung over the L.A. River, its tentacles fingering their way into the maze of industrial structures. A couple cars were parked parallel near the recycling plant, music blasting from one of them. The tang of lerium was in the air. A harmless bunch, probably. Down the opposite end of the street, a group of taggers or *street artists*, as they liked to be called, were sizing up a storage container, with little interest in me.

I hurried down the alley. The doors of the freight elevator were clamped tightly shut. Whatever had happened, I could only hope that Kanya was expecting me. The alley reeked of urine and wet cardboard. New spray painted monitors covered the old, creating an odd kaleidoscopic montage across the adjacent roll-up doors. Someone had spray-painted "Abandon All Hope" on a nearby brick wall.

I noticed a thick line of salt bordering the warehouse. Apparently Kanya had been faithful to maintain her father's rituals. At every new moon, the perimeter of the Asylum was blessed with holy water and cordoned with salt. Mind you, I have learned that there are many invisible denizens who are not stopped by either holy water or salt. Nevertheless, I now reluctantly conceded that some might be and, at least, the memory of my old friend Matisse was being honored by the ritual.

I punched the buzzer on the side of the freight elevator and stared up into the video camera high on the wall above. They had added several other cameras recently, positioned at various angles. That was a good thing. I had no idea whether someone was watching me. Nevertheless I waved my hands, hoping for entry. The buzzer sounded and I yanked the door up. The iron jaws opened and the large corrugated cross welded to the back of the elevator came into view. Part of me was not feeling very good about my descent. The dark of the alley behind me was like a vacuum, sucking away all the sound and light, heightening the moment. I stepped into the elevator, pulled the doors closed, and pushed the down button.

The Asylum was originally built as a fallout shelter, so it was considerably deeper and larger than a normal basement. This was a warehouse-sized carnival funhouse with the most exotic occult artifacts one could imagine. Think of a cross between the Ringling Bros. circus and the Library of Alexandria and you'd be in the ballpark. The elevator lurched to a stop and I yanked the doors open.

The optimistic side of me—albeit, a very small side— half expected Kanya to greet me and ask questions about my meeting with her mother, and accost me for why I'd sprung the topic upon her without warning. But Kanya wasn't there. The expanse of the Asylum stretched before me.

I stepped out of the elevator cautiously, passing through the scanners without incident. Several video cameras aimed down at this spot, as did a Centaur Singularity blaster, in the event Mothra might make it this far and require microwaving. Tall aisles stretched in opposite directions, illumined by overhead spotlights. Thick pools of shadow interrupted glimpses of iron maidens, mummified remains, and crates with bio-hazard labels. My footsteps echoed across the floor. The command center was straight ahead. A stack of wooden pallets sat behind the forklift. The light was on in this low squat structure.

"Hey! Anybody here?" My words echoed through the vast subterranean museum. "It's Reagan Moon! Anyone here?"

There was no reply.

I slowly approached the building, letting my spiritual sensors stretch their legs. On the floor next to the entryway sat several pairs of boots, much larger than anything Kanya would wear. Inside I could see tall boxes stacked unevenly. The place appeared significantly more cluttered than Matisse had left it.

"Kanya?" I said. "Hey. It's me."

But there was no answer.

The controls for the elevator were in the command center. So whoever let me in was probably still in there. Or nearby. But the vibe I was getting was not good.

A tingle traced my spine before flowing into my fingertips. My hands flushed cold, and I cringed. It had been a while since I'd felt that phenomenon. One of the last times I had, I suctioned death out of someone's body. I hadn't thought of a name for this power yet. But as quickly as it came, it subsided, leaving me opening and closing my hands trying to chase the chill out.

I scanned the warehouse again and called out as I did. The camouflage netting and rosary beads still draped the entry to the command center, just as Matisse had left them.

"Kanya. Hey, it's Reagan. You in here?"

I ducked under the netting and as I rose on the other side, someone released a high-pitched shout, spun away from the wall where they'd been backed against, and struck me with the heel of their foot on the bridge of the nose. The blow landed perfectly and sent me sprawling backwards, through the door, and onto the warehouse floor.

I knew immediately who it was.

The small, nimble figure leapt out of the door and jumped diagonally across my torso, possibly to land another blow with her foot. I was lucid enough to reach out and catch hold of her foot. The second I did, I wrenched it the opposite direction, successfully toppling her backward.

She stumbled sideways into the pallets. The stack teetered, and several crashed to the ground, taking the girl with them. In that instance, I jumped to my feet with my palms open and hands extended.

"Hold it now! Hey! Stop!"

It was all I could manage before the small, silver-white haired figure laughed, tossed aside the pallets, and leapt to her feet. She pranced toward me, shadowboxing like a prize fighter entering the ring.

"It's you again!" she said, her eyes twinkling with mischief and mayhem. "I shoulda known."

"Cricket. You need—"

I didn't have time to finish the sentence because the waif dashed to my side and jammed her elbow into my ribs, using the action to propel herself away. As she fell back, Cricket snatched my head with both hands and attempted to plant my face into her knee. I had just enough time to bring my fists up, wedge them between her arms, and pull her hands apart. This caused her to lose hold of me. We both toppled back in opposite directions.

"Cricket!" I gasped, scrabbling to my feet again. Tears streamed from my eyes, making me wonder if she'd broken my nose with the first blow. "It's Reagan, dammit!"

Cricket was already on her feet. She shook her head, swept the hair out of her eyes, and giggled. "Reagan, Shmaygun. You're all the same."

She bobbed on her toes, filled with mirth and madness. Preparing to make another move.

Pain radiated across my face. "Where's Kanya?" I said. "Bring back Kanya, okay?"

"We don't like to talk about her."

"Yes! Yes we do. We like to talk about Kanya!"

"No we don't!" Her eyes flashed with fire. "She's not coming back. Never, ever, ever again."

"She's you, Cricket!"

"Shut up, Shmaygun!"

"You know that, right? Kanya is you."

She giggled, "Cricket is Cricket, silly."

"No. She's—she's part of you. Or you're part of her. Geez!"

She grew still and then frowned, as if the thought had almost registered. Then she shook it off and smiled. "You're bleeding."

I reached up and touched my face. Blood was streaming from my nose, down my shirt.

"Look what you did," I said. "That was my favorite shirt. Now get Kanya! Bring her back. I'm her friend. I'm yours too."

"Cricket doesn't have friends. That's the only way. No friends! No friends, no enemies. And Cricket doesn't like enemies."

"I'm not your enemy!" My hands were now glistening crimson as I tried clasping them over my nose to stop the bleeding. "We're friends, Cricket! Me and you. And Kanya. We're all friends!"

She bobbed on her toes, radiating a maniacal glee. Apparently, Cricket enjoyed some verbal sparring between her sessions of whup-ass.

I scanned the area for a weapon, simultaneously trying to walk myself through the same steps that had allowed me to teleport earlier that evening. Maybe if I concentrated, I could duplicate the feat. I hurriedly sought an object or location to fix my eyes on. But if I passed through something during the jump, I could do all kinds of damage. In those few seconds of internal debate, Cricket leapt at me. It was more like a launch than a leap, and nothing at all like a jump. If I didn't know better, I'd say she was temporarily suspended by an invisible tether from the air. For as she reached the apex of her arc, she somersaulted in midair, went past me, driving her heels into the back of my head. A flash of white exploded behind my eyes. I staggered forward. I tumbled into the wooden pallets where she had lain.

Cricket was whooping it up as I hurriedly scrabbled to stand and slipped in liquid. I looked down to see skid marks in my own blood on the floor. In the second it took me to glimpse this, Cricket darted into the command center and emerged wielding the Finger of God, the ornate javelin that Matisse had kept on hand for close encounters with revenants. She pointed it at me and smiled broadly, approaching like some dark pixie about to claim her prize.

"Ha-ha!" she said. "I win. You don't."

I managed to wobble to my feet. "You win! You win!" I held up my hands. "Dammit! C'mon!"

If it was possible to die of a bloody nose, I was fairly convinced I was going to. My nose was pumping blood like a fire hydrant. She inched toward me, the tip of the javelin glinting in the light.

"Cricket! Listen!" I attempted to appeal to her while jamming my palm into my snout. "I want to help. Okay? We're friends. See? Friends."

She moved closer, swaying the tip of the javelin playfully in front of me, tracing invisible figure eights in mockery.

"I know why you're here," she said in a sing-song voice.

"Good. That's good you know."

"Cricket doesn't need her anymore," she said.

"You *do* need her."

"Oh no, silly. She died to me. When she let us go, she died."

"No. She didn't die."

"She did!" She lunged forward, swiping the javelin at me. It nicked my shirt, sending a shred of cloth flying. "She died when she gave us to the monsters."

The monsters? What was she talking about? It made me wonder if we werc talking about the same person.

56

Then I said carefully, desperately, hoping to appeal to some iota of memory inside that volcanic psyche of hers. "Cricket. Kanya isn't dead. She's alive. She's alive, Cricket. You're alive because she's alive. She's alive, and I need to see her."

Her brow furrowed and a slight apprehension seemed to pass through her features. Some memory had been pricked. She shook her head. "Not her. We don't talk about her. It's Momma. Momma's dead. Momma gave us to the monsters."

That's when I remembered. I reached into my jeans pocket and pulled out the totem that Audra had given me.

"Look," I said. "This is for you."

Cricket backed up, but when her eyes caught sight of the totem, they widened. At the risk of getting impaled. I placed the object in the palm of my hand and stepped closer, so that she could see it. Her features softened. The lunatic rage was extinguished by the sight of the five-petaled pewter flower. She studied the icon. Her hands wrung the grip of the javelin as her gaze flicked up and back at me. The mirth and cunning had left her features, replaced now by an almost child-like vulnerability. She may be some kick-ass ninja, but somewhere inside the complex make-up of this shapeshifter was a fearful little girl. And in that moment, I glimpsed something else in her eyes that gave me hope—I saw Kanya.

The javelin slipped from Cricket's fingers and clattered to the floor. She reached out and took the totem from me. She turned and as she did, I could see her hair morphing, flushing from silver-white to black. Her cheekbones were reshaping themselves.

I spotted a rag on the forklift, grabbed it, and jammed it to my bloody nose.

That's when a voice sounded from behind me.

"Step away!"

I did.

A tanned, muscular man with bleached short-cropped hair wearing camouflage pants marched in brandishing a rifle, which he had aimed at the girl. Keeping the rifle poised at the changeling, he said to me, "I see you met Cricket."

I didn't reply. I could only watch.

"Broken nose? That's it? You ain't the first, boss." He took two steps forward, rifle leveled at her. "Just hang tight. If she makes one move, she's goin' down."

CHAPTER 6

He held a well-polished, thin-barreled rifle, which he possessed with natural ease. It was aimed directly at Cricket.

"Don't shoot her!" I yelled.

The man's gaze did not leave his rifle sights. "Why not?"

A tight-fitting black muscle shirt hugged his impeccably firm upper body. A large knife hung from a canvas gun belt at his waist. His demeanor was poised with mercenary detachment. This guy was grade-A military.

"She woulda killed you," he said. "Without prejudice."

"I know, but she's a friend."

He issued a loud, sharp, mocking, guffaw. "That how all yer friends treat you?"

"Just ones like her."

"It's a tranquilizer," he said gruffly. "Easiest way to put her down."

"Put her—? She's not an animal!"

"You sure of that?" he glanced sideways at me.

We both returned our gaze to Cricket who was staring at the totem I'd handed her. Her hair had turned and her body was reshaping itself, transmuting, returning to Kanya's proportions. She did not look at us while this was happening. Her eyes were fixed only upon the icon held in her fingertips.

This did not persuade G.I. Joe to lower his weapon. "When she gets fierce like that, there's only one thing that'll stop her—elephant tranquilizer."

"You've gotta be—"

"No I am not!" He glanced at me again. "And you've got steady leakage goin' on there, mister. You should plug that thing up 'fore you bleed out."

He was right. Good Lord! The entire front of my shirt was soaked in blood. I placed the rag over my nose, and we both watched as Kanya stared at the totem.

Ripples passed through her torso, some reconfiguring her frame, others commuting color and tonal differences. Her thighs and upper body forced her clothing taut as she returned to herself.

This was only the second time I'd ever seen her morph before my eyes. But the wonder of it remained. After the things I had experienced, you would think that such phenomenon were blasé and unspectacular now. Perhaps it's to my credit that I watched, mystified by the transition of this bloodthirsty sprite into an ordinary woman. Nevertheless, I found myself wondering if I too didn't have a violent alter ego trapped inside me waiting to bust out. God help us all if that was true.

Seeing the change, the man lowered his rifle.

"Well, I'll be. She flipped." He glanced at me. "What is that? What'd ya give her?"

"I'm not exactly sure."

"Whatever it is, she's back on herself." He looped one thumb into his belt and looked squarely at me. "I ain't ever seen that before. What'd you do?"

I kept the rag pressed to my nose and just shrugged.

Kanya, stared at the totem. Drops of sweat glistened on her forehead. She finally looked up with her lips pursed. It was the gaze of a guilty child. When she saw my bloody nose, her eyes widened.

"Reagan?"

I gave her a thumbs up.

"Is that from...?" She swallowed hard.

I nodded.

She clenched her fists and turned away.

"It's all right." I removed the bloody rag from my face. "At least I'm still alive."

The man guffawed again and lifted the rifle to his shoulder.

He said, "It's a good thing you got that there, Kay. So what is it?"

She mumbled something.

"A what?" he asked.

"It's a totem," she said angrily. Then her voice softened. "*My* totem."

"Well, it pretty much saved his life."

He approached and reached out to shake my hand. But being that it was covered in blood, he withdrew his hand and simply nodded. "The name's Mace."

"Moon."

There was a hint of Midwestern twang in his speech. He was my height with probably twice the muscle mass. A good 'ol boy with an ego the size of a freight car. Dude had a rigid jawline and oozed testosterone. If he wasn't already a bouncer at a biker bar, I was sure he could be hired immediately.

"Heard some about you from Matisse. God rest 'is soul." His gaze did not waver from mine. "He believed in you, Moon."

"I know."

"On the other hand, Kay here isn't much for elaboration." He turned back to Kanya. "You probably noticed that. She has mentioned once—*once*—that you saved her life. But she did not proffer details. Keeps things bottled up. Just like that 'lil one inside her."

"Mace," Kanya said firmly. "Enough."

Mace peered at her, shook his head, and then marched toward the command center. "You're gonna kill us all someday. Mark my word."

We watched Mace enter the command center and then turned to look at each other.

"Here." She hurried over, took me by the arm, and guided me into the building.

Maps of the city still covered the walls of the command center. Another computer had been added to their arsenal; three monitors now triangulated the corner work station. Several gun racks had been mounted and were occupied by unusual looking rifles. I was not an expert in firearms. Nevertheless, these guns looked like something designed by a mad scientist rather than a gun manufacturer. Dirty dishes were stacked on a table next to the largest humanoid skull I'd ever seen. Only this one had a single eye socket, dead center. What do you know—maybe cyclops really did exist. She walked me into the hall and turned into the front room, her living quarters.

"You need to lie down," she said, pointing to the couch.

As I sat down, she went to the sink, wet a cloth, and returned to me.

"Lie back, and hold this on your nose."

As I did, I found myself looking up at her and trying to equate her features with Audra's. They definitely shared the same body shape, the angular frame and thick thighs. Almond-shaped hazel eyes, hard but immensely deep. And both of them seemed way too serious.

"I am so sorry," Kanya said.

"That's all right."

"No. Really."

"It's okay. Now I'll have a broken nose to match my broken ribs."

"She can't control it," Mace said from the doorway. He entered, still holding his rifle, leaned it against the wall near the kitchenette, and sat down at the table. "Which's one reason I counseled Matisse against bringin' her on board."

Kanya straightened; her back was to him, her lips pursed. Flipping the icon over and back in her fingertips.

"When she turns," Mace said, "she's an after-burner. Stand back or get torched. It can happen like that." He snapped his fingers. "No warning. Just stand clear and prepare for theatrics, mister."

As he spoke, Kanya's features seemed to tighten with rage. I wanted to tell the guy to shut the hell up before he triggered another outburst. But he continued, as if goading her on.

"I saw her single-handedly dispatch two Nagas. *Two.* Without a weapon. It was epic. Think we got their rattlers around here somewhere. After that, we were lucky she didn't turn on us and eat us for dessert. Apparently, she's impervious to spells in that state. And logic. A friggin' machine. Their master, some witchdoctor freak, threw the book at her. Didn't phase 'er. Hell, I think it made her stronger."

Kanya shook her head. She set the totem down on the nearby end table, went to the sink, returning to swap my bloody rag for a clean one. She began working over me, wiping my face and hands, and pressing her fingertips gently against my nose.

"I don't think it's broken," she said. "But—"

I took her hand and stopped her. Then I looked at her while asking Mace, "What do you mean, she can't control it?"

Kanya yanked her hand from mine. "That's not true, Mace."

"She can't control it," he repeated matter-of-factly. "Not that little one, Cricket, she can't. The others, maybe. But Cricket—she's a bloody terror."

Kanya glanced at me and then snatched up the other rag and took them both to the sink, where she stood wringing them out while the water ran.

I sat up on the couch. The flow of blood had finally stopped. I tapped the bridge of my nose gingerly, wincing at the touch.

Mace continued. "If she ever snaps down here, we're AFU—excuse my language. Might throw open the shutters and release everything—banshees, djinn. A regular Pandora's Box. Worse, she might flip the switch and demo the entire joint. Who knows? In that phase, she is whack, completely unpredictable. I've learned that the hard way. Why d'ya think I keep this close by?" He reached over and patted the rifle. "Matisse was more reliable. He had a way with her. Had one key, but kept it close. I attempted to persuade him to get 'er some help. She refused. Still does. Says she can handle it on her own. That's Kay. Stubborn as a jackass in a tar pit."

Kanya remained at the sink with her back to us. The muscles along her shoulders tensed as Mace spoke.

"Not sure exactly what triggers it," he said. "Threats. Bad dreams. We can be goin' along stellar for weeks, months. And then one day, *bam*—she is AWOL. Which's what you encountered today."

"So," I queried. "What set her off?"

Mace glanced at Kanya. "She was on the phone. Next thing I know, she's bouncing off the walls like a Tasmanian devil."

Kanya flung the wet rag into the sink, shut the water off, turned around, and glared at him. "That's enough, Mace!"

He spread his arms. "Do I lie? *Do I?* It's all true, Kay. All of it. Your father said the same thing."

"It was my phone call," I said to Kanya. "Wasn't it?"

She marched out of the room and crossed the hall.

Mace shook his head. "Nothin' but drama with her. If I were you, I would steer clear."

I heard her tumbling the dial to the safe in the other room. I looked at Mace, who patted his rifle and winked. "As long as I got this, we got a chance."

Kanya marched back into the room holding a key. Much like an old skeleton key, it had a long shaft and an oval head. She held the key between her fingertips, wagged it at Mace. "It's the only other key." She handed it to me. "There," she said to Mace. "You happy?"

"Hold on a second." I extended the key back to her. "I don't want this."

"My father wanted you to have it." She straightened. "He wanted you to watch after the Asylum, isn't that what you said?"

"Well, yeah. But—"

"Him?" Mace laughed. "He doesn't know the first thing—"

"Doesn't matter," she said. "If I really can't control it, like you say, then you need someone else. You can be my babysitters. How's that sound? Both of you. I can vouch for him." She glanced at me. "He's reliable."

You could say her words bolstered me. Kanya was a fiery soul. She did not wear her emotions on her sleeve. And when she did show emotion, it was usually on the scale of red hot.

"Listen. He's right. I wouldn't know the first thing about what to do down here. I'm a paranormal reporter. Remember? I write stories about ghosts and werewolves."

"You'll learn," she said.

"A paranormal reporter!" Mace snorted. "Is that like a paparazzi?"

"I'm not a paparazzi. And I don't want this."

I extended the key further towards her.

"It's what he wanted," she said firmly. "Right?"

I sighed in frustration. Then I looked up at her. "So you really can't control it?"

Mace folded his arms and looked expectantly at her.

She shifted her weight.

"Go on," Mace said. "Tell 'im."

"Most of the time," she said.

"Ha!" Mace guffawed. "It's those other times that you have to watch out for."

"I've never met a shapeshifter before, you know. Hell, I never used to really believe in them. I thought, you know, that you could, well…change whenever you wanted?"

Kanya nibbled on the inside of her cheek, her brow furrowed in icy intransigence.

Finally, Mace spoke. This time, I detected compassion in his voice. "It's some sort of traumatic break. That's what Matisse reckoned. When she was tortured."

"Tortured?" I said.

"And she don't do animals," Mace added. "Not that I can tell. Somethin' triggers that memory and—it's on."

I looked at her. "It's your mother, isn't it?"

She stared into space, without any seeming emotion.

"Did you say her mother?" Mace asked.

There was enough metric tons of tension in the room to crush a continent.

Finally, Kanya went to a small closet, reached in, pulled out a leather jacket and put it on. She reached back into the closet and pulled out a Hawaiian shirt with nifty blue Hibiscus flowers and macaws. She tossed it at me.

"You need to change," she said. "Put that on."

I caught the shirt. "This?"

"I need some fresh air. C'mon."

"You need more than fresh air, Kay." Mace watched the two of us, appearing humored.

"Um," I said, scowling at the shirt. "Don't you have something less flowery?"

"Let's go." She started to the door.

"Hold on a sec." I got up and looked down at my beloved Pink Floyd shirt. It had been drooled on, bled on, and shredded by a sacred javelin. Mace saw me staring at it and motioned to a trash can near the sink. I went there, removed the shirt, and deposited it in the wastebasket. Making sure to not reveal my scar to them, I turned away as I put the Hawaiian shirt on.

Kanya was standing at the doorway. She nodded and left.

Mace just smirked.

I hurried after her.

"You're forgetting somethin'." Mace pointed to the end table.

I snatched the totem and shoved it into my jeans pocket along with the key for the Asylum. Then I hurried out and joined her at the elevator.

Mace called out from the entryway of the command center. "Hey! You wanna borrow this?" He extended the tranquilizer rifle out to me and roared with laughter.

"Reagan!" Kanya called from inside the elevator. "Let's go."

As she yanked the elevator doors closed, Mace yelled, "Hope you know what yer gettin' into, Mr. Paranormal Reporter."

CHAPTER 7

Kanya stepped out of the elevator, into the night, bristling. Her aura was a fiery halo. Whatever nerve had been touched, it was hot and raw and ready to explode.

She looked up into the night sky and tightened her jacket around her.

I just stood watching her. Pain had begun throbbing from the bridge of my nose, radiating into my eye sockets. Before this was over, I'd have two black eyes. I felt the back of my head. The spot where she'd kicked me contained a golf ball sized knot. Maybe Klammer wasn't paying me enough for this gig after all.

She remained staring up into the night sky, breathing deeply, intentionally.

"He was a little hard on you." I said this more out of desperation than that I believed she couldn't handle an interrogation.

"No." She shook her head. "He's right. I could have killed you down there."

"You obviously underestimate my powers of self-defense."

She looked sideways at me, and wasn't humored.

"Look," I said. "I've never met a shifter before. At least, not that I know of."

"I don't like to be called that."

"Well, then—"

"I'm sick of people trying to label everyone."

I shrugged. "Sometimes labels fit."

She faced me. "And sometimes they don't."

Her words were charged with pain and offense. I acquiesced.

"I don't know what I am. Okay, Reagan? For all I know, I'm the same type of monster we're trying to stop. I can just disguise it better than others."

I wanted to object, but knew there was some truth to what she was saying.

"Okay," I said. "I'm sorry."

She glanced at me and sighed deeply.

"There's no guarantees," she said. "None. There never was. When I joined my father here, that was the first thing he said. *There's no guarantees*. Just because we sprinkle holy water and prop up our crosses, there's no guarantees. No guarantees we'll survive tonight. No guarantees I won't snap and kill us all." She paused. "And there's no guarantees that someone from your past, someone who did you wrong, won't show up out of the blue. And everything you've been trying to forget gets shoved right back in your face."

I let that sit there for a minute.

"Look, Kanya. She came to me. I didn't seek her out. I didn't even know she was here. I have no reason to go digging around in your past. Trust me, that's not my style. Anyway, she seemed honest—what can I say? She was sorry for what happened. She wants to make amends. I think it's—"

She looked firmly at me.

I swallowed. "I think it would do you good."

As I said this, I thought about the totem in my jeans pocket. Thank God Audra had given it to me. For the moment, I watched Kanya chewing on my words. Whatever conclusion she reached, I knew we'd all be better off if I kept the icon close.

"Take me with you," she said.

"Huh?"

"I just need to calm down. Take me with you."

"Well, I…where are we—?"

"You said you had an assignment?" She scrunched her nose. "What were you thinking?"

"No. Me? Nothing." I issued an uncomfortable laugh. "Yeah. I have a story. That's where I was going when I called you."

"Okay. Can I tag along?"

"Well, yeah. Sure."

"Then let's go."

She began walking down the alley toward the street. I stared after her, still rather numb from the cascade of events that had buried me. I was exhausted. Confused. My nose hurt. And to top it off, I was wearing a godawful Hawaiian shirt.

"Okay," I said to myself. "Then let's go."

The moon was long gone at this hour, taking Regulus and its companions with it. Luckily, I'd kept the passenger seat of the Cammy relatively clean since our last adventure. These days, I had to be prepared for visitors. Whether they were welcome or not. Other than a dirty jogging shirt stuffed behind the seat, the residual smell of fast food wrappers and the lingering stench of smoke and ash, the Cammy was nothing but high class.

We drove west on 3rd street, past the Little Tokyo marketplace and Angel City Brewery. Kanya was never one for small talk. Instead, she stared out the window as we went. When I felt the tension had finally left the atmosphere, I ventured a query.

"So is she your mother?"

Without looking at me, she said, "I thought we were going to drop it."

"I thought so too."

"Yeah. She's my mother."

I waited, but she did not elaborate.

I said, "She rescued me tonight."

"Rescued you?" She turned and looked at me. "How?"

"Well, it's kind of a long story. Klammer sent me to a house in Palos Verdes. A ranch. Looking for someone named the Shroud."

"Go on."

70

"Some guy attacked me there. Tried to kill me, in fact. He called me the Seventh Guardian. They were waiting for me. They knew I was coming. There was a shrine there—a Santa Muerte shrine. And a lerium lab. Jimmy said it was the Mexican mafia, but they don't know for sure yet."

"*Santa Muerte*—shrines have been popping up everywhere lately."

"More than usual?"

"Oh yeah. So how did my mother save you?"

"Right. Well there was this lady. She called herself Etherea. She knew who I was, about the Imperia, about the Tau. She knew everything. Apparently, whoever she's working for, they're worried about me."

Kanya's eyes were fixed intently upon me now.

I continued, "She said that the Tenth Plague was coming, and that I needed to get ready for it. That's when Jimmy showed up. Your mother had called him, I guess. Anonymously. And said that I was in trouble. I was. Sounds like she knows Klammer, and she's been following me. Following *us*. Anyway, she showed up at the Crescent and spilled the beans."

Kanya settled back in her seat.

"The Tenth Plague," she finally said. "You mean, like the plagues of Egypt?"

"I'm not sure. Are you saying we're going to be overrun by locusts or frogs or something?"

"That wasn't the Tenth Plague."

I searched my memory banks. Biblical trivia was not one of my specialties. Although now that I had a cross fused into my chest, breaking out the religious lexicon might be the smart thing to do.

"Don't you remember?" she said. "The Tenth Plague was the death of all the firstborn. And the summoning of the death angel."

She was right. The Tenth Plague was the angel of death. I thought about Etherea and the kiss she'd planted on my lips, and the hellish fury that radiated from the pores of her flesh. And the molten shrine that had consumed the Grim Reapress. I felt sick to my stomach.

"Saint Death," I said. "Figures."

We crested a hill, and St. Vincent Medical Center came into view. The hospital had a storied history. Built in the mid-1800s by the Daughters of Charity of St. Vincent de Paul, Saint Vincent's was the first hospital in Los Angeles. When you're around as long as St. Vincent's, you can't escape the inevitable urban legend. And St. Vincent's had its share. Supposedly, a real-life exorcism had been conducted there once. A synth was, allegedly, treated for a gunshot wound before government ops retrieved the experimental cyborg and expunged all record of the incident. And then there was Eve. Beset by scandal, layoffs, and debt, the hospital had struggled, often teetering near bankruptcy or buyout. It showed in fraying edges. Some of the lawns were dying and graffiti marred several walkways.

We pulled up at the back entrance. I was familiar with the hospital having done a story on a multiple personality case there. The victim claimed to have had nine different personalities. But when the psychiatrist he was seeing charged him nine times his normal rate, one for each different personality, the patient called foul. I usually incorporated the story into any discussion about multiple personalities or the free market.

Kanya and I exited the Cammy and walked across the parking lot to the hospital. I slung my backpack over my shoulder. It was getting on 2 a.m. and I was feeling it. I explained to her the info I had about Weeping Eve and the strange video tape that had surfaced. For reasons unknown, this seemed to add a kick to her step.

We entered and made our way to ICU.

Two female nurses were at the desk looking semi-interested in things other than our approach. When I mentioned that I was a reporter and we were there to see Alma Curtain, both nurses stopped what they were doing and looked up.

"She's been off."

They glanced at each other again, as if there was much more to their co-worker's absence than met the eye.

"I'm with the Blue Crescent," I said.

"Really?" One of the nurses perked up. "I read it all the time."

"Sure you want to admit that publicly?" I smiled semi-sarcastically.

She continued unfazed. "That story about the UFOs on Mulholland Drive—I keep telling my husband they're here. He doesn't believe me."

"A skeptic, huh? I used to be that way."

"But now you're a believer." She smiled proudly.

Kanya and I exchanged glances. Her lips were curled in a faint, knowing, smile. This, too, encouraged me. I'd never had a permanent investigative partner. But there was something about Kanya at my side that made me seriously entertain the plausibility of such an agreement.

"So is there anyone that can help us?" I asked. "I just have a few questions about a video we received."

"Of Eve." The nurse nodded. "And the deaths."

"Yeah."

"Of course," said the nurse. "Just a minute." She picked up the phone at her desk and punched a button.

In a few minutes, a middle-aged black woman, whose name tag read Trissa, approached. She had a cheery disposition, which, as a career nurse, I imagined was incredibly helpful for longevity. In my experience, grumpy nurses were the absolute worst.

We exchanged pleasantries, and then Trissa led us into the ICU. It was a large octagonal area surrounded by individual rooms with the nurse's station dead center. The sound of ventilators and monitors ticking away provided a fitting soundtrack to our investigation.

"So, this is where the image was filmed." Trissa led us into a room with an empty bed. "We're keepin' it unoccupied for the moment. Those kind of sightings always spook the staff. And once the patients find out, somethin' along the lines of panic is inevitable."

"May I?" I asked Trissa, pulling my camera out of my backpack.

"I suppose."

She pointed out the location of the security camera that had filmed the encounter and how, when the nurses hurried into the room, the temperature had dropped significantly. I asked Trissa if she had personally ever seen Weeping Eve and her feelings about the ghostly legend. Despite being deeply religious, the woman confessed being greatly unnerved by the stories. Nevertheless, I flattered her by asking her to stand at the empty bedside for a photo. She seemed eager to have her picture in the paper, provided I said only nice things about her and her employer.

I'll admit, hospitals kind of give me the creeps. You don't need supernatural power to feel the death and despair lurking in every shadow, every chart, every doctor approaching with a clipboard and a blank stare. Ellie, my deceased girlfriend and former light of my life, used to say that if we knew what awaited us on the other side, most of us would have to fight from wanting to drop dead on the spot. As much as this knowledge buoyed me, the darkness here at St. Vincent's ICU had begun to seep into my bones.

Trissa straightened the sheets on the empty bed. "The whole thing's rattled Alma somethin' terrible."

"Is that why she's off?" I asked.

"She's *been* off? Three or four days now. Said she couldn't sleep, and when she did, she started having bad dreams about Eve coming after her, swooping up from the basement to steal her soul. Gives me the chills just thinkin' about it!"

As she spoke, I allowed my senses to untwine in hopes of uncovering some new tidbit of info. This was feeling less like your typical haunted hospital tale, and more like part of a much bigger story.

"I was working that night," Trissa recalled. "It was 'round 3 a.m. I remember that because 3. a.m. is considered the Devil's Hour. That's what my aunty always used to tell us kids. Bad things always happen at 3 a.m. At first Alma thought someone was in here with her patient, a visitor or maybe the night shift custodian. But when she got here, the room was empty. Except for the patient. Who was in cardiac arrest. After he was pronounced dead, Alma came back and re-watched the surveillance tape. I watched it with her and—God's honest truth—she was in there. Eve. 'Bout scared me to death. A dark cloudy shape, it was hovering over the bed. Alma made a copy on her phone, which is against hospital policy of course. She posted it and the darned thing went viral. Course, Alma got in big trouble for that. A few days later, she called in sick. This is her third night out and, between you and me, I fear the worst."

"Why do you say that?"

Trissa straightened her collar and hesitated. "I shouldn't show you this. Some internet site. Social media. I follow her. She posted some pictures." She motioned us away from the bed, out of the sight of the surveillance camera, and produced a cell phone from under her scrubs. She tapped something on her phone, handed it to me, and I scrolled through several pictures. Most were selfies of a young attractive Hispanic woman. While several of the images were blurry, the background was clear. And recognizable. Yellow signs warning *Keep Out* across a chain link fence. Stacks of K-rails and a large subterranean entrance with the NeoKor moniker emblazoned on signage.

I handed the phone to Kanya.

"It's the downtown subway project," Kanya said.

"Oh, my Lord," exclaimed Trissa. "Why would she be down there?"

"That's just what I was going to ask you."

"I don't know. I just don't know. It doesn't seem like her. She has two kids. Lord. I thought they shut that thing down."

"I think they have."

"Then why would she be down there?" Poor Trissa was on the verge of palpitations. She took her phone from Kanya and pocketed it. "This just keeps getting weirder and weirder."

The exchange seemed to heighten a sense of dread that had crept into the edges of my consciousness. Why would a nurse sneak her way into the downtown subway project? After filming a ghost? For the first time, I could feel the ICU crawling with Invisibles. I quickly surveyed the room again. But if Eve had been here, she was long gone.

I thanked Trissa and encouraged her to take it easy, trying to lighten the mood by reminding her of the possibility of seeing her picture in print. She escorted us out of the room and through the ICU ward.

"Please," she said, "if you hear anything, would you let us know?"

"Absolutely," I replied. "If we learn anything, we'll—" I stopped in my tracks.

Standing across the lobby, I glimpsed a burnished, softly glowing figure in the ether.

"Bernard," I said matter-of-factly.

Both women stopped and looked at me.

"Who?" Trissa said.

"Really?" Kanya said.

Bernard stood at a doorway, looking into an ICU room. Room 209. At my exclamation, he turned. His look was grim— as grim as an angel's look could possibly be. In fact, he appeared to be angry. He stepped back as I approached, as if to reveal to me the object of his malice.

"What is it?" Trissa said from behind me. "Excuse me?"

My heart began to pound. The spiritual sensors inside me exploded to life. Every shadow, every whispered word, seemed heightened. Bernard stepped further away from the door as I approached. My mind was racing, spiking. And as the interior of the room became visible, I quickly realized why.

A dark figure was hunched over the bed like some demented carrion bird, perched vulture-like over the dying soul.

I have once witnessed the passage of a soul from earth into paradisiacal splendor. I'm fairly sure that few human beings have been privileged to witness such an event. In that case, the soul in transit was blissful. There were no choirs of harp-playing cherubs to serenade him. Nevertheless, the bliss that was his and the land that he ventured into could only be described as heaven.

Standing at the entryway of Room 209 in ICU, I knew I was glimpsing the shadow of hell itself.

"Can you see this?" I asked Kanya.

She came to my side. "It's freezing in there."

"You can see it, can't you?"

"I can see something. A mist, or shadow. It's hard to tell. But it's cold. Reagan, this's bad."

Apparently, the Invisible that was crouched over this poor soul was so real, so wholly evil, that even the non-gifted could see it. Or at least part of it.

I, however, could see it in its awful totality.

Hideously black. So dense that it appeared not as an object, but as a missing swath of space. Angular, as if cut from stone or volcanic rock. I'd learned that Invisibles impinge differently upon our world. Some only make their presence known through the actions of their host. But others are so despicable, so completely vile, that their presence transcends their own dimension and spills into ours. Not only was this being of the latter order, it had apparently attracted friends. For the room teemed with demons. Hunched in corners and coiling about unseen spatial crags, they waited for this poor soul to die. A distant chorus of moans and vacant cries filled my ears. A chasm to hell itself had been opened in room 209.

I stepped back as my hands flushed with power. The tingling erupted in my sternum, sending waves of energy coursing through my limbs. The scar of the Tau had awoken.

"What is it?" Kanya said. "What do you see?"

As she said this, the lights on the floor winked on and off. A collective gasp sounded from the nurses and patients. Then the heart monitor flatlined and the alarm signaled that the patient was in cardiac arrest.

Trissa pushed me aside, took two steps into the room, stopped, and shrieked.

"She's here. Lord, Jesus!" The nurse gripped her chest.

At this, the creature turned. A blast of foul breath struck me. This was no ghost. Dear God, this was something of another order, a fabulous winged monster.

I gripped Trissa by the shoulders and brought her back out of the room. Then I stood in the doorway, my body charged, studying this alien entity. Its face was concave, a sunken bowl of black in which two slits of red neon eyes hovered. A serpentine tongue whipped back into its mouth. Oddly enough, it reminded me of an aardvark sucking delectable ants from a hill. Only this tongue, I knew, was designed to suck souls from human beings.

I logged this for entry into my sketchbook *Of the Invisible Order and Its Inhabitants.* However, at this juncture, the publication of such a book would be posthumous.

For a second, I thought the Bony Lady had come to life. But then something unexpected happened. Its body swelled and large appendages sprang from its side. Raven-like wings of dense black plumage opened. The invisible monster shrieked, leapt from the bed, and flew straight at us.

CHAPTER 8

I stumbled backward as the soul-eating demon swooped toward us. With Kanya and Trissa, the night shift nurse, behind me, I tripped, and we collapsed backward onto the ICU floor in a heap.

While they could not fully see the terror that I witnessed, apparently, they saw enough of it. Trissa kept shrieking as Kanya dragged herself out from under me, staring at the thing above us.

"It's Eve!" someone yelled behind us as chaos erupted in the ICU.

But I had serious doubts that what hovered over me now was a ghost.

It passed through the wall and rose to the ceiling, buoyed there by some unseen current, looking down upon me with both hate and wonder. Perhaps this creature was not used to being interrupted during meals. But in my case, it was a sense that my proximity posed a direct threat to its very existence. Tendrils of fog wound round this devil, coiling about its body, cocooning it in a misty cloak. Its wings were open, their span forming a massive umbrella against which shone those nuclear red eyes, boring malignity into my very being.

My entire body throbbed, pulsated with energy now. It was like a fount of raw electricity had been uncorked inside me and left me stewing in raw plasma. But I had no idea what to do with it.

The commotion around me seemed to fade as my eyes fixed on this dreadful creature. Part angel, part hellion; an alien entity that gorged on human misery and despair. How many souls had this thing displaced and jettisoned into eternity?

Someone tugged at me while figures fled into nearby rooms and down hallways. The beeping of the monitor was barely audible. For the moment, it was just me and this foul harpy, two beings worlds apart, united by a single want—to somehow stop each other.

Kanya was standing, calling out to me. The ICU lights continued flickering on and off, creating an eerie strobe effect. "He's in cardiac arrest," someone yelled from Room 209. Despite the urgency of Code Blue, this demonic encounter seemed infinitely more important.

My body was humming, surging with adrenaline. I was an earth guardian. I needed to keep reminding myself of that. I'd been zapped with abilities, and I knew that the sooner I apprehended those abilities, the better. Not that everything would go smoothly. But if battling soul-sucking winged parasites was to be part of my job, then possessing some non-traditional talents would be helpful.

Yet while I sensed I could battle this thing, I had no idea what such a battle would entail. Should I lunge at it, try to take hold of it? That seemed absurd. Or was it? Maybe I could speak a word of command. You know, like some high-powered exorcist. But no such words of command came to my mind, nor confidence that I could wield them.

The stench of death pummeled me. With every beat of those infinitely black wings a Sahara of rot blasted my senses. Dry and ancient, as void of life as an atomic wasteland. Visions of the Santa Muerte shrine and Etherea's ominous warning about the Tenth Plague skittered about my mind. This was somehow part of it, a chapter in a fairy tale of death and destruction that was playing out in real-time. This monster was a player. Its eyes were piercing, radiating malice. And hunger. They turned not in sockets, but in space. Empty space. Orbiting inside a hollow cranium. As I stared, something slithered from inside that pit of a face. A serpentine root twisting and twining its way to me, aimed at my heart. For a moment, I thought I might get drooled upon for a second time that evening.

Someone in the nurses' station was on the phone yelling for assistance. Several faces peeked out of various ICU rooms, their eyes wide with shock. I could only imagine what this stand-off looked like to them. I lay on the floor staring up at what they probably perceived as a ghostly apparition roiling on the ceiling. Oddly enough, I was more concerned that Kanya would snap, turn into Cricket, and wipe out the entire floor. She didn't. Instead, she stood, urging me on to get up, and rise to the occasion. However, I was no John Wayne and unlike me, the soul-eater was without assistance. For behind me, a golden sheen rose. Much like the sun breaking through the clouds on a stormy day, a burnished glow radiated from behind me, illuminating the death angel.

It shrunk back in revulsion, appendages flailing again the light.

I turned to see that Bernard had reappeared behind me.

My guardian angel stood with his lip curled in disgust. He had no weapon, save fists clenched in adamantine resolve.

I've never seen an angel quite that pissed.

At the sight of Bernard, the demon creature turned and raced out of the ward, leaving lights flickering in its wake. I was momentarily stunned.

"There it goes!" Kanya shouted. "C'mon!"

She helped me to my feet, and we bolted out of the ICU after the creature, leaving the staff in absolute panic.

Kanya led the way, reaching an intersection where she collided with a male nurse whose tray of medical tools clattered to the floor. I looked down the opposite hallway in time to see the spirit turn, look at me, and then sweep through a closed doorway.

"There!" I pointed.

As Kanya ran to the spot, she shouted over her shoulder, "What was it?"

"I don't know. But it wasn't a ghost."

We stopped at a stairwell entry.

"A demon?" she asked.

I stood panting. "I think it was…an angel."

She stared at me.

Without thinking that the specter might be waiting on the other side, I opened the door. The stairwell was dimly lit. Empty. I entered the landing, looked up the flight of stairs, and then leaned over the handrail, hoping to catch sight of the monster.

Somewhere down below, a soft skittering sounded.

"It's down there," Kanya said.

"Let's go."

I had no plan of attack. I tried to envision myself channeling John Constantine only to be embarrassed by the idea. Modeling oneself after a character in a graphic novel was not exactly fodder for inspiration. In fact, the thought of staring into that creature's hideous face with any degree of spiritual authority was as laughable as me performing successful brain surgery. While blindfolded. Either way, if I managed to survive this experience, Haunted Hospital was shaping up to be another top-notch piece of paranormal reportage.

We descended several flights of steps, but there was no sign of our alien angel. I allowed my senses to roam. Trite reminders about health related issues were stenciled on the walls of the stairwell. *Walk Your Way to Health*, one read. Another asked if the reader knew the *Steps to Happiness*. I slowed, allowing intuition to direct me.

As we approached the bottom landing, Kanya said, "Feel that?"

"It's getting cold."

"Really cold."

A chain hung across the stairwell here with a *Do Not Enter* sign. At the end of the flight of steps was a single metal door. A rusty outline revealed where a sign used to be fixed. In front of the door stood Bernard with his arms extended. He slowly shook his head as I met his gaze.

"It's Bernard," I said. "He doesn't want me to go down there."

"Well then, don't go."

Our breath had turned to fog.

"But it's in there. I know it."

Bernard glanced over his shoulder at the door, turned back to me, shaking his head even more resolutely. He knew I was second-guessing his judgment.

"It's in there," I repeated.

Bernard folded his arms.

"Reagan, let's go."

"Hold on a sec." I directed my words to my visible and invisible friends. "So that's it? We have this...this killer ghost on the run and we just bail?"

Bernard pretended like he wasn't listening.

"I'm sorry," I said. To both of them. "But something's going on here. That thing, whatever it is, it's part of this. It's part of whatever the hell Klammer got me tied up in. Saint Death. The Tenth Plague. The Shroud. Whatever it is, it's all connected."

She mulled the possibility and then shook her head.

"If Bernard says no, then you should listen to him."

Bernard nodded enthusiastically at Kanya's words.

"Hey, I survived a lightning strike," I said. "What could be worse than that?"

"Are you itchin' to find out? Besides, what good is a guardian angel if you don't listen to him?"

It was a good point. Which I ignored. "Well, then wait here. Both of you."

I climbed over the chain and began descending the steps. If you're thinking this was a dumb thing to do, you'd be right. But if Destiny guides a man, then even his missteps and blatant bone-headedness falls to a hand bigger than his own. At least, this was a theory I thought worth exploring.

Bernard waved his hands frantically. But when he saw my resolve, he offered a look of disgust and just shook his head.

"Look," I tried to explain my intransigence to him. "I think I can beat this thing. I've got to at least try. Especially if it just keeps killing people. Okay?"

Bernard shrugged, stepped away from the door, and issued a graceful sweeping motion with his arm.

"Sorry ol' buddy. Just stay close in case things go south."

Rust blisters marred the edges of the door. I took the handle and it too was frigid. This had to be a Category Five poltergeist or some equivalent monstrosity. Angels didn't turn things cold like this, did they? The door opened into another set of stairs which descended into a darkened maze of hydraulics and machinery. Bursts of steam sounded from below. I took two steps into the room. My chest was tingling again. Energy surged through my body. Something was down here. I knew it.

"Reagan!" Kanya called from the landing above. "Be careful."

I nodded towards her, noticing in the process that Bernard was gone. Hopefully, he'd not left to find someone more compliant to protect.

When I turned back, I did not see the winged devil. To my surprise, it was a petite female wearing a pink nightgown with frilly neckline and sleeves, and shiny silver shoes. Although her shoes were not resting on the ground, but lightly hovering midair, just beyond the stairwell.

This brought me pause and short-circuited the adrenaline that had seconds ago been driving me forward.

She wasn't a woman, but a girl, with large watery eyes. They had been alive once to beauty and joy, but now were filled with sadness. Endless sadness. Her fair cheeks were moist with tears. Bruises marred her throat. For around her neck was a rope which hung taut from a large rusty pipe overhead.

It was Weeping Eve.

Here was the menace, the ghoul of urban legends. The devourer of souls. However, she looked anything but menacing. Which brought me immediate pause. This is where she had killed herself. Somewhere in the dimensional ether I

84

was privileged to witness Eve dangling there like an everlasting testament to the fateful decision she had made.

I stretched out my hand to the ghost, then returned it to my side. As much as I had pity, I knew that contact with the dead carried its own karmic repercussions. Her eyes were full of pain and sorrow, not just for herself, but for me. This greatly puzzled me and I wanted to inquire of the spirit what had happened. And why she was concerned about me. She'd served enough time and should move on. Suicide was not the Unpardonable Sin; she needed to forgive herself and let go of the pain. Of course, that was straight out of Ellie's handbook. But something other than regret had coalesced inside this lost soul. I could only describe it as militancy, a slow burn to do well or see something made right. Perhaps a plea for assistance.

Eve extended her hand. She was beckoning me, not to join her, but to help her escape from this dank crypt.

Even in my business, necromancy is not something to mess with. In this case, however, I was not required to answer the question of what to do with Weeping Eve. Because noxious gray tendrils suddenly webbed the atmosphere. The darkness of the basement grew blacker, immersing Eve in its pitch, forming a canopy of infinite space above me. From within this chasm peered neon red eyes.

The death angel!

Adrenaline seized my body again, power surging recklessly through my limbs. I couldn't compete with this thing. Who in the hell was I kidding? I needed to grab Kanya and get as far away from this dungeon as quickly as possible.

The creature's tongue unspooled from the abyss of its face and fingered towards me.

"Reagan!" Kanya was in the doorway. "Get away!"

In the confusion of that moment, I turned and launched sideways, teleporting, shearing the metal handrail, before slamming into the brick wall opposite me. Dust exploded and the wall opened, revealing a cavity of some sort. I glimpsed clothing and gloves inside this space before I dropped to the ground. The creature spun towards me with its wings arched overhead. Plumes of foggy breath filled the air as did the stench of death.

Eve was gone. My chest was throbbing, supernormal power coursing uncontrollably through my limbs. It seemed as if my mind and body were moving in two different directions, threatening to pull me apart. Half of me wanted to challenge this monster, while the other was wetting its undies. *Focus, Moon! Focus!*

The monster had me exactly where it wanted—frozen in indecision and fear. It glided towards me.

I rose to escape—white sheared my brain, a blinding nebula exploding behind my eyeballs—and materialized halfway across the room. I slammed into the ceiling. A plume of steam burst into the air as a pipe fractured overhead. Then I dropped like a rock, landing flat on my belly. It knocked the wind out of me. My chest exploded in fiery pain.

Kanya kept yelling from the doorway. But I didn't have time to attend to the pain or the demands of my sidekick. I gasped for air and rolled over as the demon creature descended upon me, smothering me in its dark icy embrace.

Somewhere in the haze of it all, in the choking, blinding confusion, a massive figure entered the room and bellowed something. The atmosphere seemed to grow stifling, dense. It was as if every mote and molecule was being pressed of its essence. Something like a dry rattling emerged from the devil's face. Was it taunting me? Or was it shrieking? Its red eyes orbited wildly inside that dense black crater of a face. The coldness possessed my bones, radiating out from this creature.

A dread certainty draped me. I did not need to breathe any longer. Nor was a beating heart necessary for survival. For I was becoming one with the godless dark. A victim of the destiny I had chosen.

CHAPTER 9

P ale light greeted me, as did a smell of burning sulfur and gas. For someone who has not always been a good person, an afterlife of burning sulfur shocked my mind awake.

I jolted upward, gripping my chest.

It was the life-sized scrap sculpture of Don Quixote standing nearby that made me realize I was still very much alive and on earth.

I was on a cot in a spacious, but sparsely furnished, undecorated room. A plain chair sat near the bed and over its back hung a towel. A small window set high on the adjacent wall revealed daylight. I swung my legs off the cot and sat there studying the immense statue looking down on me. Forged of sheet metal scraps, bolts, and random parts, it was an unmistakable rendering of the Man of La Mancha. His head was made of an overturned bucket and bed springs. A slightly curved metallic plate, perhaps from the fuselage of an aircraft or missile, forged its shield. Its fingers consisted of welded bolts and spark plugs, which gripped a large spear constructed from woven rebar and capped with the tip of a massive artillery shell.

Unless hell consisted of such odd sculptures, I was pretty sure I remained a resident of earth.

Hammering sounded somewhere nearby, followed by the chugging of a compressor. The smell of burning metal and unusual compounds tainted the air. I was in some sort of industrial warehouse. But where? And how had I gotten here?

Images of the ghastly soul eater jarred me fully into the present. Immediately, I remembered Weeping Eve, our encounter in the hospital basement, and the teleportation fiasco. At first, I felt embarrassed about the incident. Then I quickly surveyed my body to make sure that I still had all my limbs.

Once again, I seemed fully intact. Except my body ached everywhere, nowhere more than my chest.

I was still wearing the Hawaiian shirt Kanya had loaned me. I gently unbuttoned the first two buttons in hopes of seeing what the hell was happening to the Tau scar. My skin was viciously inflamed. The scar had continued to finger its way toward my pectoral muscles and abdomen. A strange, charred, red-rimmed blister now occupied the center. Either the Tau was slowly consuming my body or someone was drilling to China via my sternum.

"You're awake."

The voice from the doorway startled me. I rose to my feet, quickly buttoning the shirt.

"Careful," said a large, dark-skinned man.

The word *large* was an understatement. This man was a virtual colossus. If it wasn't for the friendly smile on his face, I was pretty sure Andre the Giant had reincarnated to pulverize me into submission.

"You've been through a lot," he said. "There. Sit back down, friend. Rest."

He approached me, and even though his demeanor was unthreatening, the sheer size of the man forced me back on to the cot. He wore a thick canvas apron that was stained by burn marks. I guessed he was of Tongan or Polynesian descent. A bandana was tied taut over curly, short cropped hair. He had thick lips and broad facial features, and a round, firm belly that would have made a Sumo wrestler envious.

I looked up from the bed as this mountain of a man stood over me.

He looked strangely familiar. I recognized him from somewhere. I traced my memory banks and then it all came back to me.

"You're the guy who...You rescued me from the—last night. You brought me here."

He brushed his hands off on his apron, and extended onc to me.

"I'm Rapha. It's fine finally making your acquaintance."

"I'm Moon. Reagan Moon."

My hand was swallowed up in his enormous grip. Good grief, this guy must be 375 pounds of solid muscle. Maybe 400! Island style tattoos traced his forearms and marked several knuckles. Needless to say, it was a firm grip, yet accompanied by a warm smile.

"You're right," he said. "I brought you here. And I already know your name."

"Welcome to the club."

He furrowed his brow at this. "Pardon?"

"I'm sorry," I explained. "But lately it seems like a lot of people I don't know already know about me."

He nodded. "You should get used to that. You've been the source of much rumor and innuendo. Perhaps that should be expected. I anticipate there will be much more."

"Oh, well," I sighed. "There goes my life as a hermit."

He peered at me. "I was told that you had a strange sense of humor."

"Really."

He nodded.

"It's a necessary life skill," I said. "Humor is the only thing that helps me cope. Especially when fighting flying monkeys."

He appeared to ponder this. "Wit and humor do not reside in slow minds, according to Quixote. Perhaps my inability to grasp your humor is evidence of my own slowness."

"Don't take it personal, bud."

I massaged my temples. My head felt like a freakin' wrecking ball. When I closed my eyes, visions of Eve and the soul eater flitted mercilessly about my brain.

"It was a death angel," Rapha said. "One of the *maelohim*, a lower caste of Harvester."

I looked up.

Mike Duran

"You were cocooned in a Delusion, Brother Moon. A spell. Paralyzed by a simple belief that you were subservient to its will and unable to contest its authority."

"You say that like I could have stopped it."

"You could have! Breaking spells is somewhat routine. At least, it will become that for you. First, you must discern the nature of the spell—its source and type."

"I don't think you—"

"If an object from the enchanter can be retrieved, typically an object of power like an article of clothing, a talisman, or something similar, one can perform a disruption and counteraction. I once encountered a warlock and used his own talisman to counter his spell. It just took—"

"I don't know how to do that! Don't you get that?"

My angry outburst surprised him.

"My apologies." Rapha tipped his head. "Yet you can do much more than stop death angels, Brother Moon. If I am correct, you can do far more." Then a gentle smile creased his lips. "But you're correct—there is much to learn."

The more I studied this man, the more I realized that something was different about him. His size was not just a physical reality. Something like mass or density, the actual physical properties, were encoded in his being. His body seemed to exude substance, impenetrability, on the verge of emitting its own gravitational pull. Upon closer look, his features appeared slightly elongated, as if he were made of clay and pressed under a rolling pin. If he were cut open, I wondered if this man would gush blood or just ooze iron.

"Is it morning?" I asked.

"It is. The new moon quickly approaches. And with it, the Tenth Plague."

I looked up at him. I was beginning to feel like a lead actor who'd forgotten his lines. The entire world seemed privy to a reality that I was ignorant of.

I groaned, lowered my head into my hands, and said, "I give up."

"Good." He placed his large hand upon my shoulder. "Giving up is the perfect place to start."

"I have no idea what you're talking about."

He removed his hand. "You will. Once the others arrive."

"Great—a convention."

"No. A council."

"Let me guess…"

"The Imperia."

"I knew it."

As much as I attempted to appear aloof, this made me a little nervous. *The Imperia.* I'd heard so much about them. But my inclusion in the group had remained a grand mystery. Was there some dues I must pay? Perhaps they believed in hazing rituals. Either way, I could not fathom what they possibly wanted with me. I'd heard so much about them, some tales being almost unbelievable. Did they, too, have unusual powers? Of course! You can't go by such a lofty title without some magic street cred. Perhaps a better question was how I could possibly fit in with a group of earth guardians. And who was this friendly giant and what role did he play with the group?

"Your girlfriend's in the other room," Rapha said.

"You mean Kanya?"

"I do. She's a fine woman. Courageous. And principled. A fine fighter too, I hear." He pointed to my face and chortled.

I reached up and rubbed the bridge of my nose when he said that. "It looks that bad?"

"I'm afraid so. If it wasn't for the changeling, you would be in far worse condition than you are. You should thank her. She's protected you in ways you don't yet know."

"Protected me? You're probably right. But Kanya's not my girlfriend."

"No? Perhaps she will be. Felix would know. He is gifted in Foresight."

"Felix?" I stared at him. "He's here?"

Mike Duran

"I'm afraid not. Not yet, at least. We are expecting him. But Felix has his own timeline, in a manner of speaking."

"Tell me about it."

"The rest will come. We have been anticipating our meeting. All but Ki." His features grew grim at the name. "Ki will not be a part of our gathering. Still, we cannot concede. The times demand it. The Imperia have slumbered far too long. Indeed, we have allowed the torch to slip from our grasp. Your deeds, your adventures, have reignited our hope. The hope that Heaven is still on our side."

"I've done that?"

"Ah, humor." A smile slowly spread across his face. "We're all knights errant, Brother Moon."

I wasn't sure what he meant by this. Although *errant* definitely described my ways. But before I could muster another witty rejoinder, Rapha said, "You must be hungry. Yes?"

He did not wait for me to answer. Instead, he waved me forward and headed toward the door.

I glanced at the Don Quixote sculpture and said, "Here's to knights errant." Then I rose from the cot and followed Rapha through a narrow hallway and past a series of low ceiling rooms. Strange artwork lined the hallway, mostly framed pieces of odd metallic abstracts. This hallway opened into a large warehouse. By all appearance, this was a welding shop. Tanks of acetylene and CO2 stood lined in a chain link cage. On this cage hung a full length mirror. Crates of soldering rods were stacked near a rack of welding torches. Barrels of water sat near heavy iron tables upon which lay large pliers, hammers, bolt cutters, and files. Sculpted pieces in various stages of construction stood about the warehouse floor. There was a Chinese dragon made from Asian coinage and a bust of unusual chain mail. But amidst the artwork and equipment were more unusual contraptions like a massive cage with iron shackles and something akin to a torture rack.

92

Rapha stomped through the aisles, tools clanking in a belt under his apron. I caught up to him and asked, "Where are we?"

He spoke over his shoulder. "This is my home."

"So, I mean, what do you do here?"

"Mostly I create original metalwork for wealthy, eccentric patrons. The City of Angels has many who enjoy such fine artwork. And are also wealthy and eccentric."

We passed a hammered copper bust of a Medusa. I stopped to admire the beauty of this piece and Rapha returned to my side.

"You did this?" I asked.

"I did. It was un-commissioned. I quite enjoy Greek mythology and fantastical tales of adventure."

"Wow," I said. "It's really cool. Have you thought about displaying at a local gallery?"

"I haven't."

"Dude, this would look boss in my apartment."

"You must have an odd apartment."

"You could say that. And what about this other stuff?"

"My talent allows me to facilitate other, more unusual, ventures."

That's when I noticed Kanya standing at a workbench with a dog at her side. She was holding a mug of steaming liquid. Her hair was slightly messy, as if she'd just woken up, but she looked great.

"You're awake," she said.

Upon seeing her, my embarrassment returned. I'd made a fool of myself last night, dissing Bernard and then bouncing around the basement like some idiot whirling dervish.

The dog also noticed me and approached with a friendly skip in its step. It was a mastiff of some sort, thick frame and large droopy face, but other than that, not very intimidating. It sat down at my side and looked up at me. I couldn't tell if it was waiting to be petted or given a command.

If this was Rapha's junkyard dog, he might have to think about investing in a real security system.

"Don't let Saucy fool you," Rapha said. "She can be very protective."

"Saucy?"

"Short for *Sausalito*, the city where we once lived. She's great at recognizing good guys."

I looked at the dog sitting there politely, wagging her tail. "Then she's obviously reading me wrong."

Rapha laughed. "You're either incredibly humble or very cynical, Brother Moon."

Kanya smiled. "Try, very cynical." She covered her face and turned away.

That's when I noticed an oddly familiar device on the workbench in front of her.

As I approached her, she said, "You know, you scared the heck outta me last night."

"I apologize. Yesterday was a rough day."

"Yeah, but whatever was happening to you—it was crazy. It was like your body transmigrated or something. I'm not sure. You hit the wall, then the ceiling. And then that…that ghost—"

"It wasn't a ghost."

"Well, whatever it was, it swooped over you. I didn't know what to do. That's when *he* showed up." She gestured to Rapha. "He did something and everything changed—the air, the space around you. Everything was being...crushed."

We both looked at Rapha, who smiled and nodded, but offered no explanation.

"Anyway," Kanya continued. "They wanted to check you at the hospital. Do you remember that?"

"Vaguely."

"We convinced them you'd be all right and managed to get you out of there before security got there and detained us. You got pretty beat up yesterday, Reagan." There was a hint of guilt in her voice, probably from knowing that she had been part of the beating I took. "Are you sure you're all right?"

"Hey, I survived a lightning strike, remember? Maybe I can survive anything."

It was a great comeback, but I was afraid its lifespan was fairly limited.

I turned my attention to the object on the workbench. It was a finely meshed cage almost the size of a milk crate. Large bolts were crudely welded at varies angles, as was an insulated device inside the unit which appeared to contain circuitry and tubing. Perhaps most strange of all was the material this apparatus was made of. Dull black, save for a slight sheen along the welded joints. Similar material comprised a large net which draped the back of the workbench. I would have thought it chain mail, except that it was the size of fishing net. Its edges were frayed and burnt, apparently a work in progress. What the hell kinds of creations was Rapha the welder producing here?

I pointed at the odd cage and said to him, "I've seen this before. Or something like it."

"Of course you have," he said. "Felix wears these. He calls it a hood. Quinn developed the design, and I've assembled it."

The material was unusually cool and smooth. I lifted it to find it was also extremely lightweight. However, the material was extraordinarily dense. Try as I might, I could not bend the material. Combine that with the absence of refraction, and I was having a difficult time discerning what type of material this contraption was made of.

"Odd," I said. "What is this *hood* made from?"

"Ndocron," Rapha said matter-of-factly.

"En…"

"Docron."

"Never heard of it." I peered at him and said suspiciously, "So where does this stuff come from?"

He paused. Finally, he motioned us forward. Rapha followed the length of the worktable. At its end, a dirty tarp lay draped over something large and bulky. He removed the tarp, revealing a black, oddly shaped boulder, maybe waist height. While its ridges were sharp and jagged, like that of volcanic glass, it seemed to absorb rather than reflect light.

"Go ahead," Rapha said. "Touch it."

I did. It wasn't nearly as slick as I expected. Or heavy. In fact, it seemed so light or porous that I was able to push the boulder back and forth.

I straightened and brushed off my hands. "Either I've suddenly developed superhuman strength or this is the lightest rock known to man."

"Perhaps both!" Rapha said. Then he grew pensive. "I may be premature in what I am about to reveal to you. But since I am here to instruct you and we have such short time, I will tell you this. Felix has created a portal through which he can transport this compound from Arcadium. You're familiar with the parallel dimensions, yes?"

"Sort of," I said reluctantly.

"Of course you are. They are well known. Well, Arcadium is not quite a parallel dimension as much as it is a higher dimension, a world influenced by ours yet independent of determined outcomes. Arcadium is Earth's higher dimension."

After a moment, I said, "So you're saying that you got this rock from…*a parallel dimension?*"

"Yes. You understand the basic laws of physics, I am told."

"I guess."

"Of course. A universal force of repulsion has long been theorized, something that acts as a barrier which keeps possible worlds from merging. Others have speculated an element, a material that comprises this barrier or membrane. It acts as a skin, if you will. We believe we have discovered such an element."

"Ndocron."

He nodded.

My legs were feeling wobbly again.

Rapha could tell I was having a hard time.

"It's early," he said. "There is much to learn."

"Yeah. So if this material restrains or harnesses anti-matter or the spread of a multi-verse, I mean, why does Felix wear this on his head?"

A smile inched the corners of his lips. He reached across and patted me firmly on the shoulder. "There is much to learn my friends. Come. Let's eat before the others arrive."

Rapha led us out of the mill and into the adjoining living quarters. Saucy followed, appearing especially interested in my arrival. Although my apartment prevents me from owning a dog, I am extremely fond of canines and owe my survival as an adolescent, in part, to the companionship of a dog. Had I lived on a ranch as opposed to a small bachelor apartment in downtown Los Angeles, I would no doubt have several dogs by my side. Seeing Saucy caused me to make a mental note—at a future date, I would become a dog owner again. Moving out of the city to a ranch would also be rather enjoyable.

We entered an area that contained kitchen appliances, where the smell of coffee greeted us. Even though I am a wizard at Mexican omelets, in my world, there is no better breakfast than hot oatmeal. Raisins and brown sugar only enhance what is already a great eat. So when I saw a pot of thick oatmeal steaming on the stove, I couldn't imagine a better way to start my day. Other than maybe not having to think about death angels and parallel universes.

Rapha motioned for us to sit at the small dining table. He then removed his welder's apron. When he did, I couldn't help but stare. A Tau draped his neck. It was similar to the cross I'd been commissioned to protect. But unlike mine, Rapha's had not been fused into his sternum. I reached up and touched the scar on my chest.

Rapha saw me looking. "Yes, Brother Moon. This is what binds us. And, indeed, perhaps will unite us in death."

I peered at him. "Yeah. Perhaps."

"As it may Orphana," he said, motioning to the doorway.

I turned to see a prosthetic leg standing alone in the doorway. In a black boot.

CHAPTER 10

I just stared, trying to register what I was seeing. Nothing about this prosthetic leg appeared unusual, save that it stood alone in the doorway. As I watched, the atmosphere around it began to thicken and to particulate into a murky form. At first, this phenomenon appeared without distinguishable shape. Then the cloud began coagulating around the leg, growing denser, and assembling into the shape of a human torso. A second leg took shape as did hips, waist, arms and upper body. In a matter of seconds, the particles coalesced from the atmosphere and took the shape of a woman.

I squinted, attempting to make sense of this marvel. Did the others see it? Apparently, they did. Both Kanya and Rapha were watching this unusual manifestation. Which meant that I wasn't hallucinating. But neither was this an issue of second sight. The materializing woman was happening in real time, not in some invisible dimension. I rubbed my eyes, refocused, and studied this strange new visitor.

A black woman with short curly hair, wearing a stylish paisley skirt, now stood in the doorway. She appeared completely solid. Anything but spectral. I could not help but gape. She was busty with a thin waist and wore 1970s style retro garb, a black turtleneck and a long paisley skirt, with a thick white belt to accentuate her figure. And tall black leather boots. She too had a Tau draping her neck, which matched her outfit quite nicely. However, she leaned upon a cane, which struck me as rather unusual.

"Friends," Rapha gestured to Kanya and me, "may I introduce Orphana, Third Guardian of the Imperia."

I wiped my mouth to make sure I wasn't drooling. "How did she—? How did you do that?"

She seemed surprised by the question and glanced at Rapha before answering. "It's just what I do, hon."

"Yeah, but…where did you come from?"

Again, she glanced at Rapha. She wasn't annoyed as much as she was uneasy. "I've been here the whole time. Over there." She pointed somewhere in the far corner. "And out there." She jabbed her thumb over her shoulder into the warehouse. "In a couple different spots, actually."

I just stared.

"Felix has a fancy name for it," Orphana said. "Particle agglomeration, I think. He has names for all our talents. I just call it *clustering*. It's got me outta quite a few scrapes. And got me into a few. But if you'll excuse me, I need to sit down."

She leaned over and adjusted her prosthetic leg, then hobbled to the table using her cane and plopped into a chair.

"So you're Reagan Moon." Orphana nodded. "Rapha's done nothing but talk you up."

"Gee," I said. "We barely met a half hour ago."

Saucy's ears perked up and she trotted off into the warehouse.

"Good," Rapha said. "The others are here."

"Are they all like her?" I glanced at Orphana.

"Not exactly," she said. "But I'll take that as a compliment."

Saucy returned, panting excitedly with more guests in tow.

"Quinn!" Rapha exclaimed. "Celeste! So good to see you." He strode to this couple, shook their hands, and embraced them. However, they seemed more interested in me than in niceties.

The man approached. A twenty, maybe early thirty-something. He wore a silk vest and high dollar shirt, with his sleeves rolled up. He had a thick mustache waxed into a masterful handlebar. Brown hair slicked back and a full, well-manicured beard to match. And he wore funky sunglasses. Oblong wraparounds that looked more like experimental Pradas than ordinary street specs.

"Nice shirt," he said. "But what happened to your nose?"

"This? Heh. Let's just say I bumped into an old friend."

"You bumped into someone all right! Looks like they did most of the bumping." The man slowly walked around me, his gaze roaming from head to foot. Then he stopped in front of me and folded his arms. "So you're Reagan Moon. You've made quite a splash."

"That wasn't my intention. Trust me."

"Oh, I trust you, all right. You don't become an earth guardian without some reservations. None of us did." He glanced over his shoulder at Orphana. "Did we?"

Orphana didn't look at him. "Please," she said, placing her cane across her lap. "He's on our side."

Quinn looked at me. I could see my reflection in his glasses. "From what Felix said, you're the next big thing. Gonna plug all the holes, pull everything together. Even get Ki back on board. Big expectations for someone so...untried."

I glanced at Rapha, who did not appear happy.

I said, "I don't know what you're talking about."

"Course you don't. None of us do, if we're honest. We usually wing it, and hope for the best. So far it's worked out. Barely. But it's worked. Apparently someone *is* watching out for us. I just wouldn't push my luck, if you know what I mean."

I glanced over my shoulder at Kanya. I could feel the tension rising in her. She wasn't thrilled with this guy. The last thing we needed was for her to blow a fuse. But I couldn't really blame her.

"The name's Quinn," the man said. "Quinn Rodgers. I moonlight for the Imperia when I'm not coding, designing high-tech polymer vests, or working for Mynx."

"The tattoo joint?"

"It's a side, side job. I specialize in script and scrolls. Birds too. Got a fondness for wings—swallows, eagles. But I'll do anything. That's where Rapha got his sleeves. Nice work, if I do say so myself."

"Yeah."

"Anyway," he said, extending his hand. "I'm the resident royal pain in the ass. If you haven't already figured that out."

As I looked at his hand there, open, waiting for my grip, I felt uneasy. There was something about this guy, his cockeyed gaze, his swagger, which made me uncomfortable. I sensed mixed motives. Or an ability to conceal what motives needed masked. Perhaps that was intentional. Or was it the air of unbridled confidence that made me hesitate. Once I shook his hand, I realized that my instincts had proved correct again. For the minute our flesh touched, a presence invaded my brain.

Quinn Rodgers was inside me.

I immediately tried to release his grip, but was unable. Or perhaps it would be more accurate to say he wouldn't let me. It wasn't just that he tightened his grip, but that something unnatural conjoined my mind to his. We sidestepped each other, hands still clasped, in a semi-dance move. Still, I could not escape. I was being watched. My thoughts, emotions, my secret fears and longings; they were all naked to him. He gripped my hand tighter, his presence bore down on me. I could smell the mustache wax, the high dollar cologne. Feel the moisturizer on his flesh. And taste the burn in his brain. He was filled with rage. And righteous indignation. I instinctively shrank back, trying to cordon my mind from Quinn Rodgers.

My chest began to tingle as power rose up in me. My thoughts became disjointed, as if he were quartering my mind for inspection. I caught my reflection in his glasses, teeth gritted, brows creased in angry resolve. I reached up, placing the heel of my opposite hand on my temple. But I couldn't stop his intrusion into my psyche.

"Quinn," someone said. "That's enough."

As much as I tried to resist his thoughts, the more I felt I was exposing something to him. I feared I was losing control of my bodily functions. He knew about my feelings of inadequacy, the growing anxiety that I'd been called into something I could not possibly accomplish. He knew about my concern for Jimmy Pastorelli. He knew that the physical changes to my body had left me feeling lost and confused. And his lips curled in delight as he burrowed into the recesses of my mind.

I'd written stories on telepaths before, but always with tongue in cheek. The highest grade telepath ever recorded was Vernon Kane Peoples. During the Vietnam War, the government had exploited Peoples and discarded him like a spent ordnance. He ended up rotting away in some convalescent home in Arizona, probably controlling the nurses with his thoughts, pinching their asses, and bribing them for extra prune juice. But if Peoples' power was real, then Quinn's was persuasively comparable.

I gritted my teeth, fighting to keep my knees from buckling. My chest was burning, my thoughts swinging from fierce resistance to complete surrender. I feared I might piss my pants.

If not for the second woman, Celeste, stepping forward and taking Quinn by the arm and pulling him back, I'd probably have become a smudge on the floor.

"Leave him be, Quinn," she said. Her voice was firm, but gentle. Perhaps it was that gentleness that persuaded Quinn to draw back and release my hand. Either way, once he did, I exhaled and stumbled forward.

I bent over with my hands on my knees. Energy raced through my body. But my head was free of Quinn and I was more focused, seemingly more in control of my functions again. However, I wasn't sure whether to thank him for going easy on me or drive my fist into his teeth.

"Guess I was wrong about you," he said.

I rose and stared at him. He smiled and twirled his mustache.

"Most people are." I squeezed the back of my neck and backed down.

"But *Vernon Peoples*? Really?"

"I researched him once," I said. "That's all."

"Peoples was a hack. And a sellout." Then Quinn wagged his finger at me. "Don't ever, ever, become that. Do you hear me?"

Celeste reached up, took his hand, and lowered it to Quinn's side.

"Don't mind him," she said to me. "He's got issues."

"Me?" guffawed Quinn, readjusting his glasses. "We all have issues. Don't we, O."

"Cool it, will 'ya?" Orphana said, barely acknowledging him.

"Friends," pleaded Rapha. "Please. This kind of discord does nothing but empower the Black Council."

"Yeah." Quinn nodded dramatically. "Tell that to Ki."

At this, Rapha straightened—all seven-foot-forever of him. His friendly demeanor vanished and his countenance grew dark. I got the sense that these two had a history and my arrival had dragged it back into the light.

Quinn appeared to sense Rapha's anger because without looking at him he exhaled sharply and turned away from me.

I swallowed hard and pressed my hand against my chest. The scar was tingling. Glancing back at Kanya, I could tell she was having the same misgivings about our new friends. I leveled my gaze at the four of them.

"Who in the hell are you people?" I said.

"*You* people?" Quinn turned around. "You mean *us* people, don't you? They have a name for us—*Nomlies*."

"As in…"

"It's short for *Anomalies* and used mostly as an imprecation."

He faced me squarely. Although this time I sensed something different—benevolence. And he stayed out of my head.

"Here's the thing," Quinn said. "If Felix is right, we don't have the time for beer and pool. All right? Maybe another year. I'm not here to be your best friend. And I'm sure as hell not going be your therapist. Although I know enough about you right now to have you committed."

He wasn't exaggerating.

"Look," Quinn continued. "In the proper settings, I can induce mass hallucinations. Once I extracted the launch code for surface to air missiles via mental reading. Last year, I used remote viewing to help the LAPD locate three victims of Brian the Brain Wagner. Remember him? I can spontaneously combust certain elements on a small scale. It comes in handy when I forget my lighter. Been doing this since I was a kid. Reading people. Feeling their anger and their regrets. Steering them to do something they hadn't actually chosen to do. And you know what? I still haven't figured out everything I'm capable of.

"So, here's the thing, Moon." He stepped closer, his features tightened with something like mad delight. "You can do the same damned things as me. Probably more. We just don't have a lot of time to babysit you. Okay?"

I stared at my timid reflection in his glasses.

Celeste gently pulled Quinn back.

They were all looking at me. I could see it now. Their auras were off the charts; rainbows of energy. Were these people something other than human? The air seemed to bristle with wild possibilities.

"He's right, Reagan."

I turned to Celeste. She was middle-aged, almost motherly. Her hair was more red than auburn, and draped over her shoulder in a long braid. A smattering of pale freckles graced her cheeks. Her eyes were kind, friendly. Quite the opposite of Quinn, her gentle gaze invited me to rest there. If

Greek goddesses were real and living in the 21st century, Celeste would be one of them.

"Don't let him fool you," she said. "Quinn's got a good heart."

"Gee," Quinn scoffed. "Thanks, Cel."

"But he's right about you. You just don't know it, you don't understand it yet. Which is fine."

I knew I couldn't dispute what she was saying, so I just nodded.

"I realize this must all seem so crazy," she continued. "Like it's happening so fast. You have to trust us. Both of you." She looked over my shoulder at Kanya. "We've all been where you're at, Reagan. Scared. Confused. But knowing deep down in our gut that redemption is possible. And that something bigger than us is behind it all."

She stepped back, unbuttoned the top two buttons of her shirt, and removed a Tau. It was bronzed, beaten up. But it looked similar to the one I'd once worn. She looked at Quinn, who unbuttoned his shirt, revealing a large similar cross resting on his chest. Rapha gripped his Tau and held it away from his chest. Orphana rose and steadied herself on her cane, turning so that her piece was also in view. She brushed her hand over its surface, causing it to glint in the light.

They stared at me.

Finally, Quinn said, "Now it's your turn."

As much as these strange new people puzzled me, I felt an unusual camaraderie with them. Celeste was telling the truth—they'd all stood where I was standing. All part of some weird succession. We were all misfits interrupted by something bigger than ourselves and tossed into the deep end. It made sense. Admittedly, there was a part of me that had hoped for the Imperia to be sleek, well-trimmed, immaculately equipped comic book heroes. Seeing these rather mundane, somewhat raggedy-looking everymen and women, I wasn't sure whether to be heartened or really concerned. But for the moment, I was emboldened.

I looked back at Kanya again. She smiled lightly, willing me forward. I nodded, turned around, unbuttoned the Hawaiian shirt and removed it, showing my scar in its entirety.

They all stood fixated at the lightning-fused Tau embedded in my body.

I tossed my shirt on to a kitchen chair as, one by one, they approached and surrounded me. Even Kanya circled around to see what now enthralled them.

"It's a Lichtenberg figure," Celeste said.

I nodded. "The lightning fused it into my body somehow. Cauterized the Tau inside me. I don't know how. I'm not sure if its elements were actually contained or whether they've bled into my system."

"You can still make it out." Celeste lifted her hand and held it open just inches from my chest. She looked up at me.

"May I?"

"You might get shocked."

"Really?"

"Kidding. I think."

"Well," she said. "I've been shocked before."

"Then sure, be my guest."

She made a fist and closed her eyes. Was she praying or conjuring her own personal electromagnetic shield? She opened her eyes and laid her palm flat against my chest, directly over the strange blister in the center of the scar. She pressed lightly, as if sounding out some inner energy. Then she removed her hand and traced her fingertip over the pale tendrils that now twined out towards my pectoral region.

She glanced back at her cohorts, smiling, and returned her gaze to the scar.

"It's beautiful," Celeste said. "There's energy of some sort. Lots of it. Unharnessed. Inside of you. I'm not sure, but it almost seems like a signal. A beacon or something. I've never seen anything like it. Does it hurt?"

"Sometimes it burns at night," I said. "And then yesterday, I—" I swallowed hard and caught Kanya's gaze.

"What?" Celeste asked.

"I think I teleported. I guess that's what you'd call it. Twice."

"Teleportation?" Quinn said in feigned exasperation. "What we need is someone who can recreate matter. Melt heavy artillery. Balance the national budget."

"No," Rapha said, a hint of annoyance in his voice. "We have everything we need, Quinn."

"That's not all," I said. "Each time it happened, the scar grew. It's…it's getting bigger."

They glanced amongst themselves. Whether concerned or just mystified, I couldn't tell. However, it was somewhat comforting knowing that others were just as baffled by my state as I was.

"Then it's true," Rapha finally said.

"Too soon to tell," Quinn rejoined. "The way things have been going, anything can still happen."

"And the Tau?" Rapha motioned to my scar. "It's the omen we've been seeking."

"Not *we*," Quinn said. "You."

"An omen of *what*?" I said.

Once again, my question was met with pensive hesitance.

"Okay, then." I retrieved the shirt and put it back on. "Now it's your guys' turn. Why am I here? And what kind of omen are we talking about?" Then I held up my hand to signal I wasn't finished. "And who's the Shroud, who is Etherea and how does she know about me, and what the hell is the Tenth Plague? And, oh, what's up with the rockabilly vampire who tried to kill me?"

I finished buttoning up my shirt and waited.

"Rockabilly vampire?" Orphana queried. "We don't know anything about no rockabilly vampire, hon. But if we get a chance, I'd love to hear the story." Then she returned to her seat at the table and placed her cane across her lap.

The others stepped back, leaving Rapha to explain.

He nodded. "It's true, you deserve answers, Brother Moon. We have been far too cryptic. And harried by circumstances. Accept my apology."

He lowered his head. Waiting.

I looked at the others. "Sure. I accept."

Rapha raised his head. "As Quinn said, there is much to accomplish in a short time. Our window narrows as we speak. The Summa Nura have grown strong. Humanity's faith has waned, as has ours. The Imperia have wearied. Our ranks have fractured, to our shame. Your defeat of Soren Volden was a great victory. It had repercussions far greater than you will ever know. Your acquisition of the Tau and its fusion inside you has given rise to hope. As our enemy grows in strength, you portend something...new. Something once foretold."

"Explain."

"So there's this prediction," Quinn said.

"It's more than that," Rapha interrupted.

"Okay," Quinn countered. "It's a map. Allegedly. A map of the future. It's Klammer's baby, so no one else has actually seen it. Anyway, supposedly it shows some fundamental shift in the war."

"Refresh my memory," I said, slightly sarcastic. "What war is that?"

"Between Arcadium and Diades. With Mankind in the middle. You really don't know this?"

"I'm almost sorry I asked."

Rapha said, "Arcadium and Diades are earth's higher and lower dimensions. Respectively. Call them Heaven and Hell if you wish, though they are quite unlike those conjured by artists and novelists. The map shows the arrival of one who will reunite the Imperia and ultimately bring an end to the War. The Seventh Guardian."

"I think I'm going to need to sit down."

Quinn said, "Everyone isn't convinced that Klammer's map is immutable." He turned and spoke to the group. "Especially if Arcadium and Diades can be breached. Which would mean that history remains malleable. Until we can stop their latest volley, the Summu Nura still have the upper hand. We have no guarantee, Rapha—none—that we're still strong enough to beat them. Or that Mr. Teleportation here can really do anything about it."

Quinn folded his arms.

"Well," Rapha said. "Then that's what we're here to find out."

"Um," I looked at Rapha and then Quinn. "You guys lost me back at Arcadium and Hercules."

"*Diades*," growled Quinn.

"Brother Moon." Rapha looked at me. "The creature you battled last night, it was a death angel. One of many that have recently been released upon the city. Someone has been summoning death angels. Yet they are only a forerunner to something vastly superior."

"*Vastly* superior," Quinn sniped. "From what we know of Etherea, she was a high-end occultist of some sort. An astrologer to the stars, seven figures. Mansion in the hills. Bodyguards. Etcetera. She specialized in astral bodies, specifically angels. Through lerium, she developed her skills and became something of an icon for the Neuro community. Queen scumbag. Started getting communique from something otherworldly. Probably Summu Nurans disguised as male strippers. Shortly after that, she vanished from the grid. She showed up sporting a thang for Santa Muerte with some mystery henchman named the Shroud. It's pretty murky."

"Santa Muerte though?" I said. "Really? I mean, it's a folk religion. Trinkets, candles, prayers to the dead. That kind of stuff. Hard to believe that this is posing some type of existential threat to humanity."

"This guy." Quinn slapped his palm to his forehead and turned away.

"Ah!" Rapha wagged his finger at me. "You underestimate the old religions. And the faith of those who practice them. Their reverence of Saint Death is just one of many portals into the heart of darkness. It is but a tool towards greater ends. And once blood is spilt, and the faith of the devout enjoined, the Bony Lady becomes a conduit of incarnate Evil."

I shook my head. Perhaps I had underestimated the power of faith. Especially when it involved death cults.

"The Tenth Plague." Kanya stepped to my side. "They're summoning the ultimate death angel, aren't they?"

"Thank God you brought her along," Quinn said.

"Yes," Rapha said grimly. "Azrael—the Archangel of Death."

"The first Passover," Kanya continued. "The death angel passed over all the houses and the ones that didn't have the blood of a lamb on the doorpost, the firstborn were killed."

"She's a rogue," Orphana interjected. "Depending on whose charge she's under, she can wipe out multitudes. Ya know, entire cities. A killing machine with one single purpose. Azrael's no garden variety death angel." She shifted the cane on her lap and looked firmly at me. "She's the queenpin."

"Gee," I said, dizzied by the implications of it all. "I didn't realize there was such a thing as a garden variety death angel."

"That's what you were rescued from last night," Quinn jabbed.

"Untold death will be released upon the city," Rapha said. "To what end, we don't know. Yet. Undoubtedly it is the Black Council's devilry. They have empowered Etherea. Few have the ability to summon such creatures, much less Azrael herself. Yet somehow, Etherea has developed such powers. At the least, she has uncovered the formula for such an incantation. We believe that tomorrow night, at the waning of Regulus, such an event will occur and the archangel will be released upon us."

Celeste smiled. "Which is why your arrival is so timely, Reagan."

"Me? What am I supposed to do?"

"Hello?" Quinn said in a sing-song voice. "You're the Seventh Guardian."

"And?"

"You're the only one here with a cross burned into their body."

"I practically killed myself last night. And you want me to stop the Archangel of Death?" I forced out a laugh. "You guys crack me up. Seriously."

"Quinn's right," Rapha said. "This is what we're called to."

His sincerity wiped the fake smile right off my face.

"There are no guarantees, Brother Moon. But come loss or victory, Heaven is with us." He thumped his fist to his chest. Then he turned his gaze upon me. "You were the one chosen for such a time as this. Not me. Or Celeste. None of us. The Tau has branded *you*. And we are here to help!" Then he grew thoughtful. "It's not to whom you are born, said Quixote, but with whom you are bred."

I stared blankly at him.

"We must see Pentecost at once," Rapha said. "Perhaps the angelologist can tell us how we can defeat such a monster. And help Brother Moon discover his true calling."

"You look kinda pale, hon." Orphana patted the chair next to her. "Come on, have a seat."

CHAPTER 11

I took Orphana's advice and sat next to her at the kitchen table. Being that she had recently materialized from thin air, I caught myself studying her body for confirmation that she was in fact real. To my delight, the stylishly dressed woman seemed quite normal, physically concrete, and very much a nice human being.

Rapha removed his tool belt and served me a heaping bowl of oatmeal, which I eagerly devoured, as Orphana tried to bolster me with encouragement and humor. I detected the slightest Southern drawl, which reminded me of my stay in Louisiana, and when she spoke of the group's escapades it was with pride and verve. Wisdom gleamed in her eyes, and the more we spoke, the more I sensed she was much older than my initial impression. Her stories were colorful and sometimes accompanied by a moral lesson. If what she said was true—and I had no reason to doubt her—this frayed group of heroes had indeed survived hell and high water. Literally. And mostly without any guarantees of reward. Save the knowledge that they applied their talents to the cause of Good. But frankly, learning how often the Imperia flew by the seat of their pants did not make me feel much better about my predicament.

We were going to see one R. G. Pentecost, an angelologist whom Rapha hoped could provide details that might help us prevent the summoning of Azrael, the Archangel of Death. I had never met an angelologist and part of me was intrigued by the opportunity. At one point in my life, I would have had a field day ribbing a nutjob with such a moniker. However, now that I had a guardian angel of my own, I feared the label of *nutjob* could equally be applied to me. But at this point, it didn't really matter. I was in so far over my head that Neptune himself couldn't save me.

Rapha busied himself in the warehouse as Quinn and Celeste spoke to Kanya. I admit I was wary of Quinn. Even a bit anxious. However, it wasn't so much anxiety about the power he wielded, but the group's conviction that I possessed similar abilities. Celeste, on the other hand, exuded benevolence and grace. Her aura wasn't just warm, it seemed curative. How these disparate personalities melded together remained a mystery. As did Ki, the Missing Guardian.

It wasn't long before Rapha entered the kitchen with Saucy at his side. It was time to leave.

As I started to get up, Orphana squeezed my hand. "There's a lot of truth to what everyone is sayin' about you, hon."

The more I looked into her eyes, the older and wiser she appeared.

"The thing to remember is this—this is *your* calling. It's no one else's. Okay?" She held my hand for a bit longer and then let go. "Now go on."

I wasn't sure what it meant, but I knew it would be worth hanging on to.

Before he escorted me out, Rapha suggested that Quinn and Orphana stay and wait for Klammer should he arrive. Frankly, I was relieved to not have to further endure Quinn.

The warehouse was surrounded by a junkyard of welded sculptures and scraps. A Hollywood prop heaven of rusty iron torsos, barrels, weather vanes, and car chassis lined the way. Old brick buildings rose on either side of the lot. The clatter of machinery sounded. Nearby, a chain link gate with corrugated metal protected Rapha's property and on a metal archway overhead hung a large welded emblem of the Tau. Bougainvillea rambled over the walls spilling into the yard. Hazy sunlight cast an orange pall about the place. It was early afternoon, but the night seemed to linger in the crevices and cool shadows.

Kanya walked beside me as we left. Saucy loped alongside and kept panting and glancing up at me with delight.

Perhaps among my other gifts was an ability to summon and control canines. If so, this could prove helpful in the event I ever entered the Iditarod or retired to become a dog whisperer to the stars.

We wove our way through weather-ravaged headless mannequins and mismatched industrial parts. The Cammy was parked just inside the gate. Apparently, someone had driven it from the hospital last night. Rapha had several workable-looking vehicles on his property, none of which would ever fit the "vintage" category like the Cammy. Until we arrived at a lifted Ford F250 crew cab, circa 1970. Dirty white with rusted pock marks. One of the side windows was cracked and the back bumper was slightly gnarled. But other than that, it was a great reminder of the age when cars were not comprised of cheap plastic and aluminum foil.

"Nice," I said, admiring the beast.

"I use it to deliver my pieces," Rapha said. "I put a new engine in. It's not the greatest on gas, but the legroom is wonderful."

"Plus," I said. "If we happen to run into any army tanks, you can just run them over."

He squinted at me and then a large smile blossomed across his face. He slapped me playfully on the back, causing me to stumble forward.

Rapha opened the back door for Kanya, and she climbed in as Celeste entered on the opposite side.

"Sit up front with me, Brother Moon. We'll spend time getting acquainted."

The truck smelled of oil and dog, and was fairly drafty. The shocks needed replaced. But sitting up that high, in a vehicle that size, with an engine big enough to power a semi, made me feel momentarily indestructible.

We were just south of Santa Monica Blvd. in West Hollywood. Rapha did indeed intend to get acquainted along the way. While Celeste and Kanya sat in the backseat talking, he asked questions about my father and Matisse, and how much I knew about spatial manipulation and the spontaneous creation of portals. In between, I ventured a question about Ki.

Rapha's features grew grim. "You needn't trouble yourself with that knowledge. Not now."

I persisted.

"Ki is the Sixth Guardian," Rapha finally conceded. "But he stumbled, became faithless. He listened to Hail, an agent of Diades. And now the very boundaries of existence are threatened. If the Imperia falter, Brother Moon, the Summu Nura will rewrite history itself."

"So…history is at stake?"

"It always is."

"And that stuff about me bringing the Imperia together?"

Rapha cast a lingering sideways glance at me.

"There is much to discover. Adventure awaits! For now, we must prepare for our meeting with Pentecost."

It was approaching noon when we arrived. R.G. Pentecost lived in Venice Beach. It figured. VB is the funny bone of California, a real freak show. There, tourists could rub shoulders with tarot readers, weight lifters, sword swallowers, and homeless veterans. The smell of ocean air was mixed with Rastafarian incense and grilled sauerkraut. The Boardwalk was like an ethnic buffet with a side of roller-skating hookers topped by the Three Stooges. If you wanted to buy tie-dyed condoms or simply watch people who do, Venice Beach was your port of harbor.

Just the kind of place you'd expect to find an angelologist.

Unsurprisingly, Rapha fit right in there. His rich, caramel-colored skin glistened under the California sun. He wore a cut-off tee revealing his massive arms. This guy's arms made my thighs look like toothpicks. Walking in public made him look even more intimidating, as he towered head and shoulders above the bustling crowd. Definitely the kind of guy you wanted on your side in the event of a scrape.

The shop was right on the Boardwalk. Large hand-painted aqua blue letters spelled out the words *Pentecost's Angelic Artifacts* in Victorian era script. Angel icons and replications of all varieties and appearances lined the large plate glass window. Porcelain, resin, crystal figurines. There were even action figures of Saint Michael slaying the devil. Rather than a wooden Indian, a life-sized guardian angel made of plaster stood near the front doors. It had been abused by the weather and disrespectful locals. Names and symbols had been carved into the statue's body. Chewed wads of gum and stickers were randomly affixed. Was nothing sacred anymore?

Rapha opened the door and ducked inside. The three of us followed. Numerous pleasant scents greeted us. Inside spread a colorful menagerie of mobiles, paintings, and statuary. Whether you wanted chubby cherubs or fierce gladiator archangels, Pentecost's had them. Tall bookshelves occupied one corner, and there were aisles of candles, incense, bath salts, jewelry, and assorted kitsch. I wondered if purchasing a personalized guardian angel visor clip for the Cammy would make Bernard a bit more helpful, but I doubted it. On the walls hung prints of angels, from Byzantine iconography to pop art. A tall, well-lit glass cabinet displayed unusual artifacts, including a carved wooden scepter from the 18th century allegedly used to summon a seraph. In the center, cordoned by thick velvety rope, was a life-sized Lego angel with a sword and a shield. I was pretty sure I could find something of interest for my apartment here and made a mental note to return if I survived this ordeal.

A tanned, grandmotherly woman with a hibiscus flower in her hair sat behind a glass counter and stood when we entered. She caught sight of Rapha and her face lit up.

"*Custode della porta!*" she proclaimed and hurried from behind the counter toward him. "Rapha. It's so good to see you."

"You too, Mother." Rapha wrapped her in a bear hug, raising her off the ground in the process. She laughed.

"We've been worried for you," she said, making sure her flower was still in place. "So many rumors. And the word has not been good."

"I know." Rapha glanced at me and said, "Hopefully, that will change."

Then the woman looked at Celeste, smiled, and opened her arms. "Celeste. You're always so beautiful. You have the grace of the angels."

Celeste appeared to blush as they embraced each other.

A wiry white-haired man emerged from a back room, fumbling at some round wire rim glasses. He too wore a white loose-fitting frock, making them both look like patrons of the nearby Self-Realization Fellowship. Or Grateful Dead refugees.

"There he is." Rapha raised his hands. "Señor Pentecost himself."

"Greetings!" The man issued a bright toothy smile. He made his way around the counter and shook Rapha's hand passionately. "My dear Rapha. I've been expecting you."

"I knew you would be." Rapha turned and said to Kanya and me, "They are friends of the Imperia."

"Oh?" I said, probably sounding more suspicious than I should.

"It's all right," Rapha assured me with a wink. "There are more than you think."

"More. Many more." Pentecost turned to me, a twinkle in his eye. "So you're Reagan Moon. Look at you! We heard about your feat, young man. Taking on the Summu Nura as you did. What courage."

"Actually, I was scared shi—"

"Of course you were! Who wouldn't be? But now you're a legend. And so young. The believers are abuzz with your exploits. We have needed such encouragement. Terrible times they are. Terrible! Thank God for your arrival."

He shook my hand firmly. The man had a nervous disposition, twitchy and slightly manic. His left eye wandered, and I thought he might be in the early stages of dementia. Or maybe he had simply reached his limit of caffeine for the day.

"This is Kanya," I said. "I guess you could say she's also a friend of the Imperia."

The woman joined Pentecost, and Kanya extended her hand to them.

"We knew your father, Kanya." The woman took Kanya's hand and cradled it in hers. "A blessed soul. *Un servo di dio.* We were heartbroken to hear of his passing. Heaven wept. As did we."

"Thank you," Kanya said. "You knew Matisse?"

"Yes, yes," Pentecost said. "A great inspiration. Many tales to tell. He sought counsel on several occasions. But for now, he watches. A witness to our exploits. And the Asylum? You've continued his mission, no?"

Kanya nodded. "It's a big job. But with Mace's help, we're back up and running."

"Sakes alive!" Pentecost exclaimed. "A big job? Ha! It's immense. Huge! You need help, young lady. It's too big for just the two of you."

I thought about the key in my front pocket and my promise to Matisse, but did not volunteer any more info to them regarding my involvement at the Asylum, or my lack thereof.

"This is Mae," Pentecost said. "But everyone calls her Mother. So tell me." He stepped closer to me and lowered his voice, as if confiding a great secret. "Mother and I have a small wager. Your defeat of the Summu Nura—something that great, I say, required direct angelic assistance. Yes? Warrior angels. A unit or a platoon perhaps. They *had* to have been engaged. Mother, on the other hand, is not so sure. Some cock-eyed conspiracy theory. A Summu Nura power struggle, she says. A house divided—that sort of thing. The woman is obsessed with conspiracy theories. She believes a rift is emerging in the Black Council—let's pray it is—a power struggle that will lead to ruin. Crazy. But still..." He smiled and winked at Mother. "So, settle the score, will you? You were joined by the holy ones, were you not?"

Mother objected, "Don't lead him, Dad."

He waved off her comment, cast his toothy smile, and peered at me, his bad eye wandering nonsensically.

"Well, I'm sorry to disappoint, ma'am," I said. "But I couldn't have done anything without Bernard, my guardian angel."

"Ha!" Pentecost clapped his hands. "Just like I said, Mother." Then he queried, "Bernard? What an odd name for an angel."

"He thinks so too."

"Does he? Hmm. Well, you're going to need him for your next adventure, young man. Of this, I'm confident."

Rapha nodded. "It's why we're here, Señor."

"Yes, yes. Of course. First—"

Pentecost marched to the front door, bolted it, and flipped the sign around, signaling that the store was now closed. He returned and said, "Now, where to begin. Let's see." He wrung his hands, squinting in thought.

"Azrael?" Rapha said.

"Yes, of course! The Archangel of Death." He crossed himself. "God have mercy. We have long feared that the elements would align. Now my calculations prove it. Of all the hierarchy, she is perhaps the most feared. Revered, even worshiped by some. Fools, they are! Her thirst is insatiable." Pentecost grew still as his gaze drifted upward. "What must it be, this Archangel of Death, her wings dipped in blood…"

Mother gripped her hands to her chest, apparently sharing in Pentecost's fearful rapture. Quickly, he returned to himself.

"The time has arrived," he said, adjusting his glasses. "All the signs are in agreement. Rapha knows. He has seen them too, yes? Here."

He motioned for us to follow him and strode past the Lego angel through the aisles to the bookshelves in the corner.

Just behind a small sitting area stood a large swivel chalkboard, apparently for advertising and educational purposes. On it was colorful flowing text announcing a weekend how-to class on creating origami angels and church services on Sundays at 11 a.m. Pentecost took the bottom of the board and flipped it, revealing an elaborate collection of symbols and calculations scrawled upon the back.

"The angels exist in hierarchy." Pentecost pointed to a triangular image of tiered figures. "Some describe it as spheres, or choirs. Whatever the name, there is order. Order." He tapped the chalkboard for emphasis. "You know this. The firmament is not a chaos. A house divided cannot stand. Yet the Archangel of Death is a rogue. Destined for blood and fire. Subservient only to the Most High. But banished from the houses of the holy. Destined to wander until it is summoned. And it is this summoning—this conjuring, invitation—that we most fear. For just as the angels exist in hierarchy, the Archangel of Death has subordinates. Minions. Those who are precursors to her appearing."

I said, "You're talking about the…"

"The maelohim," Rapha interjected.

"Precisely!" Pentecost pointed at Rapha. "The death angels."

"I was attacked by one last night," I said. "If it wasn't for Rapha—"

"Harvester angels," Pentecost said. "A caste of creatures made to transport souls, shuttle them between dwellings. But the servants of Azrael have become bent, twisted in their rebellion. Reports have surfaced—death angels manifesting across the city. That was the first sign. And then this."

Pentecost pointed to a symbol on the chalkboard.

"Hey," I said, approaching the board. "I've seen that before…"

It was an image of a crescent bowl with three droplets above it.

Mike Duran

"Where?" Pentecost asked. "The symbol, where did you see it?"

"Last night," I said. "Etherea. She was wearing a pendant like that."

"Etherea?" Pentecost queried, looking at Rapha. "Who's he talking about?"

"An occultist," Rapha explained. "A witch-priestess. A practitioner of Santa Muerte. We have followed her rise. A Neuro, apparently empowered by the drug...and Saint Death."

"Great God!" Pentecost crossed himself again. "Saint Death. The old religion. Its roots trace back to the ancients. To the blood sacrifices of old. Santa Muerte is but a gateway for the summoning."

"So that symbol," I asked. "What does it mean?"

"Of course." Pentecost adjusted his glasses and pointed to the image on the board. "The inverted crescent symbolizes the reaper's scythe. The drops indicate the blood that must be spilled at the Black Altar."

"I don't follow."

"It's a ritual, son." Pentecost looked sternly at me. "Blasted! Open your eyes. Regulus. It coincides with the Regulus phenomenon. "

He fumbled for a piece of chalk on the nearby bookshelf, returned, and sketched out a crescent moon lying on its back, bowl-like, and the three stars above it. "It's no coincidence. The perfect alignment. Symmetry! The crescent represents the sickle she wields. The stars, the blood of the living. It's why the coming of Regulus has been considered a sacred event for millennia. Those of the dark arts have long sought to release the Archangel of Death at the celestial event. For power. For anarchy. To bring in the new order. Such are the intentions of the Black Council. I fear they seek to usher in a great leader, one of their own. By destabilizing our societal structure, our safety, they can present someone—a great magician perhaps—to return order and stop the Tenth Plague. A ploy. Such is their madness! Only two other elements are necessary for such a conjuring. The Grimoire of Azrael, the tome of incantations to call forth the devils, is one of them. The appearance of the maelohim would indicate that such a document has been uncovered. Now, the only other necessary element would be an altar of summoning."

"Hold on," I said. "You're saying the Regulus effect aligns with the—"

"It's an Enochian symbol! A magical grimoire. Think, man! All things must be in place. On the crescent moon's waning phase, blood is spilled on the black altar." Pentecost grew still and stared forward blankly. "And tomorrow night is its final descent, the crescent wanes."

A disconcerting stillness fell on us.

I thought about the creature last night, its neon eyes and serpentine tongue, hypnotizing me in its spell of death. If it was but a forerunner to the main attraction, I could only wonder at the hideous majesty that Azrael was. And then it dawned on me.

"Did you say altar?"

Pentecost started. "Yes. Of course. An altar of summoning is the missing element. Such altars are extremely rare. Mythic. It was believed that only six such altars exist. Constructed from the blood of Diades. Indestructible! With the maelohim, the death angels manifesting, it suggests that such an altar has indeed been found. God help us if this is true."

I opened and closed my mouth. It couldn't be. But why the hell not? Nothing was as it could be any longer. Finally, I managed to say, "I think it is true."

"What?" Pentecost's eyes grew wide. "Tell us what you know, son."

"The downtown subway project," I said. "Our paper's been following the story. NeoKor shut the project down. The rumor was that they unearthed...an altar."

"Great God!" Pentecost slapped his palm to his forehead. "The Lizard People."

"Wait. Huh?"

Mike Duran

"An underground city," Kanya said, sounding surprised. "I remember that. It's part of the Lizard People legend."

"Precisely!" Pentecost pointed at her.

"My father," Kanya continued. "He used to talk about it. He called them reptoids. Supposedly, they unearthed an ancient altar. Matisse believed if that altar fell into the wrong hands, terrible things could happen. He wanted to remove it from circulation—that's the way he always put it. He wanted to find it and transport the thing to the Asylum so that it would never be used again. He was obsessed with finding that thing. Said it was made of a substance called…Nefarium. A material that could not be destroyed by anyone on earth."

"Hold on a second." I waved my hands in protestation. "You guys are—. That Lizard People legend was disproved decades ago."

"Was it?" Pentecost eyed me warily.

"Brother Moon," Rapha said. "Then you know of this legend."

"Sure," I said. "I researched it for the Crescent years ago. It's one of those local folk tales that never goes away. Started back in the 1930s, an L.A. Times' piece. There was some geophysicist or something, a mining engineer who reportedly invented some sort of radio X-ray machine. He believed he could locate underground tunnels with it. Supposedly, he discovered an entire underground city. Shaped like a lizard, no less. It reached from Elysian Park to downtown. Of course, when they started the dig, nothing came of it. The shafts were closed up and the kook went home with his tail between his legs."

Kanya asked, "So who were these Lizard People?"

"It was all nonsense," I said. "An urban legend. They were supposed to be some super-race, allegedly related to the Mayans. They'd purportedly fled a catastrophic meteor shower and built these underground cities along the Pacific Coast.

124

They were so intellectually and technologically advanced that they used mysterious chemicals to dig a network of tunnels."

Kanya said, "And there was treasure involved, right?"

"Isn't there always? Look, I hate to disappoint you guys, but no one has ever found any Lizard People, any treasure, or any tunnels. Sheesh. It's amazing what people will choose to believe these days."

Pentecost squinted at me. "But you're the one who brought up the altar, young man."

I stared at him.

"You obviously know your history." Pentecost nodded. "Then you might remember how the reptoids were believed to have gone extinct."

"Refresh my memory," I said dully.

"They unearthed the altar and unleashed something. It wiped out their entire race."

"That's right." Celeste had been watching our exchange with interest and appeared eager to join in. "The best record we have is from the polio outbreak of 1934. That was the last occurrence of Regulus."

"Correct!" proclaimed Pentecost.

Celeste continued, "The rumor at the time was that the mass extinction of the Lizard People—which wasn't discovered until several years later—coincided with the polio outbreak, both being viewed as part of the Tenth Plague. It led some to link the phenomenon to the possible reenactment of a ceremonial summoning. This was later confirmed when the Pacific Electric Railway—that was the group who'd signed on for the Los Angeles subway project—allegedly discovered a subterranean chamber with strange religious artifacts. It led to the closure of a large section of the dig. Reports of workers going insane, encountering ghostly apparitions, reptoid remains, stuff like that, inevitably caused that entire stretch to be diverted. From there, the reports and rumors drifted into obscurity."

She finished her analysis and smiled proudly.

"Lizard People? For real?" I shook my head, as much out of frustration as pure exhaustion. "Okay then," I sighed. "What are we supposed to do? I mean, how in the hell do you stop the Archangel of Death?"

"Yes," Pentecost said. "That's the question we come to. Terrible times. But it's why you're here, yes? Now, if the altar exists, as you say, if it's been rediscovered, and this occultist has cracked the code, then she must be stopped. Or the altar destroyed."

"Easier said than done," I said. "I have no idea where to find the woman. Or the altar. I mean, there are miles of old subway tunnels down there."

"I can get maps," Kanya said. "Schematics of the subway area. My father collected massive files and microfiche of old L.A. I'll call Mace and have him pull them up."

"And if we happen to stumble upon Azrael?" I said sarcastically. "We, what? Threaten to break her wings?"

"Why, yes." Pentecost said. "That may in fact work."

"I'm sorry. I think I'm missing something."

"Of course you are!" Pentecost proclaimed. "Here."

He hurried off, beckoning us to follow him. He led us to the lighted display case containing the staff. "Look, right there. On the second shelf."

We gathered around. On the second shelf lay a misshapen but oddly brilliant object. It appeared to be some mummified appendage, perhaps the length of a man's arm. It was angled, jointed. A ridge of bone or thick cartilage stretched along the top edge from which thick feather-like filaments sprouted. This odd object seemed to glisten in the light. However, its edges were charred terribly. Whatever damage this object had incurred, it had left it barely distinguishable. Nevertheless, by all accounts it appeared to be the partial remains of a massive wing.

"It's my most cherished treasure." Pentecost stared at the encased object. "The creature from which it was taken had fallen in battle. God have mercy. The wings of the angel are

126

rare and can be used for nefarious purposes. The Seraph's Wing is perhaps the greatest of all such artifacts."

I stepped back. "You're telling us that this is part of an angel's wing?"

"Precisely! Like every other creature of God's making, they are subject to laws. If an angel can be engaged in its manifestation, it is subject to the laws of that manifestation. To your point, yes, if Azrael manifests and you can break her wings—or shoot, stab, decapitate her, whatever—do so, by all means."

"Well, Bernard doesn't have wings. At least, not that I know of. And he's always invisible."

"As far as *you* know he's always invisible. It is possible that he has manifested in numerous ways and concealed his identity to you. Angels do that, you know? Were he to choose to manifest, he would be subject to the laws of that world. Listen—the Enochian angels were held in chains and imprisoned. Yes? So what kind of chains can hold an angel? Iron chains? Titanium? That's right. Think about that. Or take Jacob, in the Bible. How's that? Jacob wrestled the angel. Remember? Hard to wrestle an invisible entity, no? You see, when the angel manifests, it is bound to the laws of that world."

"So you want us to wrestle angels."

"You're an earth guardian, young man! Blazes! You do what you must to defeat evil. That is the calling of the Imperia."

I gripped my head in my hands and heaved a great sigh. "Okay. So all we need to do is find an underground altar in miles of unfinished subway and lock up some rogue angels before the moon sets tomorrow night." I shook my head wearily. "It's over, folks. We're screwed."

"Poppycock!" Pentecost pushed past the others and stood directly before me. "Heaven is with you, young man. Of this, you can be certain. One does not defeat the Summu Nura by luck. Or by simple strength. No. Whether we live or die, we do so unbound. Fighting for freedom. Yes?"

He stepped even closer and smiled. His wandering eye glinted madly. "Forces are at work here, son—*in* you, *around* you. As are the angels."

CHAPTER 12

W
e drove back to Rapha's for some supplies before heading to the downtown subway project to begin our search for the mysterious altar. I reckoned our odds of discovering the subterranean artifact, much less thwarting some human sacrifice while fending off death angels, was somewhere in the realm of a statistical impossibility. However, Rapha called it an adventure and rambled on about Don Quixote and errant knights seeking glory. Yet I sat in the passenger seat overshadowed by a cloud of pessimism.

Along the way, Kanya called Mace and walked him through what we'd learned, asking him to get on the computer and bring up as much relevant info on the site as possible. Entrances. Ducts. Tunnels. Especially any recent satellite footage. Or at least, what hadn't been wiped clean by NeoKor. She and Celeste eagerly discussed the best possible entry to the tunnels, where the project had run into problems, and the types of obstacles we might face reaching such a place. Celeste appeared unusually good at recalling detailed information— street names, contractors, security firms involved, historical minutiae, and dates. I had a hard time engaging in either Rapha's enthusiasm or the women's planning.

Quinn was waiting at Rapha's gate and pulled it open as we approached in the truck. Saucy came loping up, panting and smiling. As we climbed out of the vehicle, the dog nuzzled up to me, begging for attention. Which I obliged.

Quinn closed and locked the gate. I overheard him say to Rapha that Felix Klammer had not arrived. I detected more than just a little concern in them about this. Was something actively preventing Klammer from joining us? Could it be that the box-hooded billionaire played a greater role than I'd been led to believe? In a way, it was a slight consolation knowing that he kept everyone waiting and not just me. Rapha and

Quinn walked off into the scrap yard engaged in animated discussion, with Quinn doing the bulk of the animation. He glanced at me over his shoulder several times. The man did not trust me. Or, at least, he thought I was an unreliable member of their rickety superhero team. Which I probably was. Yet there was something else…something that caused me to wonder if he could be fully trusted.

As the two men walked off in conversation, I took the opportunity to call Penny, who'd apparently just arrived at the Crescent

"I need your help," I said. "Tell me everything you know about the subway project."

She didn't ask why. In fact, she was eager to share details. The project had suffered bureaucratic starts and fits for the last half-decade, more recently languishing for almost a year before a new contractor, NeoKor, was awarded. The proposed subway system would connect Metro 417 near Pershing Square with an interlocking system of subterranean rails. The holdup was due, in part, to the urban legends that had started. The previous construction attempts had generated a good share of mishaps and ghost stories. But none like this. Now the going rumor was that they'd found the altar, which had brought excavation to a standstill. Even worse were rumblings of some subterranean entity that had been unleashed, something that drove people mad. This was a detail that we'd previously not explored.

"Any pictures?" I asked. "Anything from the site at all."

"Nothing," Penny said. "Well, at least that I've found. And I've scoured the web, police reports, everything. NeoKor's covered their tracks, that's for sure. Everything I got came off the grid—a couple private interviews, a screenshot of an alleged cell phone pic. That kinda thing. But other than that, word's been scarce."

"Odd."

"Except for the victims."

"They're talking?"

"Not exactly. They probably *would* have if they hadn't been whisked away for secret 'treatment.'"

"Something along the lines of a frontal lobotomy maybe?"

"Exactly. It was a couple of workers. Tunnel rats of some sort. They'd discovered a chamber, something that wasn't on the specs. First reports were of a cavern that had collapsed. Or been dynamited and intentionally filled."

"Hold on. You're talking about a pre-existing chamber."

"Yes."

"That someone tried to...bury?"

"I guess. You remember those old stories about a subterranean city, right?"

"Ugh."

"Yeah. That one. Anyway, the crew started weirding out and NeoKor put the brakes on everything. They started unearthing the chamber. It's protocol, you know. They don't want to damage important artifacts, fossils, or what-not. Eventually, some paleontologists and a bunch of other suits were called in. So during the excavation of the chamber, religious iconography was discovered. Symbols etched on the walls. Some crude pendants and statuary. And then...the altar."

"Crazy."

"Right? That's when the reports started. Voices. Apparitions. The crew that was left started having night terrors, insomnia. Stuff like that. A buncha guys quit. They refused to work on what they believed was cursed earth. Said the signs were all bad and vowed to never set foot in that place again. Then a couple workers finally went off the deep end, threatened to kill people if NeoKor didn't stop digging. They even threatened to sacrifice people. You know, spill blood for the ground they'd desecrated."

"All that because of a silly altar."

"Not *just* an altar. Supposedly they'd seen a..."

"Yeah?"

"A ghost. A winged demon or something. With bright red eyes. I dunno. The guy I interviewed was pretty upset. He swore it was true. Said the men started speaking in other languages and voices. Real creepy stuff."

"A winged demon…" Images of the death angel hovered in my mind. "So what happened?"

"The project eventually got shut down. It's become a crime scene now, under investigation."

"A crime scene? What's the crime?"

"Heh. That's another place where it gets weird. As if it wasn't weird already. Apparently, along the way, bodies were reportedly seen. Flayed and staked. Ritual stuff. Of course, half the crew was mad at that time. So it's no telling if they were hallucinations or flights of fancy to scare away the faint of heart. And no one could confirm. So LAPD swooped in and the curtain fell. It's like a prison down there. Have fun getting info on the thing. Or getting in there."

Interesting. The entire project was on lockdown. How convenient. This was right up Jimmy and his Special Investigation unit's alley, yet he hadn't mentioned a thing about it. Unless The LAPD brain trust was re-routing this around him. But subterranean altars and winged demons were his forte. Something told me that the entire investigation stank. Perhaps the Black Council had found other, more complicit insiders to serve their purposes. Why enlist some guy in a hard hat when one with a badge is available?

"Yoo-hoo," Penny interrupted my thoughts. "You alive?"

"Mostly."

"You weren't intending to try to get in there, were you?"

"I'm debating."

"Well, plan on having to persuade L.A.'s finest. Anyway, the press is running with the firm's narrative: NeoKor ran into 'complications.' For the safety of the crew they

132

suspended further work until the issues could be resolved. They don't want to risk anyone's safety for the sake of progress, yada yada."

"And the witnesses, there's no word?"

"The crew was big, as you can imagine. The operation is currently spread out through three city blocks. It's huge. But the books aren't accessible, names, and what have you. The employees that went bonkers have disappeared basically. They're either in hiding or getting drugged into compliance."

"Or dead."

"I didn't say that. Apparently going nuts is not unusual to the tunneling profession. If you work underground that long you're bound to lose a few. It would freak me out, ya know, being underground that long. The claustrophobia, the constant darkness. The hazards. Gives me the chills just thinking about it. And, did I mention, three guys died this year alone?"

"And I thought working for the Crescent was hard."

"Arlette will want to know you said that. Anyway, it'll be a while before all the info comes out."

"An altar..." I mused. "Any idea where all this went down? I mean, where do I start?"

"Good question. There was mention about 5th Street, the Central Library—"

"That's where the project is centered, right?"

"Right. But it travels as far as Pershing Square, where the original subway station existed."

"That's about three blocks away."

"Take your pick," she said.

"Right."

"So what's with the interest, Reagan? The boss isn't putting you on the project, is she?"

"No. I'm on the Haunted Hospital. It's just...it looks like there's some overlap."

"What part?"

"I'm not sure. The nurse who sent us the video of Weeping Eve—at least, what they thought was Weeping Eve—posted a random picture of herself…at the subway project."

"Boy. You sure know how to pick 'em."

"Tell me about it."

"Well, I'll keep digging," Penny said. "No pun intended. I'm on the scanner and have a couple more possible leads. If I find anything, I'll let you know. But, if I was you, I'd think twice about trying to get down there."

"Try telling that to my new friends."

"What?"

"Never mind. Thanks, Penny."

Quinn and Rapha returned. There was tension between them. Quinn was having a hard time concealing it. One edge of his lips curled slightly in annoyance and his shoulders were taut with tension. And, what's worse, he knew that I could sense this.

"Brother Moon," Rapha said. "There's one more thing we must discuss."

At this point, I just wanted to get this over with. Rapha motioned for me to follow, which I did. He led me back to the warehouse where Kanya and Orphana joined us. Together we followed Rapha to a large framed area, a room that had been constructed at the far end of the warehouse. We entered this deep, enclosed area. Celeste was waiting there for us. She smiled as I walked in, but her benevolence was not enough to halt my growing unease.

This odd room reminded me of a large baseball bullpen. But it was eerily dark. For dense black walls or panels enclosed the room. They appeared to consist of the strange material I had been shown earlier—Ndocron. Large galvanized industrial lights burned overhead, but the surrounding material seemed to drain the light of any refractive quality. Unusual flare marks marred the surface of the walls, as well as deep pocks of various sizes randomly distributed along the perimeter. Several targets, spray-painted bulls-eyes, were on opposite sides of the bullpen. Apparently, someone had been using this place for target practice. A video camera sat on a tripod near the entry. Nearby, a metal sink, wet specimen jars, and miscellaneous medical supplies lined the northern wall. Perhaps Doctor Frankenstein was using the place on his off hours. Either that or Rapha was housing a bomb-making factory.

"My apologies," Rapha said. "But earlier you mentioned possible teleportation."

I looked at him. My stomach somersaulted thinking about the freak phenomenon. I found myself suddenly hyper aware of my body. My hands. My chest. The power that had infused me, the storm gifts—where did they reside? In my brain or my body? Or was I actually tapping into an outside source? The four of them stood looking at me and a claustrophobic fear began to creep up on me. What did they want? And could I really rise to the challenge of it all?

"Yeah," I said, suspiciously. "I teleported. If that's what you call it."

"Can you simulate that power?"

"Huh? Now?"

"Yes. We must prepare for what lies ahead."

"I...I don't know."

"Well," Quinn said. "That's something we're gonna to need to find out."

"I'm not sure," I said. "I mean, I'm still learning. Ever since the Accident, sensations come and go. If I focus my attention, sometimes just let my mind wander, I can get a sense of what people are thinking. Or feeling. And when Invisibles are present, I can see them without effort. But that power—I mean the thing at the ranch and the hospital—I'm not sure, it was a...reaction."

"And *that's* the problem," Quinn said sharply. "If it's reactive and you don't know how to control it, and you accidentally blow a fuse out there, bounce off a wall or something, you're liable to kill us all."

Rapha glanced sternly at Quinn and then said to me, "That's why we're here. To help you. To help all of us. Let me explain something. With every calling, there's an accompanying power. A gift. Or gifts. Call them talents or abilities, it doesn't matter. That was the promise of Heaven when the pact with Men was forged. We were not left to our own strength. Perhaps they were latent inside us. Perhaps they were imparted by Heaven itself. Nonetheless, those who brandish the sign of the Tau are empowered, blessed with abilities."

"Abilities or curses?" Quinn interjected.

Rapha paused, without looking at Quinn. He was annoyed with the cocky telepath. I couldn't blame him. Apparently, having superpowers did not override one's ability to be a pain in the ass. Which did not bode well for me.

"When you agreed to protect the Tau," Rapha continued, "you embraced that calling and were rewarded with the necessary tools."

Rewarded? I simply mouthed the word, not wanting to agitate Rapha more than he already seemed to be.

"Each Imperia is gifted to serve the others," Rapha said. "To strengthen the team. To form a unit. And, ultimately, to serve mankind. For example." He motioned to Celeste. "Celeste can heal. Probably a Binder at essence. You see, all disease or madness is the result of un-binding, fragmentation, a lack of holism, whether in the body or the mind. Our sister is blessed to bind what is fractured. To speak substance into emptiness, to integrate what is chaos. Absorb darkness into herself."

"It took me years," Celeste said. "I thought I was crazy at first. I was drawn to the sick, the broken. Sometimes I can absorb their suffering. But the darkness—" She looked away. "It's the price of my service."

"You thought you were crazy?" I said. "Yeah. That's how I've felt lately. Crazy."

"Brother Moon," Rapha said. "You've displayed similar powers. Binding powers. Isn't that so?"

He was right. The blue electricity, the cold energy that on occasion coursed my hands. It was the same power I'd watched bring Kanya back to life amidst the storm atop Spiraplex.

"She's also an Archivist," Quinn said. "Don't forget that."

"Which means I can remember things," Celeste said. Her eyes seemed to beam with the admission.

"No, no," Quinn objected. "You don't just remember things. You remember *everything*."

"Okay," she admitted. "I remember *everything*. Well, almost everything."

"That's right." Quinn began counting items off on his fingers. "She can remember the exact hour we met. What I was wearing when we met. The first words out of my mouth. The cologne I was wearing. And how much I had to pay for the parking ticket I got later that day."

"Fifty-eight dollars and seventy-two cents." Celeste smiled. "It was a Loading Zone infraction, wasn't it? And you used a word I shouldn't repeat."

"Show-off," Quinn snarled.

Rapha said, "The Archivist is gifted in, well, remembering details."

"It comes in handy now and then." Celeste smiled. "Combinations. Addresses. Phone numbers. Cryptograms."

"Security clearance codes," Quinn added.

"Others are gifted with clusters of psionic abilities," Rapha said. "Telepathy, psychokinesis, pyrokinesis, things like that. It's true across the board. The gifts do not exist in isolation. Brother Quinn fits this category."

"Although, regretfully," Quinn said, "the last time I tried to conjure fire I destroyed a house and sent a couple of Normals to the hospital with second-degree burns." He shrugged. "It's something I gotta work on."

"Agreed," Rapha added. "The powers have many uses. For example, Celeste's healing gifts can sometimes act as a defensive shield, a sort of protective shell."

Celeste nodded. "The same way that health makes you less susceptible to sickness, quicker to heal. Your own immunity is a shield against sickness. At least, that's how I figure it."

Rapha motioned to the entire team. "She can sometimes shield us, if need be, from pestilence and disease. All manner of sickness spells."

"Most of our talents are like that," Celeste said. "It just takes time and patience to learn how to use them. And usually years to develop."

"And I've got a couple hours?" I said.

Rapha smiled. It was a genuine effort to reassure me. "Quixote said that the maddest thing a man can do in this life is to let himself die."

I shook my head and didn't bother to ponder the latest literary quote from Cervantes.

"So if I've got certain powers," I said, "then, everyone…I mean, all of you…"

Quinn folded his arms. "He's a freakin' genius."

"That's right," Rapha said. "It is what unites us. The intersection of powers. Celeste with her binding and archival abilities. Quinn, and his array of psionics. Orphana, among other things, can cluster—disassemble and reassemble her body in various forms or locations."

"Which is a helluva fighting tactic," Quinn added. "Ever tried to fight someone who can exist simultaneously in three places?"

"How is that possible?" I said. "How is any of this possible?"

"It is the divine promise." Rapha thumped his chest.

"Or some kind of weird magic."

Rapha scowled.

"He doesn't like that term," Orphana said. "It comes with too much baggage."

"Indeed," Rapha said. "It is not accurate. Science itself was once viewed as magic."

"So," I queried, "you're not suggesting that these abilities are based in…science, are you?"

"Brother Moon, magic is often a lazy term for what man does not comprehend. Even the most fantastic of powers correspond to laws—laws of being, nature, whether of our dimension or those beyond. Magic is but a form of advanced physics. For instance, some actions appear as magic on this plane, yet are quite natural to those of another. The individual who travels between dimensions would appear superhuman to those bound by lesser dimensions. The human will itself, our freedom to choose decisions and alter outcomes, could be viewed as its own mode of magic. To the mindless, soulless, all humans possess magic." Rapha removed the Tau from underneath his shirt and placed his fingertips upon it. "It is the pact with Heaven that we be fully alive."

Orphana shrugged. "Still, the wear and tear it puts on my body? That's the killer." She shifted her weight on the cane.

Rapha slipped his shirt over the Tau and nodded somberly. "We must use our gifts wisely, Brother Moon. Great power is never without cost."

"And you?" I said to Rapha. "You're gifted at making pretty sculptures, I guess?"

"Alchemy," Rapha said flatly. "In the broadest possible sense. An elemental ability—metallurgy, particle transmutation. I can manipulate certain rudimentary spatial elements, as well. It's part of a larger gifting I've developed that relates to matter and energy."

"Let me guess, you can leap tall buildings with a single bound."

"Humor." Rapha nodded. "We need humor in these dark days."

Mike Duran

"No. Really. You want to see if I can transport again, right? How about you kick it off with a demonstration of your own."

Rapha straightened and his features grew sober. "The gifts are not something to be frivolous with, Brother Moon."

"Understood." I folded my arms. "But you want to help me, right? That's why we're here. So show me how this works, Rapha. Please."

It wasn't entirely antagonistic. I really did want to see how this crazy world of the Imperia worked. Although my unbelief had taken a serious hit over the last few months, it would be wrong to say that I had become a gullible believer in all things paranormal. Maintaining some vestige of skepticism is healthy for any human being. However, at the moment, I feared my posture conveyed far too much antagonism.

Rapha peered at me. Finally, he nodded and the smile returned to his face. "As you wish. Approach me."

"What?"

He interlocked his fingers and stretched them back, cracking his knuckles in the process. Then he motioned me forward.

I hesitated. Sizing up this giant human being made me sorry I'd ever challenged him. "You mean...?"

Rapha quickly studied his surroundings, the Ndocron walls and ceiling, the overhead lights and the nearby sink. "Just come to me. That's all."

As he spoke, I noticed Celeste reach out, take Kanya by the arm, and all of them stepped back.

"Um," I said. "Maybe I should just try to teleport."

Before I could renege on my challenge, something unusual happened. Not to me, but to the space around me. It was as if the atmosphere had turned to quicksand, dense and cumbrous. The roof groaned. The room's interior beams began to creak with stress, as if they were being squeezed in a massive vice. The nearest light bulb burst and the fixture's galvanized casing crumpled like a prune. I froze in place. Not because I was petrified by fear, but because a blanket of weight was crushing me. The air became dense, almost stifling.

And when I attempted to take a step forward, my foot remained laden.

My chest tingled as fear welled up inside me. Rapha glared at me, smiling as he did. His fists were clenched, the muscles in his thick shoulders and forearms trembled.

Whatever force he was emitting, it was crushing the space surrounding me. Or was it the actual space, the oxygen or subatomic particles, which had become dense? I tried to escape this circle of energy yet was unable to move. Power instinctively flared inside me as the Tau awakened in my breast.

And this, I knew, would be trouble.

CHAPTER 13

I didn't bother locking eyes with Rapha. I was too busy forcing myself to breath.

The density of the atmosphere had tripled. Quadrupled! Or perhaps it wasn't the atmosphere at all, but but a molecular blanket surrounding me. My shoulders, my ankles. Every part of my body was encumbered. Hell, even my bones were being compressed. It felt like I was submerged in a sub-Atlantic canyon and the pressure was squeezing the life out of me. I tried to look up at Rapha to make sense of what was happening, but even that motion required incredible effort. I strained to raise my head and stare forward. All my actions were in slow motion. Kanya and the others seemed to exist outside the periphery of this bubble of energy. Inside it, however, everything was being crushed. As if every microscopic particle was endowed with new-found density.

Rapha stood no more than ten feet away from me. But between us rose an atmospheric field of some sort. Space appeared to curve at the periphery of my sight, leading me to believe this was a self-contained blister of space. When I finally managed to fix my gaze upon him, I could see Rapha was gritting his teeth and sweating, but still managing to retain a slight air of joviality. His eyes sparkled with joy. He looked immense through that spatial curtain, a god of a man. Tan, tattooed, and almost twice my size. I grunted, attempting to trudge forward. It was impossible.

I panicked and with it a flurry of sensations erupted. I knew Rapha wouldn't hurt me. Yet the more I tried to tell my body to relax, the more the message was rejected by a deeply primal instinct.

The chill coursed my arms, my hands flushed with icy heat. And my chest throbbed. The perimeter of the Tau burned, pulsating with fiery fury. With it came that now familiar sense of flight. I could break free of this barrier, this prison of gravity. I could will myself forward and relocate. I knew it. I looked at Rapha, then I looked past him. But even doing this required maximum effort. My rib cage tightened around my lungs. Even my heartbeats seemed to labor under the force of this bizarre power.

Suddenly, multiple trajectories appeared all around me. Wormholes—space was brimming with them. I could extricate myself from this umbrella of alien power. All I needed to do was choose one and think myself through it. However, I knew I must be careful to aim away from Rapha and the others.

I engaged Rapha's eyes. This was more than just a show of supernormal talent. He was not so vain. Rapha was challenging me—challenging me to dig into myself and counter his own spell. Challenging me to harness my own magic.

I tore my gaze away from him and steadied my line of sight upon a single spatial channel that was free of visible obstructions. It crosscut my alignment to Rapha at a forty-five degree angle. Had one of the spray-painted bulls-eyes been visible, I would have aimed at it. Instead I gazed at a random gouge on one of the Ndocron panels.

Someone spoke, but their words seemed miles away. Another voice sounded, this one more concerned.

I fought to press myself forward, through the barrier. Past the barrier. I gritted my teeth, straining my gaze forward. My stomach clenched as energy welled into my solar plexus. Then I yelled. A deep, guttural primal yell that challenged the very power emanating from this man.

Two things happened simultaneously. Rapha opened his hands and flung his arms wide open. The weight suddenly dissipated and the atmosphere returned to normal. At that same exact moment I transported across the room, slinging forward with such velocity that time seemed to slow in the process.

"—in an imperfect world—"

Voices, not from my own dimension, but from another.

"—but it doesn't—look!"

"—on it—"

In that disembodied moment I was caught between two places, as if a window of time had been opened just long enough for me to intersect another realm. Or perhaps I was actually passing through another.

"—till he arrives."

My mind snapped back into my body. The black ceiling whirled through my line of sight. Then the walls. And the ground came up at my face allowing me just enough time to lower my head under, tuck my knees in, and prepare for a high-speed somersault. I had miscalculated my proximity to Rapha, because he blurred past, dangerously close, before I hit the ground, somersaulted, and slammed into the wall. The entire room rattled with the concussion.

I lay panting, slumped against the wall, perhaps ten to twelve feet past Rapha. Even though the pain in my chest was raging, at least I was free of the cocoon of density. And I was breathing again.

"Reagan!" Kanya ran to me. "Are you okay?"

As she passed, Rapha he reached out, took her by the shoulders, and spun her off her feet.

"Be careful," he said.

"Wha—?" Kanya wrestled against Rapha's grip. "Lemme go!"

I massaged the back of my shoulder where I'd struck the bullpen siding. "You better let her go."

"We don't—" Rapha struggled to maintain his grip on Kanya. "He may be—*aww*—" Kanya had one of his thumbs in both hands and was wrenching it downward "—lethal."

"Hell yes, he's lethal!" Quinn exclaimed. "D'you see what he just did?"

"Let me go!" Rapha released her, and Kanya stumbled forward and then turned to face him.

I cringed, fearing that her alter ego would suddenly appear and wreak havoc on all of us. But her anger dissipated. Instead, she turned, came and knelt over me.

"Are you okay?" Her pupils seemed lighter than usual, almost amber. For a moment, I was lost in them.

She was a passionate soul, full of complex layers of shame and sadness. She was also still feeling guilty about kicking me in the nose. But we had an unspoken kinship now. Why else would she be at my side so quickly? I thought about Audra, who claimed to be Kanya's mother. The story seemed fantastical and yet, if true, a reasonable cause of shapeshifting trauma. For the moment, her hellacious past and the horrors it had birthed were not nearly as important as her kneeling over me, concerned for my well-being. Rapha was right—Kanya would make a fine girlfriend.

The others joined her and stood looking down upon me. My chest burned, and my hands tingled.

As much as I had become of particular interest to people lately, I had zero interest in being the center of attention. I climbed to my feet with Kanya's assistance and stood wobbling.

"What was that?" I said, wincing at the searing pain across my chest.

"What was *what*?" Quinn knit his brow. "Are you talking about what *you* did or what *he* did?"

"*Him*!" I pointed to Rapha. "I could barely breathe. It would have crushed me if I hadn't... hadn't..."

"Exactly," said Quinn. "Unless you hadn't bolted through space. Or whatever it was you did."

Kanya turned to Rapha. "It's the same thing that happened last night at the hospital."

"Except I—" I looked around. "I didn't destroy anything, did I?"

"No." Rapha was also panting. "Not this time." He pulled his bandana off and dabbed the sweat off his face and forehead.

But there was something else about him. Something had changed. He seemed…larger. I walked towards him, studying his features. My chest was blazing, but I fought back the temptation to make a big deal about this. I knew that the Tau scar had grown with my latest feat. But I didn't want to entertain the thought lest Quinn pick my brain, so I focused on Rapha. What had changed about him? His features seemed…thicker, bigger, if that was even possible. As if his body had expanded ever-so-slightly.

He knew I was pondering this. He smiled slightly and then hunched forward, breathing heavily. "It's a flight gift, Brother Moon." He remained with his hands on his knees. Then he rose. "You have a flight gift. I don't mean *flying*. Not yet, at least. More like escape. You can transport across small distances of space. Possibly triggered by danger or duress. Perhaps it's some type of teleportation ability. Maybe telekinesis. Telekinites have been known to throw themselves forward. I'm not sure. But it's amazing."

I remained staring up at him. "What happened to you? You look bigger. After that thing you did, with the…"

"Gravity."

"Right. You can alter gravity," I said. "Or something like that."

"A density bubble."

"Tell me more."

"Of course. Yet I am still learning myself. For short periods, I can manipulate small spaces, flatten objects, repel and attract matter. In some situations I can cause objects to fall—if this is the proper word—to fall toward another object rather than to earth. It's very difficult to explain, but one I intuitively understand. I have not sought to explain it as much as I should. Forgive me."

"Sure," I said. "So something like that, I'm guessing it has lots of variations and uses."

"Yes. Crushing or immobilizing opponents. Sometimes decreasing gravity to lessen a blow or counter the efficiency of another's skillset. In certain settings I can anchor myself to the ground or become dense enough to withstand incredible force. But enough of me. We must seek to understand *your* gifting."

"Understand? Is that even possible?" I massaged my aching shoulder. "I'd be happy just knowing how not to break things and hurt people."

"Now that's funny," Quinn said. "It's entirely possible that that's the exact thing you'll need to do."

"You mean—?"

"You're weaponized."

"Indeed," Rapha said. "Which means you must retain some sort of mass during the jump. You couldn't damage objects unless you did."

"Which means it's not simply a flight gift," Quinn continued. "Seriously. If he flings himself into a locked door or a block wall or something, in that state, he could obliterate the whole thing."

"Either that," I said, "or lose an arm or leg in the process."

"Yeah. That too."

I turned to Rapha. "So I'm not teleporting."

"Not in the strictest sense, no. But this is the wonder of it, these gifts of the guardians. Perhaps it's some sort of spatial manipulation. A warping of space. Maybe you're generating some sort of wormhole."

"Or seeing existing ones," I added.

Rapha nodded. "Many saints and sages were said to transport. Philip and the Ethiopian eunuch, for example. Saint Philip was said to have disappeared in one place and appeared in another. Some saints were said to levitate—Aquinas, Catherine of Sienna. Other holy ones, monks and Desert Fathers, have also exhibited bilocation abilities."

"You're not suggesting I'm a saint, are you?"

Quinn rolled his eyes. "I don't think that's what he's saying."

"Ha! It's an adventure, Brother Moon. A great journey." Rapha smiled and spread his arms wide. "And we are your fellow travelers."

Then he approached and hugged me tightly. It made my chest explode in pain, so much that I almost yelped. When he released me from his grasp, I noticed Kanya smiling.

I glanced at Quinn.

"No," Quinn said. "I am not hugging you. So, are you in?"

"Do I have a choice?"

"Listen, there's no telling what we're gonna find out there. We need to be able to work together and cover each other's backsides. And try not to kill each other. You know, one for all and all for one. That kinda thing. So, are you in?"

Hmm. *Was* I in? Did I have what it took to possess such powers? Was I really willing to sacrifice life and limb for this makeshift band of superheroes?

"Well?" Quinn said.

I am not one for theatrics. Had I been, this would have been a perfect time for a rousing speech. Instead, I shrugged and said purposely nonchalantly, "Sure. I'm in."

CHAPTER 14

S ix is not the best of numbers. Nevertheless, thanks to Kanya, there were six of us. I'd tried to persuade her to stay behind, but she refused. We were in it together, she said. Besides, the rest of the team liked her. And I definitely didn't mind having her nearby.

I decided to leave my backpack at Rapha's. I'd probably regret it, but busying myself with taking pictures while trying to stop the Tenth Plague was asking too much. We piled into Rapha's truck and headed to the downtown subway project. There was plenty of room in his truck, although not nearly enough to keep me from feeling self-conscious. I hadn't taken a shower since early yesterday and with all my recent extracurricular activities, I was pretty sure I smelled as ripe as a moldy hamper.

Mace had found some old maps of the previous subway project and sent images of them to Kanya. Celeste asked to see them and spent the majority of the trip studying the diagrams on Kanya's phone, most likely logging the info into that super-enhanced memory bank of hers. Still, innumerable questions remained about the task that lay ahead of us.

"So," I said, "you're sure that going through the downtown site is the best approach?"

"Without knowing where the altar was found," Quinn said, "it's our *only* approach. A couple wrong turns and we could end up wandering around down there for days."

"They were digging southeast," Celeste said. "Along Fifth towards Pershing Square. It was somewhere near there that they intersected the original subway. It's condemned now. Thing is, it's not clear where that particular excavation began."

"NeoKor went dark right after that," I said. "So it's going to be a total crapshoot."

Quinn added, "And we'll have company, no doubt."

"Friends," Rapha said, glancing over his shoulder. "We must trust fortune to guide us."

"Well." Orphana opined. "Hopefully fortune doesn't lead us straight into trouble."

"Which would not be a first," Quinn added.

"There are a lot of entry points throughout the city," Celeste continued. "Some are definitely more accessible than this one—SoHo, Metro 417's a possibility. But at this stage, our safest bet is to trace their footsteps. And from there," she smiled, "we let fortune guide us."

Despite the obvious degree of uncertainty, everyone seemed in agreement with this.

"You guys realize," I said, "If the altar is that important, it probably won't be unguarded. I mean, Etherea seemed convinced that we posed no problem."

"Eh," Quinn brushed his hand through the air. "Wait till I get hold of her. She'll think otherwise."

"Brother Moon." Rapha looked at me in the rearview mirror. "Knights errant, remember?"

"In other words," Quinn lowered his voice. "We ad-lib."

After my last experience, I had sworn off using my handgun again for self-defense. But at that moment, I had to admit, I was reconsidering. Pentecost said that engaging angels during their manifestation made them subject to the laws of our world. Which made me wonder whether or a not a bullet to their head might be quite effective. Hell, an assault rifle might do wonders on an angel of death. I recalled the arsenal mounted at the Asylum and wondered if having Mace tag along with one such weapon would not have been a good idea. As it stood, Quinn was right—ad-libbing was probably our best plan of attack.

It was late afternoon when we arrived at the site. An entire city block had been cordoned by double chain link fencing. Sections of asphalt had been removed and the subsequent rerouting of traffic had led to nightmarish snarls and congestion. The Central library was visible from here, an architectural smorgasbord of Egyptian and Mediterranean influences replete with colorful tiled mosaics, bordered by spires of Cyprus trees. I'd frequented the Library fairly regularly, especially to explore its vast photo morgue. The Biltmore wasn't far away, containing its own trove of ghostly legends and noir-ish history. But the hole in the middle of the city was what occupied our attention.

A mountain of dirt, rebar, and cement chunks rose on one corner of the property. A flock of seagulls circled above this debris. Near it sat several earthmovers and a crane, windows dusty and vacant. Large signs emblazoned with *No Trespassing*, marred with spray painted graffiti, lined the area. Guard shacks occupied several corners with construction trailers grouped nearby. An old bowling alley had once sat on this site. But all that remained was a twelve-foot-tall bowling pin that had once crowned the old brick building. At the property's center, generators and flood lamps surrounded the excavation site. It was as if a square block of ghost town had plopped into the middle of downtown L.A.

We slogged through traffic, circling the street, debating our best approach. Cutting our way through the fence in broad daylight was out of the question. Behind the front gate sat a trailer and a guard shack. Several cars were parked near some generators. Electrical cables spooled from the generators like serpents, trailing in various directions. A large wooden sign with the NeoKor logo stood at the front gate. Although they weren't visible, Quinn said there were three guards inside, adding confidently that he could easily 'persuade' them to let us in.

Rapha chose Quinn and Orphana to go on ahead. While this saved Orphana from excessive walking, I still wondered how she would manage any length of travel into the subway. Unless one of her talents was also flying. Separating might also help us in the event of some delay, or to provide a distraction. As we prepared to stop and let them out, Rapha sternly cautioned Quinn about staying under the radar—no theatrics and, especially, no harm done to anyone. Unless necessary. Had this been a problem with him? Quinn nodded dully. It only seemed to fan the slow burn between the two. We navigated into a nearby Loading Zone as they climbed out and we prepared to find a place to park.

My stomach was grinding. My mind was preoccupied with death angels, flight gifts, and subterranean altars. I tried to remind myself of my new calling and the storm gifts. But I simply could not manage to feel anything more than a growing anxiety.

We found a parking lot around the corner and paid. Rapha retrieved a backpack that he had stuffed full of supplies—bottled water, wire cutters, flashlights, and a pair of military grade walkie-talkies—for our spelunking adventure. He flung it over one shoulder, and we hurried to the construction site.

Along the way, we passed a street preacher, pleading with pedestrians to get right with God before the coming apocalypse. Street preachers were not unusual in Los Angeles. But with the Regulus Effect in the news, paranoia seemed to linger in the eyes of the passersby. Compound this with the exhaust fumes and the snarled traffic, and everyone seemed on edge.

As we neared the site, we remained just far enough away to see what was happening with our companions. Neither Quinn nor Orphana were visible. The gate to the site was closed, and we could not see anyone in or near the guard shack. Then, just inside the property, a cargo van lurched forward, kicking up dust, and made a U-turn. Quinn waved to us from the driver's side window.

"Let's go," Rapha said.

We began weaving our way through foot traffic, speed walking to the front gate. No security guards were visible, yet we approached cautiously. Quinn pulled the van up to the gate and hopped out. He lifted a chain that was looped around the gate, removed it, and popped the gate open for us. Then he hustled to the van and yanked the side door open.

"C'mon," he said, glancing into the guard shack. "They let me borrow the van."

I did a double-take when I saw the three security guards in the shack standing zombie-like, in a tight circle, with their noses practically touching.

"Don't worry," he said. "I was nice. When they come to, they won't remember a thing."

We closed the gate, climbed into the van, and Quinn sped across the dusty lot, past a small fleet of earth-moving equipment and pipe, until we reached the perimeter of a massive trench at the center of the property. Everyone got out.

The area was cordoned with K-Rails and thick cables. Signs announcing *Hard Hat Area* and cautioning against entry were everywhere. A wide concrete ramp descended to the tunnel entrance. Conveyor belts were erected there to carry boulders and soil to the surface. Boring equipment stood silent and dusty, a testament to the project's swift closure. Alongside the colorful spray-painted monikers of taggers, other more unusual symbols marked the walls—Luciferian sigils, silver stars of the Astral Argentum, and indiscernible hieroglyphs. This piqued my interest. Perhaps the site *was* more than your standard subway dig, or a hangout for skateboarders and transients. It was exerting its own dark gravity upon the city, drawing all manner of practitioners to its occult incandescence. Security cameras stared down on us from multiple angles.

Quinn saw me looking at them. "Don't worry. I disabled those when I tucked in the mall cops."

"There's another entry point," Celeste said, staring down at the tunnel entrance. "An air shaft on the northwest corner. Maybe four or five hundred feet south of here, there's another shaft that is not as frequented and used for emergency purposes or equipment dumps, in case we need a quick exit. The remaining entries that I'm aware of are further down towards the old subway near Metro 417. And I believe there's a water main service channel that intersects the south-eastern bound tunnel. I'm just not sure of the ingress and egress."

The six of us stood staring down the ramp into the darkened entry of the downtown subway project. Thick concrete stretched before us like a runway disappearing into the bowels of the city. I peered into the entrance as if doing so might extract some secret or hint of what awaited me. There was no way around it—we had to enter this subterranean hellhole.

Rapha unlatched the cable as Quinn and Orphana jumped back in the van. We followed suit; Rapha joined us, and we drove down to the tunnel entrance. The shadows were already growing long in the city. As we descended, the sky shrank overhead as the earthen walls loomed around us. We reached the bottom and exited.

The sounds of the city had almost disappeared, swallowed by the silence of dead earth. We stood momentarily in awe of the massive project. It was like being in the middle of a volcanic crater hoping to hell it wouldn't erupt. By all appearance, this would be the main station entrance upon completion.

The entrance was framed by iron trusses and stood twenty feet in height. It was blocked by more concrete K-Rails, tightly lined end-to-end. Several boring machines were parked to one side next to sumps and other hydraulic equipment. The entry was littered with odd debris—burned newspaper, shards of clothing, and candles. The carcass of a large rodent lay teeming with maggots. Between the spray-painted anarchy symbols and skateboarding emblems were varying hand-drawn configurations of skulls, wings, eyes, and pentagrams. I sensed the shadows were seething with Invisibles, some of the variety I'd never encountered. This place was a hive of evil. Like jackals surrounding a dying beast, the Invisibles were gathering for their own last supper. A creeping sense of dread welled up in me. But perhaps what chilled me more than all of this was the large Regulus symbol—belly-up crescent moon and three stars—depicted on the entryway wall.

"Then it is true," I said, numbly.

"Of course." Rapha adjusted the backpack over his shoulder. "We are on the right track. See?"

Without further deliberation, Rapha hoisted his legs one at a time over the concrete barriers and entered the tunnel. We followed suit. Quinn handed Orphana the key to the van. She remained outside, staring into the tunnel. Rapha slung his backpack off, reached inside and pulled out the radios, one of which he handed to Quinn, the other to Orphana.

"We'll stay in touch as long as we can," Quinn said. "Just try to keep a direct line of sight, as much as possible."

Orphana nodded. "If I have to, you know I can be there."

"We know," Rapha said. He reached across and took hold of her shoulder. "Just be careful, sister."

"You too," Orphana said. "And I want to hear the whole story when you get back."

"*If* we get back," Quinn said.

Orphana clucked her tongue. "Oh, you'll be back."

The tunnel opening provided enough daylight to see what immediately laid before us. The walls were concrete, twenty-five or thirty feet in height, reaching a semi-circular ceiling strung with cables and miscellaneous colored wiring. Scaffolding rose on the far side, three stages, against a soon to be fresco area. Elaborate graffiti arrayed several walls with images of skulls, daggers, and blood-drenched roses. Open-faced, soot-rimmed barrels sat in a shadowy corner near some large cardboard boxes and articles of clothing strewn along the floor. The smell of urine and human feces mixed with that of damp earth. A bank of darkened windows without panes lined one wall, a ticket counter in the making. There was no doubt that this would be the main terminal.

Perhaps fifty yards away sat another boring device next to the train tunnel. Grooved slots for rail lines coursed the concrete, ending there. Our footsteps echoed in the cavern as we approached. Together we stood staring into the darkness of a twenty-by-twenty circular aperture. Rapha removed a flashlight from his pack and turned it on. Rebar cages lined the walls of this tunnel, preventing a cave-in. A wooden catwalk had been built, heavy plywood and two-by-fours, creating a navigable path.

"So," Quinn said, looking at Celeste. "This is our tunnel?"

"I don't know," she said. "I think so. But the maps I memorized didn't detail anything other than general stuff. This is the direction they were working—southeast. But I'm not sure how far, or what tunnel the altar was found in. There's a water main up ahead, I know that. But the location of the altar wasn't specified on any of the maps."

We stared into the darkened tunnel, without speaking. It was alive with Invisibles. I could not see them, but their slime-prints were everywhere. The faint titter of unseen voices flitted in my head. They were watching, waiting. My heartbeat rose. The sense of unease I'd felt earlier was now a malignant dread. The cool air drifting from the tunnel seemed to bear with it a toxic malaise. It coiled about my ankles, working its way into my bones. I wondered if the others were getting the same signals. The longer I stared into the shaft, the more I felt like running.

"You guys okay?" Orphana called from the entrance behind us.

It yanked me from my thoughts.

"We're okay," Quinn called back, flashing her a thumbs up. Then he lowered his voice and said to us, "We're okay, right?"

Kanya glanced at me, as if looking for confirmation. I just shrugged.

Rapha inhaled deeply. "We must trust our instincts, guardians."

He handed a second flashlight to Celeste before stepping onto the wooden catwalk. I lagged behind and waited as everyone entered. Before Kanya went, she turned back to me. I couldn't tell if she was worried about me or perhaps fearful. Our eyes met for a brief second. She knew I was nervous. She was concerned about me. In a way, I took comfort in that. However, it didn't quell the feeling that I was stepping into the Funhouse from Hell.

The wooden walkway creaked as we went, but for the most part it was sturdy. The sound of our footsteps died into the walls of the earth. The roving flashlight beam revealed cables stretching along the ceiling and strings of lights, now unlit, following the cave walls. However, the tunnel remained dark. It got warmer as we went, stuffy and claustrophobic. But no one spoke. Not even Quinn could muster his smart-ass remarks. It was as if we all sensed the innumerable possibilities of the mission that awaited us.

Quinn did not remove his strange sunglasses, which caused me to wonder about what kind of glasses they might be. Or what kind of condition he had that required them. Yet as awkward as I felt amongst my new friends, I tried to center myself along the way. I thought about Ellie and the acquisition of the Tau, which had cost her life. I thought about my father, and his desire to see me enter the fray for the love of God and man. And I thought about Matisse and his battle against demons, internal and external. As I focused on these silent witnesses, I allowed the storm gifts to untwine and come to the fore. As they did, a strange fluttering sensation stirred under my ribcage, followed by a slow burn along the perimeter of the scar. Whatever was required of me, I hoped to God I could rise to meet it.

The darkness was stifling. It seemed to drain the chamber of air and turn the atmosphere oppressive. Penny had mentioned that some cavers went mad. Even in this short time, I could see why. The claustrophobia. The perpetual artificial light. It was like a cold black ocean beating on the breakwater of your psyche.

The two flashlight beams scoured the walkway and the tunnel walls ahead. We studied our surroundings, listening and watching, but there was no evidence of an extraneous chamber or an archeological dig of any sort. Along the way, Quinn radioed Orphana to establish a connection and check in, before we settled back into silence. After maybe fifteen minutes of uneventful walking, a faint light shone up ahead.

We reached a spacious intersection. Large old water mains ran beneath the catwalk, and a service tunnel stretched into the darkness in opposite directions. The smell of mold and dank earth arose. Several old metal catwalks ran the length of this intersecting tunnel. Panels of switches and lights lined the wall further down. Past this, faint strands of daylight fingered their way from above. Apparently, this was a tunnel used by municipal workers, just like Celeste had said.

Our wooden walkway traversed this area, creating a bridge suspended from above by cables and rope. The intersection provided a brief respite to the claustrophobia of the tunnel behind us. Rapha walked to the center of the catwalk and stood listening to the rumble of water through the pipes all around us. He shone the flashlight into the tunnel ahead and then poked the beam around the grates and braces of the water access tunnel.

Could the altar have been discovered down one of these adjacent tunnels?

Everyone was sweating by now, and for once I was glad to be wearing the loose-fitting Hawaiian shirt. Rapha dabbed his brow. His arms glistened in the light. He glanced back at me and for a split second, I sensed unease in him. Did we know where we were going? Had the Invisibles penetrated his brain with their insidious languor?

As if addressing my unspoken sentiment, Quinn said, "I dunno. Something doesn't feel right."

"What is it?" Rapha asked. "What do you feel?"

Quinn stood still. Then he did a slow 360 turn, his chin slightly tilted. He stopped and said, "Getting a lot of mixed signals."

"Why?" Rapha asked. "From what?"

Quinn shrugged. "I dunno. Something's screwy down here."

"Yeah," Celeste said. "I'm feeling the same thing. Someone...something's trying to throw us off."

"Same here," Quinn added. "We're not the only ones down here."

I found myself staring into the dark, wondering what manner of exotic Invisibles were scrambling our signals.

Rapha squinted at us. Then he stared forward, in the direction we had been traveling. He let the flashlight beam linger in the tunnel ahead. Finally, he said, "I believe we're going the right way. We must proceed."

He continued in the direction we were going.

Quinn didn't budge. Which caused Celeste to put the brakes on. A pulse of anger went out from the telepath.

"So that's it?" Quinn called after Rapha.

Rapha stopped but did not turn around.

Quinn shook his head. "And here I thought we were a team."

Rapha turned. "Brother Quinn, humor me."

"Don't we always?"

Rapha stared at Quinn.

"Look," Quinn said. "Celeste is sensing the same thing. Doesn't that matter anymore? I say we take a vote or something." He looked at me and Kanya. "Let Mr. Teleportation have a say. I mean, this is still a democracy, isn't it?"

At that, Rapha stiffened. He approached Quinn. The wooden planks creaked under the weight of the massive Islander. Rapha stood before Quinn, rising six, seven, eight inches above him. Something had snapped inside the mild-mannered giant.

Quinn stared directly into Rapha's chest.

"Brother Quinn," Rapha said. His lip twitched as he spoke. Indignation radiated from him like a high-octane blowtorch. "Feel free to express your sentiments. You are a valuable asset to the Imperia. Your advice is necessary for the sake of our team. But please—" Rapha stepped closer, so close that his chin nearly touched Quinn's forehead. "Don't make this harder than it already is."

Quinn stared forward. With the energy coming off these guys, I was fearful that a quasar might erupt. A vein in Quinn's temple throbbed. What would happen if these two men unloaded their powers upon each other? There was a history here. That was obvious. But I'd be damned if I was going to stand by and watch these two superhuman guardians of earth unload upon each other.

"So is that what happened to Ki?" I blurted.

The mention of that name seemed to shock them out of their standoff. They stepped away from each other. Quinn looked down while Rapha turned to me. The water rumbled beneath us, filling this subterranean grotto with its sound.

"Yeah," I said. "Ki. You keep mentioning him. He was supposed to show up, and he hasn't. And you're all very concerned because it's evidence of the fracturing of your little team here."

"*Our* team," Quinn corrected.

"Right, Quinn. That's right. *Our* team. Well, by the looks of it, *our* team is doing fine tearing itself apart on its own. Who needs death angels or the Black Council to do us in when we can do it ourselves? I don't know about the rest of you, but I'm having a hard enough time figuring out what's happening to *me*. What's expected of *me*. And if we're here to actually, you know, defend earth and stop the Tenth Plague and all that other crap, then bickering and sniping at each other is the last thing we need. Don'tcha think?"

At that point, they were all staring at me.

I am not known as a team leader. Or a motivational speaker. Hell, I'd rather work by myself most of the time. But the mention of their wayward partner had awakened something in them. I knew it would. Something had happened amongst these fantastically gifted people that had sent them spiraling. And now I was inserted into the mix. My presence had complicated things. That was for sure. But if uniting the Imperia was some sort of mission of mine, apparently I had a hell of a lot of work ahead of me.

Rapha inhaled deeply, looked at Quinn, and rested his hand on the man's shoulder. "Forgive me, Brother Quinn."

Quinn nodded and forced a smile of concession. "I hate when that happens,"

It was a small victory, but one that only signaled other wars ahead.

We proceeded in a south-easterly direction, the way Rapha had suggested. I remained at the rear trying to calibrate my intuitive skills. Soon, tools and debris began to appear along the way—hard hats, crowbars, and miscellaneous articles of clothing. We reached another intersection, this one quite smaller than the last.

"This wasn't on any of the maps," Celeste said, shining her flashlight into the bisecting walkways.

The two catwalks intersected here, traveling opposite directions into two smaller shafts. Dead air surrounded us. Rapha followed suit and shone his light down each of the new tunnels. Both disappeared into the cave walls and were pitch black. Odd smells lingered in them, both rancid and sweet. Wherever the shafts led, we were getting closer to our destination. The rest of the crew seemed to sense this as well. Quinn leaned forward to the tunnel on our left, his head tilted in concentration. Rapha shone his flashlight into the same tunnel, and its beam caused something to glisten from within.

Several things happened in that instant. Commotion sounded ahead of us, in the direction we had been traveling. Voices and the sounds of scraping. A deep thud reverberated through the walls and the catwalk, as if something heavy had toppled nearby. Everyone turned their attention back in that direction. Because the main tunnel curved up ahead, Rapha's light was unable to identify the source of the commotion. Quinn joined Rapha at the front of the line, and they peered foreward. My first instinct was to bolt. After all, we were trespassing. Apparently, running was not in the Imperia playbook. Rapha motioned us forward, exhorting us to be on the alert, and the others hurried past the connecting shafts to see what was going on ahead of us.

But something didn't feel right, and I was about to say so when I caught a flash of golden hue from the corner of my eye.

I stopped, turned, and stared into the shaft on my left. Inside, the darkness was alive with Invisibles, demon spawn entwined in a fetid orgy. I could hear them in the back of my brain. My friends continued ahead as I remained peering into the shaft and the hideous crush of devils. If Invisibles were gathering to this degree, it was safe to assume that we were nearing the location of the altar. Yet something else was in there. Something different.

I stepped closer. The wooden catwalk creaked under my weight. I gaped into the darkness. And as I stared, the same golden aura splashed across my field of vision. I stumbled back, shielding my eyes. When I looked again, the fantastic glow had been swallowed in the pitch.

Bernard!

I blinked hard, trying to adjust my eyes. However, there was no doubt about it. My guardian angel was inside this tunnel along with a host of demon spawn.

The rest of the Imperia were now thirty to forty feet ahead. I could see their flashlight beams slashing the subterranean dark. Voices sounded from up around the bend. I prepared to call out and summon them back when I glimpsed another flash. Only this time, I was sure it was Bernard. He had tumbled past a trunk of frothing blackness and risen in a crouch. He caught sight of me, did a double take, and then frantically began waving me forward.

I hurried along the catwalk into this unexplored shaft. I reached the entrance and ducked my head inside.

"Bernard! What're you doing?"

He spun away from me. Sweat sprayed from the guardian angel's body. Oddly enough, at that moment, I wondered if Pentecost knew that angels could actually sweat. Then again, Bernard did not seem like your ordinary angel.

Not wanting to get separated from the rest of the team, I ducked out of the shaft and started to call out to them. But as I did, the sound of voices had turned to angry shouts. Rapha's thick voice could be heard resonating in the stone. They had reached the turn in the subway tunnel and all I could see was flashes of light arcing wildly about the walls. The earth guardians had problems of their own.

Dammit!

I turned back, but the angelic glow was no longer visible. I ducked back into the tunnel, moved further down the catwalk, frantically trying to locate Bernard and, hopefully, not get caught in the crossfire of whatever it was he was fighting. Yet there was no sight of the angel. The dark was absolute. Claustrophobic. And it was teeming with intangible monstrosities. Snapshots of membranous limbs and disjoined mandibles flashed through my mind's eye in a grisly montage. A bacchanalian dance of debauchery and malformation. Chills pummeled my flesh.

More shouting echoed from outside, and I caught glimpses of lights arcing wildly in the main tunnel. Whatever was going on out there, it wasn't good.

I fumbled for my cell phone as I retreated further into the dark, inching my way forward. The planks groaned under my weight, magnified by the stillness in this place. The evil was tangible, consuming.

"Bernard!" I whispered. "Are you all right?"

There was no response from the angel. My fingers reached the phone in my front pants pocket, yet something stopped me. A moan sounded. Faint. But it was clearly human. The Invisibles stirred at the sound, animated and thrilled by the painful plea. Yet it came from elsewhere, somewhere further down.

My eyes had adjusted enough to the darkness that I could now make out light in a secondary tunnel down below mine. Another shaft. The catwalk ended here. As I stared, the light below grew in intensity. Something was burning down below.

Suddenly, I caught sight of a yellow strand coiling at my feet. I leapt back and slammed into the wooden handrail.

Crime scene tape lay stretched across the chamber floor. *This was it!* Other oddities now came into view. Small pale fragments littered the ground. What the hell was I seeing? Were they bones? A shuffle of movement sounded, and I whipped around. But there was nothing behind me. Then the moan sounded again, followed by the joyous caterwaul of demons. This time there was no question—in the shaft down below, somebody was in pain.

That's when I noticed the Regulus symbol had been crudely carved into the overhead wooden joist. And I knew that I was entering ground zero.

CHAPTER 15

I stared down the shaft. It was framed by wooden braces at uneven angles and looked like the entry to some campy house of gravity in a remote roadside attraction. Penny had said that a chamber was discovered during excavation, and I was pretty sure this was the passageway to my own personal viewing. My heart thudded in my chest. Cold flashed through my arms, coiling into my fingers. The power was stirring inside me. But how it would manifest itself was anyone's guess. Whatever evil Bernard was battling, it energized the atmosphere with its presence. And ignited my senses.

I held my breath and stepped off the catwalk. In the sub-chamber down below, light flickered, sending shadows capering across a smooth floor. The smell of incense struck me. As did the stench of blood and spoilage. I picked my way past rocks and uneven soil, keeping my eyes fixed ahead. Though fear and adrenaline spiked my body, a strange curiosity seemed to propel me forward.

I reached the end of the shaft. It opened into an oval cavern with a high ceiling and a smooth dirt floor. Mining tools and lengths of discarded rope lay to one side along with dirt and debris. Odd inscriptions had been carved into the hardened earth and lined the walls, giving it the appearance of some Neolithic dwelling. Long fluted shelves, earthen bunks, rose chimney-like in another area. Some sort of burial mound perhaps. At the cavern's furthest edge burned a pyre of black candles, surrounding a massive shrine wherein stood a statue of Saint Death. However, in this case, the skeleton appeared genuine. A black velvet cape embroidered by colorful sequins draped her. She held a scythe whose blade was darkly stained. Her face glowed eerily in the candlelight.

The shrine encircled something even odder—a large squat altar made of dark stone. Immediately, I knew it was the

Altar of Summoning. It captured my attention not just because it was the fabled altar, but because it seemed to be glowing. Veins of crimson pulsated from within the strange rock as if the altar was channeling part of the earth's own circulatory system. It was massive, with enough surface space for Audra's sports car. How in the hell had something this size gotten down here? Unless it had always been down here. On its surface I could make out the symbol of Regulus. Intricate sigils and carvings glistened upon its legs and borders, a weird combination of coiled organs and celestial designs. Saint Death stared down lifelessly upon the Altar of Summoning.

Suddenly, I felt overwhelmed. If our objective was to destroy this altar, we might need several tons of TNT. Or maybe we could rent Thor and his hammer for a couple of good thwacks. Either way, destroying the Altar of Summoning now seemed somewhere in the range of impossible.

"You again?"

My heart leapt at the voice. It came from behind me. I stumbled around to see Etherea emerge from the shadows of the shaft, her pale face glowing in the warm candlelight.

She wore a short black leather skirt, spider web stockings, and army boots. This chick had all the charm of a black widow. Seeing her sent a lance through my brain. I winced and then blinked hard, trying to regain my focus. The atmosphere churned about her. Tentacles of rage and hate blistered the space she occupied. The earth itself seemed to recoil at her presence. Demons were not only attached to her, they appeared to fester there, clamoring for some delectable cleft to nestle inside her.

She stopped directly in front of me and lowered her lashes until they almost hugged her cheeks. Red glitter sparkled on her eyelids. Or was that brimstone from her travels? Her smile was as inviting as barbed wire. On her breath was the scent of despair and black licorice.

"I thought I told you this was a done deal, errand boy?"

166

I tried to muster some strength to match her diabolic panache, but I was so far out of my league we weren't even in the same galaxy.

I swallowed. "It's just starting to get interesting."

"Please tell me you've got a better idea of what's going on here."

"An idea? Yeah. It's all the details that I'm missing."

I fought to keep my gaze from drifting to her black lips. I did not want those things anywhere near me. My proximity to Etherea had caused me to sweat even more. My eyes stung. The shirt clung to my flesh. Ill-will and malice were the marrow in her bones. I wondered if she'd ever known love or if her saliva was venom. Perhaps the lerium had propelled her into a new stage of evolution. Or was this de-evolution? My knees trembled, and I had to fight to keep from crumpling to the ground and beseech her to spare my life.

"So when did you learn they discovered it?" she said.

"The altar is old news. The only thing I'm not sure about is who the Shroud is and why the hell you're protecting him. And, oh, why summoning the Archangel of Death to destroy half the city is to anyone's advantage."

She kept smiling, but I knew that she was searching my brain, gathering info. Looking for that soft underbelly in which to insert her wrath.

"I love your moxie," she said, toying with the Regulus pendant at her throat. "And you're kind of cute. In another life, I might have found you interesting. But in this one, I'm afraid you're just a broken down puppet without a future."

She released me from her gaze, circled me, and then sauntered to the altar. She was as curvaceous as they came, with a body that could send a rector racing for a cold shower. Her hips hugged that leather skirt like it was nobody's business. But I was fairly certain that what she called love was ultimately as satisfying as a bear trap doused with blight and a sprinkle of pestilence.

She stood behind the altar, Saint Death gazing over her shoulder, and traced the glowing etchings with her black fingernails.

"The Shroud is inscrutable," she said. "But I'll send a word for you. Perhaps we can schedule a rendezvous."

"Please do. But—" I pointed to the altar and the shrine. "Why? Why all this? Why kill a bunch of innocent people? I mean, are you just hard up for death?"

"Are you referring to the Egyptians? You know, all those firstborn that were slaughtered just so Moses and his crew could escape? That was the origins, you know. The Tenth Plague. You remember about that from Sunday School, don't you? Or did they skip that part to spare you the gory details? The Egyptians were innocent too, weren't they?"

"Look. That's between them and God. As a general rule, I try to keep my nose out of other people's squabbles. Especially when gods are on opposing ends."

This appeared to bring pause. "But that's exactly where you are now, sweets—between gods."

Seeing my silence, she shrugged. "Smart of you, either way. They were just collateral damage. Like people will be tomorrow night—collateral damage. Just think about it. People dropping dead in the streets, at restaurants. Hospitals will be overrun. Municipalities brought to a standstill. 'And the cry of her children will ascend to the heavens.' Isn't that how it goes? That's when the Shroud will reveal who's really in charge. Azrael doesn't care. She'll gorge herself on as many souls as she's able. She's here to serve a larger purpose. No lamb's blood on doorposts can stop her this time. She's under our orders. And when the Imperia finally recant and the city is brought to her knees, maybe then we can plot a sustainable course for universal domination. You see, the next savior is waiting in the wings. Once the world is made to grovel, they'll be begging for a real leader to step up. And we've got just the person."

"Universal domination?" I shook my head. "Figures. You're fascists. Why is it always fascists? My God. How unoriginal. Then you really don't know, do you Etherea?"

She continued tracing her fingers across the altar's carved symbols. "Do tell."

"Saint Death is a prop. You're being used just like the rest of them were. That's how they work—the Summu Nura. Ever heard of them? They're the ultimate bad guys. Astral vampires, cosmic leeches of some sort. They've been around for a long time. And they're always looking for someone to manipulate. Usually the weak-minded. Not that I'm inferring you're soft, but someone of your acumen should know this."

I thought my retort was rather keen. Yet it didn't seem to have phased Etherea. She remained nonplussed.

"You don't think I know about the Old Ones?" She shook her head. "You're worse off than I thought. Pity. Could be they revealed the Grimoire of Azrael. Could be that I've thrown in with them, you know? You can't plumb the darkness without bumping into the overlords. And from what I understand, they'd love to sink their tentacles into you. Maybe I'll get a reward for bringing you to them."

Suddenly, a great shadow passed through the room. A whoosh of air sounded overhead. I ducked, instinctively covering my head with my arms. The candles around the shrine suddenly guttered and flumed.

"What the—?" My heart was almost in my throat. Something else was in the chamber with us! Had Azrael already arrived? Were we too late? Perhaps I should call out for Rapha. No. They had problems of their own, and the last thing I needed was to draw more trouble my way. But if I didn't do something quick, I feared this would be the last trouble I lived to talk about.

Etherea was laughing. The sound was like fingernails on a chalkboard, plucking my nerves with discordant panic. I scanned the cavern above, trying to locate the source of the commotion. The shadows seemed to unfold around me, every corner and crevice birthing some new evil.

I stumbled and quickly regained my footing. Then I returned my gaze to Etherea in time to see her retrieve a burning black candle from the shrine and place it on the altar.

"This one's for you," she said. "A prayer for the dying. Or in your case, the soon to be deceased."

She emerged from behind the altar. "It's just a conduit, you know. Santa Muerte. Just about any religion will do. Only this one has already blazed a trail into the dark. Human sacrifices. Canticles of vengeance. Yeah, they ain't fooling around, are they? Not perfect, but it'll do. Most religions are like that—flimsy vessels for something much more pure. And primal. Besides, I have a thing for skulls and glitter."

She glanced into the shadows above. I followed suit. But there was nothing. When our eyes met again, I knew she was seeing fear in me.

"So," she said, "do you really think you can just waltz on stage and change the course of history? Just show up, exercise your magic powers, and we surrender?"

"I don't have magic powers."

"That's not what we hear. Last I checked, Normals don't jump. I tell you what. I'll make a deal with you, errand boy. You turn around, take the rest of those geriatric do-gooders with you, and I'll let you witness the meltdown of human society from a place of your own choosing. Hopefully very far away. Andromeda would be my suggestion."

I wrung my hands, trying to summon, much less focus, the power inside me.

She slowly blinked those thick black lashes. "The Summu Nura have already fractured your team."

I leveled my gaze at her.

"That's right," she said. "They've been compromised. It was only a matter of time. Ki has bailed. Which was smart. He's with us now. See, you were right all along. Those feelings of inferiority and unbelief you have? You should pay more attention to them. You can't reunite the Imperia. They're too far gone. Pity. I'm always up for a good brawl. Now I have to look elsewhere. And Felix—" She stepped closer. "His travels have only helped us."

Everything seemed to be closing in on me. My heart was racing. Chest burning. I looked past her, to the altar. I had to destroy it. I had teleported through flesh, through the railing at the hospital. Perhaps I could cast myself through the altar and destroy it.

Etherea shook her head. "Don't even think about it. The Table of Summoning is indestructible. What? You look surprised. Your mind is a sieve, errand boy. Besides, the altar is not from this world. The Elder Ones forged it on the other side. It's endured a lot worse than you can ever inflict upon it. Trust me. It was brought from Diades a long time back. When the earth was still cooling, I think. Its forging is what killed the dinosaurs. Or so they say. Point is, you have no shot. None. Throw in a few death angels and you've got about as much chance of knocking Mars out of orbit as you have breaking the Table."

I looked at that slab again and I knew she was right. The molten veins pulsating through this strange rock. It wasn't from earth. No wonder she was unconcerned about thwarting my access to the chamber. Hell, she practically escorted me to the altar. It was like someone had reached inside my soul and tore out every last shred of hope.

Her eyes sparkled. "We have the map, Reagan. Your future—it is written. And it can be undone."

I stared, numb.

Something like compassion glinted in her eyes. "You don't know, do you? You have got to be the lamest guardian in the history of earth guardians."

"You're probably right."

"It's a fairy tale for the children of the damned. A cautionary tale, for sure. And you're the sad, tragic hero. Once the rest of the map is acquired, we will know how the story ends. And be able to rewrite it ourselves. Knowing about the future used to be in the hands of the seers. But with the breech of Arcadium, the world is wide open to us. Thanks to Ki, your destiny is now in *our* hands."

I was past bewilderment. I'd become the poor victim of some cosmic prank. I wiped sweat from my eyes and attempted to muster a particle of resolve.

"Well," I said, "at least I'm on the right side."

"That's your only consolation? Ha! What a loser."

A flurry of movement sounded above and, this time, I felt of rush of air over my head. It was so close I ducked to the ground to avoid being struck. Yet when I tried to locate the source of the movement, I couldn't. Whispers rose from the shadows, accompanied by the titter of avian sounds. And with them, rose a moan. It was the same moan that had drawn me here. It was coming from nearby.

"The altar's yours," Etherea said. "That is, if you can reach it. Chow."

With that, she walked past me toward the shaft. I instinctively reached out to stop her. It was the only response I could think of. I grabbed her wrist, and the moment I did, she stopped and turned to me. At first, she had a look of indignation. How dare I touch her? Then her eyes softened. She studied my features looking intrigued, her lips parted slightly, almost willing me to action.

Etherea wanted me to challenge her. She wanted me to unleash my power. She was secretly goading me on.

Which put me more at a loss. Perhaps I could threaten to bind and gag her. Maybe I could fling myself against the cavern, like Quinn had suggested, and seal the exit so she couldn't escape. I frantically scanned the place for those odd quantum tunnels. But my efforts were squelched by a bizarre impulse to beg for her mercy.

Someone moaned again. This time I noticed a figure lying crumpled near the far wall, almost directly behind Etherea. I focused my attention there. It was a woman in hospital scrubs. Her eyes were sunken in their sockets. I recognized her as the nurse from St. Vincent's. Alma Curtain. Invisibles lurked nearby, unattached, but swarming as if in hungry delight. Her eyes barely registered life. But she wasn't looking at me.

Something swooped overhead again. The atmosphere in the cavern suddenly grew chill. I released Etherea and spun about trying to locate the source. This time a shadowy form materialized. It landed upon the altar, toppling the candle that was there, and hunkered down. Huge densely black raven-like wings draped to the floor. As it rose, the familiar neon red eyes glared from within its sunken skull.

A death angel.

It saw me, folded its hands as if in prayer, and bowed its head.

"Give it hell, errand boy." And with that, Etherea entered the shaft and disappeared into the dark.

Every cell in my body was screaming. I glanced back at Alma, who stared dully at the creature. Either she was unafraid or in absolute shock. I returned my gaze to the winged devil. It lowered its arms and raised its head. With unblemished hatred it glared at me. Its serpentine tongue lapped from its face as its body tensed, and it prepared to attack.

CHAPTER 16

Had I not been told that this was a death angel, I might have mistaken it for the grotesque litter of some Luciferian concubine. It was oddly familiar in the way a two-headed calf might be—both recognizable and terribly askew. I found myself equally appalled and saddened by the hideous thing. It appeared to be the same angel that had wrapped me in its spell at the hospital, and who was preparing to reenact that dining experience. I'm not exactly sure what Rapha had done to it when he rescued me, but whatever it was, the creature now had vengeance upon its mind.

For the moment, I ignored the moaning of the woman behind me to focus on the immediate threat. Fog billowed about this devil, forming a cloak or a gauzy penumbra that clung to its being. Its torso was pitch black, so dense that to focus on its breastbone was to be swallowed in a vortex of stygian dark. Perhaps even more unusual were the tatters of linen which draped its appendages, shards of fabric wrapped about its arms and legs, giving it the appearance of some demented pirate lashed to the mast of a ghost ship. Its presence was oppressive and chilled the air with biting cold. A noxious current ebbed from the angel and filled the chamber. It reeked of blighted crypts and sorrow. My flesh grew cold, my hair bristling at this evil presence.

The sigils on the altar pulsed more hotly, and in the eerie red glow I could see dark smears, layers of dried liquid that stained the Table of Summoning.

Blood sacrifices. At that moment, I knew it without a doubt. Human beings had died upon this altar.

Why was it always human sacrifice?

In a way, it figured. Power, either spiritual or psychic, is never without a cost. Even cheap-ass downtown magic—the types of incantations and spells L.A.'s jaded urban occultists used—wasn't free. It wore on you. Taxed you. And got under people's skin. Human blood was the most valued commodity. The highest of all costs. It was fused into the very fabric of the universe. It was why the primitives instinctively knew that bleeding out their tribal virgins for their second-rate gods was worth more than any amount of treasure they could assemble. Even in the 21st century, no amount of scientific knowledge or straight-up hoodoo could compare to the sheer power of a human sacrifice. Life for power. The equation never changed.

The thought immediately caused me to turn from the angel to the woman. She was here for one reason only. I ran to her, hoping to hell I wouldn't be snatched from behind by this unholy vulture.

"Hurry," I said. "Get up!"

Her languid, bloodshot eyes gazed up at me. She wanted to say something and gripped my wrist as I reached to her. But her mind seemed vacant, drained of memory. She was not going to cooperate.

Whatever I was supposed to do, I knew that rescuing this poor woman from her appointment with Saint Death was at the top of the list. If I didn't know how to stop Etherea, destroy the altar, or wrestle a death angel, at the least I could help this lady escape.

I bent over her to scoop her up and haul her out. But she pushed me away.

"Leave me." Her motions were slow and dull. Either she'd been drugged or hexed into submission. "I am the one."

After Rapha had rescued me, he'd said I was wrapped in a Delusion. The spell had left me feeling subservient to the demon, unable to challenge it. Not only was Alma Curtain probably cocooned in a similar spell, I knew I must resist the same.

Something thumped the ground behind me. I spun around to see the demon had leapt off the altar. Its wings unfolded like a huge black storm cloud whose motions caused the candles behind it to flutter in unison. I was threatening to steal its prey. A guttural rattling emerged from it, as dry as parched bone, imbued with the voltage of a den of Diamondbacks. Either it was laughing at me or preparing to strike.

Now what? Rapha said that I could do more than break spells—I could battle death angels. But how? If I knew any words of command—counter spells, conjurations, old school incantations, anything—this was the time to uncork them. Problem was, I didn't know any words of command. The words I probably *should* have known were buried under layers of ignorance and inexperience. Looking into the sizzling red eyes of the maelohim left me feeling like a boy scout staring down a pack of hungry lions with only a pocket knife. But I had to do something.

So I inhaled and with as much resolution as I could muster, I barked, "Get away!"

The death angel did not budge. In fact, it was unclear whether it had even heard me. The creature's foggy aura was now creeping across the floor, spreading out like a surreal blanket. Its red eyes radiated an inhuman, alien hatred.

Again I spoke. But this time I shouted the words. "She's mine! Get back!"

Still it didn't move.

Without taking my eyes off the angel, I said to the woman, "Can you hear me?"

She mumbled something.

This time, I angrily shouted it. "Can you hear me?"

"Yeah." She seemed barely there.

I was trembling as much from the cold as the power racing helter-skelter through my body. "Okay. I'm gonna pick you up and get you out of here."

She began sobbing.

"Did you hear me?!"

I glanced at the woman. Her glazed eyes were fixed upon the death angel.

"I c-can't go," she whimpered.

"What?"

A sad smile broke her parched lips. "I'm the chosen one." A tear streaked her dirty cheek. "I will feed her."

Her features changed. Her smile became demented and a clownish, vacant madness danced in her eyes. She said insanely, "I'm the feast for Mother, saint of the dead ones. I am blessed, highly favored. The chosen one. Handmaiden of the Bony Lady. I shall begin the great dance of death and hasten their coming."

I was temporarily stunned by her homage to the unholy.

"No." I spoke to the spell as much as much as I did to the woman. "No way!" Then I glanced back at the angel. "Stop listening to them, do you hear me? Wake up! They've lied to you. Now, c'mon. We're going."

I turned to scoop her up and make a mad dash for the tunnel.

As I did, that dry rattling emerged from the angel. It flapped its wings, and the foggy tendrils it was emitting swirled and coiled along the ground like some vast herd of serpents, spreading our way. Bringing lies and bitter chill with them.

I quickly scooped Alma Curtain into my arms. Despite the storm gifts charging my body, it was pure adrenaline that caused me to lift her with ease. Yet the woman did not want to be rescued. She fought against me. She clawed at my face, and I had to turn away to keep from getting slashed by her fingernails. When that didn't work, she started thumping on my chest, which only heightened the fiery pain there.

"Stop it!" I shouted. "Stop it! Snap out of it. I'm trying to save you."

She arched back and her eyes welled with terror. A whoosh of air sounded overhead. I didn't have time to duck. A blanket of cold immediately wrapped my torso, squeezing the breath from my lungs. I released the woman, and she fell to the floor laughing and spitting out nonsensical imprecations. A second later, my body was yanked backwards. I catapulted through the air, barely missed the altar, before striking the wall.

Flumes of dirt and rock rained from above. The breath left my lungs as I fell to the floor near the shrine. The candles sputtered from the impact. The foggy tentacles still clung to my body.

Directly across the room from me, the woman stood, her eyes wide. She was halfway between rabid glee and astonishment.

I could not immediately locate the angel. I drew great gasps of air until my normal breathing finally returned.

"Run!" I shouted. "Go! Go!"

But she still appeared to be in the spell of this devil. Her gaze passed from amazement to one of despair. Her legs folded under her, and she collapsed to the earth.

I tore at the foggy tentacles that were twining their way about me. I wasn't about to surrender to the same delusion the angel had paralyzed me with the last time.

My chest flared with volcanic heat. Rapha had called it a flight gift, but at the moment it felt more like a raging nuclear reactor in my sternum. Again I tried to locate the angel, but the cavern was an icebox of shadow and sound. I pulled myself off the floor and stood wobbling.

It materialized before the woman, facing me. Only this time, its arms were spread, either in defense or invitation. In my own strength, this god-awful creature would shred me and siphon my life essence.

But I didn't have to rely entirely on my own strength any longer.

Pentecost said the angels were subject to laws. If it was a matter of immovable object meeting irresistible force, I might have a chance. And so right there, in that candlelit cavern below downtown Los Angeles, I focused my eyes at the angel's chest. It was as black as an abyss. If angels had a heart, I would attempt to propel myself into this one's.

The Tau was throbbing now. White heat radiated through my pectoral muscles. I wanted to rip my shirt open and reveal the scar. Sure, it was probably just to bolster my own

Saint Death

self-confidence. But at the moment I didn't need that. Something bigger and nobler was behind me.

My mind piqued, fixated upon this inhuman opponent. Just like at Rapha's place, at the ranch in Rolling Hills, my focus narrowed upon a trajectory, a line of sight that could propel my body forward. With that confidence came the second sight. I could see them now—spatial channels, networks of wormholes intersecting the subterranean chamber. They were everywhere. As I set my gaze upon this dread angel, a trajectory appeared, a route through space itself. Was I creating this? I'd have to wait to find out. For now, I simply had to navigate where I would stop. If I transported too far, I could conceivably pass through a cave wall and bring the entire chamber down on our heads. At the moment, the science didn't matter. Whether I disassembled or moved at the speed of light, it didn't matter. All that mattered was that I knew now, for some fantastic reason, I could fling my body forward and demolish things. Break things. Change things. Hopefully, angels were one of those things.

I momentarily looked past the demon to the woman. We made eye contact. I willed my defiance forward. Rapha said I could do much more than just dispel death angels. And if I could intuit someone's thoughts like Quinn could, perhaps I could also bend them to my will. I pointed towards the exit, maintaining visual contact. Hopefully, I could transfer a shred of confidence, however misguided such confidence might have been, into the mind of Alma Curtain. In that brief second, a light of recognition seemed to glimmer in her eyes.

She staggered to her feet and took a step sideways, all the while staring at me. The madness was gone. Now she seemed more aware of her surroundings. Terror and wonder flitted through her gaze as she looked at me squared off against this devil. I nodded to her and even managed a wink. That made her smile. Then she took another step towards the tunnel exit.

179

It was just enough to move her out of the way of my intended trajectory.

Realizing that the spell upon its prey was breaking, the angel spread its wings, straightened, and issued its inhuman skeletal rattling. Only this was less like laughter than it was a shriek of rage or defiance, a dry, raspy peal that made my flesh cringe. As it did so, rather conveniently for me, it squarely exposed its chest.

I lowered my shoulders and fixed my eyes on that lightless breastbone. On the periphery of my sight I could see the invisible channels pulsing to life everywhere. It was as if the very molecular fabric of our world was alive to me, somehow even at my disposal. Nevertheless, I fixed my sights like a laser on the abdominal core of this reprobate Harvester, this demon of death.

Quinn said I was weaponized. Well, I was about to test his theory.

I willed myself forward, straight into the angel.

The whoosh of space filled my ears and with it came the voices. Distant. Disembodied. Yet very near.

"—moon drops burst—"

"—if the map will be rendered."

While the cavern blurred past, time seemed to slow. With it came a disconcerting sense that my mind was no longer tethered to my body, that my consciousness had been freed to roam. It was an odd combination that left me feeling both fully human and not human at all. Perhaps even more unusual was the impression that this moment was less an actual increment of time as it was a threshold to be traversed or a world to be explored. But how could I remain in such a state—in actual transit between two places—long enough to do so? Then again, perhaps time, in the four-dimensional space-time sense, was the wrong way to look at it.

"—a crisis whose nexus—"

"The realms beyond Arcadium!"

Heat exploded in my chest. I think I was screaming as the black curtain raced up to me. Or was I racing up to it? The angel's red eyes rolled back in its hollow cranium. It turned in an attempt to avoid our impact. Fierce icy blackness stung my flesh. I was immersed in it. A blackness so cold it was hellish. But there was no impact. Instead, when my body met the angel's, I simply passed through it.

The darkness vanished as fractals of light burst around me. Consciousness boomeranged into my being. When I felt my body again, my immediate reaction was to right myself. I didn't think I could withstand too many more headfirst crashes into hard objects. The impulse was smart. I managed to get my legs under me as I left the dimensional chute. However, I was going too fast and though my feet struck the ground, I skidded, lost my footing, and smashed shoulder first into the cavern wall.

A siren was going off somewhere. Or was it an anguished cry? It hurt my head. I struggled upright and covered my ears with my fists to make it go away. But the sound was so high-pitched, so full of torment, that nothing could block it.

At that point, I was unsure I'd even struck the angel. Perhaps it had dematerialized in time to make me miss. The thought caused despair to well up inside me. Until I saw the woman at the tunnel exit, staring in astonishment. Not at me. I followed her gaze. And what I saw set my heart at awe.

My body had passed through the angel and shorn it in two.

Severed at the waist, its lower extremities lay without movement. However, the angel's upper torso clawed the earth, dragging itself along in lunatic circles. Its inhuman shrieking filled the cavern. Its wings flailed the earth and finally managed to lift the upper body into the air. The half-angel swooped crazily, battered the cavern roof, before dropping again to the earth near its lower torso where it thrashed about, mewling and screeching.

But there was another layer of sound, a wailing that pierced my brain and mixed with the angelic shrieks.

It was my own screaming.

Bolts of pain radiated through my chest. It was so fierce, I fought to remain lucid. But try as I might, my knees began to buckle at the sheer agony. I was pretty damn sure that the Tau had officially created a fissure into my rib cage.

With the pain came the stark realization of my plight. If I could destroy the Altar of Summoning, I could stop the Shroud from the sacrifice and the Tenth Plague. But at the moment, I could barely remain standing. The sigils on the altar pulsated with fiery fury, as if they were taunting me to rise and do what no one else could do. Staring at that massive, dense block of otherworldly material, I couldn't help but feel beaten.

I fought to center myself and remain conscious, and cast my gaze around the chamber in search of the woman. But I couldn't focus. I clawed at my chest. My vision grew cloudy.

Voices. Someone called my name. I was fading into shock. I fought to stand and then collapsed.

Lying on my side, I managed to glimpse the death angel. Its lower torso was now standing, wobbling like a hewn tree trunk. Strands of fog bled from its shorn abdomen. To my horror, I saw the angel's upper body clawing its way along the ground to its legs. The angel took hold of its legs and began pulling its body up onto its lower torso.

It was trying to reassemble itself.

Aw, hell no.

I might have laughed at the absurdity of it. However, shadows hovered over me. They were accompanied by shouts and a hurried shuffle of feet. The cavern was filled with sound. Someone was crying. Hands grappled at me, but not for harm.

When they carried me out of the subway, the night sky wheeled overhead. I felt like such a failure. If these people were banking on me to unite the Imperia, they were sorely mistaken. If they were hoping I could save the world, they were flat-out delusional. Fresh air filled my lungs. But with every breath came pain. I glimpsed the crescent moon overhead, a thin silver bowl lying on its back. Above it shone three stars. Regulus. Tomorrow night, this cosmological phenomenon would reach its culmination and initiate an alignment of forces that would usher in the Archangel of Death and the Tenth Plague. A wave of heat tore through my chest again. And with it came anger. Because I now knew that there was not a blessed thing any of us could do to stop it.

CHAPTER 17

When I saw her face, I knew it wasn't true. It was that part of the dream when you know it's a dream, but it's just too damned good to want to wake up. The ancients believed that the world consisted of multiple threads. Like a garment woven from many strands, our dreams were the fabric of another reality being woven into our own. They were a layer of consciousness made real by our own experiences and stitched into life. Yet even with the knowledge that the figure leaning over me was not Ellie, but a residual memory, simply seeing her face again brought solace to the anguish that was tearing at my innards.

Hey, she said.

Hey.

Her long blonde hair shimmered, framing her eyes like the picture she was. She smiled. It was a genuine smile. Hers always were.

You're not really here, I thought. *Are you?*

She pursed her lips, humored by my inquiry. *It depends on what you mean, Ray. I'm always here now.*

Well, yeah. But, I mean, really *here. Like, in the flesh.*

Is that what it means to be really *here? To be 'in the flesh'?* She brushed her hand through the air. Her hair twirled up on that side of her face. *You just can't stop over-thinking everything, can you?*

Sorry. I thought I was making headway on that.

She laughed. Then her gaze turned serious. She knew what was coming.

Ellie, you didn't tell me how hard this would be. I gazed at her. *You didn't tell me how much it would cost.*

You would have chosen this way even if I had told you. See, I know that about you, Ray. But it'll be worth it in the end. Trust me on that, okay?

I stared at her. I *did* trust her. That was the weird thing about it. Even if I couldn't reach out and touch her. Even if the smell of her skin wouldn't linger. Even if things got really bad. Even if my chest caved in and my body fell apart. I supposed some things were just bigger, and more real, than the world of flesh and bone and bad angels. Ellie was a part of that world now. And, strangely enough, I was beginning to crave that world even more.

Pain lanced through my chest, and I curled in upon myself. Her face seemed to fade in and out, replaced by this excruciating fire.

Don't go, I pleaded. *I mean, not yet.*

A whirl of shadows. I felt hands on me. But they weren't Ellie's. Even though it was her eyes that I saw swell to life over me.

You can do this, Ray. I believe in you.

Ellie. Don't go.

You can do this.

Will I—? I clawed my chest and groaned. *I want to see you again.*

Soon enough, Ray. Soon enough.

She extended her hand to me. I reached for it and fire exploded in my side. I cried out and Ellie's voice disappeared amidst the sound of other voices. One in particular.

A hand made of flesh and blood took mine.

Kanya looked down upon me. She gripped my hand in hers. I could feel her heart thudding in her grasp, reverberating in mine. I'd be lying if I said it didn't feel a bit like cheating. It was impossible that I'd ever get as close to anyone as I had to Ellie. And yet here I was staring into the eyes of someone who still largely remained a mystery but who, for whatever reason, had found kinship with me.

Others were looking down at me. Their faces became clear. They were huddled around, staring, like I was some kind of lab specimen.

"Don't touch it."

"Why not?"

"Because—" It was Rapha's deep voice. "Because we don't know what it is yet."

I let go of Kanya's hand, drew a deep breath, and forced myself into a sitting position. They all stumbled back, gasping and muttering warnings.

"Brother Moon!"

I'd been spread out on the table in Rapha's kitchen. My shirt was off. A lamp stood nearby with its shade removed. Its bare bulb cast a harsh glare around the room. My Hawaiian shirt was draped over a chair in the kitchen. The rest of the Imperia surrounded me. I stared forward, trying to make everything register.

"The altar," I mumbled. "Did you…? What happened?"

Rapha shook his head. "We needed to get you out. The angel…I've never seen anything like it. It fled when we arrived. But—"

He was distracted, worried about something other than the stone altar and the death angel that had been split in two. His gaze turned toward my chest.

Quinn's head tilted my way. I didn't care that the telepath was probing my waking mind. Let him see the memory of Etherea. Let him see the death angel. Let him feel my despair.

Celeste approached. Slight tendrils of blue energy twined from Her fingertips. Healing energy. She'd let her hair down, and the long red waves brushed my skin as she drew near. She waved her hand slowly over my chest. But it found no reception in my body. The pain continued. Kanya stepped to the fore.

"Reagan," she said, glancing at my chest. "Be careful."

"What is it?" I said. "What happened to me?"

I reached for my chest and Kanya grabbed my hand. She engaged my eyes and said solemnly, "Be careful."

"All right," I said, slightly annoyed.

My flesh was hot. I probed the scar with my fingertips. It seemed larger and had inched its way into my abdomen and up my neck. At this rate, I would eventually be swallowed by the Tau scar. Then my fingers reached my sternum.

And my fingers found a cavity.

The blister had opened up and given way to a pocket. It was cold inside. Burning cold. They all watched with wide eyes as I inserted two fingers into my chest, one, maybe two inches. I did not touch bone or bodily organs. It was empty space. A crevice had indeed opened inside my body. *Good Lord!* I shouted and plucked my fingers out of the odd cavity inside me. I held them aloft to make sure they hadn't been burned off.

I slipped off the table and stood upright. When I did this, Saucy went running for cover into the warehouse. Then she poked her nose around the corner, trying to make sense of what was happening to me.

I swayed forward.

"Brother Moon—"

"Careful," said Kanya. "We don't—"

I stumbled out of the kitchen and into the warehouse.

It was night outside. I could feel cold air drifting in through the perimeter of the building. The familiar smell of solder and gas greeted me. I went to the large ornate mirror propped near the CO2 tanks. The rest of the group followed, and together we stood studying the strange condition that was now Reagan Moon.

I stared into the mirror and gasped.

Rather than an empty pocket in the center of my chest, I stared into a dark, swirling chaos. Perhaps the size of a tennis ball. The edges of my flesh had been peeled back revealing a virtual peephole into…I couldn't say. But it wasn't my body. The scar of the Tau had expanded and opened, not into flesh and blood, but into something dark and astral and completely otherworldly. The surrounding flesh had become a livid bruise webbed with tiny veins, and the flesh surrounding the former

187

blister was dry and brittle, like snakeskin being shed by a reptile.

"My God…" I looked at my fingertips, then at the hole in my chest, and back at the group. "What's happening to me?"

They just stared. Even Quinn kept his remarks to himself.

Rapha said, "You should sit back down, Brother Moon. We have a lot to discuss."

"It's like…" I swallowed. "Like some sort of an opening. Into space."

"A portal, perhaps."

"A portal." I shook my head. "Inside me? How in the hell can that be? How is that—"

I stumbled back and fumbled about for something to steady myself. The others instinctively jumped back in fear that I might touch them. All except Kanya, who rushed to my side and steadied me.

"Reagan," she said. "C'mon. You need to sit down."

She attempted to guide me back into the kitchen, but I remained staring at my reflection in the mirror.

My body was changing. I'd become some type of weird chrysalis, trapped between humanity and something else. Something new. Something dangerous. Quinn was right—I was weaponized.

"The lady," I said. "The nurse. What happened to her?"

"She's safe," Rapha said. "But she probably remembers little about you or about what happened to her. She was under a Fate spell. She believed she was destined to become the sacrifice. Brother Moon, you broke that spell."

It was supposed to encourage me, I guess. But at the moment nothing could make me feel any less lost.

"We took her to the hospital," Rapha continued. "Quinn made sure nobody remembers us. She wasn't injured. Dehydrated. Hungry. But you saved her. You saved her, Brother Moon."

"Yeah," I said. "And you guys...who was out there, in the tunnel?"

"Some NeoKor slime," Quinn said. "Burying God knows what. I wouldn't be surprised if the entire outfit is a front for Scaper wanks. I managed a neural Douse. But I'm pretty sure they were on to us."

Saucy barked and tore off around the work bench. In a moment, she returned with Blondie, Felix Klammer's personal bodyguard.

The Swede was carrying several recyclable grocery bags stuffed with items. He stopped and looked at me. Then he nodded and said unemotionally, "Good. He is waiting for you." And with that, he turned and walked into the kitchen.

"Great to see you too," I said.

"He's right." Rapha started toward the kitchen after the bodyguard, beckoning us to follow. "He's been waiting."

I didn't need to ask who it was. Even worse, with Klammer's arrival, I knew things were about to get infinitesimally more complicated. The others returned to the kitchen. All but Kanya.

"You okay?" Kanya let go of me, stepped back, and looked squarely into my eyes. "And don't say that nothing can be worse than surviving a lightning strike."

That made me smile. "I'm okay."

Kanya nodded. She glanced at my chest one final time before turning and following the others. Saucy remained watching me, smiling.

"Why me?" I asked the dog. "I wasn't *that* bad."

Even in my weird new world, dogs still couldn't talk. However, the way things were going, somewhere down the line, that could possibly change.

When I entered the kitchen, the group stood surrounding Felix Klammer. Had he been there the whole time? He was sitting in a wheelchair. Up to that point, I realized I'd never seen the man actually standing before. The group almost seemed to reverence him. Okay, perhaps reverence is too strong a word. Let's just say he was clearly recognized as something other than your run-of-the-mill Imperia.

I felt somewhat self-conscious walking around without my shirt. Especially now that a black hole had hatched in my chest. Ugh. I instinctively reached up to touch it, but pulled my hand back. What happened if it kept growing? What was the use of having supernatural gifts if I would eventually get swallowed up by using them? I removed the Hawaiian shirt from the chair and put it on.

Blondie was putting away milk, eggs, and a few groceries in Rapha's fridge. Either they were about to request an order of my famous Mexican omelet, or they were planning on staying for a while. The Swedish bodyguard finished and stepped to his boss's side, folding his hands at his waist. He seemed his usual self—as humorless as a grizzly and as conversational as a sledge hammer. Yet being that he'd saved my life once, I couldn't be too hard on the man. Besides, knowing the type of people I was falling in with, I was guessing there was more to Blondie than just his massive frame and cold demeanor.

The caged contraption was on Klammer's head, as usual. Rapha had called it a hood, and now I knew that it was made of the cold flat material they called Ndocron. In the light, I could see the device clearly. It appeared crudely welded, yet solid. It looked like an elaborate birdcage with odd gears and appendages. Cubes and oblique bolts had been welded in various spots, and its back corners were latched. A velvet cloth draped the front of this hood. Could this device really be made of a substance from a parallel dimension? How was that even possible? If so, this could realistically change the entire course of human history. Then I remembered Rapha's words about it being a protective device, a way to restrain or harness anti-matter and the spread of multi-verses. Thus, I found myself staring at this man in a new way, studying him as if my eyes alone could register some inexplicable discernment into the nature of my recruitment.

I resumed buttoning up my shirt as Klammer navigated his wheelchair so as to face me. "Let me see it, Mr. Moon. The scar." He was looking at my chest.

"More show and tell?" I sighed deeply and unbuttoned the shirt. "You sent me straight into trouble. You know that, right?"

He inched forward in his wheelchair and nodded, a clumsy movement that made that helmet of his look like something out of a B-grade horror flick. "There's no escaping it now. Every path you choose will lead to trouble."

"Gee, that's encouraging."

He was staring at my chest. "It's the path you chose when you took on the Tau."

"Yeah? Well it would have been nice to at least receive a warning clause."

"Life itself has no such clause."

"So can I opt out?"

Klammer chuckled. He wheeled himself back a few feet. "Take heart. You have done well, Mr. Moon. Even the Shroud is, shall we say, agitated."

"I haven't even met him. However, his henchwoman, Etherea—she's quite charming. I mean, if she isn't the anti-Christ, then she'd make a perfect sidekick for him. She was down there, you know. At the subway project. She was protecting that altar, whatever the hell it is. Her and her pet death angel. They had a human sacrifice, Klammer. *A human sacrifice.*"

I shook my head. The despair was churning in my gut again. "Look, I don't know what you guys have planned. But there's no way we can go this alone. Us?" I motioned to the group and snorted in mock laughter. "Look at us—broken down, needing canes and wheelchairs. And now I'm getting eaten alive by a dimensional portal. Listen, we need to get the police involved, or something. Hell, the army might even be better. If this thing really goes down, we're all screwed. And by the looks of it, we're in no position to stop it."

Klammer peered up at me. His wheezing was evident. In fact, it almost seemed to have increased since the last time I'd seen him. The cloth masking the front of the cage moved slowly with puffs of breath.

"Things are changing," Klammer said. "The drug has empowered the Neuros. They now have the ability to summon Diadetic beings, those of the Nether. The barriers between worlds have been rent. With the help of the Black Council, altering history itself is now not outside their powers."

I peered at him. "The map."

"One of many."

"Then it's real."

"It always has been. The future is never static, Mr. Moon. Our only hope is that you, the Seventh Guardian, can prevent the Summu Nura from collapsing the barriers between Arcadium and Diades, and merging our known dimensions."

If I wasn't already beyond dumbfounded, I might have kicked the dog or broken something. "I think I'm going to throw up."

"It's growing," Klammer said, motioning to the scar.

"You noticed. And every time I—I teleport or use the power, it grows a little more."

They were all staring at me. I lightly touched the skin surrounding the growing lesion. Then I shook my head. "Okay? You all had enough?" I buttoned the shirt up all the way.

I looked at them, one by one, and then my gaze drifted to Klammer.

"You guys are supposed to be helping me." I couldn't contain the slight tremor in my voice. "Rapha? That's what you said. So then what the hell is it? What's happening to me?"

Klammer sat wheezing. His hood gently nodded. Finally he said, "It's the same thing that's happening to me."

I stared at him.

With that, Klammer motioned to Blondie, who reached behind the hood and unlatched it. It separated at the seam, and the device tilted on his shoulders. Fearing that the man had severe deformities of some sort, I instinctively took several steps back. But what I saw shocked me even more than any severe deformity could.

Blondie removed the caged hood, revealing that Felix Klammer did not have a head.

CHAPTER 18

Obviously, the other earth guardians had witnessed this before. Unlike me, they did not gasp or blink really hard to make sure their eyes were seeing correctly. I looked at them, almost hoping for confirmation of what I was witnessing. Kanya was the only other one who stood gaping. The others looked on, eyes fixed mainly on me and how I would respond to this new reality. I turned back to the headless Felix Klammer.

Blondie had lowered the hood to his side, gripping it under his arm like a running back might hold a football before plowing into enemy defenses. He too watched me, remaining his unemotional self. Klammer—or at least his body—sat still, though not entirely unmoving. He was still breathing, for I could hear the rattling in his chest. Yet how could this be happening without connection to his brain? Or was his head actually still connected, just invisible?

I stepped closer, trying to discern exactly what I was seeing.

Something luminescent was fluttering in the area where his head should be. Slight metallic-like particles glinted in the light, circling round in a slow ebb and flow. It almost appeared to be a whirlpool or vortex made of faint particles, spinning and twining through the air in ghostly fashion. I stepped even closer, peering at the empty space. Then I angled myself from one side to the other to ensure that this was not some trick of light. It wasn't. At this point, my knees were nearly touching his. I bent forward, staring down into the neck and the hole that was there for I could see no spinal column, esophagus, blood, or other organs. Only a black, roiling tunnel. Its edges were a thin veil of flaky, peeling skin. Just like the skin around the Tau vortex. It was like a dimensional hole was boring into

Felix Klammer's body and slowly chewing away at the fabric of his being.

"Be careful, Brother Moon!"

Rapha's voice startled me. Only then did I realize that I was reaching toward the gauzy space where Felix Klammer's head should be. I stopped short, glanced at Rapha, and then lowered my hand. And here I thought I'd seen it all. Death angels, ghosts, spatial jumping, and gravity bubbles. This was just another anomaly to add to my strange new world.

I swallowed hard, unable to find a reasonable question to pose or a place to start asking it.

"He can't speak," Rapha explained. "A device is located inside the hood which detects the words he is thinking. Obviously, he doesn't have vocal chords. At least, not in this plane. The hood picks up the frequencies and translates them through a synthesizer developed by Quinn."

"There're electrode grids inside the hood," Quinn said. "The same kinds developed by bio-engineers and used on paralyzed patients. They decode the brain patterns—which are not purely biological—and translate them into vocalized speech. It's pretty basic stuff."

"So..." I said, "where is his head?"

"In Arcadium!" Rapha exclaimed. "But it's just his head. His body exists here. There, he is a head without a body. In this dimension, he's just the opposite."

"So he actually exists in two places at once?"

"In some sense, yes." Rapha motioned to Klammer's body. "The hood simultaneously keeps his brain and its functions tethered to his body in this dimension, sending signals to the body regarding movement and physical sensations. It also prevents further spread of the dimensional wound. If the spread is not contained, he will cease having contact with this world completely. Become a particle ghost. Felix Klammer will exist only in that parallel world, his life here—his *physical* life—will be no longer."

I continued to stare. But no amount of concentration could bring any logic into this situation. I glanced from Klammer down to my chest. If the same thing was happening inside me, then I would slowly be swallowed into a similar dimension.

This was not the payoff for being a good citizen that I had envisioned.

Blondie finally lifted the hood and returned it to Klammer's body. He reattached the device and, as he did, Klammer's body became more relaxed and animated.

"Now you see, Mr. Moon." His voice crackled to life. "Like me, your wound will keep growing, eating up the matter around it. It is our own personal cross of sorts."

"So let me get this straight." I peered at him. "I have incredible powers—"

"*We*," Quinn said.

"Okay. *We* have these incredible powers, and every time we use them they—what?—they hurt us? They destroy our bodies?"

"It's infinitely more complicated than that," Klammer said. "But, in essence—yes. Which means your chest, like my head, is transitioning. Great power is never without a cost, Mr. Moon."

I looked around the group. "So this is true? For all of you?"

"Sure is, hon." Orphana bent down. She gripped her prosthetic leg, wrenched it free, and removed it. She balanced on her cane and her good leg as she held the prosthetic up.

"So every time I cluster," Orphana said, "I lose a little bit more of myself. Molecular structure evaporates or something. Particles of mass dissipate. Quinn's been working on some cybernetic prosthetics for me. Because eventually I'll lose the other leg. After that? It's anyone's guess."

I shook my head, incredulous.

"That's just the way it goes." Orphana reattached her leg. "We didn't make the rules. Tryin' to live by them? Well, that's another story."

"So is that…?" I faced the rest of the Imperia. "That's true for everyone?"

"'Fraid so," Quinn said.

He removed his glasses. But he didn't lift them from his nose; he detached them from his face. Quinn pressed something on the side, and a click sounded as the glasses snapped from a series of plates that were embedded in his face.

Instead of eyes, a pale smooth scar wove across his empty sockets. Domino-sized plates of dull metallic material stitched his eye sockets and stretched across the bridge of his nose in a thin, uneven, band. A port or a plug was located dead center where the glasses were inserted.

"I started losing my sight in my late teens," Quinn said. "Early twenties, maybe. Course, that's when my brain started taking over. I heard voices in my head, became hyper-aware of people's emotions, their reactions. And physical sensations were off the charts. Walking into a room of people was like diving into an ocean of pain and hurt and regret and…" He shook his head. "I felt *everything*. Had to stop going out in public. Hey, who needs eyes in their head when their whole body is one big fat sensory lens? Then again, it seriously ruined my dating life. Hard to find a girlfriend looking like a sideshow freak. You know what I mean?"

He raised the glasses and a snap sounded as he plugged them back into his face.

"They're still in development," he said. "The glasses are cybernetic implants. Technically. I'm hoping to incorporate some more sensors and interface the lenses with my neural abilities. Which means I might eventually be able to develop missile capability using my thoughts."

He twirled his mustache and smiled.

"That was a joke," he said. "Sort of."

I reluctantly turned to Celeste.

She nodded. "Yep. Me too. But I'm different. My past disintegrates. At least, my memory of it does. I can remember details, things like *your* actions. *Mine*, however, are…fading." Celeste smiled, almost sheepishly. "I've tried to stitch it together with pictures, family photos and stuff. I've got a bookshelf full of scrapbooks and photo albums that I have to keep looking through. To remind myself. But the darkness just keeps swallowing more and more. I learn something new every day, and forget five other things in the process. I can't remember birthdays, graduations. You know, milestones that everybody remembers. I'm still not sure if I have any siblings. Or if I was married once. There's some evidence I might have been. I just can't remember where I encountered that evidence and what it was. Or who *he* was."

She grew quiet and stared off into space.

"Even when I joined the team," Celeste continued, "how I came on board—it's growing more and more hazy. It's kinda like Alzheimer's. Eventually, I'll end up with this archive of knowledge but be unable to remember what to do with it or how it relates to the present. When the memory of my past catches up to my immediate present, no one knows. I'll just disappear inside myself and never come back, I guess."

She smiled, but now I could see it clearly—a deep melancholy, a darkness, piercing her heart.

"My God," I said. "And you're all like this?"

Quinn held up his hand. "You mean, *'We're* all like this,' don't you?"

I was having difficulty breathing.

"So is it punishment?" I said. "Are we cursed or something? Cursed with special powers. This is insane. What have I gotten myself into?"

Rapha chuckled. "No, Brother Moon. It's not punishment. A thorn in the flesh, perhaps. But great callings are never without cost."

I turned to Rapha. "And you—" I approached him, looking more closely at his body. He smiled, inviting my inspection. "After you created that gravity bubble, you grew. Didn't you? You expanded or something."

"Yes," he said. "The price of my gift is perpetual growth."

I stared at him. "And there's no way to stop it?"

"Felix has some ideas. But, no, I've discovered no way to stop it. Not yet. Unless I stopped using my alchemical skills. Which I have vowed to never do."

"That's incredible. So, I mean, how big can you get?"

His gaze grew solemn, as if he'd pondered the question many times. Slowly, a smile blossomed on his face, and he slapped his hands on his belly. "Who's to say, Brother Moon?"

Then he peered at me. "Quixote said, 'The wounds received in battle bestow honor, they do not take it away.' Likewise, our wounds are our honor."

"Heh. Sounds more like they're our undoing."

Klammer repositioned his wheelchair so as to face the group. "Like me, Mr. Moon, the downside to your gift, if it *is* a downside, appears to involve dimensional transit or commutation of some sort. It is no cause for despair. Discomfort, perhaps. However, we are never fully of this world to begin with. Ellie said as much, no?"

"She probably did," I said. "But you've stopped it. You've kept the wound from spreading. The hood."

"Ndocron is an amazing material. There is nothing like it on earth. On *this* earth. In this dimension, it is nearly indestructible. Among other properties, Ndocron can contain or bind immaterial objects."

"You mean like—"

"Phantoms. Succubae. Cytomorphs. Only one other material exists on earth which is similar. You encountered it this evening."

"What?"

"Nefarium," Rapha said. "The Table of Summoning is forged of Nefarium."

"Explain."

Rapha pointed towards Klammer's hood. "It's another form of Ndocron. Only it comes from an opposite dimension, parallel to our own yet inverse to Arcadium."

"Hold on a second."

"Think of it as three pieces of paper stacked on top of each other—earth's dimension is sandwiched between Arcadium and Diades. Diades is earth's lower dimension. Nefarium is mined there."

"Two opposite dimensions," I pondered aloud. "Exporting matter into our own?"

"Crazy," Quinn said. "Isn't it?"

Rapha continued, "Ndocron acts as a boundary against certain dimensional intersections or intrusions. It can be used to block apertures, electromagnetic pulses, dimensional wormholes. Things of that nature. Nefarium has similar properties, but the two materials cannot exist in each other's plane. In this, the laws are different."

"Wait," I said. "So you're saying that the altar down there can't be destroyed?

"Not with anything yet at our disposal."

I just stared.

"What the hell is this?" I threw my hands up in frustration. "I get dragged into this thing, I'm supposed to save the world, and it turns out we're on a quest with absolutely no chance to even finish it?"

"Yep." Quinn nodded. "This's how we roll."

"Pfft!" I brushed my hand through the air dismissively. "You're nuts. All of you."

I turned and tromped to the doorway, causing Saucy to leap out of my way.

"Mr. Moon," Klammer said firmly.

I stopped but did not immediately turn to face him.

"There is one other possibility," Klammer said.

I turned and folded my arms.

He said, "The guardian who traverses all worlds, both Arcadium and Diades, is said to possess such powers. In its

200

raw, original state, Nefarium is impervious to destruction. Only the one who traverses that dimension can undo it in this dimension."

"So where the hell do we find a multi-dimensional interloper?"

"The wound inside you." Klammer wheeled himself to me. "The Seventh Guardian is said to possess such powers."

I looked at him, and then my head drooped in exhaustion.

I needed some fresh air. I needed a shower. Hell, I needed to get out of that shirt! But maybe more than anything, I needed to get away from these people.

"We must return, Brother Moon." Rapha thumped his chest with his fist. "This is our calling. This is our honor."

I issued a deep, tired sigh. "There's got to be another way."

"In the Bible," Kanya said, "they prevented the death angel from killing their firstborn by sacrificing a lamb and sprinkling the blood on their doorposts."

Quinn snorted. "Let's try to manage that. All we need to do is get, what, three or four million lambs passed out to every household by tomorrow night with clear instructions on how to correctly slaughter them? Yeah. That'll work."

Celeste said, "Then we have to stop her. Etherea. We have to find her or go down there and physically prevent her from performing that ritual."

"Yeah," Quinn sniped. "That worked great the first time."

"And the angel?" Orphana added. "Or angels? No tellin' what kind of things she's got up her sleeve. Especially if the Black Council's expecting us. They'll be ready this time."

It was approaching midnight. I was tired. I needed some space to process everything. Part of me wanted to run to the Chaparral and begin a week-long bender. The other part just wanted to rewind my life to when everything was normal. Or, at least, status quo.

I shook my head and said dully, "Just tell me where we go from here."

Klammer said flatly, "Our assignment is unchanged. We must destroy the altar and stop the Shroud from summoning Azrael."

I nodded.

"I need to—" I glanced at Kanya. "I need to think. And I need a shower." I motioned to Kanya. "Do you want a ride?"

She raised her eyebrows and looked at Rapha as Rapha looked at Klammer.

"He can't go," Rapha said.

"The future is fluid, Rapha." Klammer appeared unflustered. "And there are others apart from Mr. Moon with a stake in this battle. They will fight. With or without him."

I nodded and walked into the warehouse.

"Brother Moon!" Rapha followed behind. "You can't leave us now. Please. I've sought you out. To help you. To train you. You've been *chosen* for this reason."

I turned to face him.

"Look," I said. "Don't take it personal. I just need some space."

Saucy brushed up against my leg, and I reached down to pet her.

I looked up at the huge Islander and reached out and patted his arm. "Okay?"

"As you wish, Brother Moon."

Kanya stood at the kitchen door, watching.

"Do you want a ride?" It probably sounded ruder than I meant it to be.

She nodded and joined me.

As we left, Rapha said from behind us, "Tomorrow night, Brother Moon. We need you."

"I know," I mumbled. "Trust me, I know."

When we stepped into the yard, Regulus and the crescent moon were long gone, waiting to rise once more and awaken Azrael. I opened the gate and started to get into the Cammy, when Kanya said, "Look."

She was pointing at my chest. Underneath the shirt, I was glowing.

CHAPTER 19

I love the smell of diesel in the morning. It's a sign that the world is waking up. Sure, it wasn't quite morning. But by midnight, L.A.'s nightwalkers were beginning to stir, signaling the end, or the beginning, of another day. The transients wandered out of the alleys and freeway overpasses in search of food or a fix. Prostitutes flaunted their wares beside cheap motels. Truckers and delivery drivers were prepping their loads and preparing to make their rounds under the cloak of night. Of course, since Los Angeles metro had abandoned diesel fuel and switched to natural gas years ago, it left street sweepers and garbage trucks to carry the torch. They did so admirably.

Jimmy had left me a message. Apparently, they'd found something at the ranch that he wanted to show me. He seemed concerned. I could only imagine. Hearing his voice reminded me of the premonition and the fear that my detective friend was facing an enemy bigger than he'd ever battled. However, I knew that before this was over, I would need him. Paying him a visit might be the smart thing to do. Yet how could I ever hope to secure help from the LAPD without divulging the truth about what potentially awaited this city? Even Jimmy would have a hard time believing this crazy story.

I hated relying on other people. Yet I was needing a lot of people these days. It's hard for a survivor like myself to rely on others. The less you have to trust others, the greater chance of not getting let down. That was fundamental to my worldview and rather emblematic of my skewed view of humanity. Somehow, that deeply embedded philosophy of life was being quashed under the reality of my situation.

I drove to Kanya's place, but neither of us spoke. She knew the stakes. She'd seen them tearing a hole into my flesh. Besides, we were both exhausted. The last few days had been a blur. I needed to sleep. Maybe I needed a jog first. But the way my chest felt, I wondered if I'd ever be able to jog again. Is this what a suicide bomber felt like being strapped with ten pounds of explosives? The scar in my chest might as well have been an IED. I fought the temptation to touch it, to look at it. It was glowing all right. Faintly. Underneath my shirt. On occasion, an odd sense of motion would occur, as if tadpoles had hatched under my skin and were stretching their legs. Sometimes that was followed by a sense of motion, as if my gut were about to drop and I would inexplicably transmutate to a nearby location.

I watched my rear view mirror to make sure we weren't being tailed. Apparently, looking over my shoulder was going to have to become a way of life. People knew about me now. They'd read about me. Seen my picture in the paper. Now they were watching me. And even worse than all that, they had hugely unrealistic expectations about what I could accomplish.

Kanya was slightly resentful that I was taking her back to the Asylum. I softened it with the suggestion that she could help by doing some quick research on death angels and the Shroud. Surely, Matisse had archived something that could help us. It was a good move. She suggested that Mace might also be of some help, which I reluctantly conceded. Getting that cowboy involved seemed a rather risky proposition.

Either way, Kanya was adamant about staying involved. Her eyes sparkled when discussing possible danger. She seemed oblivious to the risk. After the death of her father, she'd become more resolute and steely than ever. No, it wasn't a death wish, some emotional bankruptcy tempting her to put herself out of her misery. Rather, Kanya seemed resolved about her own mortality and held it loosely.

Did Cricket share this conviction? Was Cricket really the creation of a psychotic break? Could forgiving her mother possibly allow Kanya to control her toxic alter ego?

I glanced sideways at Kanya. Being that all the cards were now on the table—and things couldn't get a whole lot worse than they already were—I hazarded a question.

"So what should I tell your mother?"

Kanya stiffened. Just the mention caused her emotions to bristle. Then she looked at me. "Why would you bring her up, Reagan? Why now?"

"Why not now? The way things are going, you might not get another chance."

Without responding, she returned to staring out the window.

"Look," I said. "I'm not trying to complicate things, Kanya. Really. I'm not trying to pry. You know that. Your mother knows something, remember? She's the one who called Jimmy, she knew I was in trouble. She knew about the Imperia, and Klammer. Besides, there's a chance none of us are coming back from this little adventure. Wouldn't you want to make amends before that happens?" I glanced at her. "Listen, I know where she lives. At least, the house she took me to. She might be able to help us."

Still she didn't respond. We sat in silence for a few minutes. I didn't want to push too much. But she knew I wouldn't forget the subject.

"I'm afraid of seeing her," Kanya finally admitted. "Not just because of what she did to me. But because of *me*. Matisse saved me, Reagan. He accepted me as I was. Audra never could. I was the outcast. That's why she gave me up."

"That's not what she said. She believed you were strong—strong enough to resist them. To fight back. It was the only way she thought she could save the others."

"Well, I survived. No thanks to her."

"I think her intentions are good. She's not trying to hurt you again. If she was, I'm pretty sure she would have done that by now. Look, she came to *me*, Kanya. That should count for something. She's initiated this. She's trying to help you. To help *us*."

Kanya appeared agitated and rubbed her hands atop her thighs, which caused me to wonder if the discussion had triggered some chemical reaction in her. I began to ponder a way of escape if she was going to flip. Remembering the totem in my front pocket brought only minimal consolation.

Finally, she released a heavy sigh.

"Audra has two sisters," Kanya explained. "Diedra and Sidra."

"Sidra. You mean the one-eyed chick that worked for Volden? The one you—?"

"Killed? Yeah."

"Then she was your—?"

"Aunt. Yeah. I barely knew her. She went bad way before I showed up. They were known as the Hydra sisters. All three of them. Audra doesn't like to talk about it. But they got talents of their own. The hydras can regenerate limbs—arms, feet, whatever. It makes them hard to kill and kinda ruthless. Only their head can't regenerate. To kill a hydra, the head must be severed. Or the heart pierced."

"Hold on a second. You're talking, like, the Greek mythology hydra, right?"

"Yes."

I shook my head. "And here I thought my family was screwed up."

"Supposedly, it traces back for centuries. A great, great someone-or-other. The family legend was that someone in our lineage had slain a hydra. They believed that drinking its blood would give them similar powers. It did, except in reverse. Cut off a hydra's head, they grow it back. Cut off a Hydra sister's arm or leg, they grow it back. Lop their head off, and they're history. Either that, or impale them. The Summu Nura knew about the sisters and sought their service. Sidra crossed over when I was just a kid. I assumed Audra followed." She looked at me. "But I could be wrong."

"Then that means that you…"

"I dunno. I've never lost a limb to find out. I'm just glad Matisse rescued me when he did." Kanya stared into space and then began unraveling her tale. "Mace was in Laos. After I escaped from the Summu Nura, it was one long game of hide and seek. The Noi—that was a local tribe, primitives almost—they were just tools. The Summu Nura had possessed them. They wanted to turn me into their own puppet. A weapon. Just like they did with Sidra. I escaped and hid in the forest. Cricket helped me stay alive."

She stared out the window, watching the darkened storefronts and sidewalks go by.

At the risk of jeopardizing a forthcoming confession, I asked, "And that's how Matisse found you?"

She nodded. "I'd been wandering the coast for about a year. Surviving. Sometimes I would flip, become a man or an old woman, anything to escape. I'd wake up somewhere unsure of what had happened, or what I was running from. I was just a kid. But I knew I had to stand against the darkness. There was so much of it. And I knew I had the power. Seeing others like myself, young girls, innocents, being abused by evil men…"

Her fists were clenched. A slight ripple passed through her forearm, and she drew that arm into herself and began massaging it. "So I went on the offensive," she said. "I just started engaging them. Prostitution rings. Drug houses. Occultists in league with the Summu Nura. I did things, Reagan. Bad things."

She fell silent, but I didn't dare probe.

"That's how I bumped into Mace," she continued. "He and Matisse were looking for some type of divining rod being used to locate burial mounds in the delta. A bunch of grave robbers had acquired it and were basically wiping out whole villages just to lay waste to their ancestral treasures. I'd been knocking off those scum as best I could, until I got captured. Luckily, Mace and his men rescued me and took the rod.

"But I was injured during the rescue. Matisse took me in and cared for me. They didn't seem to care that I was different. They genuinely wanted to help. That's the way my father was—always seeing past my differences."

It was the first significant confession about her past that Kanya had ever made to me.

"So what happened to your mother?" I asked.

"I don't know. And I don't care. She knew enough to track you down. Which means she finally got out of there. But if the Summu Nura got a hold of her, if she went over like her sisters, it can't be good."

I shook my head. "But she rescued me. Besides, if the Black Council wants me so bad, they would have taken me then."

"Unless they wanted you to lead her to me."

I thought about that for a second, but it didn't wash. "No way. If the Summu Nura were involved with her, I would've read it. I think she genuinely wants to help."

It was this possibility that seemed to frustrate Kanya more than anything. She sat massaging her forearm, mulling that possibility, and then disengaged. It was as far as we needed to go and, hopefully, the admission had released a little of the ferocity that motivated Cricket.

When we reached the Asylum, I checked my rear view mirror again before turning into the alley and parking the Cammy in the back by the loading dock. I turned the car off, and it rumbled into silence. We sat together for a minute. I felt like she wanted to say something else and gave her that minute. Whatever it was, it passed. Which left me wondering if another eruption was inevitable.

We got out, and Kanya reminded me that I was now the proud owner of the only other key to the Asylum. This was not something I relished. Perhaps it was inevitable with an operation this size and the number of enemies we were making along the way that our comings and goings could be attracting lots of attention. The warehouse had been breached once, which had led to Matisse's death. As a result, Mace had set up a few more protective measures, including additional cameras. Still, it was only a matter of time before we were tracked here. Maybe even raided again. And when that happened, I could not imagine the hell that would break loose. And I mean literal hell.

We descended into the Asylum. The first thing we heard when the door clanged open was gunfire. Perhaps bazooka fire would be a better way to describe it. Kanya and I stopped in our tracks. Somewhere deep inside the Asylum sharp punches sounded, followed by heavy thuds.

Sssht. Pmphh!

What the hell?

As I was about to run for cover, Kanya straightened and said, "It's just Mace."

"Huh? What's he doing?"

"Probably messing with his collection."

"He collects rocket launchers, or what?"

"Pretty much. C'mon," she said. "I'll show you."

She led the way through the vast warehouse towards the northeastern-most bay.

"If you're gonna be helping take care of this place," she said, "then you need to know as much as possible."

"Knowing as much as possible will probably take years."

It was not an exaggeration.

We passed statuary, shrunken head collections, and a reverse mirror. The Asylum was like a natural history museum on steroids. Perhaps an aircraft hangar-sized cabinet of curiosities was a better way to put it. Matisse had collected a wealth of the most exotic, dangerous, evil items from around the world. His firm belief, the one that ultimately drove him to his death, was that by containing all these evil memorabilia he could restrict the flow of evil in the world. I was loathe to agree with that premise. If our current situation was any evidence, evil was doing just fine, despite the incredible collection. Deep down inside, however, I wondered how long Kanya could carry the torch for her father.

Soon we reached a corridor of unusual cages. Some made of Plexiglas, others of wire or mesh, and of varying heights, some rising upwards of twelve or fifteen feet.

Sssht. Pmphh!

I stopped in my tracks. The storage racks surrounding us vibrated at the sound. We were nearing its source. We turned the corner into a jumbled group of taxidermy creatures. However, these were not your typical moose or water buffalo on display. I stopped and stared at one in particular. It appeared to be a wolf in many ways, except its torso stretched unusually long, almost seeming serpentine in nature. The creature's shoulders were thick, its upper body almost disproportionate to its frame, and its claws were twice the size of a normal wolf's. Coarse black hair draped the beast. I stepped closer, touched the hide, and examined it for signs of forgery. Had someone stitched together disparate parts of other animals, or was this for real?

"What is it?" I asked.

"An Arctic Hound," she said. "They roam the border ranges between Canada and Alaska, terrorizing those on the outskirts. Legend has it that they are part dragon, a *lycodragon* you could say. Some type of foul offspring that was banished to the wasteland."

I stepped back and stared at this bizarre taxidermy piece.

"He hunts cryptids," Kanya said in response to my fascination. "Mace. At least the ones that are a threat to humanity."

"Cryptids. You're talking Sasquatch. Mothman."

"Chupacabra. Hellhound. Windigo. Yep."

"Really," I said, attempting not to appear utterly incredulous. "A cryptid big game hunter."

"I guess you could say that."

"So he's had some luck?"

"Are you kidding?"

Kanya turned into the aisle and motioned me to follow. In between stacked crates and cages draped with tarps were odd skeletons encased in resin and dried animal corpses. Some were indistinguishable, a bundle of fur, horns, leathery skin, and bleached skulls. Others looked more like carnival props,

211

the fanciful merging of sea creature and mammal. Kanya went to a large draped object seated on the floor and took the corner of the canvas tarp. Dust wafted into the air as she lifted the cover high enough to reveal a stocky birdlike foot rising into fabulously bright feathers. Coiled at its feet was a thick reptilian tail.

I moved forward for a closer inspection. Then I put my hands on my knees and ducked down, attempting to look up under the tarp. "What is it?"

"Mace would be able to go into detail. Supposedly, it was some breed of Quetzalcoatl."

I looked up at her. "As in the Aztecan deity, the flying serpent?"

"Yep. It was terrorizing the inhabitants of a village somewhere in the remote jungles of South America. They'd been sacrificing livestock to the creature to keep it at bay, but it turned out to have a taste for human flesh. They were preparing to begin ritual human sacrifices when Mace and his team arrived."

I straightened and gaped at her. "This is incredible."

She nodded.

"And so all this—" I swept my arm before me, indicating this entire bay "—it's cryptids? Like this?"

She nodded again.

I was beginning to realize how little I actually knew about the Asylum and the treasures it contained.

"Wow," I said. "This would be a great feature in the Crescent."

"Uh, no." She released the canvas and it fell back into place, sending the dust motes fluttering again. "You had a deal with my father. Let's keep it that way."

I sighed heavily. "You're right. We did."

A voice sounded from the end of the aisle. "Did ya see the Devil?"

Mace stepped into view at the end of the bay. He was chomping gum and holding a large bulky rifle over his shoulder.

"Don't tell me you shot him too?" I quipped.

"Ha! I wish." He lowered the rifle. "No, a Jersey Devil. Bagged him on a quick turnaround. It's around here somewhere. If you'd like, I can probably dig it up. A fine specimen, I'd say."

"We don't have time," Kanya said. "We have a situation, Mace. We need your help."

We joined him at the end of the bay. As we approached, a length of gun racks came into view. They were mounted across several walls in an enclosed workstation. Behind this structure stretched a shooting range staggered with paper targets and several mannequins. A fluorescent light hung inside the station and illumined various pieces of firearms and equipment. I approached and began studying the mounted weaponry. Among it were pieces I'd never seen before. Like I said, I'm not big on firearms and have pretty much sworn off using them. That doesn't mean I'm a bleeding pacifist by any means. Guns were as much a part of American culture as was pruning shears and crescent wrenches. But some of these looked like props from the latest Aliens v. Predator incarnation.

Mace saw me studying the various pieces, walked up beside me, and leaned his rifle on the workbench near some large octagonal casings of varying sizes. "You don't strike me as a collector."

"I'm not," I said. "But I'm pretty sure you can't get these at your local sporting goods store."

"You'd be correct. Got yer basics." He pointed out the pieces as he spoke. "Standard-issue Beretta. Bolt-action sniper rifle. Others are in various stages of development. Like this smart rifle—high-tech tracking scope, guided trigger. It allows the operator to hit a target well past two clicks away. My personal favorite is this one." He motioned to a large bazooka-like contraption. "Shoulder-fired heavy anti-matter rifle.

213

Releases a charge that disrupts the molecular bonds of objects or entities. Just depends on where and what it strikes. Also depends on the molecular structure of the object in question. Still in its experimental phase, so it's not a reliable weapon by any stretch. Found that out when I accidentally melted a hole in the hull of a cargo ship. Luckily, everyone was rescued before it sank. Here." He picked up the rifle he had been holding and grabbed one of the large casings. "Been working the kinks outta this."

He motioned for us to follow him out into the shooting range. He attached the canister to the gun's muzzle.

"It's a net gun, of sorts," Mace explained. "CO_2 powered. Used to launch netting. But modified to handle larger nets, like those for T-Rexes. Depends on what yer trackin' and the degree of mesh. And distance. It can be tricky. See that over there?" He pointed to one of the mannequins, standing twenty-five to thirty feet away. He raised the rifle to his waist, aimed it in the general direction of his target, slightly adjusted his angle, and fired.

Sssht. The projectile left the muzzle of the canister and then opened. *Pmphh!* The blob of netting burst into the air, a tight bundle that opened as it went. By the time it reached the mannequin the netting had opened into a virtual parachute and fell upon its target in a tight draped bundle.

"Yes!" Mace pumped his fist. He slapped the muzzle of the piece and brought it to his side. "It can handle a much bigger load. But for now, I'd say she's about ready for live action."

I let my gaze roam the shooting range, the targets, and the workshop.

"So is this stuff legal?" I asked.

"Legal? If it was known to exist, we would be interrogated and it would be confiscated. Klammer keeps the Feds at bay or else we'd be gravy on some mustang's pork chops. If you considered the Asylum part of a covert governmental operation, you would not entirely be incorrect."

"Figures. Now we're working for the government?"

"I did not say that."

"Well, at least some of it might come in handy." I glanced at Kanya.

"You mean that situation at the subway?" Mace asked.

"Yeah," Kanya said. "But, I have to warn you, it involves angels."

"Angels!" Mace shook his head. "You know how I feel about messing with angels."

He returned to the work area, removed the canister from the rifle, and set the net gun down on the table next to the remaining canisters.

Mace turned to face us. "So exactly what are we talking about?"

"Death angels," Kanya explained. "Maelohim. Probably more than one. And..."

Mace peered at her. "Spit it out, Kay."

"Azrael—an archangel."

"Ha!" Mace shook his head. "You have got to be Article 7. If there's a weapon on earth that can stop such a creature, I have not discovered it. "

"That's not it," Kanya said. "There's an altar that we need to destroy, too."

Mace crossed his arms. "And?"

"It's made of Nefarium."

"Then you are shit outta luck. Excuse my language, Kay. But you know that that material is impervious."

"We don't have a choice, Mace." Kanya's irritation with the man had returned. "If we don't figure out a way to stop this thing by tomorrow night, Azrael will be released upon the city. It's the Tenth Plague. The biblical plague. And if we can't stop it, we're looking at a potential genocide. And all this work—all my father's work, all *your* work—has been for nothing. Nothing!"

He stared and then shook his head in disgust. "What kinda situation have you gotten yourself into?"

Mace walked away.

I glanced at Kanya, who had folded her arms in frustration. So I raised my voice. "I thought this guy was supposed to be a weapons expert."

"Listen, numb nuts." Mace turned around and looked squarely at me. "I've bagged more species than you have ever dreamed of."

"Then this shouldn't be *that* hard for you."

He marched to me. The sinews in his neck tightened as he stood chomping his gum.

"You ever fought an angel, Mr. Paranormal Paparazzi? They will eat you up. This is not like those five and dime boogeymen your outfit researches. Trust me."

If he wanted, this guy could probably rip my face off with just his teeth. However, my challenge appeared to have engaged him.

"Actually, I *have* fought an angel," I said. "I decapitated it."

He raised one eyebrow, glanced at Kanya, and stared suspiciously at me. Finally, he said, "And how did you manage that?"

"When they manifest," Kanya said, "they're subject to our laws. If it appears in our dimension and we can engage it during its manifestation, we may be able to fight it." She paused. "And besides, we might have a secret weapon." She looked sideways at me.

I groaned.

"Him?" Mace forced a loud guffaw.

"Yeah," Kanya said. "Show him, Reagan."

"Ugh. Do I have to?"

"Show me what?" Mace eyed me, smirking. "Something wrong with Clarabelle?"

"Shut up, Mace." Then Kanya turned to me. "Show him. Please."

I was starting to feel like some freak at the Venice Beach boardwalk. I guess if the earth guardian thing fell out, I could set up a booth near Pentecost's shop and charge folks to watch my chest glow at night. But she was right. We needed as many people on our side as possible. Besides, there was no way I could hide this much longer. Especially if I was soon to be swallowed by a dimensional whirlpool. Might as well use my weirdness to my advantage. I carefully unbuttoned my shirt and opened it enough for Mace to see the Tau scar. His smirk slowly faded. He approached and brushed my shirt open slightly.

"Careful," Kanya cautioned.

"What'n the hell." Mace stopped chomping his gum. "What is that?"

I shrugged. "We're not sure yet. Our best guess is that it's a micro black hole that will keep growing until it swallows me alive."

Mace slowly looked up at me, his eyes creased in incredulity.

"Either that," I said, "or I'm preparing to hatch a space alien."

Mace stepped away. When he realized I was playing, he curled his lip, approached, bent down, and peered at the Tau scar. His mouth opened and then closed. Finally, Mace stepped back. "Who in the hell are you?"

"He's one of the Imperia," Kanya said.

"Seventh Guardian, to be exact." I smiled dumbly.

"Another Nomly." Mace shook his head.

"He's here to help us," Kanya said. "He has...powers. He can manipulate space. Jump, teleport. Something like that. He went through a death angel and cut it in half."

"You don't say." Mace appeared to soften a bit. "Then why not use the same protocol on that Archangel?"

I started buttoning up my shirt. "Because of one little problem—every time I use the power, the scar grows. Next time, my entire upper body might disappear. Which would really suck."

"That's a helluva bargain, mister."

"Right?"

"The ritual is supposed to occur tomorrow night," Kanya said. "During the Regulus event. If we can destroy that altar, or stop the ritual altogether, we can keep Azrael from showing up."

"But that's a big *if*," I said. "They'll be waiting for us. And if we're not in time, if Azrael shows up, I'm guessing that she's not going to roll over. Look," I said. "We need your help, Mace."

He ran his fingers through his bleached hair and scowled. Finally, he nodded to himself. "There *are* stories about angel engagements. Though intel has it that most end badly. Humans do *not* have a good record against these creatures. It does not matter how many meat eaters are deployed. Angels may be the most lethal of all entities. Personally, I do not want to be on the wrong side of the Almighty on this one. So if you want me to engage, we must be certain as to the nature of this battle."

He moved his steely gaze from me to Kanya.

"They're being summoned by a Neuro," Kanya said. "Using a Nefarium altar. And a human sacrifice. Does that clarify the nature of this battle?"

Mace grunted. "I have heard about an angel hunter who bagged 'em with a crossbow. Harpooned 'em, basically. Wooden shafts made from the Tree of Life in the Garden of Eden. They collapsed upon capture. Allegedly. Can't say I have such exotic weaponry here. There is a sword of reckoning in C6. But it was used on swamp sirens, not mutant angels. We have a variety of sacred staffs in G. However, magic is not in my arsenal and I would not recommend attempting to wield those weapons without prior knowledge and clean underwear. Nevertheless," he sighed and nodded, "I reckon you can count me in."

I smiled. "I knew you weren't that big of a dick."

"I'm afraid the sentiment is not mutual, mister."

I detected the faintest hint of humor in his demeanor.

218

Mace smirked. "At least, not yet."

"Touché."

"Whatever you can muster," Kanya said, "bring it."

"Swords," I added. "Grenades. Pulse rifles."

"Nitroglycerin," Mace said.

"Whatever."

"Angels." Mace shook his head. "You know how I feel about angels, Kay. And the Imperia? I do not trust them either." He glanced at me. "That is one raggedy outfit."

"Frankly," I said, "I concur."

Kanya approached and placed her hand on my arm. "My father believed in him, Mace. You said so yourself." She looked at me. "I think we should too."

CHAPTER 20

K anya made a pot of coffee and persuaded me to try to get a few hours of sleep.

"You can crash here, Reagan. It's probably safer anyway."

"Sounds tempting," I said. "I'm exhausted. But there's one other thing I've got to do. Besides change this shirt."

This brought her pause. "You're going back to Rapha's, right? I mean, you're finishing this?"

I hesitated, more for dramatic effect than anything, and then nodded. "Yeah. I'm going back. Whether or not it gets finished, I don't know. But, either way, I'm not sure I have a choice."

"That's not true. Felix said that the future is fluid, remember?"

It was a perfect opportunity for a witty comeback, but the gravity of the implications legitimately bothered me. Did this mean I could truly choose otherwise, that I could turn my back on the Imperia and any perceived calling? If there was really a map of my future, as Etherea had said, did this mean my future was already scripted? Was I just rehearsing lines already written for me? Or could I indeed rewrite my destiny as I went? If we were really stuck between parallel worlds, between higher and lower dimensions, then any one choice could have innumerable consequences. The possibilities were mind boggling, and my brain and body were in no shape to ponder them. So I left it alone.

I told Kanya I'd call her when I woke up, and we could rendezvous at Rapha's. She was planning a long night of research concerning Santa Muerte, the Shroud, and creative ways to knock off the Archangel of Death. I needed to tell her how much I appreciated her help and how confident I felt with her beside me. This was not that time, so I made a mental note to do so in the very near future. At least, if we didn't become statistics of the Tenth Plague.

As I entered the elevator and prepared to leave, Mace approached holding a handgun.

"Considering how things are going," he said, "it might be advisable for you to carry one of these." He extended the gun and several ammo clips.

I was tempted. Finally, I declined. "I've gotten this far with my guardian angel and my good looks."

Mace shrugged, wished me good luck; I pulled the freight elevator doors shut, and punched the Up button.

Once I left the Asylum and had a cell phone signal, I called Jimmy Pastorelli.

"Moon." There was irritation in Jimmy's voice. "It's about time you returned my call."

"Better late than never."

"*Late* is the operative word there."

"Well, let's just say something unexpected came up."

I shifted the cell phone to my other ear as I unlocked the Cammy. I looked up into the night sky, instinctively imagining the odd celestial alignment that would occur in less than twenty-four hours.

Jimmy was on his way back to the precinct. Apparently, Santa Muerte related crimes had taken a recent spike. Another bust on the south side. Only this one had involved retribution and ritual beheadings. He conjectured whether it had something to do with the Regulus Effect and what connection the incident at the ranch played, if any, with this. Thus far, the only thing Jimmy knew about me was that I was your typical paranormal reporter. The Imperia, the Tau, and any sort of residual supernatural talents had remained close to my vest. I debated how much I should tell him. But my options were narrowing.

Jimmy said, "Whatever you bumped into over there in PV is spreading. Santa Muerte reports are soaring."

"You don't say."

"These sons-a-bitches aren't playing, Moon."

"Tell me about it."

"Yeah? Well that's what I need to talk to you about."

"I'm on my way."

"That, and your secret admirer."

"Audra?" I straightened. "I'm all ears."

"Good. Meet you at the precinct."

The precinct in downtown L.A. is in dire need of renovation. Somehow the city has managed to raise taxes every other year, while keeping the most important municipalities looking like a piece of crap. Of course, Jimmy Pastorelli was not into aesthetics. Lobbying for a new colorful fresco in the lobby was the least of his interests. Give the guy a fresh pot of coffee and a new crime scene, and he was in seventh heaven. So engaging him in any kind of campaign for renovation of this war-torn building was futile.

I parked across the street. It was pushing 1 a.m. The air was dry. Fall-like weather. A couple stood further up the street at their parked car in serious conversation. A streetlight flickered on and off. I'd compulsively checked my rear-view mirror all the way there. I carefully studied the sidewalk and its occupants. If I was being followed, I couldn't tell. Which left me mildly suspicious. I squinted, attempting to peer into whatever invisible realm surrounded me. But as of yet, the gift came in spurts and, apparently, at just the right time. It left me having to trust whatever powers or fate had orchestrated my whacky destiny.

When I walked into his office, Jimmy was sitting at his desk leafing through pictures and paperwork in an open folder. Nearby, sat several sealed, labeled, plastic bags. One contained a human skull while others had occult pendants and candles. He looked up.

"Kolchak," he said. "So you're still in one piece."

"Duct tape and zip ties can do wonders."

He rose, and we shook hands across his desk.

"Nice shirt," Jimmy said. "Where's the lua?"

"Funny."

"But what happened to your face?

I tapped the bridge of my nose.

"Ugh. I was attacked by someone's alter ego."

"You don't say. So," he said, plopping back into his chair, "you haven't burned down any more barns, have you?"

"Fortunately not. But I did stumble upon a death cult that is summoning killer angels to wipe out half the city."

"Sounds interesting."

I just stared at him.

Jimmy scrunched his forehead. "You're not kidding."

"No, Jimmy. I'm not. In fact, tonight I bumped into one of those angels, the Neuro priestess who summoned it, and I managed to rescue her next human sacrifice along the way."

Jimmy squinted at me. "Human sacrifice, huh. That seems to be going around." He pointed to the sack containing the human skull. "It's real. Some loon in Silver Lake. A power player in the movie business, I guess. So far off his rocker he'd make Manson look like a choir boy. Had a basement full of similar shit. He was into ritualistic killing. With the help of Saint Death, he was making a name for himself in the biz. Praying down bad luck and bankruptcy on his competitors. Probably made horror flicks. Bastard. And he was waiting for the arrival of something he called...the Tenth Plague."

My heart felt like a stone lodged into my chest.

"Jimmy," I said. "We need to talk."

"Wait. That's not all. Your girl Audra was the one who tipped me off. Looks like she's been conducting her own private investigation. Not a good idea. But, hey, it helps. In fact, the last message from her was that she'd located someone named the Shroud who, by her account, is some underground big shot that has the hots for her."

"The Shroud?"

"Yep."

"She found him?"

"Apparently."

I groaned. "Look, Jimmy, there's—"

"Whoa, Kolchak." He pressed his hands forward, signaling for me to slow down. "Before you dive into your stories about angels and human sacrifices, there's a piece of information that you need to know."

I swallowed. "There's more?"

"Sorry." Jimmy opened one of the plastic bags and dumped the contents on the desk—talismans, charm satchels, bones, photographs. "Got this stuff from the ranch. The one you burned down. There was a shitload of tunnels underneath the place, with a lab, as expected. They were storing lerium shipments. Equipment. Guns. It was a huge operation. Has Mexican cartel written all over it. There was also this."

He picked a framed 4X6 photo from the items and turned it over to reveal a headshot of myself.

"You gotta be kidding," I said.

"I'm not."

I reached out and took the picture. I recognized the photo as the one used by local news agencies when reporting about my last gig.

"We found another altar down there," Jimmy said. "Santa Muerte. What else. Only your picture was on it. Center stage. Black candles. Offerings. Couple of fresh chicken wings and gizzards. From what I know about the cult, someone is sending some serious bad vibes your way, Moon. Do you realize that? Any idea why an average paranormal reporter would show up on the cartel's Most Wanted list?"

My throat tightened. No wonder things had been so crazy. I was the bull's-eye of some hellacious curse. Even though I had previously discounted the real impact of such curses, now that I was the target of one, I was going to have to reevaluate.

"That's right," Jimmy said. "The Hollywood hack I just mentioned, well, he also said something about the Shroud. Said the Shroud was releasing the Tenth Plague and that everyone not under the blood of a sacrifice would be recycled for the greater good. Had a refrigerator full of human blood for him and his friends, supposed to turn away the death angel. You have any idea who that is—the Shroud? Because that's the same fella that your Unnamed Source sent you to track down. Isn't that right?"

I felt sick. My chest—or whatever was happening inside it—churned. Was there anywhere to run? Was there any way to avoid this collision? The answer was clear. My flesh began to grow clammy.

"Moon? You alright?"

Jimmy watched me twisting there. He nodded. And he tightened the screws. "Listen, you said you took pictures of the shrine that was destroyed. Well, I need to seem 'em. ASAP. And that corpse, you know, the guy that attacked you. He was mostly a charcoal briquette when we got to him. However, the forensics guys tell us that he had his leg severed and that it happened *before* the fire and was not caused by it. Being that you said you were attacked by him and escaped, I think you owe me an explanation. In fact, I need as much information as you can give me about that house, about the Tenth Plague, about your picture on that shrine, and about why in the hell you were even there in the first place." He leaned forward. "Something weird's going on with you, Moon. And now is the time I need to know what it is."

With that, Jimmy forced himself back into his chair and glared at me.

I wiped sweat off my forehead. My appendages were buzzing. There was no way this would end well. Right now, it was damn the torpedoes. So I dove right in.

"Okay," I said. "You want details. Let's start with the Tenth Plague."

"We're talking Plagues of Egypt, right?"

"Right. The Tenth Plague was the slaughter of the firstborn. The angel was named Azrael. An angel of death. She's been summoned—summoned *here*. By someone named the Shroud, who's in with the Santa Muerte cult. Who's probably in with someone a lot bigger. I'm talking about bigger in the cosmic sense. And I'm supposed to stop her before she wipes out half of the city."

"*Her*. The death angel? She's a female? Figures."

"Yeah. I'm not sure how that works. But she's being summoned tomorrow night during the Regulus event and will start wiping out innocent people. I'm not sure if they're all firstborns. Doesn't really matter. All I know is that there's lots of them."

Jimmy now stared and his jaw grew slack with incredulity. "You're losin' it, Moon. I swear to God, you're losin' it."

"I need your help, Jimmy."

He laughed. "*My* help? You need *professional* help. Death angel. Pfft!"

"You wanted to know. Well I'm telling you!" I bolted up out of my chair. "We have to stop it, Jimmy."

"Hey, calm down."

"No! No way. You wanna know why they have my picture, why they're cursing me? It's because I'm the only one who can stop it."

His palms were flat on his desk. His police instincts had kicked in. He had a gun in the top drawer and he was contemplating removing it.

"Jimmy, you know that accident? On Spiraplex? Something happened to me when the lightning struck."

"Lemme guess—you pissed your pants?"

"Almost. You know how lightning struck that tower?"

"Yep."

"How it disintegrated that old lightning rod?"

"Uh-huh."

"And how the force of it was so strong, no one could have ever survived a direct strike?"

Jimmy squinted. "Yeah...?"

"Well, someone *did* survive a direct strike."

Jimmy gazed at me.

I tapped my chest.

"You?" he said. "You were struck by lightning?"

I nodded. "But that's not the worst of it."

"Really. So what is?"

I unbuttoned the Hawaiian shirt and watched his jaw sag open.

"Holy shit." Jimmy slowly stood and walked around his desk, gawking now, staring at the black swirling void that was growing on my sternum. He reached out to touch it.

"Don't," I said.

He drew back his hand. "Why? What..." Then he looked at me. "What'n the hell is it?"

"Well, if my sources are correct, it's a possible portal to a parallel plane."

As I said that, I could feel the wheeling of forces in my sternum, tugging at me. Like some strange engine churning in my heart. No. It wasn't just my heart. It was in my being. Deep inside me. Past my bones and organs. Another dimension was aching to burst through Reagan Moon.

Jimmy just stared. I watched him. Was this how everyone would look at me from now on? Like I was a freak?

"That's weird," Jimmy said. "It's not a gash. It's...hell, I dunno what it is. Almost looks like a mirror. I can see myself in it. I'll be damned."

That was the first, but not the last time someone would see themselves mirrored inside me.

Jimmy could not dismiss what he was seeing, and his concern for me was obvious. Still, he tried to turn away and force a laugh. But no amount of laughter could erase what was right before his eyes. As though compelled by his cop instinct, he turned his hardened gaze back to my chest.

"You're not kidding," Jimmy said. "Are you."

I shook my head. "The storm gave me gifts, Jimmy. Powers."

"Powers. What are you talking about? You mean like superhero powers or something?"

"Something like that."

"You need to see a doctor." He walked away, shaking his head.

"Jimmy, you gotta believe me."

"Don't do this to me, Moon. We're friends."

"You have to listen to me, Jimmy! That Santa Muerte cult. It's a front for something a whole lot bigger. That subway project downtown. There's an altar down there. Something old. Real old. And powerful. NeoKor shut down that entire project because they found it. It's an Altar of Summoning and a ritual is planned for tomorrow night. The Shroud. The death angel. They're all involved. That's why Santa Muerte's on the rise. It's all going down tomorrow night. We have to stop it, Jimmy. Just go down there and see for yourself."

"*We* have to stop it?"

"I'll go it alone if I have to."

"You're not planning on breaking the law, are you, Moon? Far as I understand, that subway is a hazard and restricted for good reasons. And if there's some kinda homicide investigations ongoing down there, I advise you against meddling. Interference with criminal proceedings is a federal offense."

"I need to get down there, Jimmy. I can stop it."

Jimmy peered at me. My sincerity was a monkey wrench in his antagonism.

"Something happened to me up there, Jimmy. On Spiraplex. The lightning. I can see things now. I know things."

"You know things. What things? What kinda things do you know?"

I thought about that. But my answer seemed obvious. "I know about that test you took. The one for cancer."

Jimmy straightened. "What the—? How'd you—?"

I stared at him.

"I haven't told anyone about that, Moon."

"Yeah. Well, I know you're worried about that. Who wouldn't be? But you're worried about your ex, for some reason. And your son. Jimmy, *I know things now.*"

He gaped. Then he fumbled awkwardly with his shirt collar while glancing at me. That piece of info had apparently done what it needed to. He tried to compose himself while wanting to ask questions. Unfortunately for him, the latter prevailed.

"So. You know things. Then tell me..." Jimmy swallowed. "Is it malignant?"

I continued staring at him. Who would have thought a crusty old cop like Jimmy Pastorelli would have been brought to his knees by a disease.

I managed a smile. "I need to get down there, Jimmy."

"Damn you, Moon!"

"I can see other things too, Jimmy. Demons. Angels. Stuff I never used to believe in. It's true. They're out there. They're all around us. It's no joke. And I know things, I can feel things. Sometimes it's people's emotions. Sometimes it's their pain. What's more, there are others like me. These people who've been changed. They call themselves the Imperia. We're like earth guardians. Don't look at me like that. I know, it sounds crazy. But it's true. We have different powers—psionics, spatial manipulation, particle agglomeration. Hell, I'm still trying to figure it out. We're called to protect the city, to protect the earth from attacks like this. We're like—I dunno—a divine hit squad or something. They call me the Seventh Guardian because I have this." I tapped my chest. "They say that I have special abilities and I'm going to reunite them. I don't know. They think I'll make a difference. But I'm just trying to survive, really. That's all I'm trying to do, Jimmy. Just to figure out what's expected of me. And survive."

Jimmy stared. His eyes slowly glazed over. He felt his way to his seat and plopped into it.

"Jimmy, we need your help."

"I'm all outta angel bullets," he said dully.

"We need to get back down in there before the quarter crescent moon tomorrow night."

He paused, debating a response. My knowledge of his cancer had deeply shaken him. I guess it would anyone. Nevertheless, in old school police fashion, he countered. "If there's anything down there and you destroy it, you'll have the historical society, NeoKor, and the police so far up your ass you'll be shittin' out your nose."

"And if it's true?" I said. "If it's true that there's a death angel and that the Tenth Plague is going to be released on the city, then what?"

Jimmy stared at me, eyes moving from my chest to my eyes. "I need to think about it."

I growled, turned away, and hastily buttoned up my shirt.

"For right now," Jimmy said, "you need to watch your ass. And please, go see a doctor about that thing on your chest, will ya?"

I turned around, looked at him as dead serious as possible, and said, "It's true. It's all true."

He couldn't deny my conviction and did not attempt to counter my statement.

I left the station frustrated and unsure whether I could count on Jimmy or not. I'd never seen him that stunned before. But it was the revelation of his physical condition, not the Tau scar, which had left him reeling. It's true for all of us—crisis isn't genuine until it strikes home. Jimmy promised to look into the subway project, who was providing security, and what was buried down there. He also promised to dig up details on the Shroud and where, or how, he might possibly be stopped. Despite all that, it wasn't enough.

Which meant that we were going this alone.

Before I entered the Cammy, I looked out at the city. The Hollywood sign glowed ragged against the dry brush. Like everything else in this city, it was more style than substance. Seedy metal letters on a drought-plagued hill. It was sort of like us humans—even with all the bells and whistles, we were all just crumbling bits of stardust.

The sky was clear. Fall weather is like that. The smell of diesel mixed with the twill of night birds. Who knew that in less than twenty-four hours, something inhuman and deathly would yank this city from its spiritual slumber. Was it really possible that a five thousand year-old plague would be reawakened here? Perhaps the bigger question was whether or not history was fluid enough that I could change it.

CHAPTER 21

It was after two a.m. when I arrived at my apartment. I was exhausted, but convinced that I had to see this through. If I could even manage a couple hours of sleep, maybe I could better face what lay ahead.

The street was quiet, but knowing now that Santa Muerte devotees were praying down bad vibes on me, the night seemed even more alive. I punched in the code, and the security door opened. Glancing both ways, I entered the stairwell. When I reached my apartment door, I paused, allowing my mind to roam. The chatter of a television sounded from somewhere, and I could smell popcorn. Other than that, there were no red flags, so I entered.

I emptied my pockets—keys, totem, cell phone, Asylum key, wallet—and set the items on the desk next to a bronze goblet with Celtic inscriptions. The goblet was a gift from a chaos magician who attributed a stretch of good fortune to a feature I'd run on him. He said that drinking red wine from the goblet every solstice would enhance my virility, increase my wealth, and prevent hemorrhoids. Okay, so I made that last one up. I'd never undertaken the ritual, but looking at the goblet made me wonder if it might also slow down the growth of interdimensional wormholes.

I entered my room, removed the Hawaiian shirt, and chucked it into pile of clothes beside my dresser. Good riddance. If it wasn't Kanya's, I would have banished it to the Salvation Army. Instead of taking a shower, I sat on the edge of the bed, yawned, and massaged my eyes. Perhaps I should sleep. A couple hours would be better than nothing.

I lay down and closed my eyes. Even though residual adrenaline was lingering in my body, the edges of my consciousness quickly grew hazy. Within minutes, something dragged me back into the waking world and made me sit straight up in my bed. Laughter outside, in the street below. While it wasn't uncommon to hear people on the streets of L.A. at 2 a.m., this particular laughter sent my skin crawling. It didn't help that a cat mewl immediately followed. Cats are bad omens. Mewling ones are even worse.

Suddenly the room seemed alive with Invisibles. Had they been here all along? Or was the Santa Muerte curse finally kicking in? I thought about the shard from Rival's Curtain which I'd salvaged from my last big assignment. The crystalline lens had the uncanny capacity to reveal the spiritual dimension. The device had been my initiation into all things unseen. The lens was in the lamppost along with other valuables. But it would only confirm what I already knew. Instead, I went to the window, parted the shades slightly, and peered out. Two figures were walking away from the Cammy.

I grabbed a print shirt from the end of the bed and slipped it on. As I dashed past the mirror I saw that it was the Blood Run shirt I'd gotten for participating in the Zombie Mud Run sponsored by LAFD. Subtitled *Guts AND Glory*, I felt it was an oddly appropriate selection.

I grabbed the items from the desk in the entryway, stuffed them in my pockets, and left, bolting the door as quickly as possible. I descended the stairs three at a time, slammed open the security door, and ran into the street, staring in the direction I'd last seen the figures. But they were long gone. I scanned the street in both directions without any luck. If someone was after me, why not come straight for me? Unless they'd planted a bomb in my car and were hoping to blow me to shreds. That's when I noticed that the front door of the Cammy was ajar. I straightened.

I scanned the street again and approached the car cautiously. It didn't have a fancy alarm system, which made it far easier to jack than today's models. As I got closer, I was thinking it might be time for an upgrade. When I reached the car, I did not open the door, but studied the interior through the window. The nearby streetlamp sent a shaft of light angling onto the driver's seat where I noticed a fine silk cloth, possibly a handkerchief or scarf, rolled up, as if it contained something. One end of the cloth was darkly stained. *Blood*. I straightened.

Checking my surroundings again, I opened the door but did not immediately pick up the bloody cloth. Instead, I carefully brushed open the ends. The skin on my neck bristled. Inside of it lay a single human finger. An index finger. It had been surgically removed. I stepped back as the flight instinct surged to life inside of me. White light flashed behind my eyeballs, and for a second, I thought I might have transported. When I caught my breath, I could only stare.

It wasn't the finger itself that concerned me as much as it was the object on the finger. It was a ring. An ornate amber cat eye ring. And I knew immediately who it belonged to.

Someone had severed Audra's finger.

This was more than a message. It was an invitation. To which I was about to reply.

I opened the glove box and removed a half-eaten bag of Doritos. The next best thing to carrying around a severed finger in my glove box was hiding it in a bag of chips. Which I did. I rolled the bag tight around the bloody finger and shoved it in the glove box. Of course, I'd have a hard time explaining the presence of the thing if I encountered the authorities. In the back of my mind, I was hoping I could reach her in time for medical professionals to reattach it. But the more obvious question was whether she could be reached at all.

My mind was racing as I drove to Audra's. It was the only place I could think of going. Jimmy had said that Audra was on the tail of the Shroud and my guess was that she had indeed found him. Or he, her. Perhaps I could at least gather some clues as to her whereabouts from her cabana. However, if someone knew I would come to Audra's rescue, I could be playing right into their hands. I debated calling Jimmy, but he'd had a hard time believing my other stories. Asking him to investigate the possible kidnapping of an ex-queen with a therianthropic daughter seemed like asking too much. And I obviously couldn't call Kanya. There was no telling what this could trigger in her.

It was after 3 a.m. when I got to Audra's bungalow. I did a slow pass before parking several houses down. Walking this late at night in such a ritzy neighborhood would most assuredly get me in trouble, so I had to make it quick. Her lights were off and no other activity was visible. I hurried along the sidewalk, and passed several oaks and an old, boarded up water well before reaching the driveway. I glanced both ways before turning into it and walking briskly down the driveway, staying close to the high vine covered wall. A faint light burned in the front house. Audra's house was dark, but my heart quickened when I saw that her car was there.

I was prepared to climb the wrought iron security gate, when I noticed that the lock was mangled. Someone had already paid Audra a visit. This little adventure had suddenly become exponentially more risky. I pulled the gate back and slipped inside. Keeping to the shadows, I crept to Audra's house. I stiffened when I saw her cat standing near the cellar door, mewling.

"Psst!" I brushed my hand its way. "Go on. Get."

But the cat just stared. Damned felines.

I approached the front door and tried the handle. It was locked. A dry wind rattled the shed door near the back. I leaned off the porch and peered into the nearest window. No movement inside. Just the ghoulish green glow of her fish tank. I glanced back at the front house and then turned and tried the handle again. Nothing had changed. Now what?

I hurried around the side of the house, hoping to find an entrance near the back. That door was also locked. I pressed my hands against the window and peered through, but only dark images greeted me. I thought about breaking a window and sneaking inside, but it didn't sit right. In fact, nothing was sitting right. I got the nagging feeling that something was askew here. It was as if a dark cloud had drifted into my brain, dulling my perception, preventing me from knowing more than the obvious. What to do remained unclear. Perhaps I should look elsewhere. Then why put her finger in my car? As a clue? As a warning? They knew I would instinctively come here. Perhaps it was a diversion.

I wandered off the porch, letting my mind roam, hoping that chance or intuition would guide me. Yet the thick mental haze settled further upon my brain. I should leave. There was no reason to stay. But without looking inside? I walked around the opposite side of the house, debating what to do, only to be stopped by my feline friend. It perched at the steps to cellar door. It looked up at me, its eyes sparkling in the faint skylight. If I was a cat lover, I would almost swear it was trying to communicate.

I shivered. Not from the chill, but from the thought of telepathically communicating with a cat. Nevertheless, I got the distinct sense that this particular cat was at this particular door for a very particular reason.

I approached the ragged cement steps and peered into the descending dark. The mental fog almost seemed to hum now, a hive of obscurity waiting to engulf my mind. Something was down there. Without a doubt. And with that awareness came the thought that my mental thickness was being magically induced.

I retrieved my cell phone and turned on its flashlight. Soil and faint footsteps marked the area. Leaves had accumulated there. Skid marks etched the cement where the door had recently been opened.

By now, my gut was doing somersaults. Something like a hum, slightly below the level of hearing, reverberated in the air. This was not the harsh dry rattling of the cicadas in Louisiana that I had known. It was more like the drone of a witches' coven. I was supposed to go down here. I knew it.

"Bernard!" I whispered, looking right and left. "Hey. I can use some help."

There was no evidence of the golden hue that signaled his presence. Why was I given a guardian angel if he only

236

showed up when he wanted? But after what I'd witnessed in the abandoned subway, maybe he was doing double-time against creatures I couldn't possibly comprehend.

I inhaled deeply and descended the first step. Then the second. I glanced at the cat, who was almost eye level with me now. It sat erect, unflinching.

"I hate cats, you know that?"

It blinked.

"But I'm only doing this because you're here."

It just stared.

"Okay. That's not the only reason. It feels like the Brain from Planet X is down there."

The cat meowed. And then promptly stood up and strode into the darkened yard.

Damn cats.

I turned my light to the remaining steps and descended them. I was thinking about the finger in the handkerchief in the glove compartment in my car on the street when I took hold of the door handle. The door was open. It scraped the ground. The smell of mold and dust struck me. I fumbled for a light but the switch clicked up and down without response. I doubted that Audra had spent any time down here. There was no window. But a faint light throbbed from within the chilly bowels of the cellar. My light illuminated sagging shelves laden with dust and cobwebs.

"Audra," I whispered. "You down here?"

Clusters of empty mason jars lined the shelves, some toppled, some without lids. A sink sat to one side bleeding mineral stains from both handles. Just beyond several sets of shelves was another room from which a soft glow emanated.

My head was beginning to hurt, as if my brain had been put in an invisible vice. This was almost worse than Quinn's interrogation.

"Audra. Psst. Hey. It's Reagan Moon."

Light pulsated from the open doorway room ahead. Old rakes and trowels were scattered atop a rotted worktable. A wheelbarrow lay on its side, cobwebs lacing its handle.

I winced at the keening in my head. Where was this mental energy coming from? Was it simply psychosomatic, or was there a mystical power source somewhere nearby? If so, what kind of energy source could produce such a thing? It had the feel of something other than pure psychic ability. This was tainted. I gritted my teeth, fighting to remain lucid.

I reached the open doorway. It was a secondary cellar.

"Audra?" I said.

Then I stepped into the doorway.

A woman lay sprawled awkwardly on the floor, her arms spread, stretched by some invisible bonds. A ring of bones and burning candles surrounded her. But it was the six individuals behind her, dressed in black and burgundy, holding hands, murmuring, that most captivated my attention.

Six is not a good number. But it was probably fitting that this group should mirror the Imperia. The low, resonant murmuring stopped and Etherea raised her head. The individuals surrounding her followed suit.

"Well, well. So you've come to save the Queen."

"And break up your party," I said. "My apologies."

"I'm afraid your bravado is pointless. May I introduce the Shroud." She brushed back her hand, motioning to the five individuals behind her.

"This is…?"

"Welcome, Reagan Moon." They spoke the words in unison, an eerie robotic monotone.

Etherea stepped forward. The remaining five stood shoulder to shoulder, wedded by some noxious power. Their heads were abnormally large. Were they Neuros? Lerium addicts could sometimes be recognized by enlarged heads. Veins coursed their temples. Their eyes were black pools in pale flesh. When they spoke, the cloud over my brain swelled, a fug of confusion and despair. I grimaced and doubled over.

Whether a curse or from the sheer darkness of their persons, this psychic storm was emanating from the Shroud. I squeezed my eyes shut, trying to force the darkness out of my brain. But it was like someone had shoved an anvil between my ears. These weren't Neuros. They were something else.

Etherea chuckled. "The Shroud has that effect on normal folks which, apparently, is all the two of you really are."

My cell phone fumbled out of my hand.

I stood upright with some effort. "What've you done to her?"

The woman on the ground tilted her head up. It was Audra. I immediately thought of the finger and located her left hand, trying to visually identify where the digit had been removed. To my amazement, she was not missing a finger. At least, the one in its place was unusually pale and much shorter. As if a new one was sprouting. What the hell?

Etherea circled Audra. "She'll be a perfect offering for Azrael."

"For Azrael," the others said in eerie unison.

As they spoke, the clamp upon my brain seemed to tighten.

Etherea smiled.

I attempted to refocus on Audra's hand. Etherea knew I was looking at the finger.

"Oh. It's not serious. She'll grow it back. Don't you know?"

Audra was panting. She had been hit. Restrained. Operated upon. Sweat formed on her brow. But her wound…

"She's one of the Hydra sisters," Etherea said. "They're cool like that. They can re-grow limbs, you know? Regenerate. Like the hydra. Anything but the head. That's their weak spot. Cut off the hydra head, and you kill it. But in this one's case, it's already been tried."

Etherea pointed to the scar on Audra's cheek.

Audra grimaced. "Let him g-go."

239

Mike Duran

"I'm afraid not, sweets." Etherea approached me. The atmosphere around her churned with hate and hunger. "I confess, we were a tad concerned about you. Especially after you managed to escape the death angel and free our sacrifice. We were forced to take you out of the equation. Without the Seventh Guardian, your team will be what they always were— an inept, dying group."

I winced at the clamp upon my mind. "So who said I was out of the equation?"

"Do you really expect to accomplish anything in your state?"

She had a point. I looked at Audra and the circle of bones and candles surrounding her. Was this all that held her? If so, I could drag her out of here without a problem.

"It's a sacred scrim," Etherea said. "A scrim of binding. Bound by the angelic tongue. The one inside such a circle will taste of their own blood. A sort of psychic hemorrhage, you could say. Sadly, this is where we must leave you, Reagan Moon. Perhaps Azrael will choose to deliver you from your suffering when the Tenth Plague is released upon this waste of a city. If not, you will remain entombed in your own mind. A prisoner. Call it our own brand of night terrors. Only these don't last for one night. They last forever."

Audra mumbled something, attempted to rise to her knees, to scrabble to the border of the scrim, but she seemed to be moving in quicksand, burdened by invisible bonds. She collapsed face forward, her face planted into the cold cement floor.

"Get outta here," she moaned. "To the...altar."

Etherea's eyes seemed to flare. For that brief second, she appeared surprised that Audra had managed to speak at all. When Audra struggled to rise, Etherea's features turned gleefully sinister. If anything, it made me wonder if her pronouncements about the spell's implacability was more bluster than actual fact.

240

"Mind your manners." Etherea placed her boot on Audra's head and pushed her to the floor. I lurched forward, but my motions felt slow and leaden. The atmosphere was thick. A discordant hum vibrated in the marrow of my bones.

The Shroud stood watching. Pale, androgynous. Their skin was fair, and their facial features were oddly alike. Were they quintuplets? Perhaps. They stood shoulder to shoulder, swaying to some mute rhythm. A hive mind. And they were generating some sort of occult energy. Maybe this was the source of Audra's power. She was tapping into this engine of pain and bleakness birthed from these five individuals. Whatever energy they were emitting had a numbing effect on my body and mind. My head felt thick and my body encumbered by invisible weights.

"You...the Shroud," I spoke clumsily, nonsensically.

In unison they said, "We are the Shroud. Servants of Hail. Keepers of Ice." The sound of their voice was like a sonic wave in my head that caused me to sway back to front.

Etherea laughed. "They exist in perfect unity. Unlike that fractured team of yours. What fools! And, no—we don't have room for you. You have chosen unwisely, errand boy."

I slurred the word, "Neuros."

"Oh, we're so much more than that. Some say they're muses of the Netherworld, a title I quite like."

Muses? My head hurt just watching them. They'd formed some type of unified field and were projecting it upon me.

I directed my attention to Audra. Her arms were spread, but there were no visible bonds holding her in place.

"It's a spell of paralysis, slumber," Etherea explained. "Eternal slumber. The same one you're in. An invisible binding so strong that neither you, nor your comrades, can break it. Azrael will relish her essence. Really, she's quite an upgrade from the last sacrifice. Thanks to you." She put her fingertip to her lips. "I wonder if the archangel has ever dined on hydra blood?"

I forced my eyes to focus on Audra's hand, and she was indeed growing her finger back. A pale virgin index finger was budding next to the others. Of course, it was missing the amber ring. But I didn't have time to ponder this oddity. I willed my body to move, but there was a disjunction between my brain and my body.

"We're preparing the way for the Prince," Etherea said. "The great one who will arise to unify the world. He will promise to stop the plague and, when he does, his reign will commence. And the nations will worship him. You see, it's not fascism. It's so much bigger."

And with that she motioned with her hand.

Two of the Shroud stepped forward. It was unclear to me whether they were male or female. They were hairless and almost albino in complexion. As they circled the sacred scrim, the Shroud began to chant. And as they did, their spell clamped down upon my mind. I tried to lunge at them. By the looks of it, these people did not possess fighting skills. They were soft and ugly. Yet my effort resulted in me stumbling to my knees. As I did, their chanting rose, filling the cold cellar with its discordance.

They removed several large human-looking femur bones from the scrim, leaving a type of gateway, an opening in or out of the circle. Then they reached into the circle, took Audra by opposite hands, and dragged her out. She flinched at their touch but offered no resistance. Her gaze passed from brief lucidity to anger, and returned to glazed lethargy. Once outside the circle, the two muses took me under my arms and dragged me, on my knees, into the sacred scrim.

My attempts to resist were feeble. I slurred out some indistinguishable words. I think I toppled a candle trying to kick at one of my abductors. Though my senses remained lucid, my body was numbed to movement.

It made me dearly wish I'd not scoffed at the power of spells when I was with the Imperia.

They returned the bones and enclosed me inside the scrim.

"Binding muse. Binding. Arise, Lord Hail. Reveal thy Hollow."

As the weight of the curse began to settle on me, I managed to call for Bernard. It was more like a croak than a cry. The Shroud remained unfazed. They did not fear my guardian angel. Or me. Yet Bernard did not appear.

Someone stood over me. It was Etherea. "It's your own personal coma. If all goes well, your soul will be trapped. Tortured inside. No. You won't find this spell in any grimoire, Mr. Moon. Not that you have expertise in such spells anyway. Pity. You should have been less skeptical. If you're not killed by Azrael when she does her thing, you'll be trapped in your mind forever. Call it a night terror that never ends."

I tried to summon the power, to awaken the storm gifts. But the enchantment seemed to counter everything else. Even if I could focus my mind enough to teleport, I couldn't feel my body enough to do so.

The very elements around me—stone, air, and subatomic particles—resonated with the Shroud's chanting.

"Encircle thee of Nether." They said as one voice. "Blood to stone. Come hence, Hail. Hail Hollow!"

I tried to summon one last burst of energy, but I was paralyzed, trapped inside my own head. Rapha said I could break spells and have power over such enchantments. But, alas, I was an infant at such warfare. And my opportunity to learn such things had quickly come and gone. I lay helpless.

"Binding muse. Binding muse."

Through the haze, I heard someone yell. For a moment, it seemed to break the hypnotic chant of the Shroud. I glimpsed a rush of movement. More yelling. Audra and Etherea were grappling at each other. Audra flung something away from Etherea. It tumbled, sparkling, through the air. Yet the Shroud enclosed her with their voices and Audra slumped back into her lethargic trance.

Before they left, they spoke to me—whether into my mind or my actual hearing, I couldn't tell. Only that they were in perfectly awful unison.

"For the children of the damned," the voice said. "A lullaby for the lost. A world of dreams once dreamt. Fallen, they are. Fallen from their thrones. Destined to wander. The Elder Ones now send their agents. The order of Hail. Arise, Lord Hail! The coming one will dream again the dream of history. He will know the body immortal, possess its reins. The Imperia and the resistors shall be crushed. Arise, oh Hail! From the Hollow, arise! Send Azrael your servant to prepare thy way."

I heard it all with startling clarity. This wasn't sleep. Nor death. It was the night terror, the scream without an end.

They carried Audra off. Were they levitating? The world was cloudy and dark. Eternally chilly. The cellar door scraped shut.

Around me burned the candles. A thousand nuclear pinpricks in a circle of haze. Unmoving, I lay. My life did not pass before my eyes. Instead, it spread out, it pumped from the arteries of my mind like a black endless ocean. The concave face of the death angel hovered in the darkness of my thoughts, moving closer. And I knew I was to be her last supper.

CHAPTER 22

He was said to live in a permanent state of lucid dreaming. Night terrors, to be exact. But what made the case of Simon Yu one of the most popular features in the history of the Blue Crescent, was his apparent ability to torment his enemies from within a dream state. I'd visited Yu in the convalescent hospital where he'd been for almost a year. His limbs were already beginning to atrophy when we learned about the sordid tale.

He'd been a lanky boy, borderline math genius, but socially awkward. He was bullied by high school classmates, corn fed punks who measured their self-worth by the degree of fear they could generate in others. Yu was an easy target. When the school authorities learned of the bullying problem, they stalled and tried to psychoanalyze the players. Meanwhile, Yu's mother was busy burning both ends in some sweatshop in the Garment District. The kid started having night terrors, waking up in a cold sweat. Said he dreamed of taking revenge on his tormenters. Saw a therapist. Took pills. But nothing worked.

Night after night fighting bullies in his brain.

Until one night he fell asleep and never woke up. No, he didn't die. He went comatose; his face was perpetually contorted as if he was trapped in his own personal hell. After a little digging they learned that he'd been sexually abused by his tormenters, defiled with a blunt object and passed around among the boys. Real whack job shit. They even took pictures and shared them on the interwebs. And that's where it started.

One of the gang went mad. Literally. Shortly after Yu was institutionalized, this kid claimed to have been visited in his sleep. He started seeing Simon Yu everywhere—in the empty locker room, in the crowded mall. The kid stopped sleeping, started talking to himself. The guilt was catching up to him. One morning they found him in the shower, dead. Water still running. Cause of death, aortic aneurism.

Then, one by one, they all started dying. Weird deaths, too. Freak accidents and dismemberments. Final Destination type stuff. The Crescent got hold of the story, and I followed it to the end. Once the entire group had died, through various means, Yu inexplicably passed away.

I'd named him the Dream Slayer and the title stuck.

The limbo that I currently occupied brought that story to mind. For, really, my mind was all that seemed to function. In fact, I fully expected Simon Yu to appear and offer me some tips for exacting revenge upon the Shroud from within my own dream state.

My body was frozen. I could barely feel it. I fought to simply move my arms, but nothing worked. I must have been breathing because I screamed. At least, I thought I was screaming. Until I realized that the scream was stuck inside my head. It was a mute plea for help on an endless loop.

I'd researched enough out-of-body experiences to know that this wasn't one. At the moment, I was very much in-the-body. Because as hard as I tried to open my eyes, call for help, or drag my sorry ass out of the scrim of binding, I could not. I was imprisoned inside a lucid dream. Make that, a night terror.

Reagan Moon—Dream Slayer.

Several thumps sounded. Muffled, but tangible. They may have been nearby, but my sense of time and space was out of whack. I reckoned it was Etherea and her band of Netherworld muses climbing the steps, taking Audra to the Rite of Summoning. However, an odd sensation seemed to accompany the sound. A slight reverberation in my chest. Had I felt the sound? Or was the Tau stirring? With the sensation came a prickling chill spreading across one side of my body.

That's when I realized that my other senses were beginning to waken. The cold of the cellar floor burned my skin. And the smell of dust and mold—even cat spray—was becoming acute in my nostrils. However, I still could not move or animate my body. Whatever the spell was doing, it mainly affected my limbs and ambulation.

...*something. There it is!*

Strangely, without its attachment to my body, my mental acumen was cruising.

It's a person...coming through—

The voices drifted in and out of my mind. They were strangely familiar. Then I realized they were the same ones I'd heard when I'd teleported. But where were they coming from? They weren't in the cellar with me, but neither were they exclusively in my brain. They were somewhere else.

He said he would come.

And then a different voice.

He will. And he will bring deliverance with him.

They sounded close, as if they were in this very cellar, right next to me. Or at least, some space in between us. And they were talking about me. The voices. I knew it. Did they know I was here? Did they know I could hear them? But what was the 'deliverance' they spoke of?

I tried to yell. *Hey! Can you hear me? Hey, you!*

Nothing. Just my own unspoken words dying in the empty gray.

I'm here! I cried out again from the recesses of my mind. *Right here! I need help.*

But there was no response. Or was there? The voices were silent now. Had they heard me? Perhaps. So I tried again.

It's Reagan Moon. I'm—I'm the Seventh Guardian.

God that sounded corny. If I survived this, I'd have to think up a better moniker. Whatever the case, I was met with silence.

I attempted to move again. But it was impossible. Nothing had changed. I was mummified, a prisoner in my own brain. There had to be some type of magic to counter this. However, Rapha implied it wasn't magic at all. It was a combination of science, alchemy, and willpower. And divine gifting. But until I figured out that formula, I was nothing more

Mike Duran

than a corpse-in-waiting rotting away in a cellar in a Beverly Hills bungalow. Here, I would have eons to live and re-live my losses. The Imperia would probably be decimated. They stood no chance against the Shroud and the death angels. Yet they would go down fighting. I was confident of that. And I was sure that Kanya would not stay put either. She couldn't. But none of them stood a chance. When the Tenth Plague was released, I could only imagine the citywide bedlam, and the number of friends who might be taken—Arlette, Jimmy, even Mrs. Richardson, my cat-loving neighbor.

And as I lay there, the regret seemed to become palpable, living. A black maleficent thing. An entity as warped as a narvog or a cerebral slug, slowly strangling me in its grip. A perpetual twilight descended upon me, quenching any hope of intervention or release. I had entered the land of the Shadow of Death. Only here, there was no light at the end of the tunnel, only denser shades of black. And my journey was just beginning.

I remained in that place for what felt like days. Time was measured in terms of grief and helplessness. Like fossilized strata, emotional sediment became dunes along the shoreline of my being, burying me in its weight. The emptiness was so perfect there that no particle was left untainted. Every inch, every molecule had been stripped of goodness and bleached to nothing. A black hole swallowing all light, all hope. Forever.

Somewhere in that gloom, a form appeared. Its geometry was at first unclear, but gradually took shape. A slender silhouette whose features remained indistinct. It may have been there for hours or perhaps days. Waiting and watching me. But for some reason, I became aware of it. No. My eyes were not open, but I knew it was there.

Ellie? Is that you?

There was no response. Though in simply forming her name I felt guilt. I could not let her see me in this state. She had expected so much from me to only now find me lying

248

helpless in a subterranean tomb. Yet the more I trained my mind upon this person, the more I knew it wasn't Ellie. The shape remained there, unmoving. Watching.

I lay before the witness, helpless, attempting to send my thoughts forward, probing for a hint of recognition. Or communication. Soon, pale eyes took shape and came into view above me. However, something had changed. To my surprise, I wasn't seeing this with some inner awareness. This was not a premonition.

My eyes were open.

I blinked several times. My lids were thick and heavy, as if I'd been drugged. My limbs were still leaden. But something had changed. It wasn't just that I could see again, but that I could make out a pair of feet in front of me. Not six feet away. Wearing shoes, polished silver shoes.

Hovering about three inches off the floor.

The person wearing the shoes remained a temporary mystery, for as I wondered over the hovering shoes, I noticed the scrim had been broken. To be more exact, something had been pushed into the scrim from the outside in. A candle had been toppled and now lay smoking and pooling wax. Scraps of bone and a satchel were scattered helter-skelter. The scrim had been broken and with it, the weight of the spell weakened.

Though I was supremely interested in who was hovering in front of me, my immediate focus rested on an object that had been pushed through the scrim and lay on the floor, inches from my face. It was small and glimmered faintly with a dull light. I groaned and rolled onto my side with great effort. I drew a deep breath and pushed myself off the ground. Then I focused on the object before me.

It was Etherea's pendant, the one with the Regulus crescent. A broken strand of chain remained attached to it. This is what I'd seen tumble through the air in their tussle. Audra, whether intentionally or not, had managed to rip the pendant from Etherea's neck. This was more than fortuitous, for Rapha's words immediately sprang to mind. *If an object from the enchanter can be retrieved, typically an object of power like an article of clothing, a talisman or effigy, one can perform a disruption and counteraction.*

I had never broken a spell before. At least, not intentionally. The incident in the subway, freeing Alma Curtain from her delusion of Fate, was less a counter-spell than simply good old will power. But if possessing an object from the spellcaster was a necessary step, as Rapha had said, I reckoned this might do the trick.

I forced my legs to move, crawled up on to my knees, and remained there on all fours. Wobbling. Then I managed to settle on my haunches. It felt like someone had opened up my head and replaced my brain with a drawer full of socks. The veil from the magical scrim still surrounded me, obscuring my vision. Whoever had passed the pendant to me remained on the other side. The silver polished shoes were buoyed above the floor on some invisible tide. The face of this witness and its pale languid eyes were unclear.

I turned my attention to the pendant, scooped it into my palm, and gazed at it. Was there something I should say? Maybe there was a universal equation or esoteric formula I should conjure. This wasn't like betting the ponies at Santa Anita where one could combine expert opinion with gut instinct. However, I wasn't great at racetrack gambling either. Breaking the spell of some Netherworld muses had to involve more than just guesswork. I attempted to probe my thoughts for such a universal quotient. Nothing came to mind. No counter spell or sequence of words I must correctly speak to free myself from this ghastly paralysis. I weighed the pendant in my hand as if I could coax some secret out of it. I tried to free my mind and let the better angels of my nature do the talking. Still nothing.

Well then, maybe Rapha was correct—will power was the real magic. So I simply closed my fingers around the pendant, forming a tight fist. I glanced at the figure before me, as if for confirmation that I was doing this correctly. The confirmation came in the form of a faint electric blue glow twining around my balled fist. The odd, but familiar phenomenon swelled, as tendrils of energy pulsated, casting an eerie illumination in the circle. I squeezed tighter, as if by sheer will I could pulverize the talisman with my grip. The sensation grew, and my fist became a mini-Tesla conductor. I turned my head and closed my eyes, hoping I could keep from being burned by my own power. Even behind my own eyelids I could see the neon glow illuminating this once dark space. I squeezed my fist so tightly that my muscles trembled. As I did, I gritted my teeth and then yelled.

Something snapped. I toppled back.

I opened my eyes to see the proton web gone. The scrim was scattered, objects spread across the cellar floor. I was breathing normal again, and drew deep breaths just to make sure. The weight of the spell no longer held me. And the pendant was gone.

I'd done it! Not bad for a rookie earth guardian.

I quickly turned my attention to the figure before me, and when I saw who it was, my stomach dropped. A petite female wearing a pink nightgown with frilly neckline and sleeves, and shiny silver shoes. Weeping Eve, the poltergeist of Saint Vincent's, hovered there. For a moment, I thought I might puke. However, something seemed different about the ghost.

Unlike our first meeting, Weeping Eve's smile seemed beneficent.

"It's you," I said. I was still panting from the power surge. "What are you doing here?"

Her lips parted.

"No. Don't answer. Sorry. I shouldn't talk to ghosts."

Now that I was out of the scrim, my mind was flooding back and my body tingled with energy. The memory of my brief encounter with Eve and all its details blossomed in my thinking. And with it came a startling awareness.

"The accident in the cellar…" I said, drawing out my thoughts as I spoke. "It did something to free you. Didn't it?"

Again, her lips parted.

"Stop! Sorry again. I think I know. That place in the wall. They found something, didn't they?"

Her eyes widened.

"You didn't kill yourself, did you. Someone else—" I swallowed. A sickening sense of what I was about to confirm wrenched my innards. "God. Someone raped and murdered you and made it look like suicide."

Her eyes widened even more, and filled with tears.

I nodded. "They found the stuff in the wall, didn't they. Where I accidentally bashed the brick in. There were gloves, clothing. They thought it was odd that someone would have sealed those things in there. Especially because that's where your body was found. So they're doing tests. It'll give them what they need to find the killer. DNA and stuff. That's what's happening, isn't it?"

She brushed tears from her cheeks and nodded.

"Weird. I can feel everything. I mean, not really feel, but just *know*. It was a handyman or something. He used to work at the hospital, right? He knew you would walk alone and he took advantage of you. Bastard."

Eve just stared. She was probably as amazed as I was about my growing body of knowledge about her.

"He hurt others, Eve." I tried to temper the words with compassion. "He did the same thing to others. He jumped between jobs, but he never got caught. He died, but nobody ever knew a thing about his crimes."

Anger flashed in her eyes. Her air wafted about her face. The air suddenly turned chill and rage exploded in the room, a burst of electrostatic fury that curdled my flesh. Items on the nearby shelves rattled. Tin cans collapsed inwards and several glass jars exploded, sending fragments battering the walls. I ducked, shielding my head with my arms. The very foundations of the house seemed to tremble with Eve's frenzy.

252

I stayed there until the poltergeist event ebbed into soft residual energy.

When it did, I finally looked up. The ghost hovered with her chin on her chest. She was done. Maybe even a little embarrassed about the outburst. Although it made me wonder how much poltergeist activity was less about scaring people and more about righteous indignation.

"Eve," I said. "This will end it. I'm sure of it. They'll be able to trace his crimes. He'll finally be outed. Better late than never, huh? But it's over. You're cleared. They'll know you didn't kill yourself. Justice will be served. Which means you're free, Eve. You're free."

She lifted her gaze to me and nodded.

"You're not beholden to me either. In case that's what you're thinking. I mean, just because I played a part, you don't owe me anything. You're not obligated to help me. Understood?"

Her eyes sparkled.

I kicked at the scrim, sending bones and charms scattering about the cellar.

"Thank you so much for helping me. I wouldn't have escaped without you. You did a great job. But I already have an angel to protect me. And you really shouldn't be here anyway. You should go. Besides, there's others waiting for you, isn't there."

She smiled.

I nodded. "It's time for you to go, Eve. Okay? You don't need to stay here anymore."

She straightened. Her complexion changed, color and blush returned to her skin. The ghastly pallor vanished. The tears on her checks evaporated. The bruises on her neck faded. She nodded, turned, hesitated with her back to me, and then drifted out of the room.

I stood, groaning as I did. My cell phone was lying where I'd dropped it. I bent down and picked it up. Good Lord, my head was swimming. I left the sub-cellar and made my way to the exterior door. Eve hovered there. Her gaze was distant. She focused on an unknown point somewhere above us and did not acknowledge me as I went to the door and pushed it open.

It was light outside. I squinted, trying to adjust to the glare. Against the light from the open cellar door, Eve was barely noticeable. Her body appeared little more than a silken shroud. Nevertheless, I could tell that she was looking at me, smiling.

Eve was no longer weeping.

As the ghost moved to the doorway and started to ascend the steps, she turned once more as if to make sure I didn't need her.

I smiled and nodded. "You did good, Eve. You saved me. I'll make sure the truth is known. I promise. Alright? Now it's time to go home."

She gazed up the cellar steps. But her vision drifted past them to somewhere further up and deeper in. She'd served her time in the hospital. It was never her real home anyway. As she ascended the steps, her pale figure became one with the daylight. Yet as she disappeared into the ether, a thick shadow passed before the doorway, completely obscuring it. My heart practically jumped into my throat. The residual power that remained in my hands sprung to life.

I stared at a hulking silhouette which now stood at the cellar door.

CHAPTER 23

R apha stood in the cellar doorway.

"Brother Moon!"

He ducked his head inside, entered, and just as he did, the ghost of Weeping Eve wafted past him. Or through him. Her form dissipated like fog against a bright sun.

"Oh!" Rapha gasped and stumbled back. "What was that? Something—Brother Moon, are you all right?"

"Yeah. I guess." I went to the door and looked up the steps into daylight. All evidence of the apparition was gone. "It was Eve."

"The poltergeist?"

"Yeah. But she's not nearly as evil as we thought."

"What was she doing here?"

"Hmm. Let's just say that she had one more thing to accomplish before her journey home."

Rapha stared at me. "You should never have left. The Summu Nura fear you, Brother Moon. As they should. They are looking for you. They want to stop you. Which means they know that we pose a threat."

"They almost *did* stop me. The Shroud was here, Rapha. I was paralyzed. It was some type of spell." I massaged my temples. I was going to have a headache the size of Jupiter. Suddenly, I remembered our mission and my complete loss of time. "How long was I down there? Do we still have time to make it to the altar?"

"Yes. But we've got to hurry."

Rapha helped me climb the steps. I groaned as I went. My joints felt doughy. I must remember to avoid those spells of slumber whenever possible.

"They have Audra," I said. "They're planning on using her as the sacrifice."

"We assumed as much."

When we reached the top of the steps, the rest of the earth guardians were waiting for me.

"How'd you know I was here?" I asked.

"Klammer." Quinn was sitting on a nearby planter, stroking his beard. "He and Audra have a thing, and when their communique stopped, he got concerned. Apparently, he tried to dissuade her from snooping around. When she said the Shroud was on to her, he feared the worst and pointed us in the right direction."

"This fella got us the rest of the way." Orphana was hunched over, one hand on her cane, her other scratching the cat's ears. "He was in the middle of the road, waiting, and he led us straight here." The cat purred and nuzzled into her touch.

I stared suspiciously at the feline. Humph. It was going to take a lot more than that for me to change my opinion of cats. Although maybe this was a good start.

The smug feline seemed aware of my feelings because it meowed, turned its nose up at me, and trod off.

Rapha hurried us to the street. He'd parked his truck in front of the Cammy but suggested we leave it to stay together and formulate a plan of attack. For some reason, I was thinking about the finger in the glove box and the godawful smell it would create if it remained in there too much longer. Oh well, I'd just have to add rotting flesh to the list of odors in the Cammy.

I discovered it was late afternoon. *Good Lord!* I had been out of commission for almost half a day. The waning sun had turned the horizon into a basin of burning smog. It took a few minutes to regain my walking legs. Apparently, the repercussions of a spell of slumber was not unlike a hangover from a weekend binge of Jack Daniels and cheap cigars.

Rapha fired the truck up and hit the gas. The radio was blaring some news report about Regulus and pockets of panic that had broken out throughout the city.

"There've been reports," Rapha said over his shoulder. "Runs on food and water. Some looting. People are taking this seriously."

"Wow," I said. "Guess that probably helps the Shroud."

"How so?"

"Spread out the cops. Draw attention away from the site. The more thugs and looters on the streets, the less attention they turn to the subway."

"So what did you learn about him?" Rapha said. "The Shroud?"

"For one thing, I learned it's not a *him*. It's a group. Pale, weird looking creeps. Clones or something. Etherea called them Netherworld muses, whatever that is. Five of them."

"Ugh!" Quinn scrunched his face in distaste. "Shoulda known."

"You've met them before?"

"Couple times. Pretty rare, actually. They only come when asked and usually leave a mess. They're strictly top tier. Amateur occultists need not apply. Mostly upscale wizards and summoners can call them up. The muses don't come cheap. Takes someone with lots of Netherworld cred and cajones to get the muses here."

Rapha added, "Netherworld muses are gods and goddesses of the dark arts. In Diades they serve Hail and harness the whetherweres, conflagration demonias used for ruin and devastation. The muses are basically ice nymphs. It appears that Etherea's gotten powerful enough to summon a group of them. That is not a good sign."

Quinn said, "Individually, they're fairly soft. Typical dark magic stuff—phantoms, craze curses. Things like that. But together they can be a real pain. Their power grows exponentially. So with five of them? You're looking at a Wall of Despair, if not a barrage of Bleak."

"Well," I said, "it would be nice to have some kind of plan of attack. I mean, is there a way to stop them?"

"First, you gotta cut through the BS," Quinn said. "Not let them mess with your head. That's usually half the battle."

I winced just thinking about their words and the clamp it seemed to exert upon my brain.

Quinn continued, "Then you have to find a way to break their link. If you can disarm the summoner, you can disrupt them. They work together, join their minds, gain power in their unity. Disrupt their bond, and you can compromise them individually. Once they scatter, they can be picked off. So identifying the leader is critical. In this case, Etherea is the most likely candidate. Cancel her out, the muses will crack. They're usually ready to get home, anyway. They find earth too warm and rather bland for their tastes."

"Okay," I said. "Defeat muses. Then what?"

"Stop the summoning and destroy the table."

"The indestructible table?"

"Exactly. And, oh, if Azrael happens to show up, we put her in her place."

I sighed. "Might as well bring about world peace while we're at it."

"Ndocron may be the key," Rapha said.

"What do you mean?" I asked.

"Ndocron contains the spread of dimensional rifts. It acts as a barrier against passage between dimensions. It's possible that Ndocron may act similarly upon beings that move between dimensions."

"So what are we talking about? A weapon made of Ndocron? A cage? And how do you even know it will work?"

"It's like everything else," Celeste said. "We don't." She smiled.

My cell phone vibrated. It was Kanya.

"Reagan! I've been calling you. Where are you?"

"Sorry. I was busy trying to unbind a spell of binding."

"Wha—? I went to your apartment. Where are you?"

"We're on our way to the subway."

"People are going crazy down there. Are you aware of that? It's a freakin' war zone. How are you planning on getting in, where at?"

"That's a good question." I glanced at the others. "Probably wherever less cops or angels are. Either way, we need to get to that altar. Even if it means slipping in through a storm drain."

"All right," Kanya said. "We'll meet you there."

"Hey. There's something else."

"What is it?"

I hesitated. But if she didn't deal with it now, we could all be in trouble later. "They have your mother."

The line grew quiet.

"Kanya?"

"I'm here."

"They caught up to her somehow. Or she found them. Anyway, they're planning on killing her. Kanya—they're going to sacrifice her." I paused to, hopefully, let that sink in. "We've got to get there. We've got to stop them. Kanya?"

"Yeah?"

"She's on our side."

The line went quiet again. She wanted to protest, to wriggle free from this emotional conundrum. Finally, she said, "We're on our way."

I wanted to remind her that this wouldn't be easy, or that complications and changes of plan would be inevitable. I wanted to tell her to be careful, and that this was shaping into a suicide mission. But she would know all that. Really, I wanted to tell her that I empathized with her plight and sort of understood her brokenness. I wanted to tell her that it wasn't a coincidence that we had come together and that she had saved my life, and I hers. I wanted to tell her that she was beautiful and that I was beginning to get a little crush on her. Instead, I acquiesced.

"Be careful, okay?"

"You, too."

The phone clicked off and I held it there for a minute. I thought about the totem and hoped to hell I didn't have to use it.

Rapha's driving had turned borderline manic. He barely missed some pedestrians and drove over a curb. Luckily, in that tank of his, if we struck something, we'd probably be inflicting far more damage than we incurred. Celeste kept telling him to slow down. She was sounding more and more like the cautious mother of the group. We passed the Tar Pits and the Wiltern, before screaming through MacArthur Park. I was pretty sure the trip was proof of angels, because on a normal day Rapha would have been cited half a dozen times along the way.

The plume of smoke became visible miles away, spreading over downtown like a toxic umbrella. I was sure it was coming from the subway project. Then again, perhaps doomsday mongers had simply torched the city to kick things off. As we crossed under the 110 and before we even reached the subway project, the congestion started. Blocks of snarled traffic and detours. TV crews and pedestrians were clamoring for sidewalk space. Several helicopters hovered overhead. In Los Angeles, police chases are like Olympic events. We cancel soap operas and game shows just to watch hot footage of some moron trying to outwit the cops in a blaze of glory. Well, that's what this was like. TV parasites and pedestrians everywhere. By the time we caught sight of the subway project, half the police force was there. Lights flashing and radios crackling. Swat teams and paramedics. Several storefront windows had been shattered. You'd have thought Armageddon had already begun. Well, maybe it had.

I was sure Jimmy was there. Hell, he was probably leading the charge. Suddenly, letting him in on my secret didn't seem as pointless as I'd thought. Although I felt bad for bringing him into this trouble. It wasn't the first time and hopefully, for his sake, wouldn't be my last.

Rapha finally got close enough for us to see that the subway entrance had been nuked. Smoke billowed from the entryway. Charred debris lay scattered nearby, evidence of some massive explosion. We'd never make it down into the tunnel, much less travel the two-and-a-half blocks it took to get there.

"Someone torched it," Quinn said.

"No," Orphana said. "It's a diversion."

"So what do we do now?" I asked.

The traffic was at a complete standstill. Honking horns sounded and car exhaust burned my eyes. A small car, a rice burner with an obnoxiously loud muffler, squeezed between lanes, zoomed over the curb, and struck the fence. People scattered. A young girl jumped out the passenger side, cursing. A bottle arced past the car, spraying liquid as it pin-wheeled, struck the sidewalk and shattered. A police copter barked something from its loudspeaker. Other choppers hovered overhead like a flock of vultures secretly hoping for blood and carnage.

"We gotta get outta here." Quinn directed his words at Rapha, with far too much accusation in his tone.

Orphana turned around and said angrily, "Cool it, Quinn."

Rapha stared forward, grinding his teeth. Then he slammed his palm on the steering wheel.

That's when I noticed that Celeste was bent forward, kneading her forehead with her fingertips, deep in thought.

"What is it?" I asked.

She did not respond.

"Celeste." I started to reach to her when she spoke.

"There's another way in. It's so simple. Why didn't I think of it? Metro 417." She looked up.

"The apartments?" I asked.

"They used to give tours down there," Celeste said. "Of the old subway. Remember?"

"She's right." Rapha glanced back at us. "We were approaching the complex yesterday when we encountered the men from NeoKor."

"That's probably why they stopped the tours," Celeste said. "The tunnels weren't condemned. They were haunted—with death angels. When the subway project got too close, everything hit the fan. NeoKor found the altar and that's when they closed the tours to the public. The maps," Celeste continued, apparently scanning her memory banks. "Near the intersection of First and Glendale, the tunnel makes a curve toward downtown. It parallels Fourth and terminates in the basement of the grand Subway Terminal Building. We were right there yesterday, you guys. We just came at it from the opposite direction."

"We can get in through the apartments," Quinn said. "No problem."

"No problem," Orphana looked over her shoulder, "unless someone's expecting us."

Rapha looked at us in the rearview mirror. "It's a chance we must take."

The traffic on one side had begun to move. Spotting an opening, Rapha slammed the gears into reverse and veered the truck onto the sidewalk. Pedestrians jumped from the way, cursing. Rapha apologized, though they could not hear him. He steered off the sidewalk, jammed the truck into Drive, and turned into an alley. It was so narrow that the truck's mirrors almost scraped the walls. From there, we took several side streets before spilling out near Pershing Square.

The high-end loft-style apartments came into view. Metro 417 had its own unique history. Just a block away from the LA Metro's Red Line, the luxury complex occupied a 1925 Renaissance Revival structure that was originally called the Subway Terminal Building. At its peak in the mid-1940s, the Hill Street station served 65,000 commuters each day. However, with competition from automobiles and an improved freeway system, subway traffic declined. Now it sat, an abandoned ghost station, a silent testimonial to the march of progress. And a world left in its wake.

Dusk was nearing. We had to hurry.

We circled the block debating amongst ourselves the best plan of attack. Go in the front or try to avoid notice and find some other means of entrance. Rapha pulled into the large Public Parking lot off South Hill Street, bordering the apartments.

Quinn grabbed Rapha's backpack and slung it over his shoulder. No sooner had we gotten out of the truck than Bernard bolted past us.

"Hey!"

The group stared at me. Then they followed my gaze to where the angel had stopped. Bernard stood panting, glistening with sweat. Of course, no one else could see him. The angel was staring back from whence he'd come. His eyes were wide. I turned back to see what he was looking at.

The entire skyline had become a dirty brown from the fire raging at the NeoKor site. However, something else was in the sky. It looked like a thundercloud, a roiling black fog folding into itself, and was moving through the streets and between the buildings. Bursts of lightning flashed inside it. To the average person, this probably looked like some odd cloud formation or perhaps a toxic mass unleashed by the fire. But my second sight told me it was much more. This cloud was not made up of vapor at all, but of barnacles. Millions of crustacean-like organisms interlocked and churning as a single mass. It reminded me of an undersea reef. Only this reef was seething. And headed straight toward us.

I would later learn that it was, indeed, a whetherwere. It was, no doubt, being summoned by the Shroud, as Quinn had said, to assist in their apocalyptic madness. But at the moment, I didn't have the time to appreciate the awful majesty of this beast from the lower realms.

"Do you see this?" I said to the group.

"Aw, man. Yeah. We see it." Quinn tore his gaze from the cloud creature and quickly scanned the area.

Apparently, others could also see this gathering cloud twining its way through the cityscape. Parking lot attendants and pedestrians had stopped to point and gape at this aerial phenomenon.

That's when Bernard jumped into my field of view and frantically motioned for us to follow him.

"That way!" I pointed in the direction Bernard had started jogging.

"The lobby?" Celeste asked.

Quinn said, "I thought the idea was to avoid attention."

"The best thing to do," I said over my shoulder, preparing to run, "is to not ask questions. Go. Go!"

Bernard led us through the parking lot, continually glancing over his shoulders to ensure we were following him. I remained behind the group, watching Bernard and calling out directions. He led us along the sidewalk to the entryway and then disappeared inside. For a team of superheroes, none of us moved worth a damn. If my chest wasn't undergoing some strange overhaul, I could have outrun the lot of them. Instead, I remained behind, watching Rapha lumber forward and Orphana limp along on her cane. I winced nearly every time my feet pounded the pavement. Celeste and Quinn seemed far more agile, but light years away from competing against the Flash.

By the time we reached the marble entry, the electronic keypad was shorting out. Bernard had that effect upon electronics. Through the gilded glass doors, I glimpsed the male receptionist hurrying off in the other direction. My guardian angel was providing cover.

Before I entered, I glanced back down the street. The whetherwere advanced, its smoky tendrils edging their way overhead, casting a dense shadow along the pavement. Barnacles began to cluster on the windows and ledges above, reassemble themselves, and work their way into the seams and openings of the structure. Had Bernard been doing battle with this thing? I could only imagine the type of invisible skirmishes that had been going on during the last twenty-four hours. But even more fear-inducing was the thought of having to engage the creature the size of a half-city block.

I held the door open. "Let's go! C'mon!"

We entered the lobby of Metro 417. The apartments had retained the original subway architecture and its Renaissance Revival stylishness. Soaring coffered ceilings, hand-crafted woodwork, Italian marble floors, and colorful mosaic tiles were just glimpses of a much grander era. But it was an ambiance we did not have time to enjoy.

To our right stood a bank of tenant elevators. To our left was the now empty front desk, and further down the lobby, a service elevator. The *Staff Only* sign disappeared as the elevator doors retracted. Bernard was inside the elevator, frantically motioning for us to join him.

"There!" I pointed.

As we scurried into the service elevator and the door began closing, a well-dressed man and woman were simultaneously exiting the tenant elevators across the lobby. They stared at our group, and then looked up as the security cameras throughout the lobby began shorting out.

The door closed and we descended. We barely had time to catch our breath before the door opened on the next floor. Bernard was waiting for us.

"There he is!" I said, pointing, and the group exited.

We stood in a well-lit hallway. Storage rooms and offices lined this area, and there was a trace of antiseptic and steam in the air. Bernard stood at an adjacent hallway and when I made eye contact with him, he tore off down that passage. I pointed the group in that direction and, after another turn, the angel stopped at an unmarked door and frantically jabbed his finger toward it.

"Door on the right," I said.

Quinn stopped at the door and stood panting. He must not have detected danger behind it because he nodded to me, opened the door, and looked down into a brick stairwell. A rusty gate with a *Keep Out* sign stretched across the landing below. Bernard was waiting at the gate and, when he saw me, leapt it with remarkable ease. He turned and motioned us to follow.

"Down the stairs, people. Let's go."

I waited as the team quickly entered the stairwell and started their descent. Before I climbed down, I turned. Sure enough, tentacles of fog were bleeding through the air ducts under the nearby office doors. The whetherwere was following us.

The air grew thick and dank as we descended several stories. Huge rusted pipes rumbled overhead; they were interlaced with cobwebs that wafted like ghost sails as we passed.

At the bottom of the stairwell were four large rooms. They smelled of soured liquor and rat shit. In the early 1900s, seventy miles of service tunnels had been built, connecting all the major hotels and municipalities in Los Angeles, from the Biltmore to City Hall. When Prohibition was enacted, those tunnels became dens of illegal activity where the police ran the rackets for the bootleggers. We had officially passed into such an area.

Bernard rushed into one of these rooms, and I followed. He stood, pointing to what appeared a hatch or a trapdoor in a wall. It had partly been boarded over. He knelt down, looked straight at me, and jabbed his thumb at the door.

"There," I said. "He wants us to go in there."

Quinn went to the spot, dug his fingers under one of the boards, and twisted it free. Plaster crumbled to the ground releasing the smell of mold. He removed another board, revealing a small tunnel descending into darkness. Quinn angled his head; he was sending his mind along the contours of this area, probing.

"It's a delivery chute," he said. "The kind they used during Prohibition."

Rapha said, "It leads down to a basement bar most likely, and probably the subway."

266

Quinn pulled the remaining wood off. The chute was framed by a roughly four-by-four jamb, made of wood, and looked much like a polished slide. Smooth grooves and scuff marks shone where boxes, crates, and people had entered or exited the place. I approached and stared down into the chute.

"You want us to go down there?" I asked Bernard.

He nodded enthusiastically, sweeping his hands through the air in a sliding motion.

Quinn knelt before the entrance with his head cocked.

"He's right." Quinn said. "There's a room. Let's go."

With that, Quinn gripped the frame and swung himself into the opening. His footfall sounded from below as he landed. A few seconds later, he called up for us to follow. One by one, we did. Rapha was the only one who had difficulty. He barely fit and I feared the chute might crumble under his weight. When it came my turn, I squatted, preparing to slide down. Then I turned back to Bernard. He was preparing to jog back up the steps.

"Hey," I called. "You're leaving us?"

He nodded.

"Now?"

Bernard motioned upward.

"Moon!" Quinn shouted from below. "Let's go."

Bernard frantically signaled for me to get going.

I hesitated. How many creatures had my guardian angel held off in my life? And how did he even stand a chance against the whetherwere? Unless, perhaps, he had friends coming to help him. But the thought of more beings as strange as Bernard was itself rather disturbing.

"Be careful, Bernard. Okay? I'll probably still need you."

He nodded and smirked as if to say, *Ya think?* Then he took the steps in Olympian grace, leaving a wash of golden haze behind him.

I slid down the chute to find myself in another smaller room. A bare bulb overhead illuminated a single wooden table lying broken on its side, surrounded by several old crates, presumably used as chairs. This room reeked of sour liquor and sordid tales. A single door was bolted from the inside. Quinn wrestled with the bolt. As he did, I got the distinct sense that something bad awaited us on the other side. The last door Bernard told me to not go through, the one at St. Vincent's, I disobeyed. Nevertheless, red flags were everywhere. Just as I was about to caution Quinn, the bolt sprang free.

Voices erupted, echoing in a spacious area. I glimpsed the subway tunnel just beyond the doorway. We could get to the Altar of Summoning from there!

Except for the fact that someone was now blocking our way.

Flashlight beams swung wildly and a scuffle of footfalls sounded.

A large man wearing a trench coat and a fedora ducked under the door and stepped into the room. His movements were unusual, twitchy and kinetic, and his body was oddly shaped, long and slender, almost like some animated action figure. Perhaps most startling was his flesh. It was course and scaly. As he entered the room, his coat swept open enough to see a large weapon holstered at his thigh.

Sam Spade meet Velociraptor.

"This area is off-limits." His voice was gruff and guttural. "How did you—?"

His eyes widened—they were strangely yellowish—as he surveyed the group.

"Ahhh." He smiled, revealing small, sharp teeth. "Imperia scum. It was only a matter of time. C'mon, boys!" He motioned to the shadowy forms outside the door.

Two accomplices joined him, and all three removed their weapons, which they aimed directly at us.

CHAPTER 24

Normally, the sight of a gun with Komodo dragons engraved along the muzzle, mounted with a canister and a laser site, would have demanded my attention. These weren't guns; they were miniature cannons. But being that the men aiming them at us looked like human-lizard hybrids, my focus was concentrated on these odd beings rather than the strange weapons they held. These three individuals were of an order I had never encountered. Their faces were slightly compact, with short, thick noses. Snouts almost. Their mouths were unusually wide, and their jaws heavy-set. If the L.A. Zoo was looking for some mascots, I think I'd found their guys.

"This is the end of the road for ya'," the tall one rumbled, his voice a scratchy baritone.

"Jake," said Quinn, readjusting the backpack over his shoulder. "Since when did reptoids join the Summu Nura?"

"We ain't joined anyone, Brain Boy!"

The individual named Jake glared at Quinn.

"Reptoids?" I gaped, incredulous, almost oblivious to our predicament. "Serious?"

"Yeah," growled Jake, glancing my way. "Got somethin' ta say 'bout that?"

"No, I—" I swallowed. "Then the Lizard People story is true."

Now Jake turned and looked squarely at me. He took two steps closer, brushing aside the table and toppling one of the crates. His nostrils flared, and then a thick tongue protruded, massaged his lips, and slipped back into his mouth. He was smelling me. His yellow eyes peered from under the brim of his stylish fedora. Now he turned the gun on me.

I raised my hands. My heartbeat was doing double-time. To my dismay, the strange tingling awakened in my sternum. *Not now. Please, not now.*

"You're new." He inched closer and wedged the gun under my chin. This individual, this *thing*, was a good six or seven inches taller than I was. Unnervingly jittery. And he smelled oily.

"Jake," Rapha said firmly. "We're not looking for trouble."

"Too late for that, Big Boy." Keeping his eyes fixed on me, and the muzzle now pressed against my gullet, Jake the lizard-man smiled broadly, revealing his mouthful of small gleaming prickly teeth. "Yeah. He's new, boys. Greener than a cow pasture. And I'm thinking he's a person of interest." He reached out, pointed straight at my chest, and jabbed his finger into it. Directly into my blazing scar. Hard. When I yelped, he poked the pistol further into my throat. His pupils narrowed and a film of clear skin winked across his lid, as if he was changing lenses to get a better view. "Yeah. Somethin's different about this one."

"You're locked up, Jake," Quinn said, stepping toward us, clearly attempting to deflect attention away from me. "Did you hear me? You're getting played."

"Get outta my head!" Jake spun around, now aiming the weapon at Quinn. "You freaks are all the same. Damn moles. Watch 'im, boys. He'll make you go cloudy. And the rest of them, they're Stellars. They got tricks. Keep a close eye on 'em. Got it?"

His companions grunted, their yellow eyes virtual slits.

"You're already mind-locked, you idiots." Quinn tapped his temple. "The Black Council is using you. They're playing with those pebbles you call brains. You're runnin' cover for the Shroud and you don't even know it." Quinn shook his head in disgust. "Reptoids. Can you get any stupider?"

"Black Council," Jake grumbled. "The Shroud. Pffhhh! We got one side—our own."

"Yeah? Well if you were smart, then you'd know we're no threat to you. We don't care about your treasure. Have we ever? We've got other business. Important stuff that can't wait. So if you'll excuse us..."

Quinn started toward the door, and they simultaneously turned their weapons on him. Jake fired what I assumed was a warning shot because it missed so badly. The charge sounded more like a punch than a gunshot. It whizzed past Quinn and slammed the wall behind him, sending chunks of plaster smattering across the floor.

Celeste and Orphana ducked and shielded themselves from the spray. And Quinn stopped in his tracks, clearly shocked that the lizard man would shoot.

"That's right!" Jake sneered. "You ain't going nowhere."

"You don't scare me, you scaly freaks," Quinn said, not backing down the slightest. "Something's about to go down that's gonna change things around here. For the worse. For this whole city. D'you hear me? Fact is, if we don't get outta here, you probably won't have any more treasure or tunnels to worry about. Because you and me are gonna be collateral damage. That's it. The rest of us will become cattle for the Overlords. That's right, the Black Council has busted through, Jake. So if you'll excuse us, we've got to go and save the world." Quinn moved for the door.

"Did you not hear me?" Jake shouted. "You ain't goin' nowhere! None of you are. We got a score to settle."

"And did you not hear me?" Quinn refused to back down. "We're talkin' the end of the world, Jake. End of humans. End of Lizard People. You wanna be implicit in that? Huh?"

"Get yer asses over there!" Jake motioned with his gun.

"They found the Black Altar!" Quinn shouted back at him. "Now there's a real treasure for you. Except they're summoning the grim reaper!"

"You lie! No one's got those smarts. Don't listen, boys."

"Relax, both of you." Rapha extended his arms, trying to plead for calm. "We can talk this out, Jake. It's not what you think."

"Tell that to Ace." Jake turned around and glared at Rapha. "Yeah. Cuz he ain't doin' any more talkin', is he? And neither are we. It's blood for blood now. And this time the blood is yours."

"You're making a mistake," Rapha implored. "That thing at the Red Iguana—we weren't involved."

"That's a lie, Big Boy! We have it on good authority that it was one of your crew that outed Ace. Only Stellars can liquefy folks. And you're the only Stellars 'round these parts."

"On *whose* authority?" Quinn said impatiently. "Sources please?"

"We got sources!"

"And who are they?"

Jake squinted. "Get against that wall before I ventilate your head. All of you!" Jake swept his weapon at us, signaling for the four of us to join Rapha near the opposite wall.

Rapha slowly stepped back, while Quinn and the ladies stepped away from him, creating more distance between them, leaving Jake and the reptoids in the middle. This was intentional and I immediately realized why. So I followed suit, sidestepping toward Quinn.

"Hey!" Jake barked towards Quinn's group. "I said over there!"

Quinn raised his arms. "Easy. Easy. Listen, we're no harm to you. Have we ever been? No. We haven't. Which is why you're gonna let us go. Aren't you. You're gonna let us go and not even remember this little incident."

"Shut up!"

Celeste made eye contact with me. Something was going to happen. She was telling me to move.

"Ace ran into trouble," Quinn said. "There are exotics everywhere these days. New ones are constantly showing up. Nomlies and Warpers. We're not the only ones who can liquefy anymore. Which means that if someone thought Ace was a threat, you guys are stepping up the food chain. Ain't that right?"

This seemed to give Jake pause. But only for a second. He shook himself. "I know what you're doing, Brain Boy! Step down! Now!"

The air was bristling. Quinn's sensors were in full gear now. If some sort of mind control was binding these reptoids, then Quinn's counter was creating an aural thunderstorm. I winced as a burst of psionic energy pulsated from the guardian. It left the air tasting metallic. Whatever Quinn was doing, it was sending my senses for a loop and making the room hum with invisible energy.

Quinn kept talking, trying to reverse whatever orders that the Black Council had fed into lizard men's brains. As he did, I glanced at Rapha, and then did a double take. His eyes were shut, his teeth gritted, and his fists clenched.

The hair on my arms stood on end as the gravity bubble blossomed.

The atmosphere warped as this cocoon of energy took shape, emerging from Rapha like some freaky amniotic sack. I was on its perimeter, and sidled further the opposite direction to avoid being crushed in its density.

Only this time, there was no crush.

Jake and his companions suddenly lost their footing and flung out their arms in an attempt to steady themselves. Particles of plaster from the wall rose into the air. The table and crates wafted from the floor, hovering there. Following this, the three reptoids ascended, weightless.

It was an anti-gravity bubble.

Jake and his crew were yelling, trying to steady themselves. But nothing within their circle was static. One of their weapons went off, but in that nexus of space, the bullet emerged—an orb of material practically the size of my fist—and quickly died, curling into empty space like some shard of ash. They fought through the table and chairs as if caught in some invisible current. They grappled for a hold, only to begin somersaulting in mid-air, a tangle of fumbling humanoids. It was like some Marx Brothers skit gone crazy. I was seasick just watching them.

"Ha!" Quinn laughed at the comedy of it. "Shoulda let us go when you had a chance."

"Just y-you—mph!—wait!" Jake shook his fist at Quinn before glancing off one of his companions and cartwheeling into the ceiling.

"Go," Rapha grunted out the words. "Run!"

He was clearly struggling to hold this massive bubble intact.

Quinn held the door open as Celeste helped Orphana into the subway.

"Wait." I turned to Rapha, then back to Quinn. "What about—? We need him."

"Sorry, Moon. This's how we roll. Besides, at this stage, you're more important than him. C'mon!"

We needed Rapha's guidance, his help. I stood gaping. I wanted to appeal to him. Rapha was as close to a mentor as I'd had in this crazy affair. He seemed to know my qualms and hesitations. He was sympathetic to my plight and the demands of my insane calling.

Rapha had his arms spread, fists clenched. The muscles on his massive tattooed forearms trembled. As he caught my gaze, a faint twinkle sparked in his eye. It said everything I needed to know.

If we'd been given powers to help mankind, then I had to trust that being on the side of right would work in our favor. But having an idea of what awaited us made leaving Rapha all the more difficult. Still, it didn't stop me. I left Rapha standing there like Atlas. Only in this case it wasn't the earth he was holding, but a gravity globe containing three lizard men who were furious, embarrassed, and completely unable to escape their predicament.

CHAPTER 25

We stepped into the old subway station. Hazy natural light shone faintly from somewhere up above. Sunset was very near. Ornate tiles lined the walls there. Some lay cracked and shattered on the ground, and a decaying ceiling stretched overhead, complete with arches and faded murals. The tracks had long been removed, yielding to earth and broken, lichen-covered cement slabs. A rusty tin arrow hung cockeyed on the wall displayed with the words *Hill Street* station, the original terminus of the Pacific Electric Railway's Subway branch. Other signage, apparently untouched for decades, identified tracks one and two, which had long since removed.

Quinn dug in the backpack. "He can't hold them for long. Not that many." He handed a flashlight to Celeste, and kept one for himself. Before he hurried us along, I cast one last look back at the room where we'd left Rapha. *Brother Moon*, I could imagine him saying. *Knights errant! Knights errant.* That brought a smile to my face.

Celeste led the way, scanning our surroundings with her flashlight beam and giving directions. I stayed with Orphana to help her along.

"He'll be all right," she said, consoling me about Rapha. "He's managed worse scrapes than that."

"I've lost too many people lately," I said. "I don't need to lose another."

"Oh, I hear you. And I'm not sayin' this in any way to discourage you. Lord knows we can use as much hope as we can muster. But, thing is, in our line of work, it's better to not hold on to each other too tightly." She smiled, a broken smile that, I was sure, spoke from experience.

I nodded. However, I worried that the 'hope' we clung to was far more fragile than any of us dared to admit.

Despite being good with her cane, the combination of uneven terrain and occasionally loose soil made the going difficult for Orphana.

"I'd cluster if it wasn't that far," she said. "Or if I knew I wouldn't lose my other leg in the process." She chuckled.

"You're doing fine."

"Well, thank you." Then she looked over her shoulder and said to Quinn. "I'm overdue for that new leg you promised me."

"Tell you what," Quinn said. "If we make it out of this one, how 'bout I add a prosthetic flamethrower or something."

"A flamethrower?" Orphana laughed. "Maybe something a little more discreet?"

"The intersection is up ahead" Celeste said. "Soho will be to the left. The tunnel that branches north will be ours. That's where the NeoKor project connects, where we were yesterday. The chamber with the altar isn't far from there."

We passed a conveyor belt, some tools, and a portable toilet. The stench of burning oil or rubber tainted the air, and eventually smoke began gathering on the ceiling and pooling in the overhead crevices of the tunnel. Whatever was going on at the main excavation site was making its way here.

We soon reached the intersection. Flood lamps on large tripods stood lightless, like limbless trees in some subterranean wasteland. Except for water pattering somewhere, it was unusually quiet. Celeste stopped and shined her flashlight beam ahead, revealing the wooden catwalk we had followed yesterday.

"There it is," she said. "The altar is down there. It isn't much further."

Shards of clothing lay near the catwalk entrance as did charred wood and moldering animal bones. We peered into the huge dark aperture that opened before us. In that moment of silence, it seemed as if each one of us was weighing out the possible outcomes of our next steps, what the personal cost might be, and whether any of us would return.

"So," I said. "Is there a plan of attack here?"

Orphana said, "Hon, sometimes the best stories are made up as you go. Trust me, when the time comes, you'll know what needs done."

"Meaning, there's no plan?"

"We know what we have to do," Quinn said, looking past me. "Getting there in one piece is half the battle. Staying in one piece is the other half. Just promise me, if you do that thing you do, please don't aim at us. Okay?"

"Um, I'll try my best."

And that was pretty much it.

Celeste stepped up on the catwalk. I helped Orphana onto it and then looked back the way we'd come, secretly hoping for Rapha to appear. Hopefully, without angry Lizard People chasing him. But he did not.

We followed the tunnel as it angled slightly. The wooden planks groaned eerily as we went. My eyes burned from the smoke, but even worse, was the knot in my gut. I could feel her in the dark—Etherea. She was up ahead, waiting for us, building power. Klammer said that I'd gotten their attention and that they were worried about me. And now that I'd broken their spell—with the help of a misunderstood poltergeist—I was pretty sure Etherea'd be even more pissed. So, yeah, they knew that we were coming.

As we walked, the shadows grew with Invisibles. They'd come from all corners of their accursed hovels to celebrate the summoning of the Archangel of Death. Their yowls and pained merriment rose and fell in my head. Along the way, I glimpsed pale appendages wrenched at improbable angles, and faces, scabbed and fevered. Hellions. Were they in the space around me or my own head? Either their presence was oppressive. Closing in upon me. I feared I might soon reach the threshold of my own comprehension. Perhaps this was the prelude to madness. I wiped sweat off my forehead and took several deep breaths, trying to compose myself. It did not help. I wondered if I was being wrapped in some spell. Or was this simply the overflow of Saint Death and her ghastly train?

"Heads up, people." Quinn's words yanked me from my malaise. "I'm getting lots of signals here."

I nodded foolishly in response to Quinn's caution. He was right. Something was up ahead. We had entered an invisible channel that was jammed with conflicting frequencies.

Suddenly, Celeste doubled over and her flashlight clattered to the walkway. It rolled off the path, sending beams of light glancing crazily about the tunnel.

"Cel!" Quinn called.

Orphana reached to her, as Quinn squeezed past us, combing the area ahead with his flashlight beam to see if something was visible. The intersecting catwalk and the adjoining shaft were just up ahead. We had reached the chamber of the Altar of Summoning.

Quinn knelt over Celeste. "What is it? Are you okay?"

She quickly got to her feet, but doubled over again.

"It's—" She groaned. Then she pointed to the chamber. "It's in pain."

"What—?" Quinn shined the light that way, but there was nothing. "What're you talking about?"

"Inside there," Celeste said, grimacing. "I can feel it."

Suddenly, I realized what she felt. I shook myself from the funk, knelt down, and grappled for the flashlight that had fallen off the catwalk. I retrieved it and squeezed past everyone to the front of the line.

"I'll do it," I said, and headed towards the entrance of the shaft.

Forcing the darkness out of my brain, I crept forward with the light poised on the entrance. The smell of incense was growing thick in the air. They'd probably already started their ritual. I could only hope that Audra was still alive. From the dark sub chamber, far down below, I heard the chanting. The

Shroud's discordant, monotone canticle rising from the earth. What manner of evil were they now summoning?

As I reached the entrance to the shaft, my flashlight beam glimpsed something moving in the chamber up ahead. Tendrils of fog twined out from a dark form that, when struck by my flashlight beam, lurched back into the shadows. Something was lurking inside. Was it the death angel or some new monstrosity? Whatever it was, it wasn't preparing to attack.

It was hiding.

I pressed my hand behind me, signaling for the others to wait. I stood for a moment, sending my thoughts ahead of me. It was pain that I felt. Whatever was inside was radiating suffering and torment. I inhaled deeply and followed the catwalk into the first chamber, focusing my light in the direction of the figure I'd glimpsed inside.

It was the death angel. Its neon red eyes undulated inside its concave black face. The skeletal rattling sounded as it scrambled to block our path into the sub-chamber below. This was probably its assignment—to keep us from reaching the Table of Summoning. However, something was terribly wrong with the angel.

Celeste peered over my shoulder and gasped. "Oh, my God."

The death angel moved awkwardly, in stilted motions. Shambling sideways, strafing, its lower body moved in unsettling fashion. Its ankles scraped the earth. So I directing my light at its feet.

They were facing the opposite the direction.

The angel had managed to reassemble itself after my attack. However, its lower torso was reversed. While the top half of the angel faced me, its lower half faced the opposite direction.

The angel's eyes flared. As it hissed, the great raven wings unfurled, stirring dust and debris in the chamber. However, even this motion appeared spastic and abnormal.

Not knowing what the creature would do, we instinctively moved back from the entrance of the shaft. Except for Celeste. She ducked past me and entered the cave.

"Hey!" Quinn attempted to push past me. "Celeste! Hold up."

"Wait a second!" I said, preventing Quinn from following her.

"Let go of me, Moon." He had me by both shoulders. I could feel the passion, not only in the intensity of his grip, but in my brain. If this guy couldn't land a punch, he could always choke out my conscious mind. Knowing this, I tried to see what Celeste was up to while cordoning my own mind from Quinn's assault.

"She knows what she's doing." I growled the words.

Actually, it was a bit of a risk saying that. While I thought I knew what Celeste was doing, and what she was feeling, I was not at all convinced it would have a positive outcome on our current situation.

She ducked under the wooden handrail and left the walkway. Orphana and I managed to hold Quinn back as Celeste approached the death angel. He spat and cursed, but knew we were right. Celeste stopped and stood before the mangled maelohim.

The angel's wings were arched in defense. The coarse black appendages brushed the ceiling of the chamber as it hunched forward in a ghastly stature, trembling and spewing out its dry graveyard breath.

Its foggy aura began to spread, swirling gently into the air and coiling its way across the floor to Celeste. But she did not retreat. In fact, she stepped toward the creature.

"Celeste!" Quinn yelled. "Get away!"

We gripped him by opposite arms and fought to restrain him.

"Let her be," Orphana said firmly.

Celeste's actions caused the angel to rear up and advance. But with its feet facing backwards, its knees angled the opposite direction, the movement was mechanical and erratic. As awful as this creature was, it was painful to watch its tortured movement.

The angel shook itself, perhaps angered by its inability to function as it could. Its tongue lapped from its mouth, fingering forward like a vine clambering for a trellis. Its foggy tentacles wafted toward Celeste, lapped across the cavern floor, and pooled at her feet. With one flap of its massive wings, the fog billowed to Celeste, roiling about her like a gray cloak. Demons appeared to flit and tumble inside this fog. I could see them. Pale white forms, fetal cherubs spilling forth, eyeless, graceful in their corpulence. They were beautiful in a way. Looking at them made me want to stare. What kind of beings must these be, created eons ago, now given to darkness? The angel swayed. Staggered. It sucked its tongue back into its gaping face and screeched, clenching its emaciated harpy-like hands as it did.

I felt pity upon this poor creature. As, apparently, did Celeste.

She glanced at us. Her eyes glistened with tears. "It's in pain."

That's what she'd felt emanating from the cavern upon our approach—pain. As a healer, perhaps she did not view this as a monster at all. It was still God's creature—a tormented, evil creature—but nevertheless one that evoked mercy.

"I can..." She smiled shyly. "I think I can heal it."

I glanced at Orphana.

"No!" Quinn lurched forward. "Celeste. It's tricking you!"

We fought to retain our grip on him. Celeste stepped toward the hellish angel with her hand outstretched.

"Let go of me!" Quinn shouted.

I could feel his mind pummeling the atmosphere, an invisible cyclone of fear and devotion.

Celeste looked at him, appearing somewhat aghast. "It's in pain, Quinn. I can—it can be healed."

"Wait!" Quinn tensed his upper body, inhaled deeply, and threw us off. Orphana and I were flung backwards into the wooden railing. Then he leaned forward. "Cel! You do not want that thing inside you. D'you hear me? It'll kill you. Cel, it'll kill you."

As he prepared to hurdle the handrail and join Celeste, Orphana approached and gently extended her cane across his chest. He immediately stiffened. A brown, earthen radiance swelled from her cane. It no longer seemed like a simple walking apparatus, but an ancient oak—no, a forest—condensed into a single instrument. Her words were calm and measured.

"She can get us through this, Quinn." Orphana smiled confidently. "This is *her* calling, remember? It's not mine or yours. Besides, this is how we roll. Correct?"

She held her cane at his chest. A dense, innate luminosity seemed to pulsate from the simple instrument. Quinn sighed heavily, and drooped his head. As Orphana lowered her cane, whatever properties had been evoked in the instrument, subsided. Quinn stood motionless and then slumped forward. It was the same thing Orphana had said to me—this is *your* calling. However, it was her cane that drew my attention. Never once had I considered it as possessing power. But now I wondered if this common orthopedic device actually doubled as a Staff.

Celeste wiped a tear from her cheek and turned back to the death angel. She was already glowing.

The death angel stomped the ground and its wings unfolded overhead. As Celeste approach with her hand pulsing blue electricity, its trembling stilled and its wings drooped to earth. The angel did not appear defeated, as much as it did submissive. Its concave face peered toward the healer.

As Celeste approached, the fog emanating from the death angel cocooned her, twining up her thighs and her torso. Celeste outstretched her other hand. The familiar blue glow undulated within the haze. For a moment, I feared she might be swallowed and absorbed into the ghastly swathe, until I realized that the fog was not moving toward her.

Rather, Celeste was absorbing the fog into herself.

Strands of the gloomy vapor drew into her fingertips, and soaked into her pores. Her body arched as it did. The death angel and its essence were absorbed into her. Celeste had become a vacuum, a receptor, ingesting death into herself, drawing the darkness and hate and death into her very own being.

I had once also taken death into myself. The memory caused an unusual, but pleasant thought to enter my mind. Yes, the event had been discomfiting for me. But knowing that the exertion of my power had released or healed someone else, tempered the pain. I had the same healing ability as Celeste. Of course, I had never absorbed a death angel. Perhaps one day I, too, could perform such a feat. This thought did not, however, make me less amazed at what I was witnessing.

Celeste's skin turned pale and ashen. Yet her hands blazed. Her red hair wafted about her, as if she was floating on an invisible tide. All those damned souls. All of the remorse and misery. Eons of suffering were cataloged inside this angelic abomination. And my fellow earth guardian inhaled it. Tears streamed her face. Her body shook to the point of convulsion.

As the wings of mist disappeared, the angel followed suit. The veins of fog thinned. Its orifices surrendered their vitality. The creature gasped, drawing deeper breaths. Then it arched its back and staggered. It struck the wall behind it and stumbled forward. Starting at its feet, a ripple passed through it, and the angel's torso began to disintegrate. Rather than falling to the ground, the fragmenting particles clustered. Soon, the death angel's body became a throng of small, dark, winged creatures that circled and burst into the air.

The maelohim evaporated into a cloud, which sped from the chamber and rushed towards the exit we now stood at. We stumbled back on the wooden catwalk, attempting to prevent from being struck by the manifestation. We were pummeled by soft, dusty objects. I ducked with my arms over my head, trying not to breathe. When the living cloud passed, I looked up to see it fleeting into the subway. I bolted after it, and stood watching the strange fogbank flitter off into the shadows of the subway.

Orphana hurried out and joined me. We stared into the tunnel as what remained of the death angel dissipated into the gloom.

"What was it?" Orphana wondered.

"I don't know," I said. "Maybe what it always was."

That's when I realized that my fist had closed upon something living. It fluttered inside my cupped palm. I carefully opened my hand to discover that I'd captured one of the objects.

A large moth rested in the palm of my hand.

Orphana came to my side and we peered at the insect. Its antennas unfurled and it opened its wings, revealing bright red underwings.

A *death angel moth*?

It shivered. Then it flew from my hand and flitted off in the direction of its pack.

We stood momentarily breathless by the event.

"Celeste!" Orphana exclaimed, and hurried back into the shaft. I followed.

Quinn remained on the catwalk, staring. Celeste was still standing, with the healing glow ebbing away from her arms and hands. As we watched, she collapsed. Quinn vaulted the handrail, attempting to catch her, but was unable. Celeste crumpled to the ground, her skin as gray as a corpse. If I'd not seen her breathing, I would have thought she was dead.

"Aghh!" Quinn yelled. "I told her!"

I helped Orphana under the railing—keeping a close eye on her cane as I did so—and we joined them.

"She did what was necessary," Orphana said, standing over Celeste.

"Yeah," Quinn muttered, scooping his hands under her head. "Necessary and stupid."

I leaned over Celeste. My own hands were tingling with power. Not only was such an act of mercy inspiring, it seemed to awaken a sense of nobility within me. I studied her features like I hadn't before. The light freckles. The thin lips that were always perpetually poised to smile. Perhaps I was completely wrong to see my gifts as a cosmic burden destined to make me, and everyone around me, miserable. Maybe the cost was actually worth it.

Celeste's eyes fluttered and opened. When she saw us huddled over her, she smiled.

"You did it, girl." Orphana reached down and squeezed her hand.

"You did it, all right," Quinn said. "And you scared the hell out of us in the process."

Celeste attempted to sit up and we helped her. The color was returning to her skin. She spent a moment composing herself and then looked at me.

"See?" she said. "We can do this."

Footfall and voices echoed from the subway. Someone was calling our names. Quinn helped Celeste to her feet and together we turned to see who was approaching. The boards creaked as someone advanced on the catwalk. I was greatly relieved when Kanya entered the chamber and stood with her arms outstretched and body poised.

"Reagan?" she called. "Is that you?"

"It's me." I turned the flashlight to the others. "It's us."

She hurried in, followed by Mace and Rapha. When he saw us huddled around Celeste, Rapha snapped the handrail, pushed past us, and came to her side.

"What happened? Are you all right?"

"I'll survive," Celeste said. "What about you?"

Rapha nodded. He was dripping sweat, breathing heavily, and appeared greatly fatigued. "I left the reptoids at the hotel. They were still shaken. They won't stay that way for too long. They'll be here eventually. Maybe. Either way, we must hurry." He motioned to Mace and Kanya. "I found them on the way."

Mace carried a large duffel bag over one shoulder which, I assumed, contained some of his many exotic weapons. But no bullets that I knew of could stop Black Magic.

"The SoHo tunnel's been boarded up for years." Mace gestured back into the subway. "We used to practice explosives training down there. Figured we'd bypass the commotion and come at it the opposite way. Luckily, we ran into him."

"But we have company," Rapha said, pointing back out the subway.

I ducked out to see the whetherwere coiling along the ceiling of the cavern, slowly tumbling our way. Lightning burst angrily inside the churning vortex.

We'd reached the end of the road. Ground zero. Absolutely.

Rapha drew us in and like a quarterback facing fourth and long, squatted down to make eye contact with each of us. "We can do this, guardians. Our time is not up. And when it is, we still do not go gently into the night. So, onward! Heaven is with us, my friends."

Light flashed from down below. The chanting rose in intensity. Our appointment with destiny had arrived. Before we made that final descent, I said, "You're right, Rapha. Heaven's with us. And so is hell."

CHAPTER 26

O ther than hating crowded spaces and having a general dislike for human beings, claustrophobia was never a huge issue for me. Until I stepped into the tunnel that descended into the Chamber of Summoning. It wasn't courage that made me lead the way. In part, it was wonder. What must the summoning of an archangel look like? Of course, the other part was a strange concession to destiny. If a map of the future really existed, if my own destiny had already been written, then resisting that outcome was foolish. However, it could probably also be argued that racing headlong into trouble might unduly speed up the fate already waiting.

We descended the shaft. The light from the chamber below grew, as did the chanting. My breath came in short, choppy draws. A dozen scenarios played themselves out in my head, most of them about as implausible as the script for a Michael Bay film.

With Mace's arrival, there were seven of us now. Seven is a good number. Probably not good enough to prevent the slaughter of a million Angelinos, but still, a good number.

When I finally stepped into the chamber I was already hyperventilating. The scene before me only added to a growing sense of helpless abandon.

Audra lay on the black altar, bound by some of the discarded rope. She was in obvious pain, but I was unable to see any wounds. If there was any question about whose side she was on, this laid it to rest.

The Santa Muerte shrine pulsated with innumerable candles, the visage of the skeletal Saint Death glowing eerily. A scapula with a skull draped her neck. Fruits and herbal bouquets lay piled at the statue's feet, where a block of incense smoldered. The Shroud stood shoulder to shoulder on the opposite side like some hellish choir, witnesses of the ceremony. They chanted in unison, words and incantations from other tongues. A hellish haiku. The sound echoed in the cavernous room. Movement along the ceiling caused me to look up. The whetherwere circled overhead, filling the cavern roof. Ribbons of barnacles were spilling from every crevice, merging with the creature's amorphous body.

Etherea stood in front of the altar. Her visage was smoldering, her smile a toxic smack-down. Whatever connection she had to the Black Council, it was operating at max bandwidth. A black rosary draped her neck—probably replacing the Regulus pendant I'd destroyed—each bead a thorn. The cross was inverted in satanic fashion. Her face was painted like some transient character from *Dia de los Muertos*, the Day of the Dead.

The team spread out on either side of me, along the perimeter of the site.

Etherea stood before us, her back to the shrine of Saint Death. She watched as we entered, her arrogance unwavering. Clearly, she was unconcerned about us or our numbers. Or any possible powers we might possess. Hell, we could've plowed a tiger tank through the wall and she probably wouldn't have broken a sweat.

She shook her head in disgust. "That's the last time I trust a reptoid. But, hey, the gang's all here. So let's make the most of our short time together, shall we?"

And with that, she turned and retrieved a ceremonial blade—by all appearances, the same one the rockabilly vampire had tried to carve the scar out of my chest with.

"In the spirit of fairness," Etherea said. "The Elder Ones suggested we wait for your arrival before enacting the ritual. It's the old 'Killing two birds with one stone' thing, I suppose. Of course, we weren't expecting all of you to make it this far. Chalk it up to resilience, if you wish. Although, I tend to see it more as sheep being led to the slaughter. And now that the sun has set and Regulus rises, that is exactly what will happen to you, and her—you will be slaughtered. Just like dumb sheep."

Etherea raised the blade over Audra's chest.

"Lord Azrael!" she shouted. "Receive now thy sacrifice!"

"Lord Azrael," the Shroud chanted in unison, mimicking their summoner. "Receive now thy sacrifice."

"Chaos and order, between it, thou dwells." Etherea spoke the words, as if reading from some memorized tome. "Awaken, oh Lightless One."

"Awaken!" cried the Shroud.

"From the Emeralds of Eden and the Hollows of Hail, Awaken, oh *Malak al-Maut*."

"Awaken!"

It was the Grimoire of Azrael!

The muses' words were followed by song. Their voices joined in a discordant, mournful refrain. It was so unnerving, so damned dreadful, that the sound seemed to drain the atmosphere of energy and left me wanting to pull my hair out by its roots.

Etherea watched us twisting under the weight of the muses' song; she smiled, and raised the blade higher.

"La, la, la, la!" I shouted in mockery, waving my arms like some maniacal conductor.

It was a lame move. But other than storming Etherea and attempting to wrest the blade from her before she plunged it into Audra's chest, I wasn't sure what else to do to stop the proceedings.

Quinn glanced at me with a pained look, and shook his head. Apparently, he thought it was a lame move, too.

Nevertheless, it accomplished what it was intended to—it momentarily stopped the muses' hellish cantata and left Etherea gaping.

"Thank you!" I exclaimed. "Now, hold on. Can we all—let's just take a deep breath here. I mean, we can talk this out. That's right. Let's not go and—"

"Talk it out?" Etherea laughed, incredulous. "Talk what out? So would you prefer I sever her head? Is that it?" She moved the blade to Audra's throat. "Hydras are tricky like that, as you know. It's either the heart or the head. Limbs and digits can be regrown. So take your pick—head or heart? Which is it?" Her eyes fixed upon me. "Because that's all the talking I'm doing, errand boy."

As I opened my mouth to speak, she said, "Okay. Head it is."

She repositioned the dagger on Audra's neck.

With that, the chanting of the Shroud resumed. Their unholy strain had a physical effect upon the environment, bleeding it of color and vitality. The air was thick with incense; it merged with the song, becoming a toxic brew. I could not allow myself to succumb to their spell again!

The whetherwere had reached its fullness and swirled overhead, a massive lightless whirlpool. It was bearing down on us, descending closer to the floor with every rotation.

Audra's eyes were open now. She looked at us and then squirmed against the restraints, forcing Etherea to press the blade ever more closely to her throat.

"We beseech thee, oh Azrael!" Etherea shouted.

"We beseech thee, oh Azrael!" The Shroud repeated her words in uncanny unison.

"Take this your sacrifice."

Again, the muses spoke her words in their lifeless monotone.

"Saint Death!" Etherea looked squarely at me. "Awaken!"

"Okay, lady!" I yelled. "You had your chance."

As I said this, Quinn burst forward like a rampaging bull toward the altar. As much as I did not care for the guy's cockiness, I had to admit, he had balls. Yet as he barreled forward, he abruptly lurched to stop.

In fact, he hung in midair.

Quinn had only advanced five or six feet when something akin to a sheer curtain appeared. A shower of sparkling blue droplets burst to life and disappeared. An invisible veil surrounded the perimeter of the altar. I could detect a faint rippling in the atmosphere. The Black Altar was protected by some sort of a translucent barrier.

Quinn bellowed as he struck this barrier. The veins in his temple swelled as if they were about to burst. He arched his back and then doubled over in pain. He remained suspended in midair. I was unsure if everyone could see the diaphanous curtain to which he clung. But it didn't matter. Because seconds later, Quinn dropped to the floor, convulsing, seizing his gut and trembling in excruciating pain.

"Quinn!" Celeste ran to him.

"Wait!" Rapha stared at Etherea and then shifted his gaze to the crystalline rippling curtain. "A Veil of Tears. They've built a Veil of Tears."

"Oh, my God." Celeste hesitated. Then she reached for Quinn's foot, which rested outside this gauzy barrier that draped him.

"Be careful!" Rapha cautioned. "Don't touch it."

"It'll kill him," she said.

I glanced at Etherea who had stopped to watch our feeble attempts.

"What is it?" I asked Rapha.

"Hellions," he said. "A Veil of Tears is used to punish them, incarcerate the wicked. If it penetrates far enough, his heart will stop. It will freeze in place. Its touch is toxic to humans, Brother Moon." Rapha's lip curled in anger. "Unless we can stop the Shroud, it will poison him."

"Stop the Shroud," Etherea said. "By all means." She curtsied mockingly.

Celeste gripped Quinn's foot and, with Rapha's help, they pulled him out from the weird liquid-like barrier. He lay, trembling, in an apparent state of shock, curled in upon himself and muttering indistinguishable words. Thin icy veins of blue began to web his body.

"He's freezing!" Celeste yelled. "Rapha!"

"Of course he's freezing!" Etherea shouted. "They're ice nymphs, you fools. Are you that lame?" Then she spread her arms. "Be my guest. Whoever makes it through alive gets first crack at me." Her haughty gaze flicked back and forth between us. "What? No takers?"

The Shroud was now chanting words of arcane tongues, voicing some ancient grammar of the earth. Somewhere in the back of my brain, I knew this language and could twist it for my own purposes. Yet my understanding was infantile, and now served only to frustrate me. Quinn's screaming joined the Shroud's chants, and the sound rose in odd accord.

"This is how your world ends," she said, her words a withering scorn. "Not with a bang, but with its heroes' whimpers."

"Brother Moon!" Rapha looked at me, imploring some action.

"What do you want me to do?" I protested.

"She controls the Shroud." Rapha pointed at Etherea. "Stop her, and we can break their spell and pierce the Veil."

"You want me to jump. I—" I pointed to my chest. I knew I could do it. I could summon the power. If I concentrated, I could do it. If I drew out my anger. If I let myself see the wormholes, summon the spatial trajectories. But something was holding me back. Something relentlessly defensive and small.

It was fear.

It was self-preservation.

If I jumped again, the hole in my chest would become a crater. I would be history. *Man swallowed by dimensional portal inside him.* That would be the headline. Besides, how did I know I could even make it through this barrier? In reality, I might suffer the same fate as Quinn.

Rapha could see me wrestling inside myself. His words were full of compassion, but bristling with resolve. "There are no guarantees, Brother Moon. There never was. This is our calling. You're the Seventh Guardian. You've got to try."

It's difficult to describe the complete disjunction of that moment. *Seventh Guardian.* What in the hell did that obligate me to? Was this going to be a constant gamble between life and death? You know, believe you're the Seventh Guardian and throw your destiny to the wind? My next jump would surely swallow my entire torso. If Klammer lost his head, then I would lose my core anatomy. Well, maybe that was, indeed, my calling—to lose myself. Talk about a raw deal.

"The mighty Imperia." Etherea mocked. "And you're the best they can offer? It's a disgrace! You know that? The Imperia is an absolute disgrace."

God, this woman was annoying.

Yet as I stared at her, projecting immeasurable hatred and bad karmic vibes, two arms—just arms—appeared around Etherea's throat. They appeared out of thin air and formed like a cloud. Coalescing. Clustering.

I had not been with this raggedy crew for long, but at that moment, I think I got a sense for how this thing was supposed to work.

I turned to Orphana. Her cane lay on the ground beside her. Her arms were outstretched but from the elbow on, they were not visible. They were gone. She had transmigrated her arms through the barrier and was choking Etherea on the other side. It took me a few seconds to recalibrate my senses. Nevertheless, the attacker's forearms were indeed detached from her body and very much attached to the person's throat across the room.

Apparently, Etherea was unprepared for this. She dropped the dagger and grabbed those two disembodied hands, attempting to remove them from her throat.

That's when everything changed.

The chanting of the Shroud faltered. No, it didn't stop. Rather, it became more frenzied. Their unity appeared compromised. Even their tight-knit huddle that they'd been standing in started to fracture. The Veil of Tears sheared before my eyes. It didn't disappear. It dissipated. Kind of like a thunder shower that becomes a sprinkle, and then a mist.

Etherea was turning blue, and the Veil of Tears was drying up.

Quinn gasped. He lay on the floor, cocooned in a fetal state. But the change in the ice curtain affected him. He moaned, reached up, and readjusted the glasses on his head. Then he sat up.

The rest of Orphana migrated. It occurred in parts. First her head and shoulders appeared beside Etherea. Then her torso. I glanced over at her body, the space that she had just occupied. All that remained was her lower body. Her hips, skirt, and boots. This alone should have given a man pause. But it quickly dissolved and joined the transmigration on the opposite side of the Veil of Tears. Only her prosthetic leg remained standing in place.

The more Orphana passed through, the more her body materialized on the opposite side and became invested in choking Etherea, the more the Veil of Tears dried up and dissolved.

Admittedly, I was not ready for this. I had been bemoaning my role as the Seventh Guardian only moments before. But now the theater seemed wide open. This did not simplify my next decision. But what followed helped.

Cricket burst into the scrim.

She was cursing, pointing at her mother, and laughing insanely. For a moment, I thought she would retrieve the blade, leap upon Audra, and stab the woman herself. But instead, she faced the Shroud. Orphana's materialization had already caused them to falter. The five figures, upon seeing Cricket enter their circle, appeared at a complete loss. Should they assist their summoner or turn their powers to the spunky ninja chick spinning towards them?

That brief moment of confusion allowed Cricket to plow into them, breaking their chain and sending them shrieking to opposite sides. Whether it was intentional or not, by disrupting their proximity to one another, Cricket had disrupted the communal power of the Shroud with the most eloquent martial arts moves one could imagine. I watched her, captivated, and began to wonder if my role in this whole affair was more as witness than an actual participant.

I glanced back at the spot Kanya had been. Mace stood there holding a rifle aloft. It was similar to the net gun he had brandished at the Asylum last night. Only the casing on this one was massive. But why a net gun? He was visually trying to locate the unpredictable shapeshifter. However, his rifle was trained on the altar, not at Cricket. Did he simply want to stop, rather than kill, Etherea? Then why not just put a bullet through her kneecap? Mace and I briefly made eye contact, and he winked when we did. At the moment, I was hoping that he'd brought his tranquilizer gun with him, because by the looks of it, we'd need to stop Cricket's rampage. If she made it to her mother, she'd pound her into a pulp.

The Shroud was no match for Cricket. Quinn was right—muses were soft. I watched her ducking and jibing, slamming shins and separating elbows. She didn't give a shit what spell was being conjured by what person against what foe. All Cricket knew was revenge. And rage. Rage against her mother. And anyone that would stand in the way of that rage.

She cartwheeled into the group, sending them tumbling in different directions. Cricket burst onto her feet. "Ha-ha!" She clapped her hands. "C'mon, creepoes!"

She landed an elbow to one of the muses, and black blood spilled from its nose. This started a chain reaction as all the muses, whether they'd been struck or not, began bleeding from their noses. Frantically, another muse crouched and began chanting. A crack of thunder rumbled overhead. Had it emanated from the whetherwere? I wasn't sure. But its signature spread out across the floor, reverberating in the walls and beams. Cricket lost her balance and tumbled back. But just as quickly, she vaulted to her feet, a dervish of energy, and slid into the spellcaster, swiping the feet out from under them.

Meanwhile, Etherea had managed to wrest one of Orphana's hands from her throat. This seemed to provide temporary encouragement to the Shroud. Three of them frantically gathered and hunched together, extending their hands toward Cricket. They spoke a word of command which caused a layer of frost to spread and advance in concentric fashion throughout the cavern. When it reached Cricket, her feet flew out from under her and she skidded past the muses. As she passed them, she still managed to swipe at them with her feet.

"Yes!" Cricket proclaimed, as she reached the perimeter of the chamber. It was now covered by frost. She sprang to her feet. "Oh, you wanna play? Ha! Then let's do it."

Cricket leapt on the cavern wall and grappled her way up with ease. The frost circle raced after her, climbing the wall. But when she reached sufficient height and trajectory, she dangled by her fingertips and then pushed off, catapulting herself off the rocks toward the Shroud below. If they hadn't scattered to avoid her, Cricket would have landed directly upon them. As it was, she only managed to disrupt their collective spell. The frost quickly evaporated. Upon landing, she slid into the splits upon the icy cave floor. Being that she was smaller than Kanya, her pants were a little big, which may have actually kept her pants from splitting. She found her balance and scrabbled towards the fleeing muses.

One of them rose, black blood streaming from its nose, and started chanting, raising its hands towards the whetherwere. A wave passed through the cloud creature. It was responding to the muse. A whirlpool formed as the barnacle creatures coalesced, creating a funnel that was aimed at the shapeshifter. That was, until Cricket landed two lightning quick blows to the muse's throat. Something like an expulsion of fog released from its gullet, and the muse collapsed. In fact, all the muses fell backwards, as if struck by a collective blow.

"Take that, frosty!" Then Cricket turned to the others. "Now, who's next?"

But they were all on their backs, scrambling to reconfigure. Apparently, muses of the Nether have little defensive fighting skills. Their power is in words and spells. Mace had said that when Cricket was active, she was oblivious to spells, impervious to mental commands and magic. Either that or she was just too damned quick. Whatever the case, the Shroud shrieked and scrambled to congregate in another part of the chamber.

"You are bad," Cricket proclaimed. "Very bad!"

That's when I noticed that the whetherwere had changed trajectory. The swirling mass was moving toward the battered Shroud. They stood huddled in the far corner, bleeding and beaten, as far away from Etherea and the altar as was possible. They took up their chant again and, as they did, the whetherwere descended. As it did, it congealed, forming a solid stalactite of crystalline blue ice. From the top down. The muses raced to the creature, squeezing into its crevices and burrowing into its contours, becoming one with the crystalline shards.

The bloodied Shroud merged with the whetherwere.

As this sight unfolded, Cricket stepped back, tilting at the monstrous entity. That was as awed, as dumbstruck, as I'd ever seen Kanya's alter ego. Obviously, even Cricket herself was not psycho enough to attack a conflagration demon.

The whetherwere deconstructed, returning to its barnacle-like self. It rose again to the ceiling, where the dark, fomenting clouds dissipated. Smoky strands and tentacles drifted off the way they'd come, back into the crevices and hidden passageways, taking the muses of the Nether back to their icy hell.

Seeing that Cricket had contained the Shroud and that the Veil of Tears had been broken, Rapha lumbered toward Etherea. And I joined him.

But as we were about to descend upon the witch, Etherea bellowed. Invisibles were churning about her, a miasma of evil. Teeth gnashed. Pincers snapped feverishly. Glimpsing this menagerie forced me to halt my approach. Etherea continued yelling as she tore Orphana's hands free from her throat. The guardian's hands scattered, broken into tiny particulate shards, and returned to Orphana's body where they began reconstituting. In that second, Etherea retrieved the blade and thrust it at Rapha, who strafed sideways, effectively avoiding the black weapon.

"Don't try it again, baby." She spun to the opposite side of the altar, where she pressed the blade on Audra's throat. Flumes of malice and filth radiated from Etherea's being. Yet she smiled, tilting the blade so that it glistened in the candlelight. "It's made of Nefarium." She was panting from her skirmish with Orphana. "Like the Table of Summoning. They are both…indestructible. Just like the Overlords will be when they inherit the planet."

"It's over," Rapha said to Etherea. "They can't protect you anymore."

"They weren't much help anyway." Etherea drew the back of one hand across her face and checked it for blood. "They were soft. Muses always are. But it's hardly over. In fact, it's just beginning."

Audra wrestled helplessly against her restraints until Etherea grabbed her by the hair, pulled her head back, and with her opposite hand pressed the blade hard against Audra's throat.

"Don't move, or she dies." Etherea sneered at us. "And when she dies, you're history. So no tricks, my pretties. No hocus pocus. Back up!" She shouted at us. "Go on. All of you!"

Orphana, Rapha, and I followed her orders.

However, Etherea did not notice something else that was occurring. A single stream of blood was traveling down Audra's neck and pooling upon on the altar. As the blood flowed, the sigils on the altar glowed, portals of neon crimson pulsing to life.

"Go ahead!" Etherea yelled. "All the way back. That's right. Look at them. The Imperia. Guardians of the earth. Well, now you can watch what happens when the Tenth Plague arrives."

Quinn struggled to his feet. As he did, he reached up and gently touched his fingertips to the bridge of his glasses. It was unclear whether he touched a specific part on the glasses or simply pushed them tighter to his face.

Suddenly, Audra's bindings flared. The candles on the shrine behind them simultaneously burst into flame. My attention, however, was not drawn to either of these phenomenon.

Directly behind Etherea, the Bony Lady had started to move.

CHAPTER 27

The candles surrounding the Santa Muerte shrine flared, creating a brief bonfire of smoke and guttering wax. The flames sent misshapen shadows arcing wildly across the subterranean roof. Wax spilled from the shrine in rivulets, forming steaming pools at its base. Even more horrific was the fact that the entire shrine was now moving.

The life-size skeletal statue of Saint Death drooped forward. For a moment, it appeared the skull would topple from the torso and collapse into the flame. However, like some hideous plant it rose, gaunt, yet growing in stature. The torso slowly writhed and twisted in a macabre fiery dance, an unwholesome movement accompanied by the crackle of bone. The idol grew, almost doubling its size. The skeletal hands stretched from the sleeves, and the shredding of fabric sounded as it pulled taut and then burst through its garments. To my horror, something bulged from its back, shuddered, and burst outward. Appendages framed by tusks, jointed at odd angles, etched with unknown inscriptions, and draped with tattered sheets of skin; a patchwork of flesh that glistened a deep crimson. The skull changed as we watched. Serpentine hair coiled from her head, dreadlocks of a most unusual order. A penumbra of shadow framed the pale cadaverous head—a diseased halo. The skull reassembled, morphing into that of the archangel's; its hollow eyes and jaw sagged, becoming an elongated leathery mask. Locks of hair spooled forth like diseased limbs on a gallows tree. Yet upon closer inspection, it wasn't hair at all, but lengths of charred spinal column.

Saint Death had paved the way for her. The patron saint of butchers and assassins had become the forerunner for Azrael, the Archangel of Death.

Etherea turned, caught somewhere between shock and wonder. Her gaze rose, higher and higher, as Azrael now towered over her. She attempted to laugh, but only a garbled choke left her mouth.

The candles, idols, and offerings fell away from the shrine in a blazing heap as Azrael blossomed in all her terrible splendor. The scythe had morphed alongside her, as if it were an actual appendage of her being; it was made of crooked boughs of ossified wood and bone. Her wings spread. The ragged sheets of skin unfurled like a hideous banner, proclaiming a victory that would surely be hers. It was a robe stitched from human flesh, carcasses of her victims, most likely; a mast, a bloody proclamation of the waste that she wrought. She stood ten, twelve feet tall, matched in wingspan. What manner of being was this? The Queen of the Damned had now set foot upon our earthly shores. The atmosphere seemed to curdle at her presence. She stank of rotting battlefields and Bubonic Plague. Just looking at her was to know my mortality, and lose all hope.

Cold black eyes appeared. Yet it was not liquid, but sand that filled the skeletal sockets. As lifeless and empty as a wasteland; unblinking and without pupil, just sifting obsidian portals.

I was overcome with momentary vertigo and fumbled for something to steady myself on. Fear seized my members, paralyzing me in its grip. How many souls had she extracted over time, this rogue angel, oblivious to pain and regret, whose one single purpose was to take life? If there was a rank of death angel, surely Azrael occupied the dreadful summit.

An ominous thump sounded as the archangel stepped off the fiery platform. As she did, it collapsed in flames. A plume of smoke and rancid incense rose behind her. The ground she stood upon blistered and turned black.

Meanwhile, Audra wrestled against her flaming bonds. Etherea had turned away from her sacrifice and stood, tilted back against the altar, mesmerized by the angel, her features frozen in a rictus of wondrous dread. Still, she sought to invoke the magic and managed to fumble out the words of her incantations.

"Most holy d-death, empress of the d-darkness!" Etherea gulped and stared up at the hideous creature. "Take thou heavenly s-sickle. T-take this thou mortal sacrifice. From stone b-be flesh. From flesh b-be satiated."

As she spoke the grimoire, the angel's naked skull turned and looked down on her. Obsidian eyes without pupils rested upon the enchanter. Etherea stepped back, revealing Audra, who wrestled frantically against her bonds. Etherea smiled maniacally and gestured to her offering.

However, Azrael's solemn gaze remained upon the Neuro priestess.

Moving the scythe to its opposite hand, it stepped toward Etherea. Something drooled from its jaws. Etherea staggered back, unable to steady herself on the altar. Azrael hissed—a drawn-out, parched susurration—and with the sound came the smell of dust and the wind of graveyards.

Finally realizing her plight, Etherea shrieked and spat nonsensical commands as the archangel trod towards her with its insect-like mechanical gait. Its joints and sinews were reawakening from ages of slumber. Its scythe, now raised, scraped the cavern ceiling as it stalked its prey.

Azrael towered over Etherea, who fell to the ground. She was screeching insanely as the archangel stood over her, reared back, and plunged the base of the scythe into Etherea's chest. The bony handle disappeared inside the witch. As the angel drove the handle into her heart, grinding it downward, some maniacal, ancient tongue left the creature's mouth. Etherea flailed. A great plume of Invisibles gushed forth from her being. Like a cancerous polyp punctured by the surgeon's blade, vile demoniac gore spilled from innermost being. I turned away until her shrieking mercifully ended. When I returned my gaze, Etherea's back arched. She issued a silent scream, and flopped limp. Azrael remained there, perhaps draining every possible ounce of life or evil from its first victim. Finally, it plucked the shaft of the scythe from Etherea.

Those of the dark side obviously had no qualms about eating their own.

The sigils on the Altar of Summoning were pulsating crimson as Azrael turned her skeletal face towards Audra. Just as she did, the flaming rope that was binding Audra splintered. She rolled off the opposite side of altar.

"Move!" Mace shouted. He had his rifle—the same weapon he had been practicing with at the Asylum, the net gun—aimed at Azrael. "Get outta there!"

I almost wanted to laugh at the notion that a sheer net could possibly contain the Archangel of Death. What kind of half-ass outfit was this? We weren't dealing with a water buffalo here. Hell, we weren't dealing with Quetzalcoatl either! But Audra was already up and stumbling the other direction, running away from us and the angel.

It was a smart move, tactically, creating distance between all the parties. However, it didn't eliminate the fact that we were in the worst possible predicament. The archangel had been summoned. And now it had tasted blood. Nevertheless, this knowledge was not as devastating as it could have been. For one thing, by all appearances, we were engaging with a physical entity. Azrael was not invisible. She had materialized and was interacting with our dimension. She was as real as the angel Jacob wrestled. And now the adrenaline was flowing through me, spiking in my limbs. I was buzzing. It was almost as if my sense of reality had been condensed into this single pinprick of time. Somehow, beyond reasoning, beyond any human capacity, I was empowered to contest this thing. Sure, I would probably blow a hole through my torso doing so, but at the moment, the odds seemed slightly tilted in our favor. *Slightly.*

Plus, there were seven of us.

As Mace took aim, Saint Death hissed, spread its wings in awful majesty and in one swoop, rose over the altar and thumped to the ground beside Audra. Its transit was disorienting, bringing with it another wave of vertigo. The movement was less like flying—for its wings never flapped—as it was floating. Gliding. Considering the look of those tattered skin wings, it was not a surprise that Azrael couldn't use them. Maybe they were just for show. That didn't temper the fact that the creature now stood directly over Audra. The ground at its feet grew black and parched as it raised its scythe, preparing to receive its next offering

"Dammit!" Mace lowered his weapon. "Move lady!"

And that's when I noticed something unusual about the netting balled inside the rifle's canister.

It was made of Ndocron.

The large mesh net that had draped Rapha's workbench!

They'd had the idea long before I ever showed up. The rifle was *modified to handle larger nets, like those for T-Rexes*. That's what Mace had said. And because Ndocron could contain interdimensional interlopers, it would most likely serve to harness the angel. It was a brilliant idea. Capturing the Archangel of Death? Sure, why not. The old rules no longer seemed to apply anyway. Reality had taken a U-turn and was now headed back to the land of childhood fantasy. It was as good a chance as we would ever have.

Yet Audra was in the direct line of sight.

The cut on her neck did not appear serious. Again, Mace yelled for her to move. But Audra could only manage to inch herself back, fixated upon the horror, for the archangel was nearly straddling her, drooling and hissing.

The power awakened inside me and with it, an intuition. Sure, what I was about to attempt could be disastrous. But I was learning that in this life, there aren't many guarantees anyway. Besides, the wounds received in battle bestowed honor, they didn't take it away.

Rapha would have been pleased to know I had adopted such a policy.

I inhaled and focused my mind to jump. This one would be tricky. If I missed my spot, I might turn Audra into a grease spot. Or even worse, leave her quartered. Then there was another tiny detail—that the action would probably open the fissure in my chest into the size of Griffith Park. Oh well, knights errant!

I set my eyes upon Audra and as I did, the atmosphere bristled with dimensional corridors. It was a geometrician's geek dream. I was perhaps fifteen feet from her and the angel. I had a direct shot, with maybe an additional fifteen feet to navigate a landing. But I didn't have time to compute the numerological particulars of my next move. Rapha had suggested my gift might be more about spatial manipulation than actual teleportation, and in that instance, his suggestion seemed correct.

I mentally selected the space near Audra—more precisely, her shoulder furthest from the demon—and willed myself to that space. I launched to Audra—

—sent to save—

—to come into his rightful place.

—and actualized just in time to slip one arm under hers and skid past Azrael. It happened so fast that I did not at first realize I'd clipped the archangel. Flaps of loose skin exploded into the air. As did a stench of rot and canker.

We had an awkward go of it. I was hoping to scoop Audra up as I passed, hoist her upright, and land standing so that we could run. No such luck. My trajectory was such that I wheeled to my back, pulling Audra into myself with one arm. As we rolled backwards, we struck the cavern wall. We'd managed a complete rotation, which meant my back took the brunt of the impact. The very roots of the place shook. My chest exploded in pain. I yelled, as much to channel my pain as to express my pure abandonment.

Azrael shrieked, a ghastly cry of defiance. She frantically searched for her escaping prey. Her skeletal locks whipped about her face as she turned to and fro. Upon seeing us, she approached in two huge strides, raising her scythe as she came. Just under her wings, I could see Mace aiming the rifle.

"I got one shot, Moon!" Mace yelled. "Move it!"

Audra lay huddled into my chest, where we'd landed. I pulled her into myself as the Archangel of Death glared down at us.

"I'm gonna try something," I said in Audra's ear. "So hang on."

She didn't answer, nor did I wait for her to.

Azrael raised the butt of the scythe, preparing to impale both of us. Her black sandy eyes churned in their sockets.

I turned away, focused under her wing to the base of the Altar of Summoning.

As the archangel hissed and brought the scythe down, I heard the rifle sound.

Sssht. Pmphh!

A blur of space, neither material nor purely metaphysical. Time slowed to the infinitesimal.

—again!

Then it is true.

He knows all worlds.

This time I managed to control my stop slightly better. I tumbled once, but landed upright on my knees. We had separated upon landing. Audra sprawled at the foot of the altar, while I leaned back with my hands on my thighs, spitting dirt from my mouth. Up to that point, I hadn't considered what effect a dimensional jump would have on another person. While Audra appeared dazed, she looked completely intact.

Azrael's shrieking filled the cavern. It was both animalistic, yet alien. Like a massive umbrella, the Ndocron net had draped the angel. She wailed and chattered, flailing against the otherworldly sheath.

"Got 'er!" Mace shouted and pumped his fist. He tossed the rifle aside. "Quick! Pin the corners!"

Mace removed a length of rope from his pack and rushed to his prey, followed by Quinn, Celeste and Rapha. Even Orphana hobbled to help. The scythe lay to one side. Azrael struggled beneath the netting, appendages battering the Ndocron barrier. The earth where the archangel lay blanched, grew withered and charred. The team surrounded the creature and grappled for the edges of the net, preparing to pin it to the ground. As they did, Azrael screeched and flung its wings outwards. The motion sent its attackers hurtling through the air. They slammed to the earth, dazed by the force of her counter. The earth guardians were but toys and stood no chance against a creature this size.

However, the angel appeared to be struggling against the Ndocron. Its flesh sizzled as it touched the netting. In fact, its entire body trembled and appeared to recoil upon contact with the strange material. Nevertheless, the massive skeletal fingers wormed their way from under the netting in an attempt to rip it off.

Mace shook himself and staggered to his feet. "Stop it! Rapha—don't let it get free!"

But it was too late. Before Rapha could seize that edge and pull it back down, the Archangel of Death raised its arms and the netting opened, creating something like a massive headscarf draping its foul body. From under the net, the angel peered at its attackers; its eyes were draining sand. Then it opened its mouth and wailed in defiance. Rapha staggered back at the sound.

My chest was blazing, my body completely drained. I tried to rise, but collapsed. I dare not touch my chest, because I knew that most of it was gone. I had to do something to help. But I was currently about as useful as sunscreen in a nuclear blast.

The archangel was preparing to fling the netting off when I noticed Cricket retrieve the scythe, hoist it over her shoulder, and take a running start at Azrael.

She was yelling something about death and having already whipped it. Taking three huge strides, Cricket planted the scythe on the ground and vaulted herself towards the angel. She flung herself at its head. The impact rocked the struggling creature, sending it listing backward. Cricket clung to the netting and pounded her fists, left then right, into the angel's massive skull. She seemed oblivious to the moment or the chances of success, driven by a frenzy of fury and passion.

"She's mine!" Cricket yelled, hammering her fists into angel's temples. "You can't have her!"

I hate to admit it, but I was almost tempted to cheer for her.

Cricket's antics created a window that Rapha and the team seized upon. Rapha leapt up and grabbed the edge of the Ndocron netting. Using his own weight as leverage, he dragged the net back down, over the archangel, and to the cave floor. Azrael bucked against the action, flailing wildly, attempting to twist herself free. This caused Cricket to lose her grip and she sailed through the air and slammed into the cavern wall. The rest of the team quickly fell upon the net and drew its edges together. The angel shrieked as the netting tightened against its body. An awful sizzling sounded, and the smell of charred bone filled the air.

The angel began to collapse under the density of the material.

Even though it continued to thrash against the netting, the Archangel of Death began to shrink and shrivel into itself. Bones and gristle knotted together. Its limbs and appendages folded inward with sick crunching sounds. Mace looped the rope through the netting and together they drew the cage tight upon Azrael.

The angel's cries diminished and soon became little more than catty mewls. It continued to crumple inward, collapsing upon itself. Mace pushed the creature over and secured the edges, forming a thick black bundle about the size of a large refrigerator.

The others were shouting in celebration, slapping high fives and hugging. I lay buzzing, but detached from their triumph. Worlds of possibility seemed to blaze at my fingertips. The power coursed my body. Quantum realities flooded my brain. I had one more feat left within me. And I knew just what it was.

So I struggled to my feet and limped to the altar.

My body tingled. My chest was a molten stew. Audra had risen and come to my side, but I sternly ordered her to move back. I peered at the ancient altar. Ages of blood and death were imbedded therein. All the loss and torment spilled onto that Table. All the lives lost there.

Objects like the Table of Summoning should not exist in our world.

Although it would be a great addition to Kanya's collection, taking it to the Asylum and locking it up wasn't good enough.

And I had the power, as the Seventh Guardian, to do something about it.

I leaned forward and pressed my palms upon the altar.

Energy flared from my hands. I forced them onto the surface of the Nefarium altar. There were no words of command that sprang to my mind. Only pure defiance—defiance against the death that had taken so many innocent souls. I channeled that emotion into physical power. And as I did, my hands sank into the Table of Summoning. Its edges bubbled, and turned molten blue. Fumes of heat blistered my face. I turned away, biting back against the heat. The entire Table was becoming magma. The flame spread out to its edges and down its legs. The glowing ciphers and sigils disappeared as the Table liquefied. It sank into itself and collapsed inward.

Though the mass of elements broiled, my hands remained unharmed. I plucked them free as the Table of Summoning collapsed into a smoldering heap.

I staggered back to keep from being swallowed by the glowing pool. Yet I was protected. My hands were pulsating with electric blue now. I could see the veins, bones, and sinews inside myself; I had become a living, breathing Invisible Man. Neon currents twined upward from my fingertips like some mad scientist's spire. My chest burned so much I could swear I smelled flesh.

Between the mewling of the angel, the raucous celebration of my colleagues, and the conflagration that was churning in my torso, reality seemed a distant thing. I knew I was being watched and tried to say something witty. Instead, I wobbled and then collapsed. Audra ran to me.

"Mr. Moon! Are you all right?"

I was about to dismiss her query. Until I noticed Cricket was standing behind her mother. Her hands were balled into fists. Her nose was bleeding. She was visibly trembling.

And her eyes were blazing with revenge.

CHAPTER 28

Once, in Louisiana, I found myself trapped in a bar with a live alligator. The barkeep kept the reptile chained out back, sort of as an attraction for curious patrons. He fed him chicken guts and possums. How the gator escaped its leash was never discovered. But when it nuzzled its way into the kitchen, the only concern was getting the hell out of there with all my limbs. I ended up jumping on the bar to avoid the creature's chomping jaws. I was as close to pissing my pants that I'd come since kindergarten. But the fear of seeing that mammoth reptile lumbering toward me was nothing compared to watching Cricket bobbing on her toes, laughing, bleeding, and preparing to wreak vengeance upon her mother. And anyone who dared protect her.

"You—" Cricket's gaze passed from glee to malice. "We hate you!"

She tilted her head back and yelled, a tormented cry, filled with years of anguish.

Audra turned to face her daughter.

"Kanya."

"No-o-o-o!" Cricket bellowed. "We do not name her!"

Cricket's challenge was so fierce that Audra stepped back, as if physically struck by the words.

"You're wrong." Audra brushed her hair from her face. Her voice was measured, without panic. "We *do* name her. We name her because...she's my daughter. *You're* my daughter. I know you remember."

"You lost her!" Cricket clenched her fists. She wanted to hit something. "When you gave her to the bad man! You lost her. You are *not* getting her back, either. No! Not by me. Not that easy. Not at all! No! No! No!"

"Kanya, I'm sorry. I thought it was necessary."

"Necessary?" Cricket glanced at me, her face plastered in an insane smile. "Necessary?"

"I was wrong." Audra said. "I'm not sure. I think—" She swallowed. "It saved them. Kanya, you saved them."

Cricket leapt into the air with a high-pitched shout and kicked sideways, landing her foot squarely in Audra's stomach and driving her off her feet. Audra skidded dangerously close to the molten stew that had previously been the Altar of Summoning. She doubled over, clenching her gut and gagging.

I forced myself up and stood wobbling. My entire body felt like a roadside flare. At least I was still in one piece. However, the last time I faced the wrath of Cricket I'd gotten my ass kicked. But I'd received enough second chances to know there was always room for one more.

"Kanya!" I yelled, following her mother's lead. "Cool it!"

The changeling glanced at me and laughed. It was a laugh of mockery. She punched her fist into the palm of her open hand. "Reagan Shmaygun! It doesn't matter. None of this does!" She motioned to the wreckage that lay before us—the altar, the withered angel, the moldering shrine, the others who now stood watching us. "What matters," Cricket said, "is *this*!" She pointed at Audra, who was sucking air and trying not to puke.

I had kept the totem for such a time as this and began fumbling in my pocket for it.

Audra staggered to her feet. "Kanya, I—"

"No!" Cricket strode to her mother and now stood toe to toe. Although shorter in this state and more nimble in build, what she lacked in girth she made up for in fiery passion. "We remember. You left us. You gave us to the bad man. They hurt us." Her voice cracked and for a brief second, the rage disappeared into pain. "*They hurt me.*"

It was the first sign of something other than fury and reckless abandon from the shapeshifter. In fact, when Cricket

Mike Duran

said that, her hair flushed from silver-white to black. Apparently, Audra saw that as an opportunity and took it.

"You don't have to do this," Audra said. "You don't have to *be* this. You're strong, Kanya. That's the girl I knew. You can control it. You can bring her back. You can tell Cricket what to do." Audra reached out, took Cricket by the shoulders, and peered into her eyes. "You are not at anyone's mercy."

The heat from the altar framed the two of them in its smoldering backdrop.

Cricket blinked. Her mother's words had briefly registered. Her features softened.

Then she shrieked, ripped Audra's hands off her, and released a frenzy of jabs and punches. Audra countered with some fine defensive moves of her own. Apparently, they'd had these types of mother-daughter exchanges before. But Audra was no match for Cricket. Was anyone? Cricket forced her mother back. She pummeled her with blow after blow. All the while her body was flushing in and out of transition. Between cartwheels and spinning back fists, I caught glimpses of Kanya attempting to subsume her alter ego. However unsuccessfully.

"We. Hate. You!" Cricket punctuated each word with a single strike. "We. Hate. You!"

Audra finally stumbled to the ground and lay on her back. Cricket pounced on her, clenched her hands around her mother's neck, and squeezed so hard that her forearms trembled.

"Ha, ha!" Cricket spat into her mother's face. "Now you'll die. Just like I did! You will die. You and Kanya."

I had the totem out, but at this stage I doubted I could get Cricket's attention long enough to use it. The others had approached, but they also appeared at a loss.

"Cricket!" I shouted and raced to the women. "Kanya! Stop it! Don't do it! Don't—"

314

Cricket did not budge. Audra was turning blue as Cricket began slamming her head to the ground. Dammit! I had to do something.

I reared back to kick Cricket in the ribs. But I couldn't do that. Not to a girl.

"Cricket! Stop it!" I yelled louder.

I gripped the totem in my fist and with my free arm, seized Cricket's throat.

With minimal effort, and without even turning back to look at me, Cricket struck me with the back of her fist square in the bridge of my nose. It was the same spot she'd struck me in our last tango, but this time I was sure she broke it. I almost blacked out. I staggered back and steadied myself. Someone was yelling behind me, but if I didn't act in a hurry, Audra would join Etherea in the great beyond.

And after such a big victory, it would really suck to have it end this way.

I took three big steps and drove my foot squarely into Cricket's ribs. I'm not a vengeful person, but I must admit to deriving a certain degree of pleasure from the action. Especially seeing that it accomplished what I'd intended.

Cricket was ejected from atop her mother and rolled twice, yelping as she went. She jumped to her feet, her eyes still full of fury, and glared at me. But when she saw that I was holding the totem, she stopped. And stared.

I stepped closer, the totem displayed clearly in my open palm.

"Kanya," I said, approaching her with the same caution one might use while approaching a live grenade. "Kanya, you can control it. I know you can. Do you hear me? You can control the changing."

Her hair was morphing back and forth, riffing through shades of white and black. My appeal seemed to speed the process.

"You're bleeding," she said flatly.

I reached up to find blood streaming down my face. "Aw, hell. Look what you did!" I held the totem aloft. "Now, I want Kanya back. Okay? You can do it. I know you can do it."

Cricket's gaze faltered. She looked away from the totem. This could have been a bad sign. But it wasn't. Cricket was not attempting to resist the transformation; she was forcing herself to change without the help of the totem.

"That's right." I nodded. "Let it go, Kanya."

I glanced at Audra, who was perched on her elbows, bloodied, but intently watching us.

"Let it go," I said. "It's over."

And with that, I tossed the totem into the molten altar where it flared and disintegrated.

When I looked back, Kanya was almost fully there. What encouraged me more than anything was that she was looking at Audra with tears on her cheeks.

I was pretty sure she wasn't crying about her broken ribs.

CHAPTER 29

I awoke to Kanya. She wore a lumberjack flannel and leggings. I loved her style. Besides, no one could rock leggings like she could. She was standing over the kitchen table with a crook neck lamp illuminating what appeared to be wet specimens of mutant hedgehogs.

I was in the Asylum. They'd brought me here after the subway incident. That much I remembered. I'd been out of it, probably a combination of exhaustion, getting punched in the face, and having a stargate erected in my breastbone. So they set up a cot for me in their small living quarters.

Something sizzled in a pan on the stove. I smelled bacon and pastry. Mace sat nearby assembling a gun. Or was it a prosthetic flamethrower.

"Are we finally awake, princess?" he said.

I winced at the humor. That's when I realized that something was plastered across the bridge of my nose. Bandages.

"It was broken this time." Kanya said as she approached. "But don't feel too bad." She stood before me and lifted up her flannel to reveal a large brace encircling her chest. "So were my ribs."

"It was the only way I could get your attention."

She smiled. "I'm glad you did."

I swung my legs off the cot and sat up. I groaned as I did, hurting all over. Oddly enough, the pain in my chest seemed to have been quelled. I reached up to touch it. They both watched me. My hand reached something hard. Cool. Some sort of shell covered my chest. What the hell?

I lifted my shirt up to see a dark vest. Perhaps a breastplate would be a better way to describe it. It encircled my chest and back and fit snugly, yet did not restrict my motions. I would have guessed it was Kevlar until I rapped on it with my knuckles. This was as solid as stone.

"It's Ndocron," Kanya said. "Your chest—" She hesitated.

"Your chest was basically gone." Mace put the weapon aside and approached me. "What's happenin' inside you is anyone's guess. Freaky as hell, that's for sure. Quinn had the idea for the vest. Acts like Klammer's hood and keeps that thing from growing. While it's on, at least. Rapha made it. Guy's a whiz with that stuff. He came up with the idea for using the net and, sure enough, it proved a success."

He approached and extended his fist. I bumped it with mine.

"I was wrong about you, Moon," Quinn said.

"That happens a lot."

"But the jury's still out on that paranormal paparazzi act of yours."

"I'm not a paparazzi. Okay?"

"I will say, it's the first angel I've ever bagged. We got it outta there via the SoHo tunnel. That place was crawling with Summa Nuran moon dust. We are fortunate to have not been apprehended upon our exit, or else that critter would have surely been confiscated. It's a win/win. We escaped without notice, basically unharmed, and have added to our collection." He turned and gazed out into the Asylum. "Have a look."

I rose from the couch. Kanya helped me through the front room of the control station and into the warehouse. Resting near the forklift was a large Plexiglas container. Inside it was the Ndocron net which held the archangel. Only now, the creature had been condensed down to dense block of bones and crimson skin, compressed under the weight of the strange material. Amidst the scramble of joints, tusks, and rotted musculature, I could see Azrael peering at me, her skeletal face locked in its perpetual sneer.

"We can't destroy her," Kanya said. "That's not in our power. But she can stay locked up as long as possible."

"And what about that," I said, pointing to the scythe that lay nearby.

"Who knows," Mace said. "Might come in handy someday."

The elevator buzzer sounded. Mace jogged into the command center to check the monitors and see who it was.

"Looky there," he shouted. "We have visitors."

A minute later, the freight elevator door opened. The Imperia exited. Bruised and limping, but fully intact. Audra was with them. I tensed slightly when I saw her, and fought to not look at Kanya as her mother approached.

"Will you look at that." Orphana hobbled to the Plexiglas cage and studied the angel. "She is one ugly thing. Brrr! Gives me the creeps."

"Well," I said, "thanks to you, she's in there and not," I thumbed in the direction of the city above, "out there."

"Well," Orphana said, "we all played a part in the story. That's usually how it works. Everybody's got a part. Although, I must say, watchin' you do your thing was pretty cool."

"Well, it wasn't planned that way. Trust me."

Quinn approached and knocked on my chest.

"So what do you think?" he asked.

"Hmm. I'll have to give it some time. "

"You were out and that thing was just glowing. Rapha said he could see—" Quinn looked over his shoulder at Rapha. "He said he could see the universe. Or *a* universe, I guess you'd say. Inside you. It reflects whoever's looking at it, but just below the surface...I dunno, it's another world. Weird. Thought you were givin' up the ghost, to be honest. We managed to put the vest on you while you were out. Luckily, no one fell into the damned thing. We'd have never recovered 'em." He knocked on the vest again. "It should hold up. I thought about inscribing it with something. You know, like a big giant S or a full moon. Maybe we can think up a moniker for you and do it all fancy. What do you think?"

"Next you'll want me to start wearing leotards. No thanks."

They all laughed. It was a brief moment of defenselessness that provided me a glimpse into Quinn's mind. He looked at me. He knew what I was doing, and did not try to shutter his thoughts. After what we'd been through, my doubts about him had significantly subsided. Nevertheless, I was still convinced that there was much more to the telepathic tattoo artist than he was allowing me to see. That story, however, would have to wait for future telling.

Rapha approached, looking even more immense than I remembered. He placed his hand on my shoulder.

"God brings His children to heaven by many paths," he said.

"Let me guess—Quixote."

He smiled. "Only in your case, the path appears quite difficult and full of peril."

"Tell me about it."

"The prophecy was true, Brother Moon. As I believed all along. Only the one who traverses all worlds can destroy the elements of both."

"Meaning?"

Quinn said, "It means you have a passport to Heaven and Hell, buddy."

The Seventh Guardian. I was unsure of the implications and, at the moment, didn't want to know. Yet the possibilities of being able to glimpse both Heaven and Hell was a mystery that would not leave me any time soon.

"So what about the reptoids?" I asked Rapha.

"Jake." Rapha shook his head, clearly frustrated by the mention. "He had been lied to about the incident at the Red Iguana. Our relationship has always been difficult, but never so hostile. Once the spell was broken and the Shroud dispersed, they must have fled. There was far too much commotion for their liking. Reptoids prefer to stay under the radar. But I trust it will not be the last time we encounter the Lizard People. I can only hope that incident does not make things worse."

I shook my head. "I still can't believe it. I mean, the legend is actually true."

"The world's a lot bigger than you think, hon," Orphana scolded with a knowing wink.

Yeah. I'd heard that before.

"It's an adventure!" Rapha smiled. "And, what is life without adventure?"

We all managed to jam into the living quarters where we shared in spinach omelets, bacon, and massive, warm, sticky cinnamon rolls from the local bakery. There was laughter and tales shared around. Everybody had highlights of their own. Quinn described in vivid detail what it was like to be poisoned by a Veil of Tears. Orphana said that her thigh was compromised when she clustered, but that seeing the look on Etherea's face when she started choking her was worth it. Mace thought that Cricket breaking my nose was absolutely hilarious, which really bothered me. Nevertheless, the fellowship was rich. I could not recall having ever been a part of something that was simultaneously so risky, unpredictable, and potentially life-threatening, yet so rewarding. It reminded of the war stories I'd heard from my father, about the living and the dying...and the dying that made the living all the more coveted.

As the Imperia rose to leave, Audra finally approached Kanya. They'd remained a cordial distance from each other during the meal, although I'd noticed them exchange several uncomfortable glances.

"I'm sorry," Audra said to Kanya. "About everything."

Kanya scrunched her lips, appearing almost dubious about what was to follow.

"You do things when you're younger," Audra continued, "that you wish you hadn't. That you wish all your damned life that you could take back. And then somehow, despite all the regrets and all the penance, you look back and you survived, and it made you better. It worked out."

Kanya nodded, but it wasn't because she had conceded and shelved everything. She had more to say. Lots more. But hearing this, and biting back the instinctual rage, was a necessary start to her keeping Cricket, or any other alter ego, under lock and key. Until needed, at least.

"I'll be around," Audra said to Kanya. "I'll probably go back home, to our country, eventually. I miss them. And the food. But I find this city…enchanting. And Felix has promised me a role if I ever get serious."

When Kanya remained dispassionate, Audra looked nonchalantly around the Asylum. Then she cleared her throat. "If you ever, you know, decide you want to meet…"

Kanya stared at her mother. Without betraying any emotions, she said, "Maybe later. I'll think about it."

They stood facing each other. Then Audra hugged her daughter. The act was so unexpected that Kanya stumbled back as Audra held her tightly. I watched Kanya's eyes well with tears. When she saw me watching her, she looked away. They finally separated, and Audra straightened her clothing and dabbed at her eyes.

"And Mr. Moon." Audra turned to me.

"Please. Call me Reagan."

"Okay. Reagan. I need to thank you. For everything."

"It was my pleasure. I'm just trying to tweak my karma for the next life."

She issued a soft laugh.

"Well, be sure to add this one to your resume."

"I will."

When she stepped away, Celeste approached and spoke some odd benediction over me. She had one hand on my chest and the other raised. If there was healing in her touch, I wanted as much as I was capable of handling. Yet there was no change to my condition; my body still ached all over. After that, she hugged me. I liked Celeste and planned to inquire about her binding skills and how I might hone some similar talents.

Quinn followed her, stepped up, and shook my hand. "I gave you a hard time, Moon. I apologize."

I shrugged. "Whatever doesn't kill me makes me stronger. "

"Right." He smiled, shook his head, and prepared to turn. "By the way," he asked, straight-faced. "Do any of your other relatives suffer from mental illness?"

"No. They seem to enjoy it."

He playfully punched my arm, and the group of them walked to the freight elevator and ascended.

Once everyone left, I returned to the living quarters and sat on the cot. Someone had driven the Cammy back from Beverly Hills. My backpack had been removed and was lying near the cot. I checked my phone and listened to a message from Jimmy.

"Don't know how you managed it this time, Moon. But I'm guessin' you were the one who left that mess down there. Whatever the hell was going on, that Etherea freak held the reins. Tied in with the lerium syndicate. Big time. She died of a heart attack, allegedly. But toxicology said there was enough lerium in her system to power Chernobyl. It'll be a while before they unravel all the threads to this one. Apparently, some of the head honchos at NeoKor were dancing with the devil. Said something about death angels, plagues, and the merging of all dimensions. They were runnin' cover for some sorta cosmic crime mob. You know anything about that? Anyway, shortly thereafter they became slobbering idiots and are under lock and key in the psyche ward. This town is gettin' weirder by the day. In the meantime, please go see a doctor about that thing on your chest, will ya?"

I smiled at that. The message ended, but I sat for a while with the phone in my lap thinking about Jimmy. Then I rummaged through my backpack until I found my sketchbook. I pulled it out, retrieved a pencil, and began sketching another addition to my book, *Of the Invisible Order and Its Inhabitants.* This sketch was of a maelohim—a genus of death angel.

As I worked, I noticed a soft, burnished glow slanting across the sketchbook. I looked up to see Bernard across from me on the couch. He sat with his legs crossed, inspecting his fingernails.

"Hey," I said. "You made it."

He glanced at me and brushed his hand through the air as if to say *No problem.*

"And the whetherwere? How'd you manage that?"

He looked up, his face scrunched in thought. Then he shrugged and pointed upwards.

I nodded. What else would an angel say?

He rose and walked to my side where he stood with his hands on his hips, looking down at my sketch. Then he pointed at the picture and shook his head.

"What?" I asked. "That's a good likeness, don't you think?"

He curled his fingers into talons and bared his teeth.

"Scarier? You think it should look scarier?"

He nodded enthusiastically.

Once again, Bernard was probably right. Just thinking about that concave face and those neon red eyes made my stomach flip-flop. As I erased portions of my masterpiece, he turned to leave.

"Hey, wait!" I called after him.

The angel stopped and looked at me.

"I owe you one, Bernard."

He shook his head and counted off on his fingers, one, two, three, four, five, before opening his other hand and displaying all ten fingers. The angel flashed his brilliant smile.

"Ha! Okay. I owe you more than one."

And with that, he passed through the wall. I watched his golden wake dissipate into the atmosphere. Then I returned to my sketch, this time with a scarier version of the death angel.

The smart guys like to say that life, that reality, is all about matter—matter and energy. You know, we're nothing but globs of highly evolved protoplasm, which are really just globs of protons, electrons, and quantum particles. But when you strip all the jargon and academic ass-kissing away, there's a lot more to it than that. There's free will, there's good will. There's even love. And unless we want to sacrifice all those things on the altar of Science, all those things that make us different from baboons and porcupines, admitting that there's a world of invisible stuff in the mix is the most reasonable approach to life.

Now that I'd fought and beaten Saint Death herself, I couldn't imagine anything much more challenging to combat.

But I've never been quite that imaginative.

Glossary

ARCADIUM: Earth's higher dimensions

ARLETTE: Senior editor of the Blue Crescent

ASYLUM: Massive storehouse for occult and accursed items from around the world; in Los Angeles, south of Little Tokyo in the Warehouse District

AUDRA: Kanya's mother; one of the Hydra Sisters

AZRAEL: the Archangel of Death

BERNARD: Reagan Moon's guardian angel

BLACK COUNCIL: The body of Summu Nura overlords who plot the merger of all dimensions

CASEY SONG: Chinatown shop owner who possesses key to the golem prison under Third Street Shul

CELESTE: the Fourth Guardian of the Imperia; Archivist and Healer

COSMAGON: genetically enhanced henchmen developed by Volden Megacorps

CYTOMORPHS: Synthetic dimensional scouts made of Nefarium and used by the Summu Nura

DIADES: Earth's lower dimensions

DIEDRA: one of the Hydra Sisters

ETHEREA: Evolved lerium user able to correspond with the Black Council, summon ice nymphs, and harnesses Santa Muerte for releasing the Tenth Plague

FELIX KLAMMER: The First Guardian of the Imperia; exists in two dimensions -- earth and Arcadium; possesses Foresight

HAIL: A demigod of the Nether, lower realms of Diades

HOLLOW, THE: The lowest realms of Diades

IMPERIA: Seven earth guardians; empowered by Heaven to battle evil on earth and counter influence of the Summu Nura

JIMMY PASTORELLI: Lead investigator for LAPD Special Crime unit

KANYA: Matisse's adopted daughter; possesses therianthropic abilities; Audra is her mother

KI: The Sixth Guardian of the Imperia; defected to the Summu Nura

LERIUM: Smart drug being illegally produced and distributed; some users develop psychic abilities

MACE: Cryptid big-game hunter; arms / weapons expert; helps catalog and collect for the Asylum

MAELOHIM: Death angels; lower caste of Harvester angels; precursor to Azrael

MATISSE: Founder of the Asylum; Kanya's adoptive father

MRS. RICHARDSON: Moon's neighbor for whom he cat-sits

NDOCRON: Organic material mined from the dimensional skin of Arcadium

NEFARIUM: Material forged from Diades; indestructible on earth

NEOKOR: Urban developing conglomerates that re-opened the downtown subway project

NETHERWORLD: Another term used to describe the lower levels of Diades

NEUROS: A class of lerium user who has harnessed the smart drug and developed psychic abilities

NEVILLE: Moon's co-worker at the Blue Crescent

NOMLIES: Term used by the public to describe humans with supernatural abilities

NORMALS: Term used by Nomlies to describe the average human

ORPHANA: The Third Guardian of the Imperia; gifted with Agglomeration and Lore

PENNY: Moon's co-worker at the Blue Crescent

QUINN RODGERS: The Fifth Guardian of the Imperia; gifted in Psionics; coder, developer, tattoo artist

R.G. PENTECOST: Angelologist living in Venice Beach; possesses the Seraph's Wing

RAPHA: The Second Guardian of the Imperia; gifted in Alchemy, ability to manipulate matter

REAGAN MOON: The Seventh Guardian of the Imperia; possessor of the Fifth Essence

REPTOIDS: The lost Lizard People living in the tunnels under Los Angeles

SANTA MUERTE: A female folk saint venerated for healing and protective powers, beseeched by criminals and drug cartels

SAUCY: Rapha's mastiff, short for Sausalito

SHROUD, THE: Five muses of the Netherworld; ice nymphs; summoned by Etherea to invoke Azrael

SIDRA: One of the Hydra Sisters, killed by Kanya

SOREN VOLDEN: Founder of Volden Megacorps; pioneered Dream Chamber technology and Spiraplex

STELLARS: Term used by Lizard People to describe humans with supernatural abilities

SUMMA NURA: Bodiless astral vampires forever seeking incarnation and energy

TAU: A symbol of the cross of Christ, named after the Greek letter it resembles, worn by all members of the Imperia; Moon's was fused into his body from the Accident

TENTH PLAGUE: The invocation of the Archangel of Death for indiscriminate slaughter

WARPERS: Term used to describe those who can traverse different dimensions

WHETHERWERES: Conflagration demons held in the Netherworld; contained by ice muses

DID YOU LIKE THIS BOOK?

If so, there's a couple ways you can help me and we can stay connected.

Without reviews, indie books like this one are almost impossible to market. Leaving a review will only take a minute—it doesn't have to be long or involved, just a sentence or two that tells people what you liked about this book, to help other readers know why they might like it, too, and to help me write more of what you might love. The truth is, VERY few readers leave reviews. Can you help me by being the exception? Thank you in advance!

I also have a mailing list. Signing up is simple (just your name and email addy). It's called *Mike Duran's Infrequent Updates* for a reason, as I promise not to clog your email with daily or weekly info. Signing up will keep you abreast of my new projects and give you opportunity to get discounts on some of my books and products. You can sign up for my mailing list at my website: www.mikeduran.com.

If you liked SAINT DEATH, you'd probably enjoy the first book in the series THE GHOST BOX: A Reagan Moon Novel, which was selected by Publishers Weekly as one of the best indie novels of 2015. SUBTERRANEA: NINE TALES OF DREAD AND WONDER is an anthology of my short fiction that stylistically ranges from literary to pulp. It is available in ebook or in print. CHRISTIAN HORROR: ON THE COMPATIBILITY OF A BIBLICAL WORLDVIEW AND THE HORROR GENRE is a non-fiction exploration of religious themes in horror, evangelical readers' objections to the genre, and a brief apologetic for the genre's compatibility with a biblical worldview. You can find links to some of my other articles, essays, and short stories at my website, as well as links to my other social media hangouts. That link is www.mikeduran.com. Once again, thanks so much for reading!

Mike Duran